BY MANDY BERMAN

The Learning Curve

Perennials

The
Learning
Curve

The Learning Curve

·············· *A Novel* ··············

Mandy Berman

RANDOM HOUSE

NEW YORK

Published in the United States by Random House, an imprint and division of Penguin Random House LLC, New York.

RANDOM HOUSE and the HOUSE colophon are registered trademarks of Penguin Random House LLC.

Grateful acknowledgment is made to HarperCollins Publishers and Faber and Faber Limited for permission to reprint twenty lines from "The Babysitters" from *The Collected Poems of Sylvia Plath* edited by Ted Hughes, copyright © 1960, 1965, 1971, 1981 by the Estate of Sylvia Plath, editorial material copyright © 1981 by Ted Hughes. Reprinted by permission of HarperCollins Publishers and Faber and Faber Limited.

LIBRARY OF CONGRESS CATALOGING-IN-PUBLICATION DATA
Names: Berman, Mandy, author.
Title: The learning curve: a novel / Mandy Berman.
Description: First Edition. | New York: Random House, [2019]
Identifiers: LCCN 2018045609| ISBN 9780399589348 |
ISBN 9780399589355 (ebook)
Subjects: LCSH: Man-woman relationships—Fiction.
Classification: LCC PS3602.E75864 L43 2019 | DDC 813/.6—dc23
LC record available at https://lccn.loc.gov/2018045609

Printed in the United States of America on acid-free paper

randomhousebooks.com

2 4 6 8 9 7 5 3 1

First Edition

Book design by Caroline Cunningham

In memory of my grandfather,
Howard Hobbes Remaly

I have not yet determined to seduce her, though, with all her pretensions to virtue, I do not think it impossible. And if I should, she can blame none but herself, since she knows my character, and has no reason to wonder if I act consistently with it. If she will play with a lion, let her beware of his paw, I say.

—Peter Sanford in *The Coquette*,
Hannah Webster Foster (1797)

And it doesn't make sense
I should fall for the kingcraft of a
meritless crown

—Fiona Apple (2005)

The
Learning
Curve

Prologue

....

Paris, 2002

SIMONE SAT ALONE at the bar and felt herself being watched. She didn't have to turn her head to confirm it: the glare coming from behind her registered like a blast of cold air to the back of her exposed neck. She'd noticed the man when she first walked into the crowded bar on the border of the third and fourth arrondissements; he was sitting by himself in a banquette toward the front door, nursing a clear drink on ice. He'd looked up at her like he wanted to tear her in half.

On her barstool, she brought a glass of red wine to her lips and took a more delicate sip than she would have had she not known she was being watched. She was waiting for her sister in the trendy bar, not one she would have chosen herself. Vintage chandeliers hung low from the ceiling with half the bulbs burned out; the carelessness felt intentional. A bassist and a trumpeter and a drummer played jazz in a back corner, though it was hard to discern a melody of any kind below the din of the young bohemian crowd.

She felt a finger trailing down her bare neck, and in turning found herself hoping for someone other than Danièle.

Her sister gave her three *bises*, then pulled her head back to appraise the expression on Simone's face. "Were you expecting someone else?"

"Of course not." Simone took her blazer from the stool beside her and hung it on a hook underneath the bar.

"What are you drinking?" Danièle removed her leather motorcycle jacket with its array of unnecessary pockets and gold zippers. It had probably cost more than one month of Simone's rent. They were both wearing black dresses. Simone's was made from a cheap jersey material, sleeveless, one V cut in the front and another in the back. Tight. Simple enough to fool perhaps one person into thinking it might be expensive, Danièle not being that person. Danièle's dress was from the opposite realm—inordinately expensive yet not immediately obviously so (though obvious to Simone, who knew better): satin and loose-fitting, with lace detailing and spaghetti straps, like a flimsy piece of lingerie. No bra underneath, the nipples of her small breasts pointed beneath the satin. Chunky-heeled boots to structuralize the look. The gigantic diamond engagement ring on her left hand answered the money question, had it been left unanswered.

"A Côtes du Rhône," Simone said. "'Ninety-five, I think." She did not pay for drinks when she went out with her sister.

Danièle lifted the glass, stuck her nose deep into its mouth, and sniffed. "Good."

The bartender perked to attention as if he'd been waiting for her, regardless of the several other patrons on either side of them trying to order drinks. She told him she would have the same. Simone turned her head slightly, to see if she could spot the man by the front door. He was still sitting there, still alone, wearing a pressed suit that suggested he had come directly from work. She imagined him sitting in an office in a high-rise in the tenth, barking orders over the telephone. He seemed like he had the capacity to be mean. He looked up at her, as if on cue.

"Who are you looking for?"

Simone turned quickly to respond to her sister. "No one." She had thought she was being subtle, and around anyone else she might have been, but Danièle knew Simone better than most.

Danièle shrugged, lifted her glass. They clinked.

"Okay," Danièle said after swallowing her first sip. "You said you had news."

Simone steeled herself. She smoothed out the lap of her dress.

"Ariel proposed this morning."

Danièle's face brightened and widened, eyes and mouth open to capacity as she transformed into Simone's giddy little sister again—the excitable, affectionate girl she so often kept hidden now. She let out a high-pitched squeal, jumping up from her barstool as she did so. It hurt Simone to see Danièle lose all cool abandon in that moment; she let the façade down only on rare occasions. Perhaps Simone should have rephrased this news. Danièle went to throw her arms around Simone's neck but Simone stopped her, taking her sister's hands into her own.

"Sit down," Simone said.

Danièle took her hands back but still stood. There remained a glimmer of romantic hopefulness in her expression as she waited for Simone to say something else, eyes still glittering as she held out, against all reason, for a happy ending.

"I refused him," Simone said. It came out like that—not "I

said no." She'd *refused* him, because that was the truth. It felt that dramatic, the way his face and body had instantly aged and crumpled when she told him she didn't want to get married, as if she had sucked all the oxygen out of him.

Finally, Danièle sat. Her eyes brimmed with tears.

"It's okay," Simone said, clutching her hand. "I'm okay."

"Why would you do that?"

"Why are you so upset about this?"

"Because," Danièle said, wiping a tear away. "Ari is a good man. I want you to be with a good man."

"He was a good man," Simone agreed. "Is. But when he asked this morning . . . I think you are supposed to feel happy when they ask."

Danièle shook her head, as if what you felt in the moment was a minor by-product. Happiness was not the point.

"Dad wanted you to marry him," she said. Ari was a scholar, a Jew. Serious and respectable. He and her father were one and the same. "When he got sick—"

"Ari was there. And I think that was the reason I was keeping him around all these years."

"That's a horrible thing to say. You're thirty-four, Simone. Doesn't that scare you?"

"I don't know," Simone said, even though it did.

"I took this seriously. As a woman, as a Jew."

"You don't even believe in God."

"I believe in giving back."

"By marrying someone I don't love?"

"You do love him!" Danièle exclaimed. "He may not fill your storybook notion of what love looks like, but that doesn't mean you don't love him. You wouldn't have lived with him for four years otherwise."

Danièle did not love her own husband, a British banker who

traveled half the year. Simone had always suspected this, but what she hadn't understood until now was that Danièle had not married for money, not really. She married because Alex was the man she was dating when their father died. Because their father had approved. Convincing yourself of why and how you loved someone was an easy game, if you needed it badly enough.

"I'm sorry, but I won't play this game," Simone said.

"What game?"

Simone drained her glass and placed it on the bar. She gathered up her things.

"Thank you for the drink," she said, and headed toward the door.

The man in the banquette, too, was gathering up his things. Simone saw now, up close, the details of his face: pockmarked and tired, sallow bags underneath his eyes. Nonetheless, he was handsome; he would have almost been boyish looking had it not been for the obvious signs of exhaustion and age. He could have been her age, or fifteen years older: there was no sure way to tell.

He looked at her now with that same intense, almost dangerous glare as when she walked into the bar. She took his hand, in hopes that Danièle would see, and led him out through the front door. He would ravish her, and she would let him.

PART ONE

I.

FIONA DRANK FROM her bottle of Diet Coke diluted with Smirnoff and skipped ahead of her roommates when she saw the old train tracks. Already the bottle was almost empty. She finished the last gulp and chucked it in the overgrown weeds next to the out-of-service tracks. She did a cartwheel, a roundoff. She hopscotched between the rails, singing to herself—that Sleater-Kinney song Lula always blasted when they were getting ready, the last song that was in her head—as she heard the chattering of the girls somewhere behind her. She turned when the voices got close.

"Play with me!" Fiona called to them.

They laughed gamely, humored her for a minute, Lula lighting a cigarette, Marley sipping from her own soda bottle, Liv standing in silence with her arms crossed while Fiona spun, flipped, skipped. When Lula was done smoking, she crushed the butt into the ground and made for the sidewalk. Truckstop was a few more blocks that way. Marley stood and followed. Only Liv waited.

"Fiona," she said. "Time to go."

Fiona did more cartwheels. Her face felt delectably warm, her body as light and bright as if sunshine had been pumped directly into it. She looked up, dizzied, to see that Liv had also walked ahead. She ran, out of breath, toward her friend. "My baby loves me, I'm so hungry!" She sang loudly into Liv's ear. "Hunger makes me a modern girl!"

"Fiona, stop it," Liv said, turning her head away from the singing. She looked down at Fiona's empty hands. "You finished that drink already?" She said this less like a question and more like an expectation.

There it was: that air of judgment had been emanating off Liv all month like a bad smell. As if getting a boyfriend this summer suddenly made her the most virtuous of them all. But instead of delving into the shame, Fiona felt it sweetly rolling off her as if she were a duck emerging from the water.

"It's Saturday night, Livvy Loo," she said, kissing her friend on the cheek. She ran ahead to Marley and Lula, knowing that Liv was too afraid to walk in these parts of town alone, and would quickly be forced to follow.

Buchanan College, which came in at number nineteen on the 2008 *U.S. News & World Report* list of Best Liberal Arts Colleges, was in a small city in central Pennsylvania with a motley population. Besides the college community—rich liberal arts kids, the dippy professors and their mildly rebellious offspring—there was a healthy mix of townies, Amish people, working-class families, gang members, meth heads, artists who couldn't afford Philadelphia, and then, in the suburbs just outside, staunch, often religious conservatives in their gated communities. Truckstop, in a more desolate area of town—about a fifteen-minute walk from campus and ten minutes from their house—hosted an array of these groups on any given night, meaning the atmosphere was never dull. Sorority girls bought low-grade cocaine and snorted it with the dealers in the bathrooms, the floors slick from leaky plumbing, both parties leaving behind tracks of mud from the dirt-crusted soles of their high heels and their Timberlands. Lacrosse players took townies home, got them pregnant, paid for their abortions. Most recently, the quarterback of the football team, a celebrity on campus for bringing the once terrible team to more victorious seasons than they'd had in decades, had drunkenly failed to leave a tip on a pitcher of Bud Light for himself and his teammates; the bartender, all yellow teeth and shifty eyes, called the quarterback a racial slur under his breath, and a white teammate heard it and punched the bartender in the nose so hard that the crunch of his bones stopped the bar cold. Rumor spread that blood splattered directly into the pitcher, and the teammate had poured the bloody beer straight down his gullet on his way to being thrown out.

Truckstop was surprisingly hard on IDs, and there was always an unsmiling bouncer standing out front who looked more fit for a dance club than for the sticky dive bar inside. What a privilege to all be twenty-one, finally! To not have to hold breaths as Fiona, who had had her birthday in July, pulled out another fake ID to be inevitably taken from her. At some point last spring, Marley, Lula, and Liv had started playing rock-paper-scissors over who would have to accompany Fiona to a frat or loft party, lousy with underclassmen, while the other two stayed at the bar. It wasn't a nice bar—none of them believed otherwise—but it was a bar, which kept away the pimply eighteen-year-old pledges, the freshmen field hockey players who already thought they were such hot shit, and that in itself was a privilege.

Inside, they ordered their five-dollar vodka tonics, which the bartender, muscle-T'd and tribal-tattooed, handed to them in plastic cups. Lula put her card down, and told the bartender to keep the tab open.

"To senior year!" Fiona said, as if the others might forget that she was a semester behind them.

"To senior year," they all said back, and every time she was grateful for their kindness in not clarifying the truth.

In the back, there was a pool table, where Brandon, Liv's boyfriend, was playing against another Zeta brother. Liv went over there to greet him, giving him a chaste kiss on his tanned cheek, while Lula watched the game, probably calling the next one. Zetas liked psychedelic drugs and jam bands, had scruffy faces and wore tie-dye; they were the least aggressive and most tolerable of the frat boys.

Boys loved Liv and Lula, both entirely beautiful and entirely unavailable. Lula was the first femme lesbian most of them had ever known, radiating Manhattan sleekness and money, with her tight Afro, her tight black dresses, her expensive black leather boots. Then there was mysterious, racially ambiguous Liv, with a confusingly formal affect to her speech, as if she hadn't grown up in America (she had). She was in the a cappella group on campus and known for her voice, for her haunting cover of "Fast Car" by Tracy Chapman. Boys would come up to her and sing, "And *Iiii-eeee-Iiii* had a feeling I could be someone! Be someone!" and she would laugh, humor them. She dated some of them, but never for long, always becoming as quickly bored as she had become infatuated. She was picky, and prided herself on her pickiness. The relationship with

Brandon—they'd been dating for nearly six months now—was her longest yet.

Marley and Fiona drank their drinks quickly and got another round for themselves on Lula's tab. (Lula's wealthy and mostly absent father paid off every card, this his one true form of commitment, a dynamic Fiona herself was starting to understand with regard to her own father.) They looked around at tonight's crowd: rowdy, mostly guys. They stood in place as they got jostled by a big group of Sigma juniors making their way toward the bar. (Underage, most, with good IDs—it was easy for them to get real ones passed down from an older brother, especially because Sigmas had attended the same four elite Northeastern boarding schools and were bred exactly alike: narrow, deerlike faces; WASP-y pink skin and light brown hair; smarmy, moneyed grins.)

One at the back of the herd turned after passing Marley and Fiona. He had a broader face than most, a buzzed towhead, wearing one color in the pastel rainbow of polo shirts. He tapped Marley on the shoulder and smiled at her.

"You're in my neuro lab, right?"

"Oh, yeah, I think so," Marley said nonchalantly. "What's your name again?" A ruse: Marley had an incredible memory, did not forget names.

"Billy." He shook her hand. So seemingly polite, those prep school boys.

"I'm Marley."

"I know," he said. "You are brilliant in that class."

This was undoubtedly true. Marley Dorfman, from an upper-middle-class Jewish family on the Philadelphia Main Line, had been decidedly premed from the time she sent in her college applications, and never once strayed from the major. She had been valedictorian of her public high school of four

thousand students. At Buchanan, in addition to being ranked
at the top of the premed major, she managed to ace the several
literature, history, and Spanish classes that she took. She was
a Renaissance woman, in all senses of the word; she could provide you with commentary on the homosexual themes in
Swann's Way, which would be as detailed and convincing as
her nuanced understanding of and opposition to the occupa-
tion of Afghanistan, or her sound reasoning as to why she had
voted for Hillary instead of Obama in the primary. And still
she went out every Saturday night. She could drink her roommates under the table. Marley's secret was that she was not
driven by success but by knowledge, that she'd been an autodi-
dact long before she realized it was cool. And unlike the rest of
them, she didn't seem to have much interest in romantic love;
she saw sex as a primal need for now, a stress reliever, not a
tool or a weapon. When Fiona saw Billy's arm already placed
firmly on the small of Marley's back, it was clear to her where
Marley would be sleeping tonight.

Fiona was shocked to find her drink empty once again. With
no one left to talk to, she left Marley and Billy without them
noticing, and made her way again toward the bar.

There was a young man standing there in a collared shirt that
was primly buttoned and pressed, a stark comparison to the
boys in wrinkled polos. He appeared to be a few years older
than everyone else, tall, clean-shaven, alone. He was leaning
over the bar, impatient to get the male bartender's attention.
Truckstop had become unbearably crowded in the past half
hour, a line now forming outside; Marley had been right to get
there early. Fiona tapped the man on the shoulder, and he
turned.

"Do you need a drink?" she asked.

He looked her up and down once; she was wearing skinny jeans, a tight black shirt with a scoop back, and no bra. She knew she looked good, in that way she only fully believed after several drinks.

"Desperately," he said.

She leaned over the bar. It felt sticky, but she ignored it, not wanting to betray her cool. She propped her breasts over the edge as if she didn't realize what she was doing.

Mercifully, it worked. The tribal-tattooed bartender looked at her chest, and then was forced to make eye contact. She'd forgotten to ask the guy what he wanted to drink.

"Tequila soda with lime," he said into her ear then, as if on cue, grazing fingers over her hip bone. She hadn't realized he was behind her.

"Two tequila sodas with lime!" she yelled, and he slid his credit card across the bar.

"Keep it open," he told the bartender, who nodded and returned with their cheap plastic cups filled to the brim with their clear drinks.

"Do you go to Buchanan?" she asked. "I've never seen you around." They had to stay close to hear each other, their lips making contact with each other's ears.

"Kind of," he said. "I'm a super-senior. I take two classes."

She didn't bother to ask what they were; it was too loud, and besides, she didn't care.

"Who are you here with?" he asked.

"My friends," she said. "But I lost them." This wasn't entirely true; she could see Lula and Liv still over in the back room, Lula perched on the edge of the pool table, Liv lining up a shot. She didn't see Marley, though; she had probably left with Billy by now.

"Same," he said.

Soon, with small talk exhausted, there was nothing to do but dance. He put his arms around her waist and their hips moved in time to the bad song, their groins pushed up against each other. He smelled of aftershave, like the musky, sailorlike one her brother wore. His face was deceptively open and attractive, as if hiding more sinister qualities beneath it: his lips were suspiciously too pink, his skin too tanned, his smile too straight and wide—a smile that didn't convey happiness so much as charm. She wondered why she had not seen him before. He wasn't a great dancer, but she couldn't help but lean into his touch as his fingertips traced gently down her lower back and briefly to her behind and up again, such a light touch that he might have been teasing her. When they kissed—and she thought she might have been the one to initiate the kiss, finally, too excited to wait any longer—it was subtle and sensual, his tongue making just the right amount of contact with hers. It was downright sexy—a rarity among the boys in these parts.

She came up from her dizzied state when she felt a tap on her shoulder, and turned to see Liv.

"Hey," Liv said to her, briefly nodding at the guy. "Can I talk to you real quick?"

"I'm a little busy." Fiona smirked.

"Two seconds."

"Go ahead. I'll get us more drinks," the guy said, pushing through the crowd toward the bar again.

When they were alone, Liv said to Fiona: "Do you know who that is?"

"No." Fiona laughed. "I didn't get his name."

"It's Gabriel. Gabriel Benoit."

"You know him?"

"Listen," Liv said. "He's really bad news."

"What?" She looked over at the guy. His face gleamed with sweat. He towered over their classmates as he waited for their drinks. "How do you know?"

"He used to be in Zeta." Liv lowered her voice, spoke into Fiona's ear. "He got kicked out after this freshman girl came forward saying he had raped her. It went to the college tribunal and everything, and he got suspended for a year. The only reason he was able to come back and finish was because his parents donated the new science building that they just broke ground on."

"Oh my God, *that* Benoit."

Fiona looked over at Gabriel again, tapping his fingers on the bar as he waited. She had enough self-awareness, enough of an understanding of what drunkenness did to her, to understand that she was not in a place to make a good decision right now. That had not, however, stopped her from making bad decisions before. Her mind was fuzzy, as if there were a scrim of dust over her thoughts, but her emotions cut through the haziness like the sun at noon: she was feeling deliciously brazen. And attracted to this person who was supposedly bad news. Liv liked to be protective of Fiona, perhaps too much these days. She liked to be on the finger-wagging side of things; it defended her from situations in which she could, actually, be blamed. Fiona could very easily imagine a universe in which Liv heard one accusation about Gabriel Benoit and ran with it. And didn't Liv, perhaps, miss being single, miss going home with whichever stranger she pleased?

"I think I'm okay," Fiona said.

"What?"

"I said, I think I'm good."

"Fiona, you can't go home with him."

"Says who?" Fiona said.

This seemed to render Liv speechless, and Fiona turned away from Liv before she could register a response and pushed through the crowd, finding her way to Gabriel.

"Perfect timing," he said, handing her a fresh drink. In one swift motion, she pulled his head close to her mouth, made contact with his ear, and bit it.

They ended up at another bar, a quieter, more refined one in the artsy quarter downtown, where they ordered artisanal cocktails and he stuck his hand through the top of her jeans while the bartender's back was turned. They stayed until the bar closed.

"Come back to my place," he said.

"Where do you live?"

"We can walk." He took her hand. She wouldn't be able to get home at this point anyway; there were no cabs this late, and they were somewhere downtown, somewhere far from her house. She could feel her phone buzzing in her clutch; she took it out, saw that there were three missed calls from Liv. She didn't have much battery left. She threw the phone back into her bag.

They ended up in his loft apartment in an old brick building, a converted factory of some sort. He threw her onto the couch, pulled her shirt off over her head in a swift motion.

"Do you have roommates?" she asked, covering her stomach.

"No," he said, unhooking her bra.

"Not here." She looked over to the open windows and covered her nipples with one arm while the other remained firmly over her belly.

In the dark bedroom, he passed out nearly immediately, and she felt both insulted and relieved. She tossed and turned; the flannel sheets were too hot. She woke up in the middle of the night, naked, her skin burning and slick, embarrassed that she had sweated through his sheets. Her mouth was hot and dry—she could taste her own terrible breath—and her head pounded.

She groped around the bedside table for water, but there was none. She didn't realize Gabriel was also awake until he rolled on top of her—she could smell that his breath was as bad as hers—and abruptly stuck his fingers inside her. It was painful; she wasn't anywhere close to being ready. She tried kissing his neck, roaming her hands up and down his back, hoping to turn herself on, but he was panting and he smelled bad and he was dripping sweat onto her. After minutes of him jabbing his fingers into her—she could feel that his fingernails needed to be trimmed—he took them out and she felt relief before he replaced them with his half-flaccid penis. He thrust several times, trying to make himself harder, grunting and sweating, and it took Fiona a few moments, in her half-drunk, half-hungover state, to realize that he wasn't wearing a condom.

"Stop," she said, which came out rasped at first, as she realized she had not spoken a word in this middle-of-the-night interlude. She cleared her throat.

"Stop," she said, clearer this time.

"You don't like this," he said, not a question so much as a statement, with a cadence of dirty talk to it, like he was enjoying the fact that she didn't like it, still thrusting. "Give me one minute." He didn't look at Fiona.

"I said no." She pushed his hand away. "It hurts."

He looked at her, perplexed, then sighed in annoyance and withdrew from her. He flopped onto the mattress beside her. They were silent for a few moments, breathing heavily. She thought that maybe it was over, maybe he would fall back asleep.

Then she felt him take her hand, and move it onto himself. As if she were merely an instrument, he held his hand around hers, which held his penis, and moved it up and down repeatedly.

She looked at the ceiling. It didn't take him long.

In the morning, Fiona woke up first. She put on her clothes from the night before and checked her purse to make sure she had everything: keys, phone, wallet. She opened her phone to text Liv or Marley or Lula for a ride home, but it was dead. She thought of trying to find Gabriel's phone, but she didn't want to accidentally wake him—and besides, she knew none of her friends' numbers by heart. Careful to make no noise, she gathered her shoes in one hand and tiptoed barefoot out of his room and to the front door. She winced at the sound as the door creaked behind her, and she slipped her high heels on, wincing again at the pain from last night's blisters.

Outside, she found herself in a narrow cobblestone alleyway, and she walked toward the light. When she reached it, the street opened out into the main drag of downtown, and she shielded her eyes at the sudden brightness. Town was still sleepy: the streets were wet, having just been washed, and deliverymen were unpacking boxes from a bread truck and carrying them into the charming café across the street, where Fiona and her roommates occasionally came to eat sandwiches when they were in the mood to splurge. No one else was out. Cabs didn't really roam around this little city, and unless she miraculously came upon one, Fiona would have to walk two miles back to her house. Her feet throbbing, she began to climb the hill that would lead her home.

As she crossed the busy intersection at Ellsworth Avenue, a man behind the wheel of a souped-up Camry rolled his window down and whistled at her. She walked on the sidewalk against steady traffic, still spotting no other pedestrians, past St. Lazarus, the "bad" hospital (they were all told in orientation that they were to go to County Hospital in case of emergency, and *not,* under any circumstances, to St. Lazarus), past the shuttered fish market that she had never once seen open, past the public elementary school where she had volunteered to help local first-graders with their reading during the first semester of her freshman year. Several more cars honked at her; she was, after all, walking along an industrial road in a tight dress and high heels at nine A.M. on a Sunday. She desperately wanted to take her heels off and thought about doing so several times, but ultimately forced herself to resist the temptation. The pain was excruciating, but even Fiona wasn't in a low enough place to walk barefoot on Ellsworth Avenue.

The night left a sinkhole in her gut. But within it was contained the distinct feeling of an accomplishment, a conquest. This was not unusual for her after a one-night stand, that particular combination of pride and disgust in herself. For she was a late bloomer: a virgin until college, and only having slept with one person before the death of her sister, Helen (and an inconsequential one, at that—a guy on her freshman hall whom she used to get it over with). After Helen died, though, some shackles around Fiona's own virtuousness appeared to loosen themselves.

For the first nineteen years of her life, Fiona had been studious and she followed rules. She didn't feel important or beautiful—and she knew, in fact, that she was neither of these things—but she could at least do well within the parameters of a suburban, upper-middle-class life: play sports; join student council; make friends; get As; go to a good college. These were achievable goals, and she met them with aplomb. She could chalk up her overachieving state to being the middle child between a precocious older brother and a babied younger sister, though that wasn't quite fair. It was rather that Fiona had a striving gene within her, and a deep understanding that she would never be noticed or loved if she didn't excel in the only way she knew how: following the rules. Fiona lived, for those first nineteen years, in an orderly state, continually meeting the expectations she imagined the world had set for her.

And then Helen died, and rules no longer seemed to be relevant. Their family fell into disarray: her father left, and her mother holed herself up in her bedroom for months, while her older brother, Liam, took on the role of both parents. Helen had died in her sleep, thirteen years old, in her bunk at sleep-away camp. No one even knew she'd been sick—with a congenital heart defect, a dormant, symptomless malady passed on by an apparently persistent recessive gene. If Helen could die in her sleep at Camp Marigold, her favorite place on earth, before she even got her first period, then Fiona became sure there was no order to anything anymore. Life was chaos, and rules were futile. There were, in fact, no rules.

Fiona became consumed with an uncontrollable fear that she, too, had a heart problem, even though they'd all gone for advanced testing after Helen's death to ensure this wasn't the case. During that fall two years earlier, when Fiona had taken a sabbatical from school—supposedly to be there for her mother, a task that turned out to be in vain—Fiona hadn't been able to fall asleep for hours, afraid of her recurring nightmares in which Helen's body decomposed in the top bunk, putrid in the August heat, because Fiona herself had forgotten to bury her. In the daytime, she moved through the house as if in a fugue state, underslept and haunted by images of Helen's corpse, the eyes open and glassy and looking out into nothing.

Her body went into overdrive: her heart pounded with gusto and she was plagued with a giant clenching sensation in the middle of her stomach, as if all of her organs were tightened into a fist. Her body was all she could think about. Obsessed with her inability to control her own pulse, she spent hours on YouTube following deep-breathing videos, which never worked for her. She couldn't eat. The therapist she briefly saw in Larchmont suggested exercise as an antidote to her anxiety, so she began to run, and discovered that it only resulted in her heart beating twice as fast. It did stoke her appetite, though, and that made the running worthwhile, because her anxiety abated, albeit temporarily, when she ate. She came back from long jogs in the late-autumn cold and devoured three bowls of cereal, feeling the fist inside of her unclench as she chewed and swallowed, only to tighten back into place the minute she was sated. She wouldn't be able to eat again until after the following day's run.

When she returned to school in the spring of sophomore year she was thinner. She'd gained the freshman fifteen her first year but lost all of it, and then some, during the semester away. Buchanan was a small college, but plenty of people didn't know why she'd been gone, so she got some compliments on her appearance, and more attention at parties. Though she'd never been a heavy drinker, she soon discovered how convenient and effective alcohol was as a salve. It was everywhere, and drinking heavily at a party was simply what you did. It was magic how alcohol eased her rapid-fire heartbeat and opened the fist in her stomach, and allowed her to flirt more easily, and made it easier to sleep at night. Soon she began going home with guys she'd only met that night, to have mediocre sex. And every morning after, even though the guy was far less special—sometimes downright unattractive—in the daylight, she would feel good. Hungover, but good, like she was finally living a life worth mentioning. A life full of mistakes and blurred recollections and laughing with friends over greasy breakfast sandwiches the next day about the mistakes, about the things that were forgotten. She often thought of how Helen would never get the chance to get drunk at a party and sleep with a stranger. As grimy as those experiences were, they felt like *living*, like growing up. They provided the interesting stories that built your adult self. They were the things you had to do now because at some point, you'd never be able to do them again.

No one questioned her behavior at first. It didn't seem like a coping mechanism at all; in fact, quite the opposite. It was joining the fray.

Fiona's feet were numb now, past the point of pain. Finally, she turned onto her street, though she was still many blocks away from her house. She passed several bodegas, closed on Sundays, toothpaste and Café Bustelo on display in their darkened windows, before coming to a more residential area—two-family townhouses with aluminum siding, abutting each other, their front stoops in desperate need of sweeping. As she got closer to campus, she saw a senior she recognized walking her dog, who regarded Fiona with a quick, shifty glance. Passing Bagel King, she made accidental eye contact with an overweight boy who was sitting in the window, chewing.

She arrived at their home, half of a three-story two-family townhouse. The house was painted a light lavender with cornflower-blue trim, colors that had drawn them to it in the first place. When they moved in, fall of junior year, Liv had tried to make the outside porch nice, with a little patio bench and several potted plants surrounding it. Only a few weeks later, they awoke to find the terra-cotta pots smashed, soil spilled on the wooden porch, the succulents and rosemary and basil horizontal amid the refuse. "Why would someone do that?" Liv had asked, on the verge of tears. Now they never sat on the bench out there; instead they came straight inside and locked the door behind them. Liv repotted the plants, roots still intact, and placed them on the windowsill in the kitchen.

Fiona unlocked the front door and went inside. She took her shoes off and let out a deeply satisfied groan, curling her toes, lifting one foot to massage the ball with her thumb. Downstairs was the foyer, where they hung their coats and left their shoes, and a living room they rarely used: a leather couch Lula's father had donated, and a flat-screen TV he had donated, too, which Marley's father had expressed jealousy over as he mounted it on the wall. They rarely watched TV, though; the house was tall and skinny, and they mostly lived their lives on the top two floors.

Fiona climbed the carpeted steps and felt blood circulating through her feet again. On the second floor, the kitchen, with its laminate floors and speckled brown countertops, was empty. This was their usual gathering place. The natural light was strong enough that during most daytime hours the kitchen was cast in a butter-yellow hue, and it made the place feel nicer than it was. Because of the light—they had windows facing south and east and west—Liv's succulents and herbs that had been moved indoors still thrived. They lined the windowsill above the sink, where Fiona now went to pour herself a glass of water.

The light in the kitchen also unfortunately drew attention to the corners of the room, under the fridge or beside the rarely used oven, spaces heaped with roach corpses and grime. The laminate floor was caked from months of trailed-in dirt from the sidewalk on North Abbott or from the muddy quad. The wooden table where they ate, in the carpeted area where the laminate flooring ended, had not been dusted in months, nor had the bookshelf that lined one of the walls. Liv had once tried to start a chore chart, sick of doing all the work herself, but Lula quickly vetoed that, rolling her eyes and saying, "I think we're all adults here." Liv eventually gave up on the common spaces, keeping only her own bedroom particularly tidy. Fiona was personally charmed by the dust and the grime: they were signs of life to her, as was the lace underwear Lula was hanging to dry over the arm of the reading chair by the bookshelf, as were the waterlogged Anthropologie catalogs and *New Yorker* magazines accumulating on the table. Theirs were interesting, stylish young lives, at that.

Lula's and Marley's bedrooms were on this floor, opposite the kitchen; Lula's door was closed, and Marley's was open. Fiona peeked in to find Marley's bed made and no one inside. She must have slept at the Sigma house with that Billy guy. Or was it Bobby?

Fiona continued up to the top floor, which had a narrow hallway with a slanted ceiling, a bathroom, and two bedrooms, hers and Liv's. Liv's bedroom door was also closed, and Fiona felt relief that she would have to talk to no one.

She went into her room, the bed still unmade from the previous day's nap. She plugged her phone into the charger in the wall, dropped her bag and her clothes on the floor, and crawled, naked, under the covers.

In the moments before falling asleep, it dawned on her that Gabriel had felt different than the other one-night stands. The night was blurry, but as she tried to excavate the details, the net feeling coming up was less of pride than of shame. There were those few moments, in the middle-of-the-night interlude, when he wasn't wearing a condom, when he thrust a few too many times for it to be accidental. And then her staring at the dark ceiling, waiting for it to be over. In a stabbing moment of realization, it was clear to her that she hadn't wanted it. Not like that.

But out of self-preservation, or perhaps exhaustion, Fiona pushed the memory back into a place she'd be unlikely to reach again, and fell asleep soon afterward.

2.

S HE AWOKE TO a knock on her door. It opened a crack before she could croak out a response.

"Hi?" One eye squinted open at the light streaming into the room. It took a moment for her to register that her head was pounding.

"Hi." Liv handed her a glass of water. Fiona sat up and took it, swallowing it all down in one gulp.

"Thank you." She exhaled and handed the glass back. Liv placed it on the bedside table, then sat down on the foot of the bed.

"You hanging in there?" They knew the outlines of each other's hangovers as well as they knew their own; Fiona's manifested generally in thirst and pounding headaches, while Liv's were more nausea-based. It was less regular this semester, though, that Liv would check in on Fiona during her hours of recovery.

"What time is it?"

"It's two," Liv said.

"Two *P.M.*?"

"That's the one."

"That's embarrassing."

Liv was dressed in skinny jeans and a thin cotton blouse, and her face was made up. She looked as if she'd been waiting for hours for Fiona to awake.

"You spent the night with that guy, right? Was everything okay?"

"It was fine." Fiona shrugged. "We had fun." She allowed a little smile to creep in, to imply an element of mischief.

"I don't mean to say that I don't trust you," Liv said.

Liv didn't trust Fiona's judgment, though—wasn't that the point? And even though Fiona did feel a certain vague unease, the details of the night were hazy, and she didn't want to corroborate Liv's suspicions in any way. She wanted to prove that she was capable of making a good decision; even worse than something bad happening with Gabriel Benoit would have been Liv predicting that outcome. Fiona couldn't help that she felt resentful of Liv's sudden holier-than-thou attitude, which had come, it seemed, when she started dating Brandon. Fiona swore it—Liv hadn't always been like this.

"I want to make sure you're okay," Liv said. "Gabriel's reputation . . . it's not great."

"I'm fine," Fiona said, affecting lightness. "Totally fine."

"I'm glad," Liv said, sitting up straighter on the bed. "There's one other thing."

"Yeah?"

"You were sort of rude to me last night."

"I was?"

Liv looked down at her feet, which were planted firmly on the ikat rug. "Yeah."

"I don't remember," Fiona said.

"I know you don't. That's the problem." Liv took a deep breath. "Fee, I'm worried about you."

Fiona felt a mix of shame and indignation. How dare anyone be worried about her? She felt like a hormonal teenager whose mom was scolding her.

"I've tried so hard with you. To be empathetic. I mean, what you've been through, I can't even begin to imagine. And I've been trying to give you space to let you grieve in your own way. But it's been two years, and it's gotten to the point where I'm not sure your way of grieving is so healthy anymore."

Fiona's head was so heavy, and she tried to wade through Liv's words. Parts of it rang true, but parts of it not at all. Liv's perspective was unnaturally linear. There was no space for backstepping. No space for air.

"I know how long it's been since my sister died."

Liv deflated, right there on the edge of the bed. Only a monster could argue with that.

"Right. Of course you do."

"I know you care," Fiona said. "But I just woke up. I'm hungover. This is the last thing I want to talk about right now."

If not now, then when? she knew Liv was thinking. It wasn't like Fiona was so detached from reality that she was unaware that she'd become a mess. But it was always easier to put it off, to put it all off, and so she did, while she still could.

"We okay?" Fiona asked.

Liv nodded, and that was that.

Liv and Fiona had met during the spring of their freshman year, months before Helen died, in a seminar called Le Monde Francophone. Their professor was an animated thirty-something woman from Côte d'Ivoire who spoke with intense enthusiasm about everything they studied: *The Adventures of Tintin,* which Professor Djedje dissected for its white French ethnocentrism and racist caricatures, or *La haine,* a black-and-white film about racial struggles during the nineties in the banlieues of Paris. (At the tragic end of it, Fiona spotted the professor wiping away a tear.) The subject matter was a far cry from that of the old-school French-born white men whom she had studied in AP French in high school, owners of all those names with the same-sounding endings: Voltaire, Molière, Baudelaire.

In middle school, Fiona chose French over Spanish because Amy, her mother, had promised that if Fiona studied French, as Amy herself had, she would take Fiona to Paris when she was fourteen. Helen, six years younger than Fiona, had mostly taken over their mother's attention by then, so there was no question as to which language Fiona would choose.

The trip was disorienting and magical, her first visit to another country, and Amy had loved flexing her college French in cafés and restaurants. Fiona remembered her mother smoking outside a café, the wicker-backed seats facing the sidewalk for optimal people-watching, Amy making Fiona promise to keep her pack of Camels a secret. Fiona never told anyone, not even her brother, Liam. The last night of the trip, they bought dried sausages, a wheel of brie, and a baguette from the little grocery store on the corner. They ate on their hotel bed, smearing the cheese on the bread, getting crumbs on the covers, while they watched an episode of *Buffy the Vampire Slayer* dubbed in French.

As Fiona learned about other French-speaking parts of the world, and as Professor Djedje delivered impassioned lectures on Islamophobia and sexism and anti-Semitism in France, Fiona realized how sheltered her visit to that tiny, tourist-laden part of Paris had been, how much inequality existed around her that she hadn't even noticed.

Liv sat at the front of the classroom, and for several weeks, Fiona would enter five minutes before the class started to find her already there: notebook open, pen in hand, reading glasses on, silky black hair over one shoulder. She was pretty, and she spoke excellent French, her hand often shooting up first whenever Professor Djedje posed a question. Her accent was so good that Fiona suspected French was Liv's native language. It became clear some weeks into the semester that the professor grew weary of Liv's overenthusiasm, and encouraged other students to speak more. Fiona loved to read in French then, loved the satisfaction of decoding foreign sentences, their syntax backward from that of English, and of excavating meaning from them. And she was good at grammar, too: the rules were inconsistent, but she'd memorized them all years ago, knew which verbs were irregular and which were reflexive and which used *être* for the past tense instead of *avoir*.

Speaking French aloud was harder. She knew the rules there, too—not to pronounce a consonant at the end of a word; the subtle differences between *un* and *une* and between *le* and *la* and *les*—but the words still came out clunky and American-sounding, missing all those lilts and all that melody one heard when French was spoken properly, the way Professor Djedje spoke it, or the way Liv spoke it. No matter how hard she tried, Fiona couldn't get the "r" to sound right.

"*Rrrrrrevenir,*" Professor Djedje would correct her, when she was called upon in class.

"*Revenir,*" Fiona repeated, but the professor shook her head, then made a hacking sound in the back of her throat.

"*Hhhhhhrevenir,*" Professor Djedje said again, punctuating that guttural "r" a few extra times for emphasis.

"*Revenir,*" Fiona tried once more, but it sounded like phlegm was coming out of her throat, followed by a rounded, English "r." Professor Djedje sighed and moved on.

For their final project, Fiona and Liv were paired. Fiona was certain that the professor had paired them because she hoped Liv's pronunciation would rub off on Fiona (though she realized afterward that it was likely alphabetical: Langley and Larkin). The assignment was straightforward: to give a presentation about a non-European francophone country, providing historical and cultural demographics, specifically the country's relationship with France; each student would also choose a piece of literature or film produced by a citizen of that country, which she would present and then analyze at length in a corresponding paper.

Fiona suggested that she and Liv meet to discuss the country Professor Djedje had assigned them—Algeria—on the second floor of the on-campus coffee shop. It was Fiona's favorite place to work, and it seemed that not many other students had discovered it. She was often alone among the sun-baked leather couches and reading chairs, the floor-to-ceiling windows overlooking the main thoroughfare for students walking to and from class. Fiona liked the din of students chatting and cappuccino machines hissing downstairs; she worked better in places with background noise. She liked to be reminded that she was not alone, unlike in the partitioned-off carrels in the silent library, which often sent her into an isolated spiral of despair.

When Fiona suggested the meeting place over email, Liv had replied, "You study there, too?" Now Fiona arrived to find Liv already reading on a couch, a fat novel open in her lap. She looked up as Fiona sat next to her.

"Hey!" Liv said.

"What are you reading?"

Liv held up the cover: *Vaste est la prison,* by Assia Djebar. "For the project," she said. "It's *amazing.*"

"Oh." Fiona immediately felt like an underachiever for not having started her book. In fact, she was planning to simply review *L'Étranger,* which she'd already read in high school. They hadn't even discussed their author choices with each other. "You're really far already."

"I'm sorry. I got ahead of myself. It's just so good. Do you know her?"

Fiona shook her head.

"She's cool. Really anti-patriarchal and anti-colonial and all that."

"I was thinking of doing Camus," Fiona said, suddenly ashamed by the obviousness of her choice, the most famous Algerian writer there was—and one who'd spent most of his life in France, anyway.

"That's a great choice," Liv said. Fiona couldn't tell if her enthusiasm was genuine or put-on. "I really like this class," she added, leaning in, as if it were a secret. "My French classes in high school were so boring. I went to this prep school where everything was just *so.* You know, all the early white men. Voltaire and Molière and all of that. Now I realize we were reading the colonists, not the colonized."

Fiona didn't think Voltaire and Molière were actually colonists, but she understood what Liv meant.

"You know, Voltaire was all about religious freedom, but he actually was a huge anti-Semite and Islamophobe," Fiona said, parroting a more politically active girl than herself from her AP French class.

"I believe it," Liv said.

Up close, Fiona could see how striking Liv was, with her

dewy olive skin and big, dark eyes, the lashes slanted dramatically and diagonally toward the outside corner of each eye, as
if they'd been drawn on. Despite her teacher's-pet persona, Liv
was actually quite sexy, Fiona realized now, in her formfitting
black turtleneck, schoolgirl skirt, and knee-high boots. Being
somewhat average-looking herself, Fiona often thought about
the intoxicating effect that beautiful women had on her. She
knew this made her an internal misogynist or whatever, but she
was doubly impressed when a beautiful woman was also smart
and hardworking and didn't rely on her looks the way Fiona
was sure *she* might have if she'd had them herself. In this way,
the thing that drew her immediately to Liv was quite shallow.
Fiona wondered, then, what circumstances went into making
Liv as industrious as she was.

"Where are you from?" Fiona asked, hoping to piece aspects of her story together.

"D.C. area," Liv said. "You?"

"Westchester. So your parents work in politics?"

"Sort of. My mom's a translator at the Japanese embassy.
And my dad's a lobbyist. What about yours?" Somehow, Liv
was lobbing Fiona's questions just as quickly back at her, as if
Fiona were even half as interesting.

"My dad's a lawyer. My mom . . . well, my mom is a mom,
I guess. Kind of lame."

"I don't think that's lame at all," Liv said, shaking her head
emphatically. "It's the most important job there is." This
sounded like a line, but Fiona was grateful for Liv's generosity.

"So where does the French come in?"

"What do you mean?"

"You're French, right? Is your dad French?"

Liv shook her head. "He's American."

"So your mom's a polyglot."

"Just Japanese and English."

"You mean you're not a native speaker?"

Liv shook her head again.

"You had me fooled," Fiona said, and Liv appeared to be blushing, genuinely flattered by Fiona's mistake.

When they were done brainstorming for the project, Liv said, "I'm supposed to go to this soccer party tonight. There's this guy I've been . . . And my roommate just told me before I got here that she has to study for a chemistry exam. Like she hasn't already known about this test for weeks." Liv rolled her eyes. "Anyway. You wanna come?"

Fiona was surprised that Liv deemed Fiona interesting enough to spend more time with. Most of Fiona's friends at Buchanan so far were potheads from her hall—funny, goofy girls who ordered a lot of delivery pizza and didn't leave the dorm too often. She agreed at once.

They'd gotten an A on the project, Liv delivering a presentation on *Vaste est la prison*, focusing on the subordination of women in Arab society. Fiona felt immensely, somewhat inexplicably, proud of her new friend.

They went out a few more times together before the semester ended, and then Fiona left to work as a counselor at Camp Marigold. They promised to write letters to each other, but they fell out of touch during the summer months. It was that August, when Helen died, that Liv came back into the picture.

She called Fiona often at the house in Larchmont—sometimes simply to tell her about her day, when Fiona didn't want to talk—and sent care packages filled with nail polish and magazines and face masks and Reese's cups. There were always handwritten notes in the packages, too, often about nothing important, but the sentiment in them felt genuine and heartfelt and gave Fiona a small amount of comfort.

When she returned in the spring of sophomore year, Fiona felt sheltered by Liv. She emerged as the kind of person one needed in a crisis: steadfast and unceasingly generous, becoming Fiona's tutor, therapist, and drinking buddy rolled into one Dr. Frankenstein creation of a selfless friend. Liv insisted they live together, and used her charms and Fiona's particular circumstances to get them an apartment off-campus in the spring, normally a perk only available to juniors and seniors. There wasn't a meal that semester that Fiona ate alone, whether it was Liv's home-cooked pasta primavera on a Tuesday night or bagels picked up on a Sunday morning. Liv also seemed to have an endless reserve of booze for Fiona's grieving purposes, and she offered it up constantly, supporting Fiona's drinking habits wholeheartedly and engaging in them herself. They drank so much pinot noir that year and smoked so much pot, and stayed in and played gin rummy, or went to parties arm-in-arm, Liv ferociously protective of her friend, leaving when it was lame, or dancing until the morning, or going home with fraternity brothers, hooking up with the boys in adjacent rooms and meeting at the bathroom at dawn, hardly having slept, bursting into hysterics. They were both English majors and French minors at the small college, and they had three out of four classes together that sophomore spring, so Liv helped Fiona with schoolwork and often briefed her on readings, knowing that Fiona was too bogged down by grief and anxiety to do much herself.

Liv seemed to have an uncanny knowledge of how to be with someone who was in mourning. The times when Fiona broke down—try as she might to keep it all in, sometimes it felt like the tears had an agenda of their own—Liv rubbed her back and shushed her until she calmed, like a mother would a child, sometimes even putting her to bed and staying there until Fiona fell asleep. When Fiona threw up from drinking too much, Liv held her hair back. When Fiona wanted to be alone, Liv busied herself with other things, managing to seem totally independent and not at all smothering until the exact moment that Fiona wanted to be with her friend again, at which point Liv would become instantly available. Fiona knew that friends like these were rare, although a part of her was scared that Liv had drawn closer to Fiona *because* Helen had died—because there was some strange novelty and celebrity attached to being the person whose sister died unexpectedly at the age of thirteen. Sometimes Fiona had to wonder why Liv had chosen, in the first place, to be friends with her. Did she invite Fiona to that soccer party that night, back at the end of freshman year, only because Fiona had complimented Liv on her French skills? Or because her roommate had dropped out at the last minute and she needed a new wingwoman? And would they have even remained friends after that semester had it not been for Helen's death? After all, they hadn't been in touch at all that summer. Why else would she return with such full force?

Fiona then cast these thoughts aside, feeling immediately ungrateful and guilty for even having them. The point was that Liv was there with more gusto than anyone else at Buchanan had been. And that was what she'd needed—someone to be there.

In the spring of junior year, after Liv got back from her semester abroad, they moved into the house with Marley and Lula, a pair of girls from Liv's freshman hall. It was fun to have more roommates for their card games and movie nights and weekend outings. Marley and Lula, too, were sensitive to Fiona's needs, though perhaps never so much as Liv was. Liv was a particularly loyal brand of friend, the likes of which Fiona had had tastes of before, but never to this extent. Fiona was used to being the loyal one, not the one who called the shots.

This year, that all seemed to change. Liv, Fiona, and Lula had done internships in New York that summer, where they fell in with a group of other incoming seniors from Buchanan also in the city, many of whom they didn't know well. It was then that Liv started spending time with Brandon, a preppy, pre-law, kind of cute, kind of boring fellow senior. Their ramp-up to dating was quick, and Liv simply became less available to her friends. These first few weeks of senior year, Fiona had to ask Liv for help with the few assignments they'd been given, when her anxiety was acting up too much for her to be able to focus on a reading; Liv no longer took the initiative. She also wasn't around as much; she slept at the Zeta house about half the nights of the week. Fiona tried to recalibrate what she needed from her friendship with Liv and accept that things necessarily had to be different, that a year and a half was long enough to be babied, that she would have to be better now, get back to being a fully functional college student. But then her needs bled out to others, to Marley and to Lula. Maybe, she was starting to realize, she needed too much from people. Maybe she needed to do a better job at relying on herself.

That evening, with both of them eager to move on from the day's earlier conversation, Fiona agreed to accompany Liv to the annual English department Welcome Back party, which was set up in the hallway on the fourth floor of Leviathan Hall, an area far too small for the occasion. They got to the top of the stairs, winded. Shiny plastic tablecloths were draped over the folding tables that lined the hallways, punch bowls and platters of store-bought cookies atop them. Seventies-era folk music played faintly from someone's office. Fiona's classmates, predominantly female, wore flowing embroidered blouses, boot-cut jeans, heeled boots, feather earrings. The professors were in their usual drab attire: wool, tweed, moth-eaten cable-knits. Fiona felt boring in her V-neck sweater and skinny jeans, while Liv looked pretty, as she always did; she'd changed into a sweaterdress since the afternoon, wore her long shiny hair down her back, and had applied a fresh coat of lip gloss, her full lips gleaming.

They waved to a few people they had classes with as they pushed through the crowd to the drinks table, where most everyone had congregated.

"Hi, Fiona." Her Shakespeare professor from sophomore year, a chubby and pink-cheeked British woman, was pouring white wine into plastic cups. The woman extended a cup across the table, and Fiona accepted it with a close-mouthed smile.

"How's your semester going so far?" the woman asked. Because Fiona had taken a leave of absence her fall semester of sophomore year, and then missed several deadlines upon her return in the spring, this professor—like so many of them at this point—knew the intimate details of Fiona's particular situation. Eventually Liv had caught Fiona up to speed in classes, though Fiona guiltily knew she could have ridden the wave of sympathy as long as she needed. Because it was a small school, nearly everyone in the department knew everyone else, and even though none of them had ever known Helen, the way she had died, so young and unexpectedly, was enough to soften even the most hardened hearts. (This was true of everyone but the Larkins themselves, of course, whose hearts contracted and chilled in tandem as if drawn as the inverse correlatives on the same chart.)

Now the woman was looking at Fiona with those pity eyes she knew so well at this point, all droopy and puppylike. Even older adults who had lost parents or friends didn't know how to deal with a loss like Fiona's, such a young woman having to experience the unexpected death of her even younger sister. It was novel, almost. It was the kind of thing one only heard of in movies or on the news. And for two years now Fiona had been able to discern the difference between those who cared for her grief and those who were putting on a show—those who perversely thrived on the novelty of it, for it made them feel so much better about the fortunes of their own lives. This professor would go home to her husband and say, "I saw that poor girl from the department whose thirteen-year-old sister died a few years back. Remember her? She looks so thin."

"It's fine," Fiona said humorlessly, and turned away from the table. Liv was holding a glass of red wine and already engaged in a conversation with Professor Roiphe.

Joan Roiphe was both Liv's and Fiona's advisor. Two courses in pre-nineteenth-century literature were required for the major; they were far less popular than the more modern offerings, but Professor Roiphe's animated nature and cross-references between the subject matter and contemporary pop culture made her early American lit class palatable, even interesting. Her love of the English language was contagious, and anyone who had grown up staying up past bedtime to read novels in bed—as Liv and Fiona both had—felt an instinctual kinship with her.

"How are you two ladies liking the seminar?" she asked, a cookie lodged in one cheek. Joan Roiphe was in her midfifties; she wore slacks and sweater-vests and kept her gray hair cut close to her scalp. There were rumors that she'd slept with female students over the years, though none that Liv and Fiona definitively knew of.

"It's amazing," Liv gushed. "Actually . . ." she started, the wheels turning. Liv had this weird thing around authority figures, always had to be so *on* around them. "I've been thinking a lot about George Eliot in the context of the class, her having to hide behind the pen name in order to be taken more seriously. I was wondering if it's absolutely necessary that the woman we write about be American? There's so much there with Eliot, especially in comparison to her female contemporaries who were writing lighthearted novels about the marriage plot. I think I could really make a case for the fact that the male name was not a personal choice but a political necessity."

"Well," Professor Roiphe said, and Fiona was suddenly embarrassed for Liv. "I'm not so sure, considering we're only reading from the American canon." Liv's face was blank. "We can explore it in one of our meetings," Professor Roiphe offered, perhaps to save the rejection of Liv's misguided overzealousness for another, less festive occasion.

"Great." Liv beamed, taking this as encouragement.

"Hi, Joan." A hand clapped Professor Roiphe on the shoulder, and she turned.

"Oliver," Professor Roiphe said brightly.

Liv straightened as if in the presence of a celebrity. Around these parts, he was. He was the department's prize catch this year, having signed on at the last minute after Professor Bernstein's sudden death (well, not *that* sudden—the man had been old and overweight). When Liv had learned that Oliver Ash was coming to Buchanan this year, she immediately tried to switch into the Holocaust literature seminar, but it was, of course, already filled to capacity.

Fiona thought she had heard his name before, but didn't know anything about him or his writing. As Liv reported to

Fiona on their walk to the party, Oliver Ash's first book, published when he was a mere twenty-six years old, simply titled *Adolf*, was a dystopian novel about the second coming of a Hitler-esque leader—an American man by the name of Adolf Kinder—growing up and rising to power in early-1990s America. It was published to acclaim, won him a few prestigious awards. Gus Van Sant had made it into a film, Nirvana soundtrack and all, a critical favorite and a moderate box office success.

Fiona had first seen Oliver Ash's face on a poster outside one of her classrooms, advertising an upcoming reading of his on campus. She'd stopped to look at the headshot: early forties, all seriousness and fury, gray-blue eyes pointed at the camera with sexual intensity. A thinning head of salt-and-pepper hair. In the picture, he'd looked as she'd expected him to look: like an ex-wunderkind who had aged into a smoothly predatory professor.

He was taller in person than Fiona expected, broader. He wore a tweed blazer and a wool tie, overdressed for the warm September night. He looked around the room as if checking for approval. He held his plastic cup of wine uneasily as he brought it to his lips, which were surrounded by gray scruff, and took a long sip. The word that came to mind was "self-hating," but that might have been too harsh. He had good posture, which Fiona could sense was a front; she imagined him actively practicing standing tall for public-facing occasions like this one. He was not smooth at all, but rather awkward, as if the wunderkind had woken up that morning in a body much larger and older than the one he was accustomed to.

"These are two of my brightest advisees," Professor Roiphe told Oliver Ash. "Olivia Langley and Fiona Larkin."

"Liv is fine," she said eagerly, shaking the man's hand.

"Liv, then," he said. "Hi," he said to Fiona, stretching his hand out to her now.

"Hi," she said, taking it.

Oliver Ash had an odd accent; Fiona wanted to call it British but it wasn't, quite. It was a gentle mélange of European accents, or something. Pan-European, if that was a thing. And now he was looking directly at her and he was saying something else.

"What?" she asked, having missed his question altogether.

He smiled. His teeth were small.

"I said, Are you enjoying yourself?"

"Oh," she said. "Yeah. We just got here."

"Where are you from?" Liv asked, cutting off any possibility of organic conversation as if she were tasked with interviewing him. Though she of course probably already knew the answer. Fiona saw the way Liv was looking at him, wide-eyed, chin tilting up in adoration.

"Oh, all over," he said. "Not far from here, originally, actually. I grew up in the suburbs of Philadelphia. Now I'm based in Berlin."

"I *love* Berlin," Liv said. Fiona knew that she'd been once, for a weekend, during the semester she was studying abroad in Paris.

"It's a pretty special place," he agreed. "What brought you there?"

"Oh, just visiting," Liv said, as if casually ticking off European cities were a hobby of hers. "Quite the scene."

"Did you do the whole clubbing thing?"

"A little," she said. Fiona knew that Liv and her friends had waited on line for two hours, in the dead of November, outside the biggest club in the city, only to be turned away at the door.

Fiona wondered then if her derision of Liv was too cruel. She was, after all, just trying to impress someone.

"I certainly haven't." He smiled. His little teeth reminded Fiona of Chiclets gum. "I'm about twenty years too old for it."

He asked Liv and Fiona if he would have the pleasure of teaching either of them the following semester.

"Maybe!" Liv said. Fiona knew that Liv would register for his fiction writing workshop the minute spring registration opened. "Are you enjoying your time at Buchanan?" she then asked, so eager with the follow-ups.

"I am," he said. "Though I thought I'd be taking more advantage of being in the Northeast. I had all of these plans to enjoy the fall foliage and take the train to Philadelphia or New York on the weekends and visit museums and see plays. Instead I mostly watch baseball in bars by myself. It's been so long since I've been able to watch a sport I care about in a bar."

Everyone politely laughed, as if that had been a joke. Liv was rapt as he went on about his classes this semester. Fiona drained the mini plastic cup and felt her cheeks warm. It was at this moment that she felt the telltale signs of rising anxiety, which still plagued her these days. It was as if there was not enough oxygen to go around for everyone. The answer was, usually, more alcohol, but the number of people surrounding the wine table added an additional lurch in her stomach.

"Are you all right?" Oliver Ash asked her, interrupting Liv in the middle of a monologue.

She hadn't realized her anxiety was so obvious to an outsider.

"I'm fine," she said. "Though I may go soon."

Liv looked over at her, surprised.

"Why is that?" Professor Ash asked. "There's free alcohol here, which there surely won't be wherever else you are going.

And the company is all right, too." He said this last bit in a self-deprecating way.

"Because communal joy and merriment have the opposite effect on me," Fiona said, "and if I don't leave soon I might hurl myself out the window."

This elicited a chuckle from Professor Roiphe.

"You can use my office," Oliver Ash said without skipping a beat, pointing to one of the oak doors toward the quieter end of the hall.

Liv had also mentioned, on their walk to the party, Oliver Ash having been the subject of a controversy when he taught at Columbia, ten years earlier. Something to do with sleeping with a student.

She looked between the two of them now, confused.

Professor Roiphe pointedly turned to the girls. "You two should come to Professor Ash's reading on Thursday. It's rumored he's going to read some new work."

"Yes, it's looking that way. In fact, perhaps it's best you all stay home." More polite laughs.

"I'll be there!" Liv said.

At that point, some other professor came and tapped Oliver Ash on the shoulder, and Fiona took the moment to duck out of the conversation. Liv, seeming torn, eventually followed her friend.

"You okay?" Liv said.

"I'm getting my claustrophobia," Fiona said, which Liv knew was a recurring theme. "Too close and hot up here."

"Want me to come with you?"

Fiona knew that Liv only asked this because she was supposed to, not because she actually wanted to leave with Fiona.

"No, you're having fun," Fiona said.

Liv paused. "You sure?"

"Definitely." Fiona truly wanted to walk home alone, to not have to talk for a minute.

"Let's go to his reading on Thursday," Liv said. She moved closer to Fiona, lowering her voice. "Isn't he sexy?"

Fiona looked over again at the man, who was speaking with a new group of professors and students. She supposed he was attractive in a dark, brooding way. His eyes were quite focused on whomever he was talking to at the time, which had a sexy net effect.

"I don't see it," she said.

Liv shrugged and hugged her goodbye, then made her way toward the wine table to refill her cup.

Fiona walked quickly down the hallway, but she paused at the top of the stairs, noticing the office door, slightly ajar, that had Oliver Ash's nameplate affixed to it. It was noteworthy that they had taken the time to make that, considering that he was only here for a year.

Fiona peered toward the professors and students in a clump at the other end of the hallway; Liv was now chatting with the Shakespeare professor at the refreshment table. Fiona slipped in through the open door and shut it quietly behind her.

The green banker's lamp on the mahogany desk was turned on, illuminating a disorganized pile of papers and Post-its. There was an open paperback, facedown on the desk to save its place. She rounded the desk to see what it was: *The Periodic Table,* by Primo Levi. She pulled a Post-it from a clean stack and marked the page, then closed the paperback. You weren't supposed to treat books like that. She peered at the papers on the desk, which were short stories by students with Oliver Ash's notes in the margin, sloppily written. ("What do you mean by this? PUSH.")

The bookcase behind the desk was filled with books by Jewish men: more Levi, Elie Wiesel, Saul Bellow. An entire row of Philip Roth, all the titles printed in the same font. She had never read any of the books in his bookcase, except for *Night,* which was required in high school. Everyone always told her to read Roth. She should really get on that.

There was also a single framed photograph, of Oliver Ash, a woman, and a young boy. The three of them were sitting on a couch, the boy between the two adults, looking up at Professor Ash, and the adults looking at each other, their hands clasped over the back of the couch behind the boy. The light was yellow and orange; the photo must have been taken in the evening, the space lit by soft lamps and a candle on the coffee table in front of the trio.

Where were these people—back in Berlin? Why weren't they here with him? Was it possible he was no longer with the woman? Why would he leave a child for a whole year? Or maybe they were, in fact, here. No one had brought significant others to the party tonight, and none of them, in that short conversation, had discussed their personal lives.

She heard a door open and she froze, sure she was about to be caught. Then it clicked shut, and she relaxed; it was the office next door. She moved toward the door of Oliver Ash's office and put her ear to it, to make sure no one was approaching. She turned the handle and slipped out; indeed, no one was on the other side, and no one spotted her as she left the door slightly ajar, the way it had been when she entered, and descended the four flights of stairs to the main entrance of the building. She pushed open the front door and breathed in the air of the unseasonably warm night. Her heartbeat, she realized, had slowed completely.

3.

B EFORE HER EYES could open, Simone smelled the distinct odor of fresh piss.

"I did it again, Mama."

As she roused herself, she saw the boy standing at the foot of her bed, his blue-and-white-striped pajamas soaked around the crotch and down one pant leg.

She sat up, put one foot on the ground. *"C'est pas grave, mon chéri."* She knew not to fuss. It was common at this age, especially for children with separated parents. Not that she and Oliver were separated. Not technically. To a five-year-old, though, a month without a parent was an eternity; Oliver's presence was probably such a distant memory to Henri that he might as well no longer exist at all.

Simone peeled herself out of bed, her bones aching the way they did every morning. This never used to be a problem. It was as if she'd woken up on her fortieth birthday a few months earlier and suddenly felt that her entire infrastructure was cracking. Forty wasn't all that old, but she supposed living in

this city, surrounded by young people and knowing she no longer had viable eggs, had something to do with it.

She knelt down to her son's height, one of her knees making
a quick popping noise, and kissed him on his forehead.

"Can you take those off for me, love? Mama needs to wash
them."

He peeled them off, one leg and then the other. The underwear followed. As he crumpled both damp articles into a ball,
he began to sob.

"Shh," Simone said, taking the soiled clothing from him.
She looked at his tear-streaked face. Though she was partial,
she knew he was pretty, feminine in his beauty. He was tall for
his age, but hadn't lost his fat pink cheeks yet, which got pinker
in the cold. His eyelashes were long and glossy, so thick that in
the right light, it looked like he was wearing eyeliner, and his
lips were so comically plump that when he pouted, she couldn't
help but laugh at her luck. *This* was the boy she had been
given. She must have done something right.

"Little boys have accidents all the time," she said. "Even
your father did when he was your age."

This was a mistake. The wails got louder. Henri, naked from
the waist down, flopped his head heavily onto Simone's shoulder, as if his neck could no longer sustain its oppressive weight.

"I miss Papa," he managed to say into her shoulder between
hiccups and sobs.

"Breathe, my love," Simone said, stroking his head while
biting her tongue. Who knew it was so hard to keep your true
feelings from a five-year-old? "Do you want to take a bath
with Mama?"

"No." Henri pouted. "I want to take a bath with Papa."

"Okay, we'll shower then," she said, snapping into action—

all traces of maternal sweetness abruptly gone from her—
taking him by the wrist as he wailed all the way.

He wailed all the way through breakfast, too, and on their
walk from their apartment in Neukölln to the U-Bahn, and
throughout the fifteen-minute U-Bahn ride—commuters rolling their eyes and *tsk*ing endlessly at Simone as the train am-
bled over the canal. He kept screaming as they got off the train,
down the wide tree-lined streets of Kreuzberg, the leaves turning toward their first hints of oranges and yellows and reds,
past mothers with their well-behaved children, mothers who
looked upon Simone with a mix of smugness and pity. She
knew this look because it was one she had often employed
when Henri was a younger, more agreeable boy. *Glad that's
not me,* she used to think when the roles were reversed, passing
a little girl throwing a temper tantrum in the middle of the
sidewalk and squeezing her own son's hand a bit tighter. How
quickly mothers forgot to be sympathetic when their own children were having a good day.

Simone had never been so relieved to get to Henri's school,
a French *école* hidden behind a canopy of trees and a tall
wrought-iron gate. She handed him off to his teacher, a kindly,
stout woman, at the entrance of the classroom.

"I'm sorry. We've had a rough morning."

"Not to worry," the teacher said. "We'll have a good day
today, won't we, Henri?"

Almost instantly, a friend pulled Henri away for an arts-
and-crafts activity, and his tears dried up. As he disappeared
into the sea of children, Simone felt near-immediate sorrow
and regret. Now she had to go to work.

....

Simone and Oliver had moved to Berlin four months earlier, following a particularly rough period in Paris. When Simone was offered a fellowship through the Berlin Museum for Jewish Studies, it felt like ideal timing. She needed to leave Paris, for that was where she'd had three miscarriages. It had become almost regular, the cycle of grief and hope and grief again: the initial physical pain, the realization, and the fallout, sinking depression one day and dissociation the next and the manic need to scrub down every centimeter of the apartment the day after that; the eventual rehabilitation (never complete; she was never quite herself after each one) and the cautious desire to try again; Oliver's growing distance after each loss, the gulf widening between them; and the final verdict from the doctor after miscarriage number three that, at Simone's age, it might be in their best interest to start pursuing alternative options. Had they ever considered adoption?

Oliver supported the choice to take the fellowship and said, in fact, that he'd had a book rattling around his brain for a while that took place in Berlin. So they went in June, to enjoy the summer before her fellowship and Henri's new school started, subletting their apartment in the Marais for an unthinkable amount of money to a British couple, and renting the spacious, airy place in Neukölln, in the former West, for a fraction of the cost. And then came Oliver's job offer from Buchanan College, a tiny but prestigious school in the middle of Pennsylvania. It was extremely last-minute, after the unexpected death of a beloved tenured professor. The head of the English department had been a colleague of Oliver's at Columbia ten years earlier, which already gave Simone pause, considering how things had ended for him there.

"Why would someone from *Columbia* want to hire you?" she'd asked at their new kitchen table in Neukölln. Henri was asleep, and they shared a bottle of wine as Oliver broke the news to her, still-unpacked boxes surrounding them.

"The man was a major scholar in contemporary Jewish lit and Ruth thought I could teach the seminar he was slated for in the fall," he'd said. "Plus a writing workshop."

"Surely there are other writers out there who also study Jewish literature? Why you? Especially in light of what happened last time."

He shot her a look as if to say, *Don't go there,* even though they had, of course, gone there many times before.

"That was ten years ago."

"Have you even interviewed at this school before?"

"You know how American universities are," he said. "It's timing and politics. She said she thought of me first. They're offering an insane amount of money."

Their money situation was thus: they were running out of it. Once, Oliver had had seemingly unlimited funds from his first book and film royalties. Over the past year or so, though, the checks had slowed. Were for smaller, sometimes laughably minuscule amounts. Oliver's place in the cultural canon was becoming less and less relevant. It would be unwise not to take the job.

"We just moved here, though," Simone said. She knew this would be good for Oliver's career, too. He was being given another chance in the States. But he would need to be there and she would need to be here. What about this new start, which was meant to be taken together? It had all been so easy these first few weeks, like Berlin had wiped the grief from Paris clean.

"Should I not go?"

She shook her head. "You have to."

Later, she looked up the program and clicked on the link for Ruth Alpert, the head of the English department at Buchanan College. Ruth Alpert was a name for an old Jewish lady, but she looked to be around Simone's age. In her headshot, she wore a swipe of red lipstick and a sleek dark braid over one shoulder. Her areas of study were feminist theory; twentieth-century English literature and culture; modernism; Virginia Woolf. In another life, they might have been friends.

The museum was within walking distance of Henri's school, and she took her favorite route down Schöneberger Ufer, a winding street with wide sidewalks that ran along a canal, where weeping willows dipped their branches into the water. They'd had such a good summer here, before Simone's fellowship started, before Oliver left, picnicking in Körnerpark, a Neo-Baroque garden with fountains and manicured hedges. (It was incredible how many green spaces there were in this city, nearly everywhere you turned.) She remembered a summer day watching Oliver chasing Henri across the grass and feeling, for the first time since the miscarriages, a sense of contentment. That maybe her one son, screaming with glee as his father spun him in the air, was exactly enough.

Now Simone took Henri to parks on the weekends, but she was never as much fun as Oliver. She was a single mother for the first time in her life, and she had little energy to chase Henri around when the workweek was over. It was probably why he resented her so much—she was no fun. And now there was starting to be a chill in the air; Berlin moved quickly from summer to winter, and the sun set so early these days, and soon they wouldn't be able to play outside at all. She worried about the onslaught of the deep freeze, which apparently lasted from October to May, often unceasingly. She might go crazy shuffling from one indoor space to the other, with no one to call a friend besides her five-year-old son. Maybe she should try talking to some of the other moms at the *école* or in the playground. But she was shy. And tired. Wasn't it strange, how loneliness begat loneliness?

She crossed the canal and passed an abandoned brick building on the other side, covered in graffiti. She cut through a park and came to a busier road, turning onto one of the side streets that were so characteristic of Kreuzberg: eighteenth-century residential buildings, almost Parisian with their wrought-iron balconies, French windows, and carved façades, juxtaposed with brutalist Cold War–era structures, with their slate-gray exteriors and their rectangular, ornament-free windows. Berlin's lack of identity was, in many ways, its identity: a long history of libertinism followed by decades of chaos, of Nazi and Soviet rule, of bombings and ruins, and then of rehabilitation, and shiny modern buildings erected as replacements amid the vestiges of Fascism and Communism. And it thrived amid the turmoil: the city was constantly building and rebuilding itself, thrumming with sexual energy beneath a gray and green expanse. The people were in charge, the gorgeous young people, like the blond woman who rode her bicycle past Simone now, or the man in black leather crossing the street who managed to look handsome with a septum ring. They seemed to come here from every corner of the world—not necessarily for the history of this place, but for the weirdness, for the repurposing of spaces and identities, for the parties in Soviet bomb shelters and the art museums in Nazi bunkers. They came, too, because it was cheap. The city itself was their blank slate.

And Simone, the forty-year-old mother, she of the unviable pregnancies, she who did not have the courage to make friends, felt impossibly weary, and impossibly old.

The Berlin Museum for Jewish Studies was a giant Baroque complex with a stone walkway and a burnt-red roof. It had been used as Prussia's supreme court in the 1700s, and was most recently repurposed as the largest Jewish museum on the continent. Simone went through the metal detector, past the front doors, as she did each morning, and waved at the guard as she gathered her bag from the X-ray machine and took the elevator to the top floor. She used her ID card, on a lanyard around her neck, to get into the library.

"*Guten Morgen,* Greta," she said to the archivist, who was reading a newspaper behind the front desk. Greta grunted and did not look up.

Simone passed rows and rows of stacks and long, unoccupied reference tables, until she came to her office, hidden in the back. She closed the door and sat down at the desk, settling in and opening her laptop, preparing to review what she'd written the day before. She already knew, without looking at it, that it was going to be crap. This project was, so far, complete and utter crap.

Simone was translating firsthand accounts of Jewish women from Ravensbrück, the all-woman concentration camp, who were raped or forced into sexual slavery, as well as the non-Jewish female prisoners forced to work in the Third Reich's brothels. Her field of Jewish studies was still an emerging one in France, and even now, in 2008, it was an area largely dominated by men, and thus, stories of male victims and survivors took center stage. But the women—who were raped by SS officers, impregnated, and then forced to have abortions, or to give birth in makeshift nurseries where the babies would never survive—were regularly sidelined. Simone had already written a book about pregnancy and abortion in the Holocaust, with a great focus on Gisella Perl, the gynecologist who saved hundreds of women's lives in Auschwitz by performing abortions, despite the lack of access to antiseptics or running water, before Dr. Mengele could get to them for medical experiments.

Recently, in her otherwise all-male department at the university in Paris, Simone had been feeling self-conscious about having spent so much time writing largely about a woman whose memoir had been published, who was well-known enough to have a Wikipedia page. In this way, she was no better than her male colleagues, who wrote over and over about Eichmann and Goebbels and the banality of evil (a term that, ironically, had been coined by a woman); about the most famous survivors, Primo Levi and Elie Wiesel; and, on occasion, about Anne Frank, who was a safe choice for Holocaust scholars because of her sunny sheen and secular nature. At the university—not a particularly reputable or prestigious one— Simone had been relegated to the lower-level Introduction to Judaism and Introduction to Holocaust Studies classes. The students were almost entirely men, and the courses were never filled. In graduate school, she'd done her dissertation on the intersection of feminism and Judaism in modern France; then she'd written the book on Perl, which secured her the teaching job; but after the birth of Henri, and a full teaching load, and all the failed attempts at having a second child, research had taken a back seat in her life.

Sometime after the second miscarriage, in the interval before they decided to try once more, Simone began more heavily researching the 35,000 women from Ravensbrück and other camps who had been forced into sexual slavery. The topic had been gnawing at her for a while now because of the lack of scholarship revolving around it—scholarship nearly nonexistent in France. Only a few books on the topic existed now, written by Germans and Americans, but there were still people out there—Holocaust scholars, in fact—who denied that women had been sexually violated during the Holocaust.

She applied for the fellowship on a whim; she was always applying for fellowships. This one, at the Berlin Museum for Jewish Studies, was brand-new, in conjunction with the recent renovation of their archival library. She saw online that the museum had a significant archive of primary accounts by women who'd been in Ravensbrück—letters and diary entries, many of which had not been translated. Many of the primary accounts were in Yiddish or German, languages she could read well—and Polish, of which she had a basic grasp. She argued that France, in particular, desperately needed more scholarship on misogyny and the Holocaust, and she proposed a book that would use the Ravensbrück letters and diary entries to reveal the horrors of sexual slavery during the period, while drawing a clear connection between the neglect of women's Holocaust narratives and the lack of scholarship on the intersection of Jewish studies and women's studies in the twentieth and twenty-first centuries.

Simone's fellowship acceptance coincided almost simultaneously with her third miscarriage, and that final, deafening decree from the doctor: she was too old. She was quite fertile still, so IVF wasn't going to help anything; the problem was that her eggs were not as young as they had once been—or, as the doctor put it, they were "chromosomally abnormal." She would almost definitely keep having miscarriages as long as they kept trying.

The timing for the fellowship acceptance, then, was exactly right. She so desperately needed to do something again that brought her joy, something that would make her feel useful, because she'd recently been feeling the exact opposite of useful. She missed poring over primary sources under a dim lamp, the way she did in graduate school and as she wrote her first book, pages spread on the large reference table in front of her, her eyes buggy from overuse. She wanted to make connections that wouldn't otherwise be made, to tell the stories that wouldn't otherwise be told, to discover it all for herself. She wanted to dig, keep digging, into more stories of women in the Holocaust who'd been forgotten.

So far, here in Berlin, she was coming up short. The letters and diary entries were there, but the content was vague and inconclusive, or—most frustrating of all—written illegibly. And so many more of the documents than she was expecting were in Polish, and she had perhaps overestimated and over-sold her proficiency in the language. It had been more than ten years since graduate school, and she was rustier than she'd anticipated. The sources in Yiddish and German that she *could* read were mostly mundane in nature, likely because these women were censoring their content for fear of their letters being found. She was angry with herself for not having anticipated this sooner, and angry with the museum for not warning her that the sources she was planning to use might not be fruitful. She'd been so eager to start a new project, and so convincing in her application, that she did not stop to consider the possibility that she might not find anything. There was, after all, a reason these sources hadn't been translated: they said very little.

There was one Polish woman with several diary entries in which the word *Sonderbauten* was repeated several times. The word meant "special places"; it was the euphemism SS soldiers used for their brothels, of which there were outposts at several camps. This woman had, as far as the archives showed, died in Ravensbrück, so it was curious that she learned about these brothels, which were elsewhere: Auschwitz, Buchenwald, and Mauthausen-Gusen, to name a few places. Perhaps she had been receiving letters from a woman in one of the brothels? Or perhaps she herself had, in fact, come from one? Simone had been working for several days now with a Polish-French dictionary, but the translating was painstakingly slow. So far she only had a series of words that had yet to be strung together to create any meaning.

After a few hours of moving back and forth between the nearly illegible Polish writing and her dictionary, her eyes tired from squinting, her phone began to buzz, snapping her out of the moment. She looked at the caller ID: Henri's school.

"Is this Madame Simone Klein?" a woman's voice asked.

"Yes. Who is this?"

"This is Madame Bouchard, Henri's headmistress." Simone remembered her from their tour of the school that summer; she had taken an instant dislike to the unsmiling woman in her drab blazer.

"Yes?" Simone said. "Is Henri okay?"

"He's fine," the woman said. "But we need you to come to school and pick him up."

He was sitting in Madame Bouchard's office, his arms crossed over his chest. His face was red, his lips pursed, his eyes narrowed: an expression landing somewhere squarely between shame and defiance.

The headmistress stood when Simone stormed into the room.

"What happened?" Simone asked. "Is he okay?" She looked to Henri. "Are you okay?" He kept his head down.

"Hello, Madame Klein," the headmistress said from behind her desk. She was a tall lady—one might have called her handsome. "I'm sorry to tell you that your son hit a girl in his class today."

"He hit her?" To her son: "You hit someone?"

Still he looked at his feet.

"It was in the playground, during lunchtime," the headmistress said, her face remaining stoic and cold. "I suppose the girl said something that antagonized him, and he hit her in the face."

"In the *face*?"

"It left a bruise."

Simone rubbed the bridge of her nose. Henri was big for his age, unaware of his own strength.

"Look at me," she said to him, and finally he did, the skin around his eyes even redder than the rest of his face. Not from tears, though. His eyes were dry. From something else. Something like fury.

"He has never done anything like this before," she said to the headmistress. "His father has been in America for the past month, and Henri has been acting out because of it. Extremely childish behavior in order to get attention. Reverting to infancy and so on." It occurred to her that she was talking about Henri as if he weren't sitting right there. "Tell me what I can do to make this better."

"Madame Klein, with all due respect, I'm not here to teach you how to discipline your son."

Simone was too shocked to respond.

"What we ask is that he have enough control over his"—
Madame Bouchard searched for the right word—"*faculties* to
be able to conduct himself in a mature and respectful manner
in school."

Simone had been hoping that a French school would feel
like home. They were only going to be here for a year; there
had seemed to be no point in putting him in a German school
for such a short amount of time. She didn't want him to feel
jerked around, and she thought that keeping him among
French or French-speaking teachers and children would make
the transition less abrupt. This hostility felt like the opposite of
home.

"This is the first time anything of this nature has happened,"
Simone said. "I promise it."

"That may be the case, Madame Klein, but we do not toler-
ate physical violence of any kind. It does not matter how many
times it has happened."

"What exactly did this girl say to him?"

"Maybe Henri will tell you in private, but he will not tell
me."

"Madame Bouchard, my son is hardly a threat to society. I
would imagine this young girl would have had to say something pretty incendiary to get him in here."

"We really can't let this happen without some kind of a punishment," Madame Bouchard said. "You're going to have to
take him home today, I'm sorry to say."

"Aren't you supposed to figure out the punishment here?"
Simone said. "I have a job." She thought about all the sources
on her desk, the Polish diary entries waiting to be waded
through.

"We have a zero tolerance policy when it comes to violence."

The phone on Madame Bouchard's desk rang, shrill and disruptive enough to make Henri jump slightly from his seat, and she picked it up without hesitation. She spoke with someone for thirty seconds in German before she realized that Simone and Henri were still in her office. She put her hand over the receiver.

To Simone: "You may go."

Simone grabbed Henri's wrist, pulling him up from his seat, and dragged him all the way home: the same way the day had started. Only, no wailing this time. Just a weighted silence while she figured out what to do next.

They lived on a quiet street, two blocks from the canal, two blocks in the other direction from Sonnenallee, a wide two-lane road, home to the best and cheapest Turkish and Lebanese food in the city. Dinner was take-out *shawarma* and *fattoush* on more nights than Simone would have liked to admit.

Their flat was on the second floor of a building painted a baby-diarrhea yellow-brown. It had been terribly decorated, with shag rugs and fluorescent overhead lighting—an old lady had died there just before they moved in, which made Oliver uneasy—but the bones were all there: shining hardwood floors beneath the rugs, south- and east-facing windows. They replaced the overhead lighting and splurged on a new stove (nothing, Oliver reminded her, compared to what it would have cost in Paris) and bought a mix of thrifted and Ikea furniture; they'd left all their own stuff at the apartment in Paris. She brought along only the framed black-and-white photographs of her parents and both sets of her grandparents and covered one wall with them, the one wall that felt like home.

"Sit down," she said to her son, pointing to a chair at the cheap kitchen table which Oliver had frustratedly constructed following the wordless Ikea diagrams. Henri did as he was told. She pulled out her own chair and sat across from him.

"You need to tell me what happened."

"Madame Bouchard already told you," he said.

"No, she did not."

He moved his head back slightly, as if he were afraid of her. Sometimes she had the tendency to do this: come off as stronger, scarier, than she meant to. She experienced it with her students, too. When she spoke of the Führer or Goebbels or the high-ranking Vichy officials during a lecture, she could see them shrink into their seats, like she had the power to do more to them than just teach.

"What did the girl say to you?" Simone tried it more gently now. She had to put the disciplinary self away if she was going to get anything out of him. Beneath her anger at him she still wanted to believe that her son was somehow justified for hitting the girl.

"She called me —" Henri stopped. "I don't know if I should say it."

"You can tell me," Simone said, putting one hand over his. She wanted her son to be justified. She also hoped it wasn't what she suspected. Tears were brimming in his eyes.

"Go on," she said, her heart racing.

"She called me," he started, and hiccupped. "She called me *Jewish*."

"You *are* Jewish," she said, composing herself. "That isn't a bad word in itself, *chéri*."

"It was she way the said it!"

"How did she say it?"

"Jewish boy. She kept saying that! *'Jewish boy, Jewish boy!'*" He imitated a high, girlish voice.

She hugged him and rubbed his back, unsure what to say. Was being called Jewish in and of itself anti-Semitic? She supposed it was, if the word had been lobbed at Henri in such an antagonistic manner. In a way, she was glad to have concrete evidence to go back to that awful headmistress with. If there was anything they ought to take seriously in Germany, this was it.

"It felt really mean," Henri said as she held him.

"I know it did." She pulled her face back and looked at him. "But you can't hit, Henri. There's never an excuse to hit someone."

She put her son in his room then, unsure what to do with him.

It was eight in the morning in Pennsylvania. She knew that Oliver's class wasn't until eleven, and she would be waking him up.

"Henri hit a girl in school today," she told him in French when he answered the phone. These days, since he'd been gone, she only spoke French to him. It was her way of preserving what little she had left from her country. Oliver, who was fully immersed back in his America, tended to respond in English anyway.

"He hit a girl?"

"That's what I said."

"What the fuck happened?"

"Apparently she was teasing him, calling him 'Jewish boy' over and over. Antagonizing him."

"Christ."

"At least she didn't call him a *dirty* Jew."

"I don't know," he said. "Did he hit her hard?"

"She has a bruise."

"A bruise? Where?"

"On her cheek."

Oliver let out an exasperated exhale on the other end. "What are we supposed to do?"

"I had to take him home. That headmistress, I swear—"

"Shouldn't we fight this?"

She took umbrage with the use of the word "we." "You mean me. I'm not sure how you're going to be able to help much from over there."

"Or what about a new school? If the headmistress is really that bad—"

"And how would I manage that?" Simone said. "The next closest French school is in Prenzlauer Berg. It would take an extra hour out of my day. It's too much."

He took another deep breath to steel himself. "I can't help the fact that I am here, earning money for our family."

"Right. Money. When does your first paycheck come in, by the way?" She had yet to see any of the money. "Is Miss Ruth Alpert going to hand-deliver it to you personally?"

"Jesus Christ," he hissed.

She heard herself now; she heard how ridiculous she was being, but she couldn't help but keep prodding.

"I think you wanted to be there without us," she said.

"Simone, come on," he said. "I just woke up."

He always made her feel so demanding, like she wanted too much from him.

"There's nothing shameful about needing to process things

by yourself," she said, and she could hear the passive-aggressive tone in her voice. "I know this year was hard on you, too." He had cried, briefly, after the third miscarriage. He wasn't entirely unfeeling. But there *was* something wrong with his leaving nearly the minute they moved to Berlin; he should be processing with her, he should have insisted he stay. She knew she had told him to go, but part of her wished that he'd refused to.

"It's not that," he tried.

"Oliver," she said. "He misses you."

Which was to say: they missed him. She missed him. Only, it was easier to use Henri as a proxy.

—*//*—

Simone had met Oliver in a bar in Paris six years earlier, the night after she had refused Ariel's proposal. They barely spoke in his palatial, sparsely decorated apartment in the third arrondissement, so intent were they on the physical: grabbing and bruising and gnawing and digging. She didn't sleep there; he was meant to be one time only, a clearing of her system, an erasure of her slate so that she could start anew. Afterward, it was late but she felt like taking the nearly hour-long walk to her apartment in Montmartre—which she was still sharing with Ariel; she would have to move out as quickly as she could—her insides pleasurably sore. Who was this man who could afford to live in such a large apartment in the Marais? It didn't matter anyway. She'd never see him again.

She slept on the couch, and in the morning, awoke to a text message.

"It's Oliver," the message said—in French, although they'd been speaking mostly English the night before. "You forgot your necklace." Wrong gender assigned to "necklace."

The emerald necklace, the one that contained the gem from her maternal grandmother's engagement ring. She couldn't leave it, much as she didn't want to see him.

"I'll be over in a little bit," she replied in English.

Late in the afternoon she took the Métro back to his apartment. When he answered the door he was wearing glasses, a nice V-neck sweater. Without a word he beckoned her toward him and clasped the necklace around her bare neck.

"I was wondering if you'd like to go to dinner with me tonight," he asked.

He took her to an upscale bistro in Saint-Germain-des-Prés and ordered a 1991 Saint-Émilion.

"Did I give you my number last night?" she asked. "I don't remember doing so."

"You did," he said, swirling his wine.

"That's extremely disconcerting," she said. She rarely blacked out.

"Your English is extremely good," he said.

She asked him what he did.

"I'm a writer," he told her.

"What do you write?"

"Novels, mostly," he said.

Family money, perhaps. "Anything I would know?"

The escargot they had ordered arrived at the table. Oliver took his time in answering, first picking out a snail with the miniature fork.

"My first book was a novel called *Adolf*," he told her.

She took her own escargot, chewed, swallowed, feigned a look of searching into the far reaches of her memory. God, she'd read that book when she was, what, twenty-four? They were around the same age; he must have been so young when he wrote it.

"I think I did read that," she finally said. "Quite dystopian, no? Darkly funny?"

"Pitch-black," he said. "Did you really read it?"

"Yes," she admitted, putting her fork down. That book was everywhere in the midnineties, and as a graduate student in Holocaust studies, she practically had an obligation to read it. She was a harsh critic of most fictional Nazi or Holocaust narratives, because alternate histories of the subject matter brought about a whole new slew of problems. As long as there were Holocaust deniers, it was dangerous to reimagine the history at all—fidelity to and respect for the whole truth were of the utmost importance when it came to something as monumentally serious as the slaughter of nearly an entire race of people. And yet—she had liked *Adolf* in spite of herself. She'd felt as if she'd been in confident hands, ushered through a novel by an American Jew who had done his homework. The satire, some critics argued, co-opted Eichmann to make a statement about American capitalism and identity politics. She disagreed. She thought that this second coming of Eichmann was perfectly rendered as an American; it made sense, seeing him as a boy in rural Pennsylvania, working his way through college and up the American political ladder, and capitalizing on the economic recession of the early 1990s. It ultimately, she felt, made the argument that any man with great enough ambition, at the right place and the right time, could be dangerous. Fascism wasn't only in the past; it wasn't exclusive to Germany in 1939—or Italy in 1925, or Russia in 1931. It happened before, and here was how it could happen again.

"I liked it," she told him, with pointed, measured approval, this being all that she would, for now, allow.

The day after that dinner—and the night that was rather more tender, the night she accidentally fell asleep in his bed—she bought his second novel, *Dispatches from a Half-Breed,* and read it in one sitting. Had his father really killed himself? Had his mother, a shiksa, really abandoned him when he was a toddler to start a new life? Had he really slept with a seventeen-year-old student, and lost a tenure-track job at Columbia because of it?

She wanted to hate the protagonist—almost definitely a proxy for Oliver himself. She'd known men like Oliver, men who used women and drinking as a cure-all, men who got away with wretched behavior because they were charismatic and handsome and intelligent. Usually, she detested these kinds of men.

Only, she felt too sorry for Oliver to hate him. It was the following paragraph that had punched her in the gut, and had made her rethink the man who had seemed sexy and full of himself and slightly chauvinistic as, in fact, deeply wounded:

I remember my father's face as he drove us to shul every week in his Ford Fairmont: grim and gray, as if he were driving us toward our own deaths. He sat through services with clenched teeth and fists. He complained constantly about the duties that Judaism imposed on him. But when I asked him, when I was old enough to understand his hatred for the religion, why we kept going to shul, he looked at me as if I'd just slapped him across the face. "It's not an option," he had said. "And don't you dare begin to treat it like it is."

Simone also went to shul with her family every Saturday as a child, but her parents' relationship with Judaism, though still dutiful, was filled with reverence, too. They taught her the things they loved about the religion along with the responsibilities: the sense of community, the meaningfulness of ritual. They leaned back on Pesach and drank goblets of wine, and ate honey and apples on Rosh Hashanah, and dressed up for Purim, and there was joy along with the sorrow, celebration amid the loss.

Simone's mother, Joséphine, had been born after the war to parents who were able to hide in Paris due to the kindness of their fellow countrymen, and therefore considered herself French first and Jewish second. She moved seamlessly through the non-Jewish world in a way that Simone's father, Hugo, never quite could.

Hugo had spent his childhood and adolescence in a children's home in Geneva that was funded by wealthy Jewish donors, and attended one of the best schools in the city, also at the donors' expense, eventually coming back to Paris for university. During Hugo's time in Switzerland, the Jewish refugee children he lived with became his family, as did the rich Swiss Jews who housed them. He was freer to be Jewish there, removed from everything happening at home, even though he never stopped thinking of his parents, about the rumored gas chambers and crematoriums, never stopped hoping those rumors weren't true. He lived better in Switzerland than he ever had as a child of Austrian immigrants in Paris; he ate better, went to better schools—and it was thanks to the benevolence of well-meaning Jews, and, paradoxically, to those poor immigrant parents, who managed to find a contact with the underground Oeuvre de Secours aux Enfants in the first place, who saved his life but lost their own. Though he was grateful for their sacrifice, he could not cut off the thoughts he had of them dying of starvation or exhaustion, or suffocated in a gas chamber, or shot for sport. He didn't even know where they had died, whether they were eventually taken to Auschwitz or killed right away at Drancy. Which was worse: an immediate death, or a prolonged uncertainty? How did one believe in a God who had saved him but hadn't spared his parents? He never came up with an answer to that, but what was certain, at least, was that Jews saved his life, and Gentiles killed his parents. Judaism would always be, for him, synonymous with goodness.

So when Hugo had his own children, he did whatever he could to make sacrifices for them, in the way that his parents had sacrificed for him. This was, Simone came to realize later, a quality of her father's she respected deeply, and she hoped to repeat his selflessness when her time came.

Oliver's father, on the other hand—or, at least, the father in *Dispatches*—had a directly opposite approach to parenting Jewish children. The protagonist's father escaped to America from Berlin with his mother in 1938; his father and his older brothers stayed behind to work, because there wasn't enough money for all of them to go. They, of course, never made it to America.

The unnamed father in *Dispatches* constantly tells the narrator that his own problems aren't big enough, that nothing can compare to the pain of saying goodbye to your father and brothers. Nothing compares to not knowing what happened to those family members: maybe they were gassed to death, or worked to death, or starved to death; maybe, for all they knew, one of the brothers had to bury the other before his own time came.

The father treats the boy with disdain whenever he complains: about missing his mother, who left when he was young; about not wanting to do his homework, or go to shul, or scrub the bathroom clean; about wanting to see his friends, which the father rarely allows him to do. The boy thus grows up believing that he deserves nothing, that he should want nothing, simply because he should be grateful to be alive, a Jew in America in the 1970s and not decades earlier, across the Atlantic.

And then, when the narrator is in his midtwenties, his father hangs himself. The narrator then sleeps with a seventeen-year-old student at Columbia, loses his job, and runs away to Paris, which is where the book ends.

Simone began sleeping at Oliver's place most nights, mostly as a way to avoid Ariel and put off having to find a new apartment, despite the fact that she knew it was wrong to sleep with someone she felt sorry for. She wondered what it was about these damaged men that made them so good at sex. It was almost like he was not fucking her, but fucking away something that haunted him, some ghost looming in the middle distance. She noticed his drinking, of which there was always a bit too much, and the Xanax he had to take to fall asleep every night. She was not in love with him, but he was smart, and kind, and great in bed, and she enjoyed his company. Rebounds were, by necessity, supposed to be a little bit unhinged.

Simone was terrible at remembering to take her birth control pills; she often forgot to take them at the same time every day, and sometimes she skipped several doses altogether. With Ariel, at least, she would tell him that he needed to pull out on days she suspected she was at a higher risk. With Oliver, though, there had been a few drunken nights when she hadn't been as careful as she could have been. It was part of the allure with him, the knowledge that she was making one long bad decision. The reckless sex was simply an extension of that.

When she first realized her period was late, she was surprised to find that she didn't feel dread. She hadn't known that she ever wanted a child, and never really put much thought into the matter. But once she knew she was pregnant, the idea of aborting it—which had seemed, at first, to be the obvious option—set her into a fit of uncontrollable, violent vomiting. It was the morning sickness, of course, but it was almost always set off by those thoughts: imagining a fetus being wrenched from her, *her* baby, bloody and lifeless in a kidney-shaped steel pan. Once she knew the baby was there, she couldn't reckon with the idea of its absence. She couldn't help but understand that this was *her* baby.

She was thirty-four. If she didn't have this child now, then when would she? At thirty-eight? Forty? Her chances of a healthy pregnancy were only going to diminish as time went on.

She knew that having a baby with this man she hardly knew was misguided, to say the very least. A child was a lifetime commitment, and she treated it as such. She thought of raising it by herself, with Joséphine and Danièle's help for childcare. She was in her third year of professorship, still building a career for herself, but she technically had the money if they lived modestly. She still had some of her inheritance from her father. She thought of simply disappearing from Oliver's life before she began to show. He wouldn't even miss her when she went.

Toward the end of her first trimester, right before she would start showing, she admitted to Oliver that she had read *Dispatches from a Half-Breed*. Before disappearing for good, she wanted to know how much of that book really reflected the life he had lived.

"Oh," he said. He sounded terrified.

"Is it all you?"

He let out a sigh, as if he'd seen this conversation coming and had been dreading it.

"More or less."

"Your father? He was really like that."

He nodded.

"And the girl?"

He nodded again.

"And your mother?"

"I just said it's all true." It was the first time he'd raised his voice with her. He got up and went to the bathroom.

When he returned, several minutes later, his face was mottled and red.

"I'm sorry I yelled," he said, standing at the foot of the bed in his boxers. "Do you want to ask me more questions?"

She wasn't sure she did.

He sat down on the bed next to her. "I thought writing it all down would help me heal, or absolve me. Then these editors wanted to give me a bunch of money for it, and I took it. It only made everything messier."

"So you sold yourself out."

"Something like that." He smiled at her, and as she looked at his face, she felt a wave of nausea overcome her. She got out of his bed, ran to the bathroom naked, and barely made it to the toilet.

He followed in right behind her, held her hair back.

"Don't look at me," she said, head hanging over the toilet.

He took a washcloth from under the sink and dabbed around her mouth, wiped the sweat from her forehead. He ran a glass of water under the tap and lifted it to her lips. He sat cross-legged on the floor, silent, periodically giving her sips of the water. He didn't fuss over her the way Ariel would have, didn't ask what was the matter. He waited for her to tell him.

Didn't they also stay up for hours sometimes, talking about Kafka and Modigliani and every artist and writer that Ariel, a biochemist, had not known a thing about? Wasn't Oliver, in fact, very kind? Didn't he make her laugh sometimes, too? Didn't he also give her more orgasms more often than any man she'd ever been with? Were those things not enough, strung over a lifetime, to make her happy? Compounded with the happiness that this child, this thing she suddenly felt she couldn't imagine life without, would bring? Wasn't it possible that they might, actually, make very good parents together? Their child would be smart, and bilingual, and Jewish. Their child would know so much about where his people came from. Their child could have two parents, like she did—not one parent, the way Oliver had had. She could not bear the thought that she, alone, might fuck parenthood up the way his father had. Two parents could atone for each other's mistakes.

"I'm pregnant," she said.

His face softened, became putty, glowed.

She couldn't help it; she was crying, and she wasn't sure if it was from happiness or resignation or a mix of the two.

"What are you thinking?" he asked, pushing a strand of sweat-matted hair away from her forehead. "For what it's worth, I would be here. If you wanted me to be." Then he kissed her, vomit on her breath. She had not imagined such a uniformly positive response, not an ounce of anxiety or dread seeping from him. She supposed she hadn't felt any anxiety or dread, either. Was it meaningful that the two of them were ready at the exact same time?

And so she ignored the gnawing thing, the thing that said his trauma would be passed on to their child like bad blood. The thing that said he might have wounds himself that had yet to be healed, that might never be healed. And she said okay, and they had the baby, and got married so Oliver could stay in France, and for a while, actually, they were really quite happy.

—#—

"I thought we both understood that I was doing this for us," Oliver said now on the other end of the line.

"After today," she said, "I feel abandoned."

It was quiet on the other end.

"I miss you," she said.

"I miss you, too," he said. "It's only a few more months until Christmas. Why don't we Skype later this week, all three of us?"

"All right," she said, even though she knew seeing his face would only make her more resentful.

A few hours later—she had let Henri out of his room to watch television—Simone called Danièle, after she would have gotten home from her school day in Paris. She was a primary school teacher at a posh private *école* in the tenth.

"Horrible day," Simone said when Dani picked up.

"You want to talk about it?"

"Not particularly. I only wanted to hear your voice."

The sisters' kinship was singular: they were each other's best friends. They were the kind of women who tended not to make many other female friends, because—Simone knew—they were somewhat intimidating, closed off with new people, hard to get to know. Simone was distrustful with strangers, and her sister was the only person she really confided in. She missed her tremendously.

"How are you?" Simone asked.

"Trying to teach European geography to nine-year-olds is an uphill battle."

"Did your period come?" Simone asked, as tentatively as she could. When they had talked over the weekend, Dani had been a few days late, which was met with cautious excitement by both of them. Like Simone over this past year, Danièle was having trouble conceiving—although Dani and Alex didn't have any children at all, and had been trying for several years now. There were no pregnancies to speak of, no miscarriages. She'd been on hormones for years, and most recently, they had gone through a few rounds of IVF treatments.

"What do you think," Dani said.

"Sorry."

"It's fine. It's gorgeous here today. How's my boy?"

Simone sighed. "Causing trouble. He's got quite the rebellious streak."

"He certainly didn't get that from you."

"I didn't say it was a bad thing."

Danièle had never approved of Oliver. She liked that he was Jewish, but did not like *him*: she was reproachful of his moody affectations and the playboy lifestyle of his past; she thought that he drank too much, that his writing was dark and strange, that he was not a good role model for her nephew. She would have much preferred that Simone marry Ariel, and she had never seemed to be able to come to terms with Oliver being the polar opposite of him. Danièle herself had made the practical, steady choice by marrying Alex, who was gone for work so

often that it made Simone suspicious. Then again, she supposed, she was no longer an authority on present husbands.

The sisters themselves remained close despite Danièle's dislike of Oliver—and, if Simone was being honest, her own dislike of Alex. Oliver did not like Danièle, either: he thought she
was too prissy, too uptight, too judgmental—not exactly inac-
curate, but Simone never verbally agreed with him, feeling defensive of her sister. Oliver didn't have siblings, and he might
never understand her bond with Danièle. And Danièle was
particularly invested in Henri: it was important to her to keep
up with her nephew, the child who remained the closest to
being her own.

"When are you coming to visit?" Simone pleaded.

"You know how I feel about Germany."

"Berlin isn't Germany."

"That language. How can you stand it?"

"It's my job."

"I know," Dani said. "And I'll never understand it."

Later, Simone and Henri went to pick up dinner from the Lebanese place on the corner. They took it to go and ate silently at
home, Henri watching her, waiting for her to speak, but she
had nothing else to say. She had to admit that she was, in her
core, quite proud of him.

4.

OUTSIDE THE AUDITORIUM were a few young women holding signs that read EXPEL RAPISTS and BELIEVE VIC-TIMS, chanting, "Hey hey, ho ho, the patriarchy has got to go."

"You should join them, Marley," Liv said, as they walked past. They'd been bickering about the reading all day. Marley was appalled that Oliver Ash had been invited to Buchanan after the sexual misconduct at Columbia, and was determined to speak up about it. And as a Jew, Marley hated that Oliver Ash might be considered at all a representative voice of her community. Liv was obviously on the other end of the spectrum, attracted not only to Professor Ash himself but also to the prestige he brought to the college. She also, so she said, genuinely loved his writing. ("Why come if you hate him so much?" Liv had asked, to which Marley didn't respond.)

"Nice work, ladies," Marley said, cheering on the protestors while ignoring Liv. Fiona hadn't realized she was going to be playing mediator tonight over this relatively inconsequential issue.

"Maybe you shouldn't show them that you're about to walk inside," Liv said.

"I think everyone understands that I don't have to be a fangirl in order to attend a lecture."

"An affair is not the same thing as rape," Liv said under her breath so Fiona could hear it but Marley couldn't.

They were there fairly early, at Liv's insistence, and they settled in seats a few rows from the stage. Here was what Fiona knew so far about Oliver Ash's Columbia controversy, as Marley had explained it to her before the reading: two years after he was hired to teach in Columbia's undergraduate creative writing program, tenure track, he was fired for sleeping with a freshman. (She was also, it turned out, seventeen, which was a horrible revelation, though it was not *technically* illegal in the state of New York.) Then he fled to Paris and published his second novel two years later. It could hardly have been classified as fiction: the story of a professor having an affair with a student after his father, a Jew who'd fled Nazi Germany as a child, had killed himself. "Thinly veiled" would have been a generous description of its relationship to his own life. It didn't sell the way *Adolf* had, and critics were split on it: everyone found it self-indulgent, but some were willing to look beyond this and acknowledge his mastery of language and his unique voice. Some even called him the next Philip Roth—though not always in a complimentary fashion.

The auditorium began to fill up with students, professors, and community members. The college often hosted prestigious speakers, but Oliver Ash was their first big name of the school year. At seven P.M., the lights dimmed, and the English department chair, Professor Alpert, in an A-line dress and sexy leather boots, took the lectern. She looked over her reading glasses at her printed speech, said phrases like "stormed onto the literary scene," words like "dystopian," "cynical," "Holocaust," "haunting."

Fiona wondered what it might be like for your ideas to be so valuable that other people would pay to read them, or would show up on a Thursday night, when they could be drinking or having sex or sleeping instead, to hear them. And what was it like to have your ideas cemented in print, unerasable? To not be able to go back and change them? She was so mutable, the things she felt and knew changed so quickly from one moment to the next; she couldn't imagine putting a single one down in ink, to be published forever.

"We are so grateful to have Professor Ash here this semester," Professor Alpert was saying, and Marley turned to make a face at Fiona, who sat between her two friends.

The audience applauded. He walked out from the wings, shook the department chair's hand, and took the lectern.

"Hello," Professor Ash said to the audience. "Thank you, Ruth"—he turned toward Professor Alpert, who had now taken his place in the wings—"for the incredibly kind introduction." He was wearing a starched white button-down, top button undone, a navy blazer, navy slacks, no tie. Like those he'd worn at the department party, his clothes looked expensive. The slacks fit him well.

"I'm going to read the first chapter of my yet-untitled new novel," he said to the audience. "Please be kind to me."

He offered a weak smile and began:

"No one had prepared Michael for Berlin in winter."

He cleared his throat, and read on.

He'd spent Decembers in New York, Januarys in Edinburgh, even Februarys in Montreal, but the dark, gray expanse that

was Berlin from November through March was unprece-
dented in its ability to impress upon him a deep, unrelenting
sadness. He was not one to follow the rules of staying up
late and rising early in order to beat jet lag, and so, during
the first month, he would remain awake all night and then
sleep until three in the afternoon, only experiencing an hour
of sunlight through the window of his apartment—if one
could be so bold as to call it sunlight, the sun already single-
mindedly determined to set—before the sky began to turn
that charcoal blue again.

Michael's life was permanently charcoal blue. He saw
charcoal blue behind his eyes as he closed them to sleep in
the very early morning. When he went for walks after dusk,
when he finally got himself out of the apartment in Neukölln, he passed the doner kebab shops on Sonnenallee but
did not eat anything. In Kreuzberg, where his father was
born, he thought inevitably of a childhood in an attic, of
Berlin winters in an attic, winters that were strung on top of
each other like nesting dolls. He stuffed his hands in his
pockets instead and tried to keep himself warm while the
unforgiving East German wind worked its hardest to carry
him up, out, and away.

He read the rest of the chapter from the book and finished
to steady applause. Fiona found it engrossing, and less intel-
lectually dense than she had expected; it was about this man
trying to reckon with the memory of his father, a Jew who had
escaped from Berlin in 1938, while retracing his footsteps
throughout the city seventy years later.

The house lights were raised. Liv didn't look at either of
her friends—she was too focused on the man at the lectern.

Marley looked over at Fiona and rolled her eyes, mouthed, "Clichéd." Fiona nodded; she wouldn't admit to Marley that she'd liked it.

Oliver Ash said he believed that there was time allotted for a few questions, and several hands shot up. An usher walked a microphone out to a girl sitting in one of the rows in front of them. She was young, round-cheeked, a freshman or sophomore, the microphone wobbling in her hands. Oliver Ash smiled at her in a way that looked kind and unintimidating, a smile Fiona imagined his publicist or someone else who worked for him had encouraged him to practice.

"I was wondering?" the girl said in a high-pitched voice. "Do you have a writing routine? I was wondering if you could share it with us?"

Fiona had been to a few of these readings, and someone always asked this question.

"I find that establishing a routine is extremely important for me when it comes to getting work done," Oliver Ash said. "I try to sit at my desk from nine until five, with around an hour-long break for lunch and a walk. My wife teaches full-time and my son is in full-day school and then I'm in charge of the child-care after school, so that concrete gap of time while I have the apartment to myself is pretty much taunting me each day to get work done. Some days I find the words pour from me. Others I can barely eke out a sentence." Several audience members emitted small, familiar chuckles. "On those days, I read authors that I admire, and I drink a little extra coffee, and my lunchtime walks are a bit longer. The key, I think, is to keep your ass in the chair for as long as you can each day, and eventually your brain catches up with your body."

Bullshit, Fiona thought, and mouthed this to Marley, who nodded in assent. If he followed that routine every day he would have published at least one more book since his last, almost ten years ago. The underclassman girl seemed grateful for the answer nonetheless, perhaps emboldened by it, and Fiona felt content that this girl would keep trying hard, keep writing, a thing she clearly loved to do, because of this answer. The girl, giddily starstruck, passed the microphone back to the usher. A few more questions went along like this—who are your favorite writers, how do you get inspired, et cetera, et cetera.

Then Professor Alpert announced that there was time for one last question.

Marley's hand casually went up. Fiona and Liv both turned their heads and were surprised to see the microphone being immediately delivered to her, almost as if she'd conspired with the usher ahead of time. Marley stood, confident, prepared for something Fiona could not begin to predict.

"Your second novel is obviously largely autobiographical," Marley began. "I was wondering about your relationships to reality and fiction in your own writing. Do you ever grapple with the balance of fidelity to the facts versus fidelity to the story? In other words, where do you draw the line between fictional narrative and truth?"

Oliver Ash nodded, clearly considering the subtext to this question and how to tiptoe around it. The second book, of course, was the one about the affair. Fiona loved that she had friends like Marley, unafraid to confront a man in power. Marley was intimidated by no one.

"To me, 'truth' does not live so much in facts as it does in the realm of emotional verisimilitude," he began. "What's important to me is that my reader feels some sort of human recognition of the narrative. So whether or not I'm recounting things that have happened in so-called reality feels irrelevant.

That is, if we are defining reality as events that have happened in the course of human history. Which is, of course, relative, since we're always repeating ourselves in one way or another." He seemed to stop himself there from digressing further.

"Okay," Marley said. "That doesn't answer my question, though."

Fiona couldn't help but let out a wide smile, full of nervousness. She always laughed or smiled when she was uneasy, when awkwardness abounded. Liv's face was pink, and she was not looking at either of her friends.

"I'm sorry?" he said. "Perhaps you could rephrase it."

"Pardon my crassness, but I'm not talking about a bullshit version of 'truth.'" She used her fingers for air quotes. "I mean in the most basic way, aren't you actually betraying truth by blurring its outlines so much?"

The audience shifted their gazes back to him.

"No," he started. "I don't believe that I am. Fiction springs from life, but it's also dynamic. The borders between facts and fiction are entirely up to each writer. When a reader decides to read fiction he is giving the author the power to determine—"

"Or she."

"I'm sorry?" he said again.

"The reader. He or she."

Fiona swore she saw him roll his eyes. "When *he or she* reads fiction, *he or she* is granting the author permission to take liberties. This is the unwritten contract of novels. The reader doesn't have to like what he's reading, but so long as he has the book in his hands, he continues to be complicit in whatever version of fiction he's being served, no matter how much an amalgamation it is with a recognizable version of reality."

"So do you not care if people believe that that character is you?"

Titters came from the audience, nervous whispers.

"That's an entirely different question," he said.

"Well," she said, "if that character *is* you, this reader would rather not be complicit in our college hiring someone who abuses his power and sleeps with his students. But . . ." She shrugged. "Who are we to judge. As you say, truth doesn't really 'live in the facts.'" She handed the microphone back to the stunned usher and sat down. From the back of the auditorium, there were a few hoots and hollers and spurts of applause. Fiona, sitting so close to the man himself, stopped herself from joining in.

Marley had left Oliver Ash dumbstruck. Professor Alpert, flustered and red-faced, rushed out from the wings and toward the lectern. Fiona had to admit that it was entertaining, the way Marley's question had punctured the politically correct air of the largely white, largely liberal auditorium.

"That will be all for tonight," Professor Alpert said into the microphone, forcing Professor Ash to step off to the side. "Thank you so much for coming, and for your . . . probing questions. Please get home safely." She walked off the stage then, beckoning for him to follow her, and the audience began applauding in staggered numbers. Oliver Ash offered a small wave on his way out.

—*//*—

"Incredible. Honestly incredible."

Fiona was shaking her head in disbelief and grabbing three cups from the cabinet above her head. She, Liv, and Marley were in the kitchen, jackets still on and bags slung over their shoulders.

"I don't see why any man should get away with that kind of behavior," said Marley, throwing her purse on a chair.

Fiona grunted in assent, dropped her jacket and bag on the counter, and took the half-empty handle of vanilla vodka from the freezer.

"I'm not drinking," Liv announced.

"What?" Fiona said. "Why not?"

"I'm staying in tonight."

"You said earlier you were going to come out."

"I changed my mind."

Liv took a cup from the counter and filled it with water from the tap.

"You should stay downstairs with us for a bit," Marley said. "It's Thursday night."

"I have work to do," Liv said, and made her way up the stairs to her bedroom.

Fiona and Marley looked at each other, glances weighted with judgment, and after Liv was out of earshot, Marley said in a low voice, "Why does she care so much about him?"

"I think she might be trying to sleep with him."

Marley's eyes widened. "Are you serious?"

"She was fawning over him at the department party," Fiona whispered.

"What about Brandon?"

Fiona shrugged. Maybe she was being too harsh on Liv, but she suspected she was right. Brandon did not seem to make Liv really *happy*, not the way she used to be when she was single. It was like she was with him out of some sense of duty, because she felt she ought to have a boyfriend, not because she wanted one.

"Well, if that's the case," Marley said, "I don't understand why me saying what I did would put a damper on her chances with him."

"I think she's trying to make as strong an impression as she can. And she thinks he might have thought less of her because she was next to you. It's silly, but that's the way she operates. You know. She cares a lot about appearances."

Fiona felt bad immediately. She and Liv used to be a pair, Marley and Lula the other duo. She felt, confiding these things to Marley, like she was cheating on Liv.

"Well," Marley said, "I can't think of anyone I'd less like to fuck."

"Same." Fiona opened the fridge. "Let's make a drink." She pulled out a big bottle of Diet Sunkist.

"Did we forget to get Fanta?"

"I love this," Fiona said, pouring the bright orange soda into her cup. "It tastes like orange sherbet."

"Blech," Marley said, but held her own cup out anyway, allowing Fiona to pour the soda into her drink.

Marley leaned against the counter, took her first sip, made a face.

"Hey," she said to Fiona. "Have you heard from that guy?"

"Nope."

Fiona hadn't expected Gabriel to call, but she hadn't expected him to not call, either. The night had left a bad taste in her mouth, so why would she even want to hear from him again? But she did, despite all logic. Hearing from him would have made her feel she was valuable to him, would have been a way to prove herself and her own suspicions wrong about the night. If he had contacted her, then maybe what she'd imagined had happened didn't actually—because calling her would have meant that he wanted *her*, specifically her, and not just who-ever happened to be in his bed in the middle of the night.

It was better, she was learning, to have no expectations

whatsoever, to go on as if you were impervious to hurt or hopefulness. Her not being called after a one-night stand wasn't specific to Gabriel.

The distinct pain of not being called: one would say that this so-called pain was not really pain at all; it was a sting, a bruise, a pique. To not be called was not heartbreak, let alone tragedy. She knew all this, and still she wanted desperately to share it with someone—to just once be able to cry to Liv or Marley or Lula about her profound and never-ending well of loneliness and disappointment without having to attribute the feelings to her sister. Grieving was not linear or predictable—everyone always said this to her, when she took so long to cry in the first place, to even talk about it. The subtext there, though, was *Take your time, but you'll be sad eventually, about the exact thing you're supposed to be sad about.*

And she had done all that. She still dreamed of Helen nearly every night. She still woke up sweating or crying or screaming or all three. And then, at other times, she was sad about things that had nothing to do with her sister. She was sad to be alone in her body every moment of every day. She was sad when, once again, she realized in the morning that she had been the drunkest of them all the night before; or when she woke up in a strange bed and learned once again that the crash was more painful than the rush was enjoyable; sad when she pretended to not wait for a call. But it was predictable and girlish to care; you were meant to enjoy your freedom, to be happy with casual sex. To crave attachment from a man was desperate and old-fashioned and uncool.

"What about your guy from last week?" Fiona asked. "What was his name?"

Marley furrowed her brow, thinking for a minute. "Oh,"

she said. "Billy. He's been texting me, but I'm not really into it. The sex was pretty bad."

This, *this* was the pose you were supposed to take, the way you were supposed to feel. It never even dawned on Fiona to think about the quality of the sex. It was about the being wanted, and continually being wanted, which was proof that you were something, proof that you were not nothing, proof that you existed at all.

Lula slipped out of her bedroom and closed the door behind her, walking into the kitchen.

"Do you have company?" Fiona whispered.

Marley laughed. "Guess someone enjoyed having the house to herself tonight." Lula often had a rotating cast of girls coming in and out of the house—often girls who had never slept with other girls before. Lula had that effect, of turning them, or at least getting them to stray from men for a little.

"You can invite her to join us, you know," Fiona said quietly.

"I don't think she wants to be seen," Lula said under her breath. "What are we drinking?"

Fiona's phone buzzed on the counter and she picked it up too fast, feeling caught after her conversation with Marley about Gabriel, after affecting a certain indifference to whether he contacted her.

It was only a message from Liam: "Mom says she hasn't heard from you all month. CALL HER."

Well, Fiona hadn't heard from her mother, either. All the platitudes about death bringing a family closer together, Fiona had learned, couldn't have been further from the truth. Because there was no way to fill the space Helen had taken up. In the weeks and months following her sister's death, Fiona had become the revered child. As if, retroactively, everyone had assumed that she and Helen had been close. That her parents had it the hardest but she had it the second hardest: what's worse for a girl than losing her sister? What no one understood was that their attention was unwanted: it made her feel more guilty than she'd ever thought possible. She was unworthy of it. Fiona had once hated Helen for taking attention away from her, the forgotten middle sibling, but after Helen's death, Fiona got the attention back. Over time, she'd hoped, Helen would be catapulted into sainthood, forever the youngest, and while this had happened, Fiona, too, had been catapulted into martyrdom, though she'd done absolutely nothing to deserve it. While she had once thought she hated being the forgotten middle child, she would now have given anything to be forgotten again. Being pitied and revered for being "brave" or "courageous" only made her hate herself more for all the ways she could have been kinder and better to Helen when she'd been alive.

Her phone buzzed a second time, a reminder of Liam's scolding.

Helen was born when Fiona was six; by that point, Fiona had thought she would be the youngest forever. She even remembered asking her mother, when she was around kindergarten age, if there would be any more babies. "No, sweetie," Amy had answered, smiling, "you're my baby," only to start showing a hardened belly mere months later. The memories that Fiona had of ignoring her baby sister were spotty, surely, but Liam and her parents regaled her with them often. How she used to put on shows for them, singing and dancing in costume to her mom's Elton John cassette tapes, hoping to regain their attention. It was supposed to be funny, how much Fiona was jealous of infant Helen, but the tales made her uneasy, because the sentiments still felt true when they told her these stories during her teenage years.

The clearest of her own memories began around the time Helen was three and Fiona was nine. Fiona was old enough to get herself ready for school, and in the mornings, her mother would go into Helen's room first, clip barrettes into her blond curls, put her in a pink dress. On her way to brush her teeth, Fiona would often pass the open door, through which she saw Helen in her mother's lap, her mother playing with Helen's hair, talking to her in a hushed, singsong voice, sharing secrets only the two of them were in on. Helen made Amy happy in a way that Fiona had long ago stopped being able to. Everyone was so proud of that hair, wondered how Helen managed to be born with curls despite having straight-haired parents and siblings. They had yet to cut it, they were going to keep growing it for a long time—for forever, it felt, to nine-year-old Fiona. Fiona soon realized that as long as Helen had that long curly hair, Amy would come to Helen's room first in the mornings to clip barrettes into it.

So, one night after everyone had gone to bed, Fiona took a pair of scissors from her mother's sewing table, crept into Helen's room, and snipped all of those perfect yellow coils from her head, guided only by the nightlight next to the bed. Helen was a sound sleeper; she tossed and turned a bit as Fiona snipped the strands, once or twice making a moaning sound, but never fully woke up.

The act of shearing brought Fiona deep satisfaction; wielding the scissors, she felt capable and powerful in a way she never had before. The ringlets fell onto the pillow, rearranging themselves around Helen's tiny head like a crown. Fiona gathered them and threw them into the bathroom trash, did not even think at the time about hiding the evidence. The act itself was the only thing she'd planned for, having thought about it for several nights before actually doing it. She had not once thought about the consequences, aside from the one she'd been counting on—that her mother would come to her room in the morning first, instead of Helen's.

Fiona was awoken to the sound of her mother's screaming, followed by her reddened, tear-stained face above her own bed. She'd never seen Amy so angry. She had not considered this possibility. And there was little Helen, toddling in behind her, crying, too, but mostly out of confusion, her hair cut at all sorts of odd angles, some strands dangling a few inches from her head, others cut almost dangerously close to the scalp. Fiona had not been able to see well with only the nightlight in Helen's room guiding her.

That was the start of their real rivalry, probably, and the start of Amy's and every other Larkin's deep mistrust of Fiona. And Fiona's own mistrust of herself, too. What other evil was she capable of?

"Who was it?" Lula asked Fiona now. She was holding her phone, open to the message from Liam.

"Doesn't matter," she said, and put the phone back, face-down, on the counter.

5.

In the unforgiving light of the morning, I felt ugly. My breath was terrible; I knew there were violet circles under my eyes. I hadn't wanted her to spend the night, but she offered to stay after I told her about my dad. I assented. What was that about? There's safety in anonymity, I suppose.

THE PHONE BESIDE Liv buzzed. A text from Brandon appeared on the lock screen: "You coming to party tonight? Sleepover here?" Brandon lived in the drafty fraternity house, with its sticky surfaces and the endless sound of bedroom doors being slammed, either by careless, drunken brothers or by their girlfriends leaving to throw up the contents of last night's keg. The first time Liv woke up in Brandon's room on the third floor, with the slanted ceiling and chromatic posters from DMB and Phish concerts on the walls, she found the silence eerie. She'd only known the house during parties from her first three years at Buchanan: a busty girl from her eighteenth-century French literature class retching

over a banister, a table of shouting boys in the basement lined
up to chug and flip their Solo cups in record time, wooden
floors so slick with dirt and beer you could skate on them. At
dawn that first morning, needing to pee, her stomach churning
from the previous night's sugary punch, she went into Brandon's bathroom, which he shared with the overweight boy they
cruelly and sardonically called Stretch. No toilet paper, of
course. She squatted over the seat and shook the excess urine
from herself; she could hear Stretch's heavy snores from the
adjoining bedroom. The inside of the bowl was crusted with
the remains of someone's vomit.

When she left Brandon's room to head back to her own
house, seeing the frat house in that early-September light was
stark, depressing. The floor was imprinted with marks from
sneakers and high heels, littered with the red cups. Some had
been half full; stale beer had spilled from them and seeped into
the already stained hardwood. It was a graveyard of collegiate
debauchery and regret, and now she did all she could to avoid
sleeping there, at least on the nights there were parties.

She put the phone facedown on her bedside table now. Kept
reading.

> As I watched the girl sleep, I felt certain, not without some
> self-awareness and apprehension, that I was going to sink all
> my hopes into her, and that I would, in consequence, take
> her down with me.

Liv had purchased *Dispatches from a Half-Breed* at the college bookstore the day after she met Oliver Ash at the department party. She'd read *Adolf* years ago, and had enjoyed it,
though dystopian fiction wasn't really her style. She preferred
classic narrative literature: a linear storyline with compelling

plot points; clean, intelligent prose; relatable, fully fleshed-out characters. Often romance was involved. She liked Jane Austen, Edith Wharton, the Brontës. She had read *Madame Bovary* three times (and for the fourth, was currently reading it in French).

Although Professor Ash's second novel skipped around chronologically and was narrated by a highly unlikable antihero, it was changing her perspective on what kind of literature she thought she liked. It was largely autobiographical, everyone knew, and dark and sexual and depressive. Maybe she should have known, after seeing him at the party, that no matter what the book was like, she was going to like it. Was going to be turned on by it. He was so broad and imposing despite his shyness, so witty yet careful in the way he spoke, it seemed impossible that any woman could look at him and not imagine his hands on her. She'd had to picture him to finish with Brandon that night, which made her feel deeply ashamed afterward.

And his writing was exactly how she'd hoped it would be: cynical, sparse, adult. Every sentence, even in the scenes that weren't about sex, dripped with a quiet masculine sexuality, some latent need to lose himself that simmered beneath the surface of the controlled prose.

The phone beside Liv buzzed again. Brandon was calling now. She let it go to voicemail. The vibrating stopped, and then a minute later, began again. She sighed and picked up.

"Hello?"

"Hey, babe!" In the background she could hear males shouting, the bumping of a bass, tonight's party already under way. "Whatcha doin'?"

"I'm reading," she said.

"You gonna come out?"

"I told you. I have too much work to do this weekend."

"You said you *might* have too much work. It's only Thursday."

"Well." She flipped over the paperback on her lap to look at the photograph of Oliver Ash. It was an old headshot: his face lacked the pockmarks she'd noticed at the department party; the bags under his eyes were less pronounced, and his head of hair was darker and fuller than the short, graying cut he sported now. His mouth was closed tightly in seriousness, but his eyes flirted with the camera. One more button on his shirt was undone than she might have expected, a hint of chest hair peeking out. "I forgot about this paper due Monday."

"No you didn't. You never forget about papers."

"Okay, I didn't," she said, her voice dripping with sarcasm. "I'm lying for no reason. Do you think I'd rather stay in than spend the night with you?"

"I don't know what you'd rather do."

She let the silence sit there for a minute, unable to come up with a good enough retort. At some point over the last year or so, as she could see the end of college and the start of adulthood nearing, she found herself panicking about being cut loose without a job, without a boyfriend—without any "prospects," as her mother would say. She knew that she had a safety net in her parents, but that didn't stop them from putting pressure on her to settle down anyway; her whole life had followed a tidy timeline, and now she was about to graduate from college during America's worst economic period in nearly a century, as her father never failed to remind her. She had enjoyed her single days, freshman through junior years, when she had the luxury to sleep with whomever she wanted: sinewy soccer players and brooding poets and Parisian university students during her semester abroad and, once, a girl on the volleyball team. Those days were supposed to be behind her now. It wasn't only her parents, either: in truth, *she* was also worried about how it would look if she didn't start getting serious about all aspects of her life. What would she tell people following graduation if she had neither a job nor a boyfriend? What would her parents tell people? She would have never, ever said this out loud. It was incredibly old-fashioned and uncool. But there was something to be said for security. She had never lived a day of her life without it.

And yet: here was Brandon, her PBF ("perfect boyfriend," a term her mother had lovingly coined), supportive and handsome; and here was Oliver Ash, married and by all accounts a terrible decision. She had never cheated on a boyfriend before, and she was surprised at herself when she first felt the desire to, when she first started to think about the practicalities of it: how she could make it happen, how she could get away with it. It was so wrong, and the guilt she felt ate at her, had kept her up at night over the past week. She tried to find the logic to it: Did she want Oliver Ash *because* he was a terrible decision? Because there was something exciting about infidelity? About sleeping with a professor? Didn't every college girl want that? She supposed it didn't matter, really, why she wanted him, only that she did. It could be one last fling, another part of her reasoned, one last chance to sow her wild oats. And then she would settle down with Brandon for real. Then she would be good.

"I just want to see you once in a while, okay?" Brandon said on the phone now.

This was enough to make her feel bad. She knew how much he cared for her. She knew she had the capacity to break his heart.

Then she thought of the frat house, of waking up in that sad morning light. She thought of how dutiful the sex had felt lately; she kept doing it, insisting she liked it, but was this all sex was, and all it ever would be until the end of time? Him working on her manually, almost clinically, until she had a modest orgasm—never as big as the ones she gave herself—and then missionary style, lying there and waiting for him to finish so she could go to sleep?

She thumbed the pages of the book in her lap. She didn't feel bad enough to stay with him tonight.

"I do, too," she said, not without regret in her voice. "But not tonight, babe. Let's get lunch tomorrow?"

He said okay, because what else could he say? She put her phone facedown on the bedside table and opened the book in her lap.

Downstairs, Liv could hear her roommates pulling out chairs, laughing.

"Bye, Liv!" Lula called from the bottom of the stairs, and Liv yelled goodbye back. She wasn't surprised that the other two didn't say anything; they would be mad or at least disapproving that she wasn't coming out. But Marley had been so embarrassing tonight. The undergrad thinking she was fighting patriarchy by standing up to a man she knew nothing about? What a cliché.

With Fiona, it was more complicated. They'd become close at the end of their freshman year, working together on a French project; Fiona was smarter than she realized, humble and self-deprecating about her own knowledge of the topic, but then went on to deliver a nuanced, seemingly off-the-cuff presentation on intersectional Muslim-feminist identities in contemporary Algeria, earning them an A from their Muslim-feminist professor. When they went out together for the first time—to a lacrosse party where they ended up rummaging through the

kitchen cabinets instead of talking to anyone, then later drunkenly pealing with laughter over a greasy pepperoni pizza at the
late-night campus café—she felt that she'd found one of *those*
friends: the kind you were supposed to find in college, a relationship that felt effortless and intimate and that would last
your entire adult life, the kind that she had been searching for
in vain all year.

Liv did not make friends with other women easily; much as
she tried, they were mostly wary of her, and the ones she did
become friends with were often beautiful and vapid. She hated
to use her looks as an excuse, but she had yet to find any other
evidence to support it: most unglamorous women were intimidated by Liv.

Fiona wasn't. She joked with Liv, poked fun at her, as if Liv
were nothing special. She wore oversized blouses that hid her
body, and no makeup, and she never brushed her hair; she
often looked like she had overslept and was running late for
class. She also had a giant, unhinged smile, and a too-loud
laugh, and her seeming indifference to what other people
thought about her actually made her exceedingly likeable. If
Liv could spend time around someone unafraid of the opinions
of others, maybe she, too, could learn to care less.

Liv was quick to claim Fiona as her new best friend, writing
her letters when she went away for the summer to be a camp
counselor in the Berkshires. Then, when Helen died, Liv suddenly found herself Fiona's only actual friend from Buchanan.
Liv was good at helping people in a crisis, and she felt it was
her duty to stand by Fiona. She was happy to do it, really,
though "happy" was perhaps a callous term for the circumstances. Liv had always thrived on being needed. She liked to
cook for Fiona, or bring home bottles of Sancerre from the
boutique wine store downtown, or even sleep in the same bed

with Fiona on the nights she was afraid to sleep alone. Some weekends, they went to frat parties, Liv keeping one eye perpetually on her friend, making sure she always had a drink in her hand, a boy to dance with. Or she would get them weed from her boyfriend *du jour*—the joints always pre-rolled; Liv had never learned how to do that herself—and they'd stay in and smoke, order Chinese food, and watch *Mean Girls* for the eight hundredth time.

Once, Fiona's drinking had felt like a reasonable coping mechanism—how else was she supposed to escape when the unthinkable had happened?—and Liv had never witnessed any over-the-top public displays of drunkenness. Liv supposed she had drunk more, too, during their carefree sophomore and junior years, when college felt like it had the capacity to last forever. Things felt different now. Fiona seemed to be getting sloppier, more unhinged. Liv worried about her, but also began to feel that Fiona didn't want her help anymore. Just the week before, Fiona had gone home with Gabriel Benoit after Liv had warned her not to, but Fiona had been defiant when Liv tried to intervene. It was clear that Fiona didn't want Liv's input, didn't appreciate Liv's good intentions. If she didn't want help, maybe Liv needed to stop offering it. Why waste so much energy in caring for a friend who spat it right back in your face?

Then, at the department party the other night, Liv watched Fiona down three plastic cups of cheap wine, one after the other, her cheeks turning pinker as she made irreverent comments in front of Oliver Ash and Professor Roiphe. It was embarrassing; Liv had wished she was talking to the two adults alone. Liv was trying to plan for her future in this horrible economy—she wished she could figure out how to telegraph to Fiona how important it was to start planning for her post-graduation life, too, and how cavalier she was being about her own future, but Fiona would immediately get defensive, using Helen's death as a way to end the conversation, the way she always did. Because what, ultimately, could be said in response to that? What did Liv actually know about losing a sister? About losing anyone, for that matter?

She heard footsteps, and the faint sound of the front door shutting, two flights down.

She exhaled. The sudden silence both freed and scared her. She didn't love being home alone; their house was old and rickety, and not in the safest neighborhood. The floorboards creaked when they weren't supposed to. Her laptop was sitting at the edge of her bed, and she folded in half to grab it. She opened her iTunes and put on Fiona Apple, because she could never think of anything better to listen to.

Her browser was open already, and she went to check her email. No new messages. In her drafts folder, there was a (1). She clicked it.

Still an empty message addressed to o.ash@buchanan.edu. She'd looked up his email the night of the department party, had written it out in the address bar, then found herself at a loss for words.

She looked across to the framed photographs hanging on the wall opposite her bed: Liv, standing between her parents on the football field, the night of high school graduation, a National Honor Society cord around her neck; Liv and her roommates, drunk at Waffle House late one night, sophomore year; Liv and Brandon, in a black-and-white photo that she recently had printed. It had been taken on a hot night in New York last summer; she was in a skimpy sundress, Brandon in his khaki shorts and boat shoes. They were on the sidewalk outside the bar they frequented on the Bowery, Brandon standing behind her, his arm around her neck like a vise, her hands tightly gripping his forearm. The pose gave the impression that she was holding onto him, but she knew that in that moment she had been pulling his arm away. Wasn't the beginning of a relationship supposed to be fun and exciting? Or had she understood, even from the very start, that choosing to be with him was equivalent to a life sentence? They'd only been dating for five months. Why, then, did it feel like the relationship was going to last an eternity?

"He said 'it's all in your head,'" Liv sang along. "And I said 'so is everything,' but he didn't get it." The draft waited in front of her.

"Dear Oliver," she began to write. Too informal. Delete-delete-delete.

"Dear Professor Ash," she rewrote. As she typed, she found herself grateful to Marley. Marley's escapade at the reading might have embarrassed Liv at the time, but it also gave her a reason to send this email.

To: o.ash@buchanan.edu
From: l.langley@buchanan.edu
Thursday, September 25, 2008, 10:26 P.M.
Subject: Tonight's reading

Dear Professor Ash,

I don't know if you remember me; we met last week at the English department back-to-school party. I have long black hair parted down the middle and I was wearing a black sweater-dress; we talked for a bit with Professor Roiphe.

Tonight, my roommate and friend essentially accosted you at your reading, and although I know she isn't my responsibility,

I felt somewhat obligated to email you anyway and offer my apologies on her behalf. I was mortified, not only because it was extremely inappropriate, but also because I think you've written two beautiful books. I also think that fiction, as you said tonight, deserves to be taken at face value.

Anyway, I really hope that I have the chance to study with you before I graduate. I have been working on a novel and would love to be able to workshop it in your fiction writing class in the spring.

Sincerely,

Liv Langley

She clicked Send, her adrenaline coursing, and picked up his book again. She kept the laptop open while she read. She knew he probably wouldn't respond until Monday, if at all, but she found she couldn't concentrate on the words in the book because she kept looking up at the laptop screen anyway, refreshing the browser every two minutes. When her phone vibrated she jumped; it was a text message from Brandon: "Missing you."

After half an hour of trying to read, she got up to brush her teeth, the floorboards croaking in complaint as she walked to the bathroom.

She shared this bathroom with Fiona, and was glad to have it to herself tonight. She washed her face, moisturized, inspected her skin for any blemishes; there were none. She brushed her teeth, flossed, and inspected her teeth, too, in the mirror, with a wide, joyless smile.

Returning to her bedroom, she put on her pajamas and climbed into bed. As she went to close the laptop, it made a dinging noise. She reopened it to find a single white subject line in her inbox above the read emails.

To: l.langley@buchanan.edu
From: o.ash@buchanan.edu
Thursday, September 25, 2008, 11:53 P.M.
Subject: Re: Tonight's reading

Dear Liv,

Thank you for your thoughtful note. It was awfully unnecessary, but nonetheless kind of you to write. I can't say I blame
your friend. By all objective accounts, I am a scumbag, and I
expected something of this nature to happen upon my return
to the States. Buchanan has been very kind to me, and I can
only hope that I'll be able to prove myself again, somehow, to
the community here.

And, yes, of course I remember you. As for the class: I've
been told that entrance into my senior fiction workshop next
semester will be by permission only. Why don't you come to
my office sometime next week and tell me a little bit about
what you're working on?

Best,

Oliver

"Of course I remember you"? 11:53 P.M.? Was Liv reading
too much into this? Surely, he couldn't be the one to make the
first move, not with his track record. This would be up to her.
With her heart racing, Liv responded: "Wonderful—I would
love to come by your office. Monday okay?"

Two minutes later came his reply confirming the meeting:
Monday at 1:30, after his class.

Liv ducked under the covers of her bed and let out an un-
abashed squeal. In the hours before she could fall asleep, she
lay motionless with the lights on, clutching her teddy bear

safely to her chest. When Brandon called for the third time, she unceremoniously turned off the phone.

—— // ——

On Monday, Liv got to Leviathan early, and the English department secretary told her she could wait in Professor Ash's office until his class got out.

She sat in the chair across from his desk, crossed her legs and then uncrossed them, smoothed out her hair. She'd thought for a long time about what she could wear to this meeting, tried nearly everything in her closet until she finally landed on what she always ended up wearing: a dark turtleneck, a flannel schoolgirl skirt, and knee-high boots. A look that was professional, that would assert her seriousness about this class—because she did, in fact, want to study with him—but also a nod to the fact that she was interested in other ways, too.

The bookcase behind the desk was filled with books by Jewish men: Primo Levi, Elie Wiesel, Saul Bellow, Philip Roth. Over a summer break a few years earlier, she had read *Goodbye, Columbus,* and found herself angry on behalf of the girl by the end of it, which probably meant that Roth was doing something right. The girl, Brenda, did everything she could to get the boy she loved to stay with her, including getting a diaphragm, which was illegal for unmarried women then—and she didn't even want to, she only did it because he pressured her to—and still she ended up getting caught and in trouble for it, while the boy got away scot-free. *Isn't that life,* Liv had thought, turning the last page of the novella. She'd been disappointed to learn that the short stories in the collection following the novella were male-centric and more heavily focused on Judaism, dry and unrelatable. She soon gave up trying to finish it.

"Hello?" Oliver said from the doorway.

She turned. Her stomach dropped in excitement at the sight of him: at his height, at his professorial blazer and glasses, at his hair haphazardly askew. He looked confused, and then had a moment of recognition. He'd forgotten about their meeting.

"Hi," she said, with what she hoped was a shy, alluring smile. "Is this a bad time?"

"Not at all," he said. "I'm just getting out of class. We went a few minutes over, got caught up in a rousing discussion about one of the students' short stories."

He rounded the desk and sat. She noticed again the pock-marks in his face, signs of age or acne scars. It felt strange try-ing to reconcile the crush she'd been working up in her head for weeks with the man in front of her now. Sometimes, in her fantasies, she'd forgotten what his face looked like and would need to look at the back of the paperback again to remember. Now he was in front of her, and he still looked radically differ-ent from the photograph. He was so much older now. There wasn't quite a seamless way to marry her own image of him with his actual, real-life face.

"So, you're interested in taking my course next semester?" he asked. "Is that right?"

"Yes," she said. "You mentioned it's by permission only? I guess you're in high demand."

"I'm at a loss as to why," he said with what was obviously false modesty. He must know he was a name here, and that she wasn't the only undergraduate to have a crush on him. "So why don't you tell me about this novel you're working on?"

"I've been writing it for some time," Liv said, "but I've never shown it to anyone." There was, of course, no novel.

"Okay," he said. "Why don't you send me a chapter? And I

can take a look." He paused for a moment, his brow furrowed. "I'd like to see, if that's all right with you."

Her lips pursed; this wasn't the response she was hoping for. She'd foolishly thought the fact that they'd emailed before about this, close to midnight on Thursday, was entrée enough, and that talking about the novel was just a formality.

"Okay," she agreed. "I can do that." The novel lie had been a tactic to prove her seriousness, but clearly it had backfired. She would send him a short story from last year, backtrack and say she wasn't quite ready to show the novel to anyone. She knew the story was good.

"Great," he said. "I'm really looking forward to reading it."

Liv's eyes traveled again to the bookshelf above his head, a photograph now catching her eye. She pointed to the frame behind him.

"Is that your family?" she asked.

It was a picture of Oliver and what appeared to be his wife and son, sitting on a couch together. A picture of domestic bliss. He turned to look at the photo himself.

"Yes, that's my family," was all he said.

She was disappointed; she wanted more information about the woman and the boy. He had mentioned his wife and son during the lecture, but she was curious about details. Why wouldn't they have come to Buchanan with him? Maybe there was some sort of recent break that would explain him being here.

He did not offer any more information, and Liv suddenly felt apprehensive. She was used to being the one pursued, and not the other way around. And how did one come on to a professor, a power figure—especially when that professor might still be in a relationship, when there was a *family* involved?

And then she thought, sharply, of Brandon. Did she only want this because it was some rite of passage she felt she had to experience, a bucket-list item of sleeping with a professor? Was it worth hurting Brandon for an experience that would probably prove to be insignificant in the long run? Brandon wasn't a bad person. He didn't deserve to be cheated on. If it was to happen, the thought of him ever finding out made her feel queasy.

Oliver Ash stood and Liv followed suit. He offered his pleasantries, and promised that he would read Liv's work as soon as she sent it to him. Maybe this was all for naught, she was thinking. Maybe she should let this go.

But in that moment, as she was thinking of dropping this entirely, she felt his hand on the small of her back. He held it there for a few moments, a beat too long for it to be accidental. She felt her heartbeat quicken and sank her lower back into his hand.

She turned, and he took his hand away, and looked at her.

"Goodbye," he said.

"Goodbye," she said, and he shut the door behind her.

6.

Fiona emerged from Franklin Hall after finishing her shift at the communications office and walked out into the central quad. It was finally, truly fall, and she was glad for it. Campus had more or less burst into flame: gigantic orange-leaved trees obstructed the views from the taller windows of the brick academic buildings; scarlet and yellow foliage littered the grass around burnt-red Adirondack chairs. Heat was no longer tolerable for Fiona: warm weather reminded her of camp, of what had been lost. Every summer now she longed for the day the weather would turn, and then she could breathe again.

She worked ten hours a week in the communications office; although her father covered her tuition and her books and her rent, Fiona liked being able to have her spending money, however paltry, apart from his funds. This didn't change the fact that every month he plopped another thousand dollars into her checking account for no specific reason. She lived modestly, only spending money on groceries and booze, and did her best not to touch what he wired to her. He'd gone back to work two weeks after Helen died. He had cheated on her mother, and now they were divorced. Fiona saw no need to maintain the emotional aspects of that relationship.

She checked her phone to find a message from Liam: "You still haven't called Mom, have you?" It was probably two weeks since he'd last probed her. He was right: she hadn't talked to her mother since the first week of school, when she was still settling in. Time somehow both expanded and contracted at college. The days went painfully slowly, and then one day you looked up and a month had gone by, and it felt like you had learned nothing new at all.

She parked herself in one of the Adirondack chairs and dialed home. Her mother picked up on the second ring.

"Well, hello," Amy said, already on the defensive.

"Hi, Mom."

"Did Liam tell you to call me?"

"He might have."

"Whatever it takes, right?"

"You know the beginning of the semester is always a bit of a shit show."

"Language."

When Fiona and her siblings were younger, her family had a "language jar," and every time any of them said a bad word they would have to put a dollar from their allowance into it. Amy had supersonic hearing—Fiona and Liam and Helen could be in the TV room without any adults, and one of them could say "fuck" or "shit" or "asswipe," and Amy would call from the kitchen, two rooms away: "Language!" Now it was only a knee-jerk reaction. There were, of course, no longer any repercussions.

The money from the language jar went to charity—a tradition so privileged, Fiona realized now, she would be embarrassed to tell anyone about it. Her family was not charity-minded in any other ways. It was just that they didn't *need* that money.

"Well, how are your classes?" Amy asked.

"They're fine," Fiona said. Two boys with backpacks slung over their shoulders walked past her, en route to the library. One glanced in her direction. She caught his eye, and he started for a moment, recognizing her. He offered a slight wave, and turned away, continuing toward the library. Muttered to his friend, who chuckled. She had hooked up with him last Thursday night, when they went out after the reading. They went to a lacrosse party, and at the time he'd looked cute, in a sort of stocky, preppy way. And the fact that he was hosting the party allowed for an added sense of attraction, like being in charge of it gave him power, however small. The details were a bit hazy, but she remembered him making her drinks in the kitchen from his own liquor, instead of dipping her Solo cup into the vat of red jungle juice that everyone else was drinking, and this had felt valiant and romantic. She had given him a blow job, and it was messy, because he didn't warn her when he was finishing. He didn't reciprocate. She didn't sleep there.

Now, in the middle of the day, she would have described him as husky, not stocky. His face was wide but his mouth small and puckered, and his chin was round and pink and jutted out a bit from his face.

"Just fine?" her mother said.

"Sorry," Fiona said. "Um. The French lit class is hard. I need all of Liv's help that I can get. I'm completely worthless."

"I'm sure that's not true."

"No, it is." She kept talking. "The feminist lit seminar with Roiphe is great. Modernist lit is fun. Easy. Poetry is fine. It's required."

"You have a really heavy reading semester," Amy said.

"It's not so bad."

"Roiphe is your advisor, right?"

"Yeah. We're supposed to do this term paper at the end of the semester about an American woman whose narrative was destroyed by the patriarchy. I think I'm going to write about Monica Lewinsky."

"Really? That's an interesting choice."

"What do you mean, interesting?"

"I mean, interesting. That's all."

"It sounded loaded."

"Don't do that, Fiona. Don't edit me."

"I'm not. I just don't know what you meant by that."

"I just mean that she's certainly controversial."

"Well, that's the point."

"I'm not going to take the bait on this, Fiona."

"Huh? There's no bait."

Amy took a deep breath on the other end, preparing to change the subject and, consequently, be the bigger person. In always giving Fiona the last word, Amy was actually the winner. She ended up coming off as the more emotionally healthy one, the one who could let arguments go, while Fiona floundered, holding on to disagreements that would be insignificant to any reasonable person.

Fiona reported on Marley, who'd scored high on the MCAT and was now working on her med school applications, and Lula, planning to apply for museum jobs in New York.

"And Liv?"

Fiona examined the unpolished nails on one hand, holding them out in front of her.

"I don't know."

"You don't know?"

"I mean. I don't know how to explain. She hasn't exactly been around."

"That new boyfriend of hers?"

"Yeah."

"What's he like?"

Fiona lowered her voice.

"Preppy. Rich. Republican, pre-law."

"Sounds perfect for her."

"I think that's what she thinks she wants, but it's not actually what she wants."

"It's hard to know what you want in a partner when you're twenty-one years old."

One year ago, Fiona would have said, "You did," because Amy and Fiona's father had married in their early twenties, but that was no longer relevant.

"Speaking of which," Amy said, clearing her throat. "One of the reasons I wanted to talk to you is actually to let you know something sort of, well. Sort of exciting. Exciting to me, anyway."

"What?" Fiona said. "You met Richard Gere at ShopRite and he asked you to run away with him?"

"Close," Amy said.

"You met Richard Gere at Target?"

"I met someone, Fiona."

"What?"

"I met someone," she said again. "A man. His name is Ed. He's a biochemist. He's very smart and very kind. He lives over in New Rochelle." Again, that unnatural affectation. Like she'd practiced this. Perhaps with the therapist she saw twice a week.

"What? Ed?"

"Yes. That's his name, Fiona."

She let out a snort. "Liam is going to have a field day with this."

"Liam knows, actually."

"What?"

"He met us for dinner in the city, in fact."

"What?"

"They got along famously."

"What? *Famously*?"

"Could you please stop saying 'What'?"

"Sorry," Fiona said. She tried to put herself in her mother's shoes, but found herself unable to cross the line into empathy. "I'm at a loss. I'm twenty-one years old and my mother has a boyfriend and I don't."

"That's right," Amy said, lowering her voice to a stern whisper, as if someone nearby was listening. "Your dad moved on a long time ago and I had to, too."

Did her dad have a girlfriend, too? Was he with the woman he'd cheated on her mom with? Fiona didn't ask, didn't want to know. She didn't really want to know any of this. She found it nearly impossible to imagine her parents as sentient people apart from each other, with desires and sex drives. It was only when the divorce was finalized a year ago, and she learned about her dad's cheating, that the reality of that had sunk in. For so long she thought her parents' separation was temporary, a by-product of grief, not also a result of infidelity. She'd never thought the separation would last forever. She knew this had been an immature response; it was the way children, not college students, thought of their parents being separated.

"My dad can go fuck himself, as far as I'm concerned."

"Well, yeah." Amy didn't call out Fiona for swearing this time.

This was the one thing that Amy, Fiona, and Liam could all

agree on now. It was almost nice, at that point in time, to have someone to blame. To have someone to be angry with. It became extremely easy to believe that most of this was his fault, that his cheating could have somehow, impossibly, caused Helen's death, and for that, Fiona—and her mother and brother, she was sure—had been grateful.

"I'm happy, Fiona."

If Fiona died, would Liam, a short two years later, have to endure this kind of conversation, hearing his mother say she was not "starting to feel like herself again" or "getting a little better every day," but downright "*happy*"? It was one thing to experience happiness now and again, but the gall it took to admit it.

"I don't know what to say." A group of skinny freshman girls walked by, laughing and oblivious. Fiona suddenly felt uncomfortable sitting outside, in public. This conversation felt particularly private. "It's a strange thing for you to spring on me."

"Well, if you ever answered your phone or called me back, I could have told you sooner."

"How long have you been seeing him?"

"Three months now."

"Three months? And you're just telling me now?"

"Like I said. If you answered your phone—"

"I was in New York three months ago! That was the summer! And you kept it from me all that time?"

"I didn't want to tell either of you until I knew it was serious."

"But now it is."

"Could you find it in your heart to maybe, somehow, not be totally miserable about this?"

Fiona understood that her experience of loss could never

compare to her mother's. She had not lost a child. And yet, how was it possible that Fiona felt so desperately alone in her own grief? She did not want to try to be happy. She felt entirely incapable of it. And the fact that her mother was moving on, and Liam was moving on with her, and Fiona was left behind— well, this made her feel not only lonely but incompetent, *less than*. How were they so healthy in their mourning? How did one even begin to try?

"Please," Fiona said. "I've always been miserable."

She knew that was an exaggeration. But the line worked in the moment, and was powerful enough to stun her mother, followed by Fiona ceremonially clicking the red hang-up button before Amy could respond. She knew it was childish, but she forever wanted to get the last word.

Seething, she stormed across the quad, past the library, crossing Phillips Avenue. Her car was parked a block before her house, and without much thought, she climbed into it. She threw her bag on the passenger seat and, with both hands on the steering wheel, let out a noise she could only make alone, deep and anguished.

When she thought of where she might be able to go that wasn't home, she couldn't come up with anything. This town was a wasteland, managing at the same time to feel both insular and unimportant.

So she drove forward, every now and then wiping her furious tears away with the back of her hand so she could see the road in front of her. It was six P.M.; the sun was just setting, and she lowered her sun visor to shield her eyes from the orange glare. She drove past the old cork factory and the new boutique hotel and made her way through downtown. She sat at a traffic light watching Amish women stream in and out of the large brick building where the market was held. She drove down the hill, past the nice restaurants and the Irish pubs, past the two-screen movie theater, past the loft where she had spent the night with Gabriel Benoit, and hit the traffic light that separated the "good" part of downtown from the "bad" part. On the other side of the light, the restaurants grew sparse and the houses grew shorter, pushed up next to each other like the houses on her block, only more ramshackle, paint chipping from the exteriors, flat fronts and plastic-shingled awnings, pickup trucks with their hoods open in the driveways, no one tending to them. After passing an empty lot, an abandoned church, and an overgrown field with a "Property for Sale" sign staked into it, she spotted a bar. It was called Rudy's—she'd never heard of it. It was a shack with a neon sign out front. It was exactly as anonymous as she needed it to be.

She parked in the lot out back, checked her reflection, wiped away the mascara that had ringed around her eyes. She made her way to the front of the building. When she opened the door, the half-dozen men inside turned and looked at her as if they'd never seen a young woman before. Two burly middle-aged men sat at a table on the other side of the room, dirty from a day of construction work, still in their boots. There was a pool table in the back of the room, and two younger men in flannel shirts were playing each other. The pregame show for a baseball playoff game played on the old TV mounted in a far corner, and the old man sitting at the bar alone seemed to be watching it without paying attention.

Fiona sat on an empty stool at the end closest to the TV and rested her elbows on the surface of the bar. It was sticky.

The bartender wore a plaid shirt, his dirty white undershirt peeking up at the neck. The shirt, untucked, only barely covered his gut, which looked as firm and round as a basketball. He had broken capillaries on his nose and several days' worth of gray scruff.

He pushed a coaster over to Fiona. "You waitin' for someone."

"No," she said, noticing her smeary reflection in the dirty mirrored wall behind the bottles of liquor. "Double well whiskey." She pushed a ten across the table.

"You twenty-one."

"Yeah."

He grunted, poured.

The old man at the other end of the bar seemed to be talking to himself. "Nothing wrong with that," he kept saying, shaking his head and peeling the label off his bottle of beer. "Nothing *wrong* with that."

Wordlessly, the bartender replaced the man's bottle.

"Thanks, Danny," the man said, and he immediately began to peel the label off that bottle, too.

The knocking of the cue against the billiard balls on the pool table, and the balls against each other, was comforting. It sounded like the rituals of youth, or something like that.

Her drink was going fast. She hadn't always been like this. Once she had been a lightweight, had hated the feeling of being too drunk. Her friends used to make fun of her for it; her friend Rachel, from camp, who drank early and efficiently and capably, used to say, "Fee, the goal is to drink the beer *before* it gets warm." They emailed every now and then. Rachel was thriving now, on track to graduate magna cum laude from Michigan, in a serious relationship with a fellow psych major. Was taking the LSATs and planning to apply to law school. An example of how you can turn your life around, Amy would say, because after Rachel was sexually assaulted and her dad died, all during the course of that one unforgettable summer, she did, indeed, turn her life around. Sometimes it felt like Amy wouldn't have minded having Rachel for her daughter instead of Fiona.

She signaled the bartender, pushed her glass toward him, and put a finger up. He nodded, refilled.

The door opened again and from inside the bar Fiona now found herself squinting at the person walking through it. The sky outside had darkened; the tall, broad figure, whom she was sure she wouldn't recognize, stepped into the blue neon of the bar. In fact, she did recognize him.

He sat down, two stools away from Fiona.

"Hey, Danny," Oliver Ash said, his strange accent out of place in the blue-collar American bar.

Danny nodded, and poured Oliver Ash three fingers of Stoli into a glass filled with ice.

"Thanks."

Oliver Ash squinted up at the TV, and in turning his head in that direction, noticed Fiona.

"Hey," he said to her, a friendly affectation to his voice. "Have we met?"

"We have."

"You go to the college?"

"Yeah."

He nodded, still trying to place her.

"We met at the department party last month," she said.

"That's right," he said. "You were there with that girl. Liv?"

"Yeah."

Of course he remembered Liv's name and not hers. She had that effect on people. In fact, Fiona always seemed to surround herself with girls like that—girls who were prettier than she was, whom men liked more, as if she could somehow catch their allure. When she thought of it, all of her roommates and

Rachel, too, were this way; they seemed to charm their romantic interests with little effort. Fiona, on the other hand, felt as if she had to bend over backward to make someone desire her.

Professor Ash looked at the empty stool between them. He gestured to it, and cocked his head to the side.

She nodded, and he moved over. Put his hand out. "I'm Oliver," he said. He was dressed down from how she'd seen him previously, in a chambray shirt with sleeves rolled up, tucked into dark jeans held up by a braided leather belt. No males her age tucked in their shirts.

She took his hand and shook it, even though they'd done this before. "Fiona."

"Right," he said.

He looked up at the TV behind her. He had such a peculiar sense of weariness to his face, as if he'd seen the future and it wasn't pretty.

"Playoffs," he said. "You like baseball?"

"No."

"Me neither."

"Why do you come here to watch it, then?"

"Americana, I guess."

"You're from Berlin, right?" she asked him.

"I live there," he said. "But I'm from Philly originally."

"So what's with the accent?"

"I've lived in Europe for over ten years. I'm one of those people that picks up accents through osmosis."

"I haven't been to Europe since I was a kid," she said.

"Your parents took you to Europe when you were a kid?"

"My mom took me to Paris when I was fourteen."

"La-di-da."

She rolled her eyes at him.

"No, it's great," he said. "That you had that opportunity. Why haven't you gone back?"

She was always going to go to France for her semester abroad, fall of junior year. She had always planned on that. But taking the semester off after Helen died put her a semester behind, meaning she wouldn't be able go abroad at the same time as her friends, meaning she wouldn't see them for an entire academic year. So she skipped it, and stayed at Buchanan with Marley during the fall of junior year, waiting for Liv and Lula to regale them with their European adventures when they returned.

"Reasons," she said.

He nodded, not pressing any further, and drained his Stoli, signaling to Danny for another.

"So you must live with the other girl. The girl that . . . at the reading . . ."

"Marley. How did you know?"

"Oh, Liv mentioned it in her email to me."

"Oh?"

"Oh," he said, taking the refreshed vodka from Danny. "I'm already getting myself in trouble."

So Liv was working on him. The fact that Fiona was now privy to this information, without Liv knowing it, gave her a perverse sense of satisfaction.

"No, it's fine. Why did Liv email you about that?"

"I guess . . . I don't know. I guess, without sounding like a prick, it was her way of talking to me." He looked guilty. "I didn't, though," he said. "I mean. I wouldn't."

"You don't have to explain yourself to me."

"I do, though."

Fiona could feel herself growing drunker as she drained her

whiskey. She slumped over the bar, the weight of her torso resting there; it was a comfortable place to land. She lifted a finger to order a third drink from Danny. She noticed that Oliver had drunk his second vodka exceptionally fast.

Oliver gently touched her hand while discreetly shaking his head at Danny. "Should we make it water?"

She looked at him stone-faced. "Beer."

He considered, conceded. "Two Amstel Lights," he told Danny, and she scoffed.

"I'm watching my figure," he said, patting the small gut folded over his lap, and she smiled.

For a few minutes they were quiet, watching the Phillies game. Someone on the Phillies hit a home run, but no one in the bar reacted.

She looked up at Oliver, who remained upright.

"Why aren't you drunk?" she asked.

"I'm bigger than you," he said. This pleased her; she loved allusions to her smallness, no matter how oblique.

"So why are you *here*?" she asked.

"At this bar?"

"No, like, *here*." She used both hands to wave all around her, as if to imply, *Here Buchanan, here Pennsylvania, here America.*

He flipped over the cardboard coaster in front of him. "It's a job," he said.

"But so *far* from home. There are jobs in Berlin! Aren't you married? Isn't she mad?"

"My wife—Simone—she's not mad I'm here, no."

"Why not?"

She tried signaling Danny for yet another drink but Oliver gently pressed his hands around hers, shook his head once, almost imperceptibly.

"Come on," she whined.

"How about water," he said.

"I hate water."

He drained his own beer, put more bills on the counter for Danny. A water appeared, and he raised it to Fiona's lips.

"Drink, please." He said this with such the right mix of confidence and care that she did as she was told, swallowing the plastic cup of water down in one gulp. There was too much ice in it, and she cringed.

"Brain freeze."

"I feel," he said, "that I would be remiss to not take you home now."

"I don't want to go home."

"I'm going to take you home," he said, patting her hand once more. "Where do you live?"

"Doesn't matter," she said, but she followed him outside to his car anyway.

Fiona could feel the tinge of an early headache, biding its time. The clock on the car radio said it was only 8:33 P.M. They were near campus, and she told him when to turn left onto North Abbott. He pulled up across from her house and put the car into park.

"Thanks for the ride," she said. Only she didn't get out of the car yet.

"You have someone to go with you to pick up your car tomorrow?"

"Yeah," she said. It would have to be Marley; Lula didn't have a car, and she certainly wasn't explaining this situation to Liv. "I don't want to go inside yet."

"Okay," he said, and turned the engine off.

She looked at him. "Did you really do all that stuff that you were accused of?"

He stared out the windshield.

"The girl. Was she underage?"

"I really don't think it's a good idea we have this conversation," he said slowly, measured.

She was feeling brave, less drunk than before, but still with an ounce of carelessness in her.

"She was, wasn't she?"

He sighed deeply. "I think you should probably go now."

"Listen. Sometimes the cards get stacked against you," she said, suddenly feeling very wise, and suddenly feeling like she knew this man, like she could feel sympathy for him, in a way she couldn't for, say, her own mother. Strangers were easier. "And you have to wonder if you had anything to do with it. *I* wonder how much I had to do with my own life turning out the way it did."

"Turned out? You're what, twenty-one? You're only getting started."

At this she could not control the tears.

"It doesn't feel that way."

"Oh shit." He scrambled for tissues or napkins in the console. He only came up with a crumpled paper napkin, and handed it to her. "I'm sorry. I didn't mean to."

"No, it's good you don't know," she said, wiping at her face with the dirty napkin. "It feels like you're the last person on earth who doesn't know."

They sat for a few more minutes, not saying anything. Cars drove up and down her street, and students passed by on foot, walking to their off-campus homes. Some were walking in the other direction, already dressed up for the night, toward the frat houses on Phillips Avenue.

When she was ready, she unbuckled her seatbelt. "Thanks again."

"Water," he said to her as she shut the passenger door.

It was only then, as Fiona crossed the street to her house, that she looked up and saw a light on in the third-floor window, and Liv, holding a curtain open, standing and watching from it.

Fiona almost made it to her bedroom without being confronted by Liv. Almost.

"Are you sleeping with Oliver Ash?" she asked from the top of the steps.

"I have to go to sleep," Fiona said, passing Liv into her own room and crawling under the covers with all her clothes on. Liv followed her in.

"Why were you in his car?"

"Water," Fiona groaned, eyes already closed and head on her pillow.

"Take your shoes off, at least."

Liv was quiet a moment, and Fiona thought she might have gone.

"If I get you water," Liv then said, "will you tell me?"

Fiona made a sound that might have meant yes.

Liv returned with the glass and sat at the edge of Fiona's bed.

Fiona sat up and finished the water in two gulps. She exhaled, caught her breath. This was a pattern lately, it seemed: Fiona was drunk and Liv was taking care of her. Or had this always been their relationship, that of competent caregiver and helpless girl-child? Only, Fiona wasn't actually that drunk anymore. Just thirsty and tired and headachey and desperately uninterested in talking to Liv about Oliver Ash.

"Okay, spill," Liv said. She was trying to sound excited and casual, Fiona knew, to disguise her own possessiveness over Oliver. Fiona again felt that hit of perverse satisfaction in knowing more about the situation than Liv realized she did.

"Nothing happened. We ran into each other at a bar, and he drove me home." Fiona felt slightly protective of Oliver now. He had been kind to her. He had not hit on her, and would not say anything about his sordid past when she asked him. This impressed her, perhaps more than it ought to. She knew that men like him—that is, men in power—were considered laudable for maintaining the bare minimum of decorum. And yet knowing this did not stop her from liking him more.

"What bar?"

"I don't remember the name."

Liv looked skeptical, waiting for another piece of information.

"Can I please go to sleep now?" Fiona said.

"Be careful," Liv said. "You know what happened last time he was teaching."

"I'm an adult," Fiona said, "he's an adult."

Liv seemed even more intrigued now, as if the mention of two adults suggested adult activity.

"I promise you," Fiona said. "Nothing happened. I was too drunk to drive, so he drove me home," she repeated. "That's it. I'm not interested."

She could have asked Liv: *If you're so worried about his past, then why are* you *emailing him?* But she stopped short, out of some innate need to protect Liv's feelings or ego. She wasn't sure, if the roles were reversed, that Liv would do the same; she might, in fact, be brutally honest, tell her all about their conversation and make it clear that Oliver wasn't interested, as a way to gain power over Fiona, couched in an aura of protectiveness and way to give Fiona some "tough love."

But Fiona would not stoop to that. She felt it was important to let Liv think her secret was her own. Out of some sense of generosity, she wanted to let Liv have her fantasy. She understood the joy fantasies could bring, especially when they weren't brought down by the hard thud of reality.

"Okay, Fee," Liv said, seeming satisfied. She stood and walked toward the door. "Get some rest." She turned off the bedroom light and left.

"I will," Fiona said, though for a while she lay there with her eyes open, entertaining her own fantasy about Oliver Ash.

The next day Fiona stayed in her room, studying. For Roiphe's seminar, she was reading *The Coquette*, a late-eighteenth-century novel about a New England woman whose illegitimate pregnancy leads to her social downfall and, ultimately, her death. The novel was based on the story of a real woman who died at a roadside tavern after giving birth to a stillborn infant. The author had published it under a pseudonym to protect her own identity, because the content of the novel was so scandalous for its time.

Without much of Liv's help this semester, Fiona was doing her best to keep up with her reading. She knew that her passion for literature had largely dissipated after Helen died, and her anxiety, especially when she was faced with nothing to do but read, was still a challenge. (Wading through French lit, in particular, was a gigantic struggle.) In Professor Roiphe's class, though, she felt competent, even smart. It gave her the sense that she might be on an upswing.

She had not always done well with pre-nineteenth-century literature, with its antiquated language and often outdated storylines, but the subject matter here—women wronged because of their sexual decisions—was one that newly interested her. Sex had lately taken on a different meaning for her: as an outlet of some kind. She wouldn't go so far as to say it was an avenue for validation, though she knew her friends thought that. She could admit that the attention from men themselves was validating—it was like a hit, a rush of euphoria that never lasted long enough. And though she'd lost weight out of grief and anxiety, the attention to her body from men had grown since she'd gotten thinner, and perpetuated itself, until she got to a point where it was easy to not eat a lot because being thin meant she would always feel this desired.

That and sex were two different things. The attention, she wanted. The sex, that was simply the next logical thing to do. It was not particularly enjoyable. It was a physical expression of what she could not express in any other way: her bottom. The bottom of her grief and the bottom of her guilt. In having not-particularly-enjoyable sex, she felt she was getting what she deserved.

She couldn't totally square that with the women in these early American books, who seemed to be making sexual decisions out of romance and love. Fiona had never been in love, but she had had a series of extreme crushes that felt like love for weeks on end, until another crush introduced itself and took the place of the first. Or, sometimes, the crushes lived in tandem with one another, and she would rank them in her head, their positions changing constantly. Even she knew these crushes were not love, though she wasn't quite sure how love would feel different—was it not intoxicating, all-encompassing? Did it not keep you happily awake at night, give you the jitters in the daytime, squash your appetite, make you perk up when you heard his name? When she didn't have a crush—as she didn't at the beginning of this semester—her life felt empty, joyless, half-formed.

And now: she had a new crush. He was one of the two men in her Roiphe seminar: a long-haired, bearded poet whom she and Liv called Mountain Man. Mountain Man's real name was Dave, which was unfortunate. He was not from the mountains, but he looked as if he'd been hiking for days. For Liv, the nickname was not intended to be complimentary, though Fiona liked that unshaven, unwashed vibe. He was, in fact, from New Jersey. He barely talked in class, but when he did, the comments he made seemed profound. He did the readings. Perhaps he sounded more profound than he was because he spoke in a soft, husky voice and tucked his hair behind his ears as he did so. He wore wide button-down linen shirts with no collar, reminiscent of Indian kurtas, and ragged jeans, the same pair always, frayed at the ankles, and filthy canvas Converse low-tops.

Fiona had tried clicking through his Facebook pictures, but she could only see a limited number, since they weren't Facebook friends, and she didn't want to add him—at least not until they had had one or two conversations. There was a photo of him holding an electric guitar, standing in front of a microphone, a stage light casting him in a pink glow. Another of him climbing up a steep rock, big bushy green trees up ahead, wearing long denim shorts, hiking boots, and no shirt. The photo was geo-tagged at a mountain in the Adirondacks, taken by a girl named Erin Kingsley. Fiona had clicked Erin's profile: she was petite and cute, had short, dyed-red hair and a nose ring, and was from the same town in New Jersey as Dave. The rock picture had been taken nearly a year ago; she was a high school sweetheart turned long-term college girlfriend, Fiona surmised, but it was very possible they'd broken up in the last year, since there were no pictures taken by her or with her on his Facebook since then. On his profile, the relationship status field was left blank.

Now Fiona entertained daydreams about herself and Mountain Man: going on hikes themselves, taking a weekend trip to the Poconos to see the foliage. Standing in the front row at one of his shows, him singing a song he had written for her, introducing it vaguely ("This one is for a girl I know"), and then winking at her so fast only she could see it. Having sex for the first time, both tender and hot, slow and sweaty, his hair getting all over her, him making sure she finished first.

She did not have a game plan about how to talk to him, because she never saw him at parties; in fact, she never saw him around at all, except in class. The issue was, she was scared to flirt; she didn't know how to do it; she always felt incredibly self-conscious partaking in an act so obvious that both people knew it was happening. This was why her sexual encounters tended to be initiated only at parties; alcohol made everything easier.

And, she did admit, if only to herself, that a second, in-tandem crush on Oliver Ash was forming. She'd been thinking a lot about that picture with his family in his office, and about the fact that he was a father. What was more powerful, more sexy, than a man having a child? Having to provide for a family? She'd never had a crush on a dad before, and now she wondered why not. She began, without even realizing that she had feelings quite this strong, imagining his wife dying in a tragic accident and him taking Fiona back to Berlin to be his child's nanny, a Maria von Trapp. Then, slowly, they would fall in love. Was Fiona ready to be a mother figure? This would be the central crisis, but ultimately she would find that her love for the child and for Oliver far surpassed anything she could have imagined, and over time she would step into the role with tenderness, care, and aplomb.

There was a knock on the door. Fiona looked up from her book; Marley was in the doorway, holding a mug and wearing her Saturday clothes: gray sweatpants and a gray tank top.

"What are you reading?" Marley asked.

Fiona showed her the book cover.

"Is it good?"

"Yeah," she said.

"Didn't you need a ride somewhere?"

Both of them still in their sweatpants, the two girls got into Marley's car—a used two-door Toyota that Marley had bought with her own savings from her summers lifeguarding (her parents, though they had some money, were big on their kids paying their own way)—and drove back to the run-down bar.

"Are you sure this is the way?" Marley asked, seeming skeptical when they crossed the train tracks.

"It's a mile farther or so, I think," Fiona said, and then recognized the big plot of land for sale, the empty lot.

"What were you doing over here, anyway?"

"I was just getting a drink."

Marley glanced over at Fiona.

"It's up ahead. Here, on the right."

Marley turned into the lot and pulled up next to Fiona's car. Fiona opened the passenger door of Marley's car.

"Thanks," she said, though she could tell she was not free yet; Marley had something to say, and Fiona would have to listen: her fee for the ride.

"You should be careful," Marley said. It was no surprise that Liv had already shared with their roommate what she'd seen. How many times did she have to be told to be careful? Did her friends really think her so irresponsible, so lacking in good judgment? Sure, she'd been promiscuous the past few years, but it wasn't as if she hadn't made these decisions for herself, hadn't *chosen* to go home with this guy or that. She was an adult. She had agency.

"Marley," she said, careful to be particularly measured and calm. "I'm not sleeping with him. Not that that should matter, actually."

"You can sleep with whoever you want," Marley said.

"So what are we talking about?"

Marley's hands were still on the steering wheel.

"I guess I'm worried about the reasons. I mean, it's no secret that I think Oliver Ash is a bad person. But what's more concerning to me . . . It's, well, do you actually *want* to sleep with these guys? Because if you do, then, by all means, that's your prerogative. It seems, from the vantage point of a concerned friend, that you have this wound—a gaping wound, actually, which anyone in your position would have—but you aren't taking care of it. You are just covering it with Band-Aids, little by little, in hopes that it might heal on its own, that those small bandages are enough."

"Original, Dr. Dorfman. I already told you. I'm not sleeping with him."

"Okay." Marley seemed stung that her metaphor, which she'd perhaps practiced, had been shut down.

"Sorry," Fiona said, squeezing Marley's hand once. "I appreciate your concern. But you have nothing to worry about. Everything's under control." She didn't like this; she didn't like her friends trying to constantly control her behavior. Why didn't they trust her judgment? Why couldn't they give her the space to make her own decisions, even if they were wrong?

"I have been thinking," Marley said, "maybe it's time to . . . Have you ever thought of seeing someone, maybe? I know you did when Helen first . . . but maybe again?"

"Like a therapist." Fiona had, of course, thought about this. She saw the way her mother had become since therapy, full of platitudes that had been spoon-fed to her by this woman she overpaid. Didn't Fiona have people like Marley and Liv and Lula to talk about her problems with?

Marley nodded.

Where was this coming from? The drinking? The fact that she had hooked up with, what, two guys since school started?

No: it was Oliver. No matter how much she denied it, neither Liv nor Marley believed that she wasn't having an affair with him.

"Who are you to judge my motivations for sleeping with people?" Fiona said, beginning to go from annoyed to angry. "How can you possibly judge *why* I do the things I do? You sleep with random guys all the time."

"I didn't—"

"Since when are you the Virtue Police?"

"I'm not."

"I'd expect this from Liv. Not you."

"Enough," Marley said. "I'm only trying to help. I love you."

"If you loved me, you'd believe me."

Marley sat for a minute, quiet. She looked as if she was about to start crying.

"I'm sorry," Marley said, shaking her head. "I'm not trying to slut-shame. You can do whatever you want. I just want you to be happy." This was the first, really, that Marley and Fiona had ever had a conversation of such substance.

Fiona hugged her friend, told her it was okay, then got into her own car to drive home. For some reason, the harder parts of the conversation dissipated, and she was left only with this refrain: *You can do whatever you want.*

That night, she sent Oliver Ash an email to thank him for driving her home.

> To: o.ash@buchanan.edu
> From: f.larkin@buchanan.edu
> Friday, October 3, 2008, 9:47 P.M.
> Subject: thanks
>
> hey-
>
> it's fiona from last night. just wanted to say thanks for the ride.
> i got some weird news beforehand & was kind of a mess. do
> NOT drive drunk, usually. so was glad to have you there. &
> also embarrassed. but mostly glad.
>   registration for next semester closes next week and i'm
> thinking of taking your workshop. is that weird?
>   f

As soon as she sent the email, she second-guessed it. Was this a bad idea? It was innocent, she reasoned; she would have thanked anyone who had done what he had. And knowing that Liv had been emailing with him as well catapulted her into a state of action. It was immature, but she wanted to prove to herself that Liv wasn't the only one who could garner his attention.

And then he responded. Almost immediately.

To: f.larkin@buchanan.edu
From: o.ash@buchanan.edu
Friday, October 3, 2008, 10:04 P.M.
Subject: Re: thanks

Fiona,

Don't worry about it. It happens to the best of us. I'm just glad
to have been in the right place at the right time.

I don't see why taking my workshop would be "weird." The
fact that we ran into each other once socially should not ex-
clude you from being in my class if you're indeed interested in
taking it. I only hope that I don't disappoint you too much.

I'm happy to give you permission to enter the class, and I
look forward to reading your work.

Best,
Oliver

Delighted and satisfied with this response, she decided to
leave it there for now. She wasn't going to pursue it any further.

7.

Simone walked along her favorite canal route to pick Henri up from school; it was early November, and at 3:15 the sun was already threatening to set over the tree line, not to return for another fourteen hours. She'd been deep into Polish translations, finally excavating some meaning from a diary entry, when she realized the time. It felt like there were never enough hours in the day to get her work done, especially when she didn't have Oliver here to help out. She spent most of the mornings in Berlin getting herself into the right frame of mind for translating, often clearing the hurdle of switching off her mom mode and no longer thinking about her son and worrying about whether he was having a good day—especially in light of the incident back in September. By the time she was finally able to focus and get into that sweet spot, that zone where her mind was singularly focused on the work in front of her, she only had two hours left before she had to leave. And then the challenge was transitioning back, from work mode to mom mode again. She was always toggling between the two, never fully in one or the other; at work, she thought about Henri, and when she was with Henri, she thought about work. When she picked him up, he was often—like her—exhausted, and the rest of the day was more a matter of enduring his grumpiness than of spending any remotely enjoyable time with him.

Occasionally, Henri had playdates with classmates after school, which bought Simone another hour or two of work time; but then, these playdates had to be reciprocated eventually, which resulted in her having to manage two children on her own instead of one. Once, the mother of Henri's closest friend, Jean, invited Simone to stay for tea while their children played. She'd been optimistic about it—the woman was an artist whose husband worked for the French Embassy in Berlin, and Simone thought she might have been an interesting person to become friends with. Instead, Jean's mother gossiped about other parents at the school while their children built with Legos in another room. She had awful things to say about everyone: Claude's mother had gotten so fat, and Gabrielle's father had a drinking problem, and did she know that Isabelle's father was having an affair with Mathieu's mother? Simone decided she preferred dealing with her moody five-year-old alone to enduring and engaging in vapid conversation with an adult for two hours.

These days she wondered how people raised more than one child. Just one was a second full-time job. Before motherhood, she could never have imagined how much it took over her thoughts: worrying about Henri, where he was at any given point in the day. If he was happy. If he was safe. The worries were mind-numbing, repetitive, too boring to share with anyone. Even Oliver seemed to have the capacity to turn off the anxieties about their son in a way that Simone couldn't. Out of sight, out of mind, for him. Look at how he had run away this year, as if he were single and childless.

Belaboring this thought as often as she did didn't do anything. It didn't make Oliver magically reappear. But he was coming home in six weeks for winter break, for an entire month, before returning for the spring semester. And as angry as she was with him, she couldn't wait to see him. She missed his smell, like peat moss and Marlboro Lights (even though he'd quit smoking years ago, the smell lingered, like it had been embedded in his skin). She missed his presence around the house: on his good days, playful and efficient, fixing a drip in the sink, carrying Henri to school on his shoulders. She missed how he made her come, quickly and powerfully. She even missed the bad days, the ones when he didn't leave his office, when a certain darkness permeated the house and kept her and Henri away.

She turned away from the canal onto a cobbled street that looked wet and gleaming from the glare of the setting sun. Her phone buzzed, and she looked down to see that Danièle was calling.

"Simone?"

Danièle's voice was high-pitched and excitable, but Simone could not tell if it was on account of good news or bad.

"Are you all right?"

"It happened!" Danièle squealed. "We're pregnant!"

All this time they had been trying, Simone had assumed they would eventually give up: stop with all the treatments, which were becoming emotionally exhausting, and decide on adoption or surrogacy. Five years of trying was a long time, and Simone herself knew the toll that could take on a person. Simone immediately felt a deeply confusing mix of jealousy and joy. Hadn't she just been thinking about how hard even one child was?

Then there was being pregnant itself. She'd loved being pregnant with Henri, the magic in it, that this body that she'd been carrying her whole life was now working in a brand-new way. It made her feel powerful, purposeful, and utterly ethereal. And then, when he'd arrived, all of those little fingers and toes, and his baby laugh, and his smell. She'd never felt as content as she did when she fed him. He needed her; she'd never been needed before, not as desperately as that, and now she never would be again.

Danièle was her sister, though, and her happiness was big enough to trump Simone's envy. Now Simone would have someone to share all the mundane motherly things with, all the worries and anxieties that she kept to herself.

"I wish I could be there to hug and kiss you," Simone said, and she could hear that Danièle, like her, was crying. "How far along are you?"

"Only six weeks," Danièle said. "I'm due at the end of June. I wanted to wait to tell you but I couldn't hold it in."

"I'm so glad you did."

"You're the second to know. We just saw Mama. She's completely beside herself."

This, now, made Simone sad. She wasn't home to receive this news in person. She was missing everything. And she missed her father, who would never get to meet any of his grandchildren.

"I'm so happy for you, Dani," she said again, even after the tears turned sour.

She called Oliver next.

"My love," he answered in French, which made her smile.

She told him Dani's news.

"That's wonderful," he said.

"It is."

"How far along is she?"

"Six weeks."

"Early."

"Yeah."

There was a pause. Two out of three of her own miscarriages were several weeks later into the pregnancy than that.

"It seems very soon for her to tell people," he said.

"I'm not just 'people,'" she said.

"Well. A loss for her would also be really hard for you."

"I'd rather be there for her during something like that than not."

A pause. "I'm trying to be realistic."

He wasn't wrong—Danièle's odds, considering how long they'd been trying, weren't great. But Simone felt fiercely protective of her little sister. Why assume the worst for her, too? She couldn't stand to think about Dani enduring what she had.

"It is very exciting news," he said stiffly. "Please tell her I said congratulations."

"I will," she said, and then: "It's a little sad, too. For me."

"Why?"

"It feels final. Like now I really never will be pregnant again."

"What does Dani's pregnancy have to do with that? I thought we had come to that conclusion months ago."

Come to that conclusion? There was no official conclusion here, only a sad inevitability. And where was the *we* in this situation? He wasn't the one who had to endure the miscarriages, not in the way she did. He wasn't the one who let out a piercing scream that third time, the worst one, ten weeks along, as she doubled over in pain as the bloody clot of fetal tissue fell out of her body and into the toilet so wholly it made a *plop*. She'd stayed in bed for days afterward, not only out of physical pain but out of a legitimate inability to work or to move or to think. She didn't sleep. She couldn't close her eyes without seeing the beginnings of a person floating in the toilet water—the stringy tissue among the remains of a broken, bloody sac. At ten weeks, the baby would have already had kidneys and intestines, a brain and a liver, fingers and toes.

No: Oliver was able to keep working. He'd checked in on her, and comforted her as well as he could, but kept working. Unsure what else to do, he had flushed the thing—their child?— down the toilet.

"I'm both happy for Dani," she said now to her husband, "and sad about myself."

"I see," he said.

"I don't think you do," she said.

He sighed. He would never get it: the envy and happiness and fear all wrapped up into one singular emotion. Since the miscarriages, she felt like she needed too much from him, like she had *too* many feelings, which overwhelmed him and confused him. He used to be attentive to Simone's needs, but recently she had the sense he'd started to give up on her. Like at some point he was tapped out, leaving her feeling bad and wrong for having those needs in the first place.

"I'm at Henri's school now," she said, even though she had ten more minutes left in her walk, and hung up the phone.

Simone got to Henri's school at exactly 3:30, politely smiling at the other mothers waiting for the classroom door to open, saying hello to the headmistress, who walked through the hallway now. She had spoken to Madame Bouchard after Henri's incident in the playground and told the headmistress what the girl, Isabelle, had said to Henri. Madame Bouchard was shocked and appalled—or at least she feigned being shocked and appalled—and said that she would speak to Isabelle and her parents at once.

Simone had heard nothing else about it, and when she asked Henri, a few weeks later, if there had been any more problems with Isabelle, he had said no; in fact, he'd told her that they were friends now. She'd been eyeing Isabelle's mother at pickup ever since the incident, a petite Alsatian woman who was always chatting with the other mothers in that ugly accent. She seemed friendlier with them than she ever was with Simone, for reasons that seemed fairly obvious. It made Simone ill to think about the kind of rhetoric that went on in that household.

When the door to the classroom opened, she looked over the tops of the children's heads for her son. Several kids streamed out, their mothers or nannies greeting them at the doorway with big hugs and smiles, as the children handed over their backpacks and whatever art projects they were taking home and asked for help with their coats. At the end of the line, finally, was her son. Holding hands with a girl. With Isabelle.

Simone saw now that only she and Isabelle's mother were left waiting for their children, and they stood on opposite sides of the doorframe. The boy and the girl paused inside of it.

"Isabelle is my girlfriend now," Henri announced to Simone. They were kids; this was what kids did. It would have been silly to react in any way other than pleasant complicity; they'd be uninterested in each other in a week.

Isabelle's mother was looking at the children with her mouth pinched into a closed circle. Perversely, Simone wanted the woman to say something. She longed for ammunition, she longed to have someone to be angry with other than Oliver. For someone to understand *why* she was angry, because everything she expressed to him, everything she wanted, everything she cared about, seemed to go misunderstood.

The woman grabbed her daughter's hand and, when she saw that Simone was looking at her, changed her facial expression to one of placidity.

"Well, isn't that nice," the woman said to her daughter.

"It is, isn't it?" Simone said, and stared at the woman, unsmiling, until she was forced to look up. Simone was much taller than the woman, and towered over her. She grabbed her own son's hand. He was still holding on to Isabelle's hand, so that now all four of them were connected in a chain, like paper dolls.

She called me Jewish.

Jean's mother over tea: "Isabelle's father is having an affair with Mathieu's mother."

People like this woman were allowed to make children, and bring them up in this world. Pass down to them whatever they believed. It was entirely random, who got to become a mother.

Maybe Isabelle was nice to Henri now, but the woman would still retain her beliefs. She would still point out Jews, or any "others," when she saw them, to or around her young child.

Simone could tell her right now: *Your husband's cheating on you with Mathieu's mother.*

Then she'd hate Jews, if she didn't already. It shouldn't be Simone's responsibility to be a virtuous Jew on behalf of all Jews, and yet—she felt that it was. It was possible that Simone and Henri were among the only Jews this woman had ever met.

Simone leaned in close and very quietly, so the children

couldn't hear her, said into the woman's ear: "It would be wise to be careful, next time, about how you choose to talk about my son in front of your daughter."

It was satisfying to watch Isabelle's mother become visibly shaken, to see her pull her head back in shock and say to her daughter with fake sunniness: "Time to go, my love."

Simone and Henri walked outside after the mother and daughter, ambling out of the school gardens and into the darkening German city. Simone felt a deep sense of contentment, of power reclaimed.

"I wanted to have a playdate with Isabelle," Henri whined as they walked out of the school.

"Maybe another time," Simone lied, and held onto his hand a little bit tighter.

8.

THE STUDENTS IN Professor Roiphe's seminar Sex, Sentiment, and Sympathy were mostly young women, mostly
keen and overzealous, their notebooks open to a fresh page
before the start of every class. They were the kind of girls who,
like Fiona, had fallen in love with language early, who'd holed
themselves up in their teenage bedrooms but were afraid to
share what had really allowed them to love books in the first
place: the romance of Austen and the Brontës, or the sisterly
bonds in *Little Women*, or, for the moodier girls, the glorified
depressiveness of *The Bell Jar*. But they were afraid to be
marked as too feminine or drippy or suicidal, and Fiona understood not wanting to be identified by what you loved.

So when Professor Roiphe had asked, back on the first day
of class, what they'd all read over the summer, they hid behind
the safe and plot-centric, emotionally withholding voices, the
men who wrote like men and the women who wrote like men:
Salinger and Welty and Hemingway and O'Connor. The two
young men in the class threw in a Faulkner and a Cormac

McCarthy to assert that they had an interest in the gothic, that they weren't afraid of violence. Fiona told the truth: that she'd read the entire Gossip Girl series over the summer—the only stuff she managed to get through—to which the other students were unsure how to react. (This was, after all, a class about women being punished for their sexual and romantic choices in a patriarchal society. It stood to reason that the students in it ought to start not being embarrassed for liking feminine literature.) Liv simultaneously defended and one-upped her friend's summer reading, sharing that she had read the more highbrow but "thematically similar" *Anna Karenina* during the month of July. Professor Roiphe had appreciated both of their answers, had said that, in fact, the course would be focusing on similar themes of societal and class constraints, and these were strong examples of how the sentimental novel has persisted over centuries and into today.

The seminar took place at a round table in Leviathan. They sat in gray-blue plastic chairs around the wooden table, which showed decades of wear: initials carved into the sides, varnish gone where strips of adhesive tape had been peeled away. The off-white walls, too, were peeling in the corners. On one wall, there were four black-and-white photos, appearing to be from the seventies, the frames slightly askew, of professors teaching, fingers up in the middle of pontificating, of a trio of diverse students—one black girl with an Afro, a Latino boy in bell-bottoms, and a white girl with Farrah Fawcett–blown hair—leaning forward in their seats, rapt. Fiona had no idea the significance of these photos in this particular classroom. Considering that Buchanan cost as much money as it did, she often wondered about the shabby nature of the rooms, about how no attention whatsoever was spent on maintaining them.

Where did all that money go? Probably to fancy visiting professors like Oliver Ash.

Today they were discussing *The Coquette,* and Professor Roiphe had written on the board, "Is Foster subversive?"

She was lecturing: "On the surface, the novel is purely instructional, no? Eliza Wharton sins and dies, and in this respect, she satisfies the conservative moralism demanded of the time period in which it was written. Foster could not have publicly penned a novel that questioned the patriarchal demands on women in 1797; this was a time in which, at the formation of our brand-new nation, many believed that gaining control over women would lead to a prosperous and, perhaps more important, *virtuous* republic. And one way control was gained was through books: women could and should read, because they were the educators of our future generation, but they shouldn't be *too* well-read. A learned woman was a dangerous woman.

"So a book that came out and said 'Women should not be punished for wanting love—for wanting more than the life of a homemaker, or, God forbid, sex'—would flat-out never have been published. But there's an argument to be made that Foster's novel does, in fact, say this. The real Eliza Wharton— Elizabeth Whitman was her name; Foster doesn't take many pains to disguise her—died in 1788, and the New England papers turned her death into a moral allegory, blaming her demise on the reading of romance novels. This was Foster's response; it paints Whitman in a more sympathetic light, and allows room for a more sensitive reader to understand the impulses that might lead Whitman to make the decisions she does."

She wrote "moralism" on one side of the board, and "sympathy" on the other. Liv, sitting next to Fiona, was taking prodigious notes, barely looking up from her notebook.

"And an even *more* sensitive reader," Professor Roiphe continued, "might infer that Foster's novel is a sort of secret message to all the other women of the time reading romance novels. It satisfies the guidelines of the moral conservatives, but it also is a romance novel itself. The epistolary form, with all of its different points of view, would allow a shallow reader to be satisfied with the book as a cautionary tale, but there are also times in which Eliza appears as a victim of the marital standards heaped upon her. Structurally, politically, Foster is perhaps criticizing societal norms, and the republic itself, for leading Eliza to this point. And, still—still—even though it was disguised within itself, Foster published it under a pseudonym. This was how tightly the reins on women were held."

Fiona looked over at Dave, who was doodling in his notebook, apparently not listening to Professor Roiphe. Today he was wearing an oversized flannel shirt, rolled up around his elbows, the dark hair on his forearms showing. He hadn't trimmed his beard in a while, and the hair around his mouth had spread wildly to his cheeks.

"Do you believe the novel is subversive?" Professor Roiphe asked the class. "How did you read it?"

Liv raised her hand. Professor Roiphe waited for a few moments to see that no one else was volunteering, and gave in to Liv, whose hand was always shooting up first.

"Yes," Professor Roiphe said, sounding somewhat resigned. "Liv."

"I did," Liv said. "I thought the epistolary form gave us some insight into her decision-making in a way that was meant to make us sympathetic toward her."

"Okay," Professor Roiphe said. "Can you point to an example?"

"Yes, so, she has these really modern desires to simply enjoy herself for the experiences themselves." Liv leafed through the pages. "Here, on page thirteen: 'I am young, gay, volatile. . . . Let me then enjoy that freedom which I so highly prize. Let me have opportunity, unbiased by opinion, to gratify my natural disposition in a participation of those pleasures which youth and innocence afford.' She says things like this throughout the book, and we're supposed to relate to that feeling."

Dave suddenly perked up and raised his hand.

"Yeah, but that's a really modern reading," he said. "I'm not sure we are supposed to relate to her, because all along the way, there are dissenters, there are people who are morally rebuking her, and I think those are the people we're supposed to take the side of. Because right after Eliza says that, Mrs. Richman responds to her, 'Of such pleasures, no one, my dear, would wish to deprive you. But beware, Eliza!—Though strowed with flowers, when contemplated by your lively imagination, it is, after all, a slippery, thorny path.' She gets the last word in that conversation."

"What about all her letters with her friend Lucy?" Liv said.

"What about them?" said Dave.

"Why else would the author include such personal correspondence as a confidential one between a woman and her best friend?"

"Because Lucy is supposed to be the voice of reason," Dave said, as if this were the most obvious thing in the world. "And we're supposed to align with her, not with Eliza. She's the one who gets married and has a happy ending. That's what readers of this time are supposed to want."

"I don't know," Liv said, shaking her head. "On the surface, yes. I think the tragedy of Eliza's death is supposed to be critical of the patriarchy, though. It's tragic that she dies *because* the patriarchy forced this upon her, because awful men like Sanford gave her no choice but to give in to him."

"I'm not sure why that's Sanford's fault, though," Dave said. "Eliza could say no to him, but she doesn't."

Liv was full of passion and had lots more to say, but Professor Roiphe interceded.

"She *could* say no," she said. "That's right. But what about the idea of female agency? Is Foster for or against it? Look to page forty-eight." As they paged through their books, Fiona looked up to see Liv looking over at Dave with admiration, or fury, or a mix of both.

After class, Liv stayed behind to ask Professor Roiphe a question about her project. Fiona thought that maybe this was her chance: maybe today would be the day that she talked to Mountain Man after class.

"Dave," she said, following him out. He turned, surprised to hear his own name.

"Yeah?"

"I wanted to say, I thought that was interesting, what you were arguing about with Liv in class."

"Oh," he said. "Thanks."

"I think I agree with you," she said, though she hadn't finished the book. "I think it's unwise to take too modern a stance on a book that was written over two hundred years ago."

He nodded, as if this topic was now so far beyond his radar that he'd already forgotten about it the minute he left the classroom.

They were crossing through the quad outside of the library now, past the Adirondack chairs where she had sat and talked to her mother a few weeks earlier. Since then, leaves had fallen from the trees and were crunching under their feet as they cut across the lawn toward Phillips Avenue.

"Do you live this way, too?" she asked, which she knew as soon as she said it was a dumb question, because all upperclassmen lived off campus, and almost all of them lived on Phillips Avenue or on one of the side streets stemming from it.

"Yeah, I'm on North French," he said.

"Cool," she said. "I'm on North Abbott. Neighbors." The streets were two away from each other, not really closer to or farther apart from one another than your average seniors at Buchanan would live.

"What are you up to this weekend?" she asked.

"Not sure yet," he said, not reciprocating the question, as she had hoped.

They walked down Phillips together, toward her block.

"Anyway, this Saturday," she said, trying to sound casual, "there's a party at Zeta they do every year. It's Hawaiian-themed. They fill the basement with sand."

"Sounds messy."

"Yeah, it is."

"Um, I'm not sure what I'm up to," he said. "My roommate's in Zeta, so he could probably get me on the list. You gonna be there?"

Inside, Fiona delighted. This was the first clue he gave that he might, in any remote way, be interested in her.

"Definitely," she said. "You should come."

"Cool," he said. "Maybe I will."

"All right," she said.

"Wasn't that your street?"

"Oh, yeah," she said. They'd walked half a block down Phillips past Abbott. "Whoops." She pivoted. "I'll see you Saturday, then?"

"Cool," he said, and gave her a little wave as she walked back in the direction they came from.

All day Saturday, she labored over what she might wear. Should she go casual, in jeans and a black top? More dressed up, in a tight dress and heels? Marley and Liv were at the library, so Fiona paraded her outfits in front of Lula, who seemed more disapproving with each new one than the last.

"Trying too hard," she said to a floral dress that highlighted Fiona's bosom.

"Too boring," she said to jeans and a cotton button-down.

After Fiona's own closet was exhausted, they went down to Lula's. Lula had better taste than Fiona did: her closet was filled with vintage flared jeans, silk scarves, never-worn suede heels, Frye boots, sturdy motorcycle and army jackets, and a dozen Diane von Furstenberg dresses that had belonged to her mother in the seventies.

"What about this?" Lula said, pulling out one of the DVF dresses: a classic wrap, deep V-cut in the front, with three-quarter-length sleeves and a short, flared skirt. It was black with small beige teardrops patterned throughout, and a matching belt to cinch the waist.

"Will it fit?" Fiona said. It was elegant yet flirty, refined yet effortless: the exact balance that she wanted to strike. But Lula was a good four inches taller than she.

"Try it," Lula said, and Fiona undressed to her bra and underwear.

"You've gotten so skinny," Lula said, in the cadence of a

compliment. Fiona felt herself blush with pleasure; Lula herself was thin, though always had been. She had fewer curves than Fiona did, and her thinness took a more natural form, that of the tall, gamine Manhattanite. But it was additionally rewarding when a thin person recognized Fiona's own thinness.

"How do I do this?" Fiona said, with the dress open, fumbling with the tie. Lula helped her to pull one end of the belt through the hole, wrapping it around the back and toward the front, joining it to the other end in a tight bow right of center.

Lula stepped back to appraise her friend.

"You look hot," she decided.

Fiona checked the full-length mirror on the back of the door. Despite the two women's different body types, the dress had somehow molded to Fiona's form. Her breasts were highlighted, but not as obviously as with the floral dress; rather than pushed into the bodice, the V-cut here dipped only to the middle point of her cleavage, and narrowly so, allowing for the right amount of allure. Her waist looked tiny, and the flared skirt lightened up the look, making it more playful than serious.

"I do, don't I?" Fiona allowed herself to say. "Do I wear heels?"

"God, no," Lula said. "Wait." She disappeared into the back of her closet and resurfaced with a pair of ankle booties, camel colored, with a block heel.

"Have you even worn these?" Fiona asked, picking up one of the shoes and inspecting its unscathed surface.

"And this." She took a black leather motorcycle jacket from its hanger and threw it to Fiona, who caught it.

The boots were a bit big, but not obviously so; only Fiona would notice the small space between her heel and the back of the shoe. And the jacket pulled the whole look together, as

Lula knew it would. Lula took a long look at the completed outfit. She put her fingers to her mouth and kissed them, like an Italian chef.

"You're getting laid tonight," she said. "The dress can be dry-cleaned, but don't spill on the shoes. They're suede."

—— // ——

Wow-ee Maui was one of Zeta's most popular parties of the year. Every fall, the first weekend of November, they filled the entire basement of their house with a foot of sand, poured rum punch into coconut shells, and "lei-ed" every girl that entered the frat house with a plastic version of the real thing. The fraternity brothers wore grass skirts over their jeans, and some girls dressed for the theme in tropical dresses, though this was mostly what underclassmen did, since older girls knew it was better to wear what you wanted than to conform your outfit to the theme of a frat party.

Fiona had managed to get all four of them to come out, which hadn't happened since the night they went to Truckstop at the start of the semester. Brandon, who seemed to have radar on Liv, appeared the moment the four of them walked through the front door, running down the wide steps and scooping her up in the main entryway. She squealed with faux annoyance as he spun her around; then he let her down and kissed her.

"Hey, girls," he said to the three of them, pulling Liv close to himself. "Who needs to get lei-ed?" He laughed at the play on words, as if he were the first person to come up with it. He lifted an arm, which held a dozen or so of the plastic garlands. Liv and Marley each took one, but Fiona and Lula declined, too conscious of their good outfits to ruin them with a prop from Party City.

Fiona looked around at the young girls streaming in behind

them, already tottering on their heels. At the boys: some serving punch from a table in the entryway, others moving toward the basement, where the party really took place. Fiona could hear the bass pumping. She was looking for Dave without trying to make it seem like she was obviously looking for him, though she knew she'd be preoccupied with thoughts of finding him all night, worried that she might miss him if she wasn't paying close enough attention.

They headed downstairs, where it was busy and loud but not too packed, not like it would be in an hour, and Brandon handed them all coconuts filled with fruit punch. It was mostly brothers and their girlfriends; they'd gotten there fairly early. Fiona took a sip: it tasted like red Kool-Aid. Marley and Lula ran into a girl they knew from rugby—they used to play, freshman and sophomore years. Liv was making out with Brandon. Fiona stood with Marley and Lula for a while, not quite able to follow the rugby-centric conversation—people she didn't know, terms she didn't understand—and she drank her fruit punch quickly. She looked over at the beer pong table on the other side of the staircase, at some frat brothers playing, yelling things across the table at each other, but it wasn't beer pong: there was no Ping-Pong ball. It was some game only they understood, and it appeared that girls weren't allowed to play: some girlfriends were standing around the table next to their boyfriends, who were ignoring them. The girlfriends, with leis around their necks, were chatting with one another, holding coconuts and watching the game. Fiona told Marley and Lula she'd be right back, and walked over to the bar behind the pong table for a refill. There was already sand inside the too-big-for-her booties.

The guy working the bar took her coconut. "You're in my modern lit class, right?"

He was wearing a purple-flowered lei and a fake grass skirt, with shorts on underneath. He was tall and smiley, skinny, Asian American, with black hair buzzed close to his scalp. He talked often in that class, sometimes offering to Fiona what seemed like pretty obvious insights, but he seemed nice and genuinely interested in the course. She wouldn't have pegged him as a frat boy.

"Yeah, I am," she said. "What's your name again?"

He ladled the bright red punch into her coconut and handed it back to her.

"Ben," he said. "And you're Fiona."

"Yeah." She was surprised. "Good memory."

He shrugged. "You're a senior, right?"

"I am," she said. "What about you?"

"Sophomore," he said. "That's why I'm stuck manning this table. Go tear it up on the dance floor in my honor, okay?"

"Okay." She smiled at the phrase: "tear it up." Who said that? "I'll see you later," she said.

She felt a tap on her shoulder then, and perked up, hoping it would be Dave. It was only Liv.

"Fee-bee!" Liv's cheeks were blotched pink, as they always were when she drank even a few sips of alcohol. She, too, was sipping from a filled coconut. "Did you see your Mountain Man yet?"

"Not yet," she said. She looked up at Ben, who was already serving punch to another girl, and smiling at her, too. "Is he here?"

"I dunno." Liv shrugged. "Let's go dance!"

Marley and Lula joined them on the dance floor when their favorite song came on: *I fly like paper, get high like planes.* They cocked their fake pistols at the sound of the gunshot in the chorus: *And take your money.* The four of them were grinding up against one another, taking each other's hands, spinning and twirling and dipping. Marley was doing silly pantomimes now, her versions of the running man, but with everyday activities: the microwave (ticking a finger to her chin, to the beat of the music, as she waited for her invisible food to be ready), the shopping cart (pulling down canned goods from invisible shelves, inspecting them). They were in stitches, they were drunk, they were gleeful, they were just kids. Fiona forgot, just for a moment, that she was at the party to see someone, at the party to do anything but dance with her friends.

The joyfulness that came with forgetting inevitably ended every time she remembered: that is, every time she thought of Helen. Fiona could never be happy for long, because whatever Fiona was doing that brought her joy, Helen would never do. Helen would never have a senior year of college. She would never go to a frat party hoping to see a boy. Fiona kept dancing, to do what Helen could not, though it was not out of happiness now but out of guilt. Helen would *want* you to be happy, so many people had said to her over the past two years. *Helen doesn't want anything,* she always wanted to say back to them. *Helen is dead.* Why should she, of all people, be the one to understand this? Because people didn't want to dive deep into the specifics of loss, least of all the loss of a thirteen-year-old girl. That was why her parents had had Helen cremated. No one wanted to look at a miniature coffin.

"You okay?" Marley mouthed to Fiona.

Fiona's heart was pounding, a sign that her anxiety was starting up, even though the alcohol was supposed to counteract that.

"I have to pee!" she yelled over the music.

"Me too." Marley took Fiona by the arm. They wound through the crowd, which had thickened, past the bar, where

Ben was no longer serving drinks, and up the old steps to the main floor.

"You really okay?" Marley said when they could hear themselves.

"Really," Fiona said. "But thank you for asking."

They had to go up another flight of stairs to the bathroom, where there was a long line of girls waiting, as always. "No toilet paper!" a redheaded girl shouted as she left the bathroom, crookedly winding her way past Fiona and Marley.

"Wanna see if Brandon's up here?" Marley asked.

"Genius idea," Fiona said, and they walked down a hallway that smelled like marijuana, all of the bedroom doors closed. Fiona stopped at the third door on the right. "I think it's this one?"

"Let's try."

Marley knocked on the door.

"Go away," they heard on the other side.

"It's Marley and Fiona," Marley tried.

"Who?"

"Marley and Fiona!" she yelled again.

The door cracked slightly. It wasn't Brandon but a tall, overweight guy they only vaguely recognized.

"Is Brandon here?"

"Wrong room." The guy was about to shut the door on them when Fiona spotted Dave sitting on a futon on the floor next to another frat boy, taking a bong hit.

"Dave!" Fiona yelled through the crack in the door. "Hey!" She watched him exhale a giant puff of smoke.

"Dave, you know these girls?"

He coughed, squinted his eyes at them.

"Oh, hey, yeah. It's cool, Stretch," he said. "You girls wanna toke?"

Stretch looked at the girls and shrugged, opening the door wide and letting them in. "It's your weed," he said to Dave.

"Can we use your bathroom first, please?" Marley asked.

"It's there," Stretch said, gesturing to the doorway on the opposite side of the room.

They went in together. There were two doors—one, presumably, to Brandon's room on the other side—and they locked both of them. And there was toilet paper, mercifully.

"That's him," Fiona whispered as Marley sat down to pee, letting out a deep sigh of relief.

"Who?" Her eyes widened. "Oh, Mountain Man? Which one?"

"Shh," Fiona said. "Dave," she mouthed.

"Well, he doesn't know that's his nickname."

"It's a pretty obvious nickname."

"He's cute," Marley said, wiping, standing up to give Fiona her turn.

"Will you stay and smoke with me?"

"Yeah, of course."

They sat in a circle on the futon, Fiona and Marley squeezing in between Dave and Mike, his roommate, who was also a Zeta brother. The room was plastered in posters—mostly Grateful Dead bears and Tarantino movies. Stretch and his girlfriend, a petite underclassman, were taking hits from the bong. Fiona wondered about the mechanics of them having sex: he was about three times her size.

"'Sample in a Jar,'" Marley said about the music playing, some live album of a jam band. "I love this song."

"Right on," Mike said. "This girl knows her Phish." Mike was also cute—scruffy like Dave, though not quite as unkempt. He had dark features and thick eyebrows, and he was wearing a bright pink Talking Heads T-shirt.

The bong—a gigantic one, the biggest Fiona had ever seen, green glass painted over in swirling reds and blues—was passed to Dave, and then to Fiona, who took it awkwardly with both hands, trying to set it down sturdily between her crossed legs.

"Careful," Stretch said, looking at her suspiciously. "That thing cost me two hundred bucks."

"Can you light it for me?" she asked Dave, and he assented. She was mostly used to bowls and joints.

"Pull in," he coached her, as he took the bowl from the stem, and she did, a bit too hard, erupting with a hacking, smoky cough, like this was her first time getting high. He laughed, though it felt a bit more like he was laughing at her lack of expertise than in any inclusive, good-natured way.

She passed it to Marley, who was a natural at the bong and needed no help whatsoever from any man. Fiona watched the way Mike watched Marley: with admiration and interest. Marley, for her part, seemed unaware that his attention was fixed on her. She looked at Fiona after inhaling and laughed a little bit at her sudden highness, squeezing Fiona's hand.

Then Mike asked Marley another question about Phish, and Marley turned to answer, a conversation that Fiona could not participate in if she wanted to. Dave, on the other side of her, was staring straight ahead.

"This stuff is good," she said to him.

"Yeah, it's all right." He seemed to hear what Mike said about a certain Phish show, and began arguing with him across Fiona. Soon the three of them—Mike, Dave, and Marley— were in a heated debate about which of two performances of some song was better, and Fiona tried desperately to follow it but could not, even if she had been sober. Her mouth was dry; she realized she still had her coconut with her, and she sipped from it. The sugary Kool-Aid tasted so good. Sometimes all she ever wanted to do was eat and drink, forever and ever. She wanted a snack but she felt too high, and too embarrassed that she was high, to ask Stretch if he had anything to eat.

She watched Dave, engaged in the Phish conversation, watched the way his mouth moved, his pink lips surrounded by a full, dark beard. She resisted the urge to take a finger and trace them.

"What?" he said to her when he noticed that she was staring.

"Nothing," she said, and shifted her gaze straight ahead.

Marley put a hand on Fiona's leg. "You okay?" she asked quietly.

Fiona nodded. "I'm too high," she whispered back.

At a certain point, Stretch and his girlfriend starting making out.

"Hey, can you guys leave?" Stretch said, his girlfriend now sitting on his lap.

They all made their way downstairs to the main floor, which was now sticky with punch and filled with careening girls and red-faced boys, many of them making out, and Mike and Marley kept heading toward the basement. The bass from downstairs sounded even louder now, and was vibrating the floorboards beneath their feet.

"Dude," Dave said, grabbing Mike's arm before he was out of reach. "I'm gonna go."

"All right." Mike barely glanced back at Dave, fixated as he was on Marley. "See you at home."

"Oh," Fiona said. "I was gonna see if you wanted to dance."

"I'm pretty tired," Dave said. "I'll see you later."

In one fluid moment, convinced that this was her only chance, Fiona grabbed Dave by the arm, pulled him toward her, and pressed her lips against his. She felt his beard against her face, wiry and itchy. But before she could open her mouth and he could open his and they could *really* kiss, he pushed her away.

"What are you doing?" He extricated himself entirely from her, taking a giant step back.

"Kissing you?"

"I have a girlfriend."

"Oh." She was mortified. "I'm sorry. I didn't realize. I thought—"

"Thought what?"

"Well, I invited you tonight. I thought you came to see me."

He looked confused. "You did?"

"Yeah, when we were walking back from class the other day."

He tried to recollect. "I don't remember," he finally said. "I just came to smoke from Stretch's bong."

"Oh," she said again.

"I'll see you later," he said, and made his way out through the front door.

She felt that she might begin crying at any moment, but she wasn't quite sure where to go. She couldn't go outside yet, because he had just done that. She couldn't go downstairs, because that was where all her friends were, and she couldn't bear to pretend that nothing had happened, or worse, tell them the truth, so she stood there in the middle of the lobby. She felt the rum punch heavy and thick in her gut, the cloying sweetness in her mouth, her face hot from drunkenness or shame or some combination of the two. She walked over to the alcove where all the coats were and tried to find Lula's motorcycle jacket. It took what felt like hours of wading through identical black North Face fleeces before she found it.

"Going so soon?" said the extremely tall fraternity brother

manning the front door. There was a line of underclassmen waiting to get in, the girls barelegged and shivering. Fiona made it all the way down the front steps before throwing up a deluge of bright red, Kool-Aid-flavored vomit all over Lula's spotless suede shoes.

——//——

When she woke up on Sunday, her head pounding, her mouth parched, the house was silent. She checked her phone to find a missed call and several texts from Marley:

where did you go?

did you leave with dave?

shit, mike says he a has a gf. i'm sorry :(

are you ok? i hope you got home safe.

ok, i'm staying @ mike's. PLEASE text me when you get these.

Squinting, Fiona typed into the screen:

got home fine. just hungover. will give deets in person. hope you had fun ;)

In the kitchen, she filled a cup with water from the tap. The house was silent. Liv must have crashed in Brandon's room at Zeta, and who knew who Lula had gone home with. She fixed herself two rice cakes with peanut butter and jelly smeared on top. She sat at the table, eating silently, downing her water. The light streamed in from the one window in the kitchen, which looked out onto the puny plot of grass behind their house. The sky was completely blue.

Fiona returned to her room. Marley hadn't texted back. She watched several hours of TV on her laptop in bed, her brain turning soft and spongy, until she decided she might as well do something she felt good about. The final project for Professor Roiphe's class—a thirty-page research paper, plus a presentation—was due in less than a month, and she'd hardly made a dent in it. Still in bed, she opened her laptop and googled the Starr Report.

Fiona had been only eleven during the Lewinsky scandal; she'd more or less learned what "sexual relations" were because of the repetition of that phrase in the media, the constant replaying of that particular sound bite, the president dismissing Monica as "that woman" in his Arkansas accent. When Roiphe announced the assignment on the first day of class—to write about a woman who'd been publicly shamed by the patriarchal society in which she lived—she'd immediately thought of Monica. They were supposed to support their papers, on whichever woman they chose, with evidence from the novels they read: seduction novels from two hundred years ago, like *The Coquette,* that warned against the devilish temptations of sexual impulses (or, depending on how you read it, subverted that warning). Over two centuries later, women were still being punished for sleeping with too many men or sleeping with the wrong man—or, in the case of Monica, falling in love with that wrong man.

Fiona couldn't help but feel that same kind of judgment pressing down on her. She thought of the conversation with Marley the day she drove Fiona to get her car—Marley saying she wasn't worried about Fiona sleeping with all these guys but about the *reasons* she was doing it. As if that made some kind of difference. She thought about Dave; about Oliver, who was forever sitting in the back of her head like her threat to herself: *You could do this, you know.* She felt like mourning Dave, but knew there was nothing of any substance to mourn. It had all been in her head, in her active fantasy life. Still: she felt pain from it, from the shame of his rebuffing her, from vomiting in front of all those people. She felt pain that Gabriel had never called her and neither had that lacrosse player that she'd given a blow job to. And then, different from all of these rejections was Oliver Ash's last email to her, still hanging there. She had never responded.

The Starr Report was all legalese, hard to get through, and she found her eyes glazing over a lot of the content. What was becoming most interesting to her was the Linda Tripp aspect of the story. Linda had betrayed Monica by taping their conversations about the affair; as Monica was confiding in her friend about the love she felt for the president, and the heartbreak when he broke off their affair, Linda was using this information to boost her own reputation in Washington. When Monica told Linda that she was being encouraged to lie about the affair under oath, Linda contacted the notoriously right-wing Kenneth Starr. Although Linda's recording of their phone conversations without Monica's knowledge was illegal, Starr encouraged her to continue recording them, and agreed to grant her immunity from prosecution if she did so.

This was news to Fiona—she had had no idea that there was also an element of betrayal here, that Linda Tripp, supposedly one of Monica's closest friends and confidantes, ended up stabbing her in the back in order to save her own ass. Fiona spent nearly an hour sifting through the transcripts of Linda and

Monica's wiretapped phone calls. She was floored by an ex-change in which Linda convinced Monica to keep the blue Gap dress that had Clinton's semen on it:

Nov. 20, 1997

MRS. TRIPP: O.K. So one other thing I want to say to you
   that you can do what you want with—
MS. LEWINSKY: Oh.
MRS. TRIPP:—but I want you to think about this—and
   really think about it, instead of always just dissing what
   I say, O.K.?
MS. LEWINSKY: I don't always dis what you say.
MRS. TRIPP: Well—
MS. LEWINSKY: But sometimes you're such a—
MRS. TRIPP: You're very stubborn. You're very stubborn
   (sigh). The navy blue dress. Now, all I would say to you
   is: I know how you feel today, and I know why you feel
   the way you do today, but you have a very long life
   ahead of you, and I don't know what's going to happen
   to you. Neither do you. I don't know anything and you
   don't know anything. I mean, the future is a blank slate.
   I don't know what will happen. I would rather you had
   that in your possession if you need it years from now.
   That's all I'm going to say.

What if, every time Fiona confided in her friends, they were using her confidences for their own benefit? Sometimes she felt that was the case—not that they were going to use her words in a court of law, but that they gave her shit about her grief and her drinking and her sex life because doing so meant they were able to exercise a certain amount of control over her. As a way to prop themselves up, to feel better about their own lives.

Everyone left Lula and Marley alone when it came to their sex lives. Because they hadn't lost a sister, so their sleeping around didn't stem from grief the way Fiona's must. This was what angered Fiona most of all: that, in her friends' eyes, there was a direct line between Helen's death and Fiona's promiscuity. As if her brain, her emotions, her *grief* were that simple. As if Helen had died and Fiona immediately said to herself, *Time for me to sleep around—or stop eating, or drink too much—to fill the new void in my life.* It was like they'd each taken one psychology class freshman year and then spent a year around Fiona post-tragedy and concluded that they understood human behavior in its entirety. What did they know of grief? Of self-loathing? Of the need to punish oneself, over and over, until the pain finally became severe enough that the punishments felt sufficient?

She checked her phone; still no messages. She texted Liv, feeling desperate for social contact:

are you coming home anytime soon? lunch @ bagel king?

Fiona opened another tab and soon found herself on another set of transcripts, these from Monica's grand jury testimony in August 1998.

JUROR: Your relationship with the President, did your
    mother at any time try to discourage the relationship?
LEWINSKY: Oh, yes.
JUROR: Well, what kept it going? I mean, what kept it—you
    keeping it active or whatever?
LEWINSKY: I fell in love.
JUROR: I beg your pardon? I couldn't hear you.
LEWINSKY: I fell in love.

JUROR: When you look at it now, was it love or a sexual obsession?

LEWINSKY: More love with a little bit of obsession. But definitely love . . .

JUROR: You said the relationship was more than oral sex. I mean, it wasn't like you went out on dates or anything like that, like normal people, so what more was it?

LEWINSKY: Oh, we spent hours on the phone talking. It was emotional.

JUROR: Phone sex?

LEWINSKY: Not always. On a few occasions. I mean, we were talking. I mean, interacting. I mean, talking about what we were thinking and feeling and doing and laughing. We were very affectionate, even when—after he broke the relationship off in May, I mean, when I'd go to visit with him, we'd—you know, we'd hug each other a lot.

You know, he always used to like to stroke my hair. . . . We'd hold hands. We'd smile a lot. . . . I just I thought he had a beautiful soul. I just thought he was just this incredible person, and when I looked at him I saw a little boy and—I don't know what the truth is any more. . . .

JUROR: I'm not understanding these two different things because one time you're sentimental but then again you do just the opposite of what you say you're thinking. Did you ever think that . . . anything real could—and truthful and honest—could have come from this relationship?

LEWINSKY: Yes.

JUROR: With this married man?

LEWINSKY: I did.

Poor Monica. Linda Tripp, Kenneth Starr, everyone was out to get her. She was just in love—or thought she was in love—with a man in power, and everyone wanted to punish her for it. Fiona began to write.

Monica Lewinsky is living proof that sentimental stereotypes of women still exist. After her affair with President Bill Clinton in 1998, the media portrayed Lewinsky in a variety of different ways: as a victim, a slut, a femme fatale, a feminist, an innocent flirt. Countless interpretations of Lewinsky exist, and many journalists did come to her defense when the affair went public. Nonetheless, she is remembered as "that woman" who lied for the President, and whom the President lied about to the American people.

This week for Roiphe's class, they were reading *Amelia; or, The Influence of Virtue*. She hadn't finished the book yet, but she remembered a particular passage that reminded her of Monica early on, and paged through until she found it.

She marked the page, then wrote some more. She felt pleased with herself for getting some work done despite being hungover, despite the dull pain in her temples.

Lewinsky's case made me think that Americans are most comfortable sticking to sentimental stereotypes, labeling them virtuous if they're virgins, and sluts if their sexuality is referenced. This is, it should be noted, two hundred years after the classic vixen and virgin were created and portrayed in sentimental narratives.

Conveniently, Lewinsky fits the mold of the classic sentimental villain to a T. Sally Wood's *Amelia; or, The Influence of Virtue,* written in 1802, contains two women who represent these two classic characters. Amelia, the heroine, is described as "tall and beautifully shaped . . . grace[ful] and elegan[t]," with small features, a "complexion fair and soft," and "eyes . . . blue and mild" (10–11). Harriot, on the other hand, is described thus:

> Harriot . . . had, from the moment of her birth, been considered a beauty. Indeed there was a brilliancy in her fine black eyes, and her very florid color charmed one at first sight; her features were regular, her brows arched, and she had a great luxuriance of fine dark hair; she was lively even to pertness: at the age of thirteen, she had the appearance of a complete voluptuary, all her limbs were finely turned, and she could look gay or languishing at pleasure (10).

Descriptions of Lewinsky during the scandal do not stray far from this image of a dark-haired, voluptuous, and manipulative vixen.

Her phone buzzed, interrupting her flow, and she reached for it. Two messages from Liv:

> hey! hope the rest of your night was super fun! wanna hear ab MM :)

> I already ate with B, sorry! I'll be home in a little!

Fiona was starving now; the rice cakes weren't nearly enough, but she didn't have anything else to eat in the house.

She didn't want to go to Bagel King alone. She texted Lula next, even though she was terrified to tell Lula that she'd thrown up on her suede booties.

hey! hope you had a fun night ;) r u coming home soon? bagels?

She wondered if the girl whom Oliver Ash slept with at Columbia had been in love with him. Maybe she had thought she was at the time. She wondered if every girl who slept with an older man, or a married man, or a man in a position of power over her, thought she was different. Did Monica? Did the girl who got Oliver Ash fired from Columbia? Did these girls believe that their love was new, that no one had ever felt that way before, that it would stand the test of time, despite the odds stacked against pairings like theirs? That he would leave his wife for her, run away with her, give her babies? Or was it only about sex, about wanting someone you knew you weren't supposed to have? Was it possible they were the same thing? How could you even know, under such forbidden circumstances—which, by extension, were hot circumstances—if love was even a possibility?

In her inbox there remained one white subject line among the gray messages. She'd left her email from Oliver Ash marked unread, and would check back on it from time to time, marking it again as unread when she was finished, in case she ever decided to respond.

She opened it again now. It was a completely perfunctory email, one that required no response. Professional except for this one line: "I only hope that I don't disappoint you too much." There was a tinge of playfulness in that, wasn't there? Or was it literal? Either way—when was the last time anyone else in her life had expressed their interest in her approval? She thought of how kind he had been that night driving her home, and generous, and respectful.

What would happen to her if she tried? Or to him?

She had nothing worthwhile to say, which was what had stopped her from keeping this interaction going many times before. It would have to be subtle, skirting the line between flirtatious and professional, so that she could play down her intentions should he not reciprocate them. It would have to be couched in her interest in the class. Even if he knew it was bullshit, she would still be able to claim her innocence in a court of law.

She clicked Reply. In her email, she asked him how he'd been; she said she was looking forward to their class next semester, that she had been working on some new short stories, and asked to meet with him to discuss them. She would figure out what to say about these nonexistent stories if he agreed to the meeting. One thing at a time. In her signature, she added a smiley face for good measure. She clicked Send.

She checked her phone. No new messages, and still no roommates home. It was well into the afternoon now. She closed her computer and turned the TV back on. Maybe she'd order delivery.

9.

I T W A S T H E Larkins' third Thanksgiving without Helen. They decided to skip the hoopla with their extended family this year; they'd gone to Fiona's uncle's house last year, but it had been too much. All the fawning over the three of them—Liam, her mother, and herself—and all the talking about Helen, sharing their favorite memories of the girl. They acted like there was a ranking system for their grief—who mourned longer, who cried more, who brought up Helen's memory more often during family gatherings. Like someone might be keeping track.

There were new additions this year to their nuclear-family Thanksgiving: Ed, and Liam's new girlfriend, Rebecca. Five people, like it had once been, but now with replacements of the originals.

When Fiona pulled into the driveway of their colonial in Larchmont, both Amy and Ed—a balding man in a burgundy sweater, only a few inches taller than her petite mother—were standing at the front door. Fiona laughed at the sight, the suburbanness of it, though it also warmed her. Her father would never have waited outside for his children. He wouldn't even have been home yet at 5:30 on a Wednesday.

Ed and Amy walked down the front steps and toward the driveway as Fiona got out of her car.

"Let Ed help you with your bag!" Amy called.

"I got it," Fiona called back, opening the trunk.

They arrived at the car, Amy squeezing her first, and then, with some fanfare, introducing her to Ed. They hadn't spoken of their argument on the phone in October but instead pretended that it had never happened. Still—Fiona wasn't sure how much of the fight Amy had shared with Ed. She hoped, upon seeing this pleasantly avuncular man, that she hadn't shared any of it.

To her surprise, Ed drew Fiona in for a hug.

"It's an absolute delight to meet you," he said.

"Oh," she said, halfheartedly hugging back. "You, too, Ed."

"Let me get that," he said, gesturing to her duffel.

"It's really not that heavy," Fiona said.

"Nonsense," he said, insistently taking the bag from her.

"How was the drive, sweetheart? Was there a lot of traffic?"

"Kind of," Fiona said.

"What time did you leave?" Amy said.

"Not till one or so. I should have left earlier."

"Yeah, it's a busy traffic day. The earlier you leave, the better."

"I needed to pack."

"Why didn't you pack the night before?"

Fiona didn't respond, attempting to pick her battles.

"Shall we go get warm?" Ed said. "It's chilly out here. Your mother made a feast!"

. . . .

They waited for Liam and Rebecca to eat. The two of them arrived around eight, having taken the train in from the city. Liam bounded through the front door like a golden retriever.

"Sis!" He took her in a bear hug. Fiona missed Liam, missed his hugs. She wished it wasn't so painful to stay in touch with him.

Rebecca, following behind him, was not what Fiona was expecting. She was probably around five ten, and stunning; she had the kind of face that one rarely saw in real life, so symmetrical and structured and filmic, like it had been drawn, and it left Fiona without words for a moment.

"Hi," she said, looking over at Liam with big, disbelieving eyes. "Are you sure you're in the right place?" she said to Rebecca.

Rebecca laughed, crinkling her nose, her cheeks flushing; Fiona couldn't tell whether the cause was real bashfulness, or not.

"Oh my gosh," Amy said, coming to the door. "The famous Rebecca. Liam showed us pictures, but you're somehow even prettier in person."

It was true that Amy had made a feast, resplendent with a mix of their favorites: homemade gnocchi in a mushroom cream sauce (Fiona's favorite); a sirloin steak (Liam's favorite); and a giant salad of mixed greens with candied pecans, dried cranberries, and goat cheese (Ed's favorite, apparently). It turned out that Rebecca was an actress, and as she answered all their questions about what she'd been in (a few off-Broadway plays, a Pepsi print ad that went up in some major subway stations), Fiona watched her push the food around her plate. Fiona, who hadn't eaten all day and had been shoving the gnocchi into her mouth at a lightning rate, now felt self-conscious and slowed down, remembering that overeating would always make her feel worse later, and resolved that she would go for a run in the morning. It felt unfair that no matter how skinny she was, she would never be as pretty as Rebecca.

"How's work going, Liam?" Ed asked across the table. "You've got a front-row seat to the insanity."

Liam swallowed his steak. "I've been working crazy hours," he said. "It's a wonder we even got here tonight."

"It's a holiday," Amy said.

"Banking's not an industry that values time off, Mom."

Liam was twenty-four now, going into his third year working for Goldman Sachs. He'd been extremely lucky after the crash, a few months earlier, not to get laid off. He worked in technology mergers and acquisitions, but no matter how many times Fiona heard him explain it, she still didn't quite understand what he did. All she knew was that he didn't necessarily like the ins and outs of his job, but he was good at it, earning a huge paycheck every two weeks and an extremely generous bonus at Christmas, and this made his work tolerable, even enjoyable, as a means to an end. Fiona had a hard time understanding doing work for money's sake, which she knew was somewhat naïve. Most people worked because they had to, not because they wanted to. Even she would, very soon, have to work for money, but she would only be supporting herself. For Liam, it seemed there was an inherent pressure to not only support himself, but a future and so far nonexistent wife and family as well. This was, after all, what had been modeled for them.

"Well, money never sleeps," Fiona said.

"Neither does Liam," Rebecca responded, and the girls smiled at each other.

. . . .

After dinner, Ed insisted on doing the dishes, despite the fight they all—especially Rebecca—put up.

"You've been traveling," Ed had said. "I barely lifted a finger today." Fiona suspected this wasn't true, but there was a kindness in his humility, in his making sure they could all spend time together tonight. He knew, most of all, that it was important to Amy. As he shooed them out of the kitchen, Liam and Rebecca making their way toward the living room already, Fiona turned to grab her wine from the counter by the doorway and saw, from the edge of the kitchen, her mother lingering by the sink, and Ed wrapping an arm around her waist and pulling her in for a deeply romantic kiss. When Amy pulled her face away, it was flushed with what could only be described as joy. Fiona hurried into the living room before Amy saw her.

Fiona hadn't wanted to like Ed. Part of her felt he was trying too hard; part of her wanted to resist his kindness and his love for her mother. She hadn't seen her mother this happy in years, though—not even, she realized, while Helen was still alive. It was hard to see Helen's death and her parents' divorce as two separate events, but she was going to try to now, because what was becoming quite clear was that Amy had not been happy with Fiona's father for a long time.

And Fiona was surprised at herself, too, because she didn't find her mother's happiness unwarranted. Instead, it was a comfort to her. She hadn't realized, perhaps, that Amy's well-being—or lack thereof—rubbed off so much on her. Though why wouldn't it? It always had when she was a kid; when Amy was in a bad mood, undoubtedly due to something Fiona's father did, young Fiona instead believed it was her own fault. And even when Helen died, Fiona felt she was failing by not being able to put her mother back together again. What she realized now was that she'd perhaps never had the capacity to do that. And there was a freedom in letting go of the conceit, and letting someone else take over.

"He's nice, Mom," Fiona said quietly when Amy joined them in the living room. They all held fresh beverages: more wine for Fiona and Liam; mugs of herbal tea for Rebecca and Amy. Amy looked contented at the mention of him.

"He's great, isn't he?"

"Can you imagine Dad ever doing the dishes?" Fiona said, turning to Liam.

Amy shook her head. "No," she said. "I cannot."

Liam didn't say anything, and seemed instead to be intent on the wine that he swirled around in his glass. Rebecca, sitting on the arm of his chair, put a hand out to steady his wrist. It looked like an expression of something private, like there was an anxiety here that Fiona wasn't privy to.

She had become, seemingly overnight, the fifth wheel in her own family. She didn't even have any prospects. She thought back to the email she'd sent Oliver the week before, and was filled with deep shame. He'd never responded—of course he hadn't. She should have known better than to think he would humor her, would see her as anything other than yet another undergraduate with a crush on him. It was an inappropriate, deeply pointless message to send. Especially that fucking smiley face. She regretted it immensely.

She sipped her fresh glass of wine and began to ask Rebecca more questions about herself.

Later, Fiona caught Liam while en route to the bathroom. He was walking back to his bedroom, fresh out of the shower with a towel around his waist.

"Cover it up," she said, faux-shielding her eyes.

"Har har," he said, continuing to walk past her.

"Hey," she said from the open doorway of the bathroom.

"Yeah?"

"What's up with you and Ed?"

"What do you mean?"

"I mean . . ." She lowered her voice now. "Do you not like him? You seemed weird in the living room."

"I never said I didn't like him."

"I know you didn't *say* it."

"I'm tired," Liam said.

Her brother, who liked nearly everyone, worried her. What if Ed wasn't as good as he seemed?

"Did he do something?"

"What?" Liam said. "No. God, no."

"I don't understand, then."

Liam looked down the hallway to the closed door of their mother's—once their parents'—bedroom.

"It's just weird."

"Yeah, it's super fucking weird."

"Right?"

"Yeah."

"I keep feeling like," Liam whispered, "I hear her talking in a sweet voice to a man, I assume it's gonna be Dad. Our whole life there was one dad figure. How do you recalibrate that? Seeing Mom with someone else?"

"I haven't figured it out, either," Fiona said. "But he seems to make her happy. And that makes our lives easier." She was surprised by her own one-eighty on Ed, though she suspected that Liam's hesitancy about him made her more enthusiastic, as if she felt the need to make up for it. When she had thought that Liam was okay with Ed, she'd felt more freedom to disparage him. She couldn't quite handle the idea of her mother being entirely alone in her happiness.

"Yeah," he said, looking down at his bare feet. If he were done with the conversation, he would have left by now.

"What?" Fiona said.

"I need to tell you something," he said.

"What?"

"Let me get dressed. I'll come to your room in five?"

They sat at the foot of her bed. Her heart was racing, and she felt that hot claustrophobia that came back so often these days: the clammy hands and the tense neck and the feeling like her intestines were bunched into a tight wad.

He was in his pajamas now—a Yale T-shirt and sweatpants. His brown hair was cut so short these days, it was already almost dry. He put his hands on his knees to prepare to speak.

"I saw Dad," he said.

"When?"

"A couple weeks ago. We had lunch in the city."

"That bastard," she said, without yet hearing why they had met or what they talked about or what he was doing with his life these days. She still felt so much anger toward him, and even the mention of his existence, in anything other than vague terms, catapulted her into a state of rage.

"That bastard is still paying your college tuition," Liam said.

"As he should."

"I'm feeling a little . . ."

"What?"

"Conflicted."

"What's there to be conflicted about?" Fiona said. "Why did you meet with him?"

"He asked me to," Liam said.

"And you just . . . said yes?"

"Not right away, but . . . eventually, yeah. He's our dad."

"So what?"

"So he can still bankroll your existence, but you don't even feel the need or responsibility to talk to him anymore? To give him a shot?"

"It's not a two-way street, Liam."

"Fine, we don't, technically, owe him anything. I *wanted* to see him. Is that okay?" He said this last part sarcastically.

"Well, how is he?"

"He's fine," Liam said. "He's living in a high-rise on the Upper East Side."

"Oh, well, I'm glad he can enjoy his bachelordom now that he's in the city."

"He's in a relationship, actually."

"I don't want to hear any more." Fiona waved a hand, trying to keep Liam from sharing new information. "You shouldn't have told me this."

"I'm going to keep seeing him," Liam said.

"He cheated on Mom! He went back to work two weeks after Helen died! Does all of that not tell you anything about the kind of man he is?"

"It's complicated. Marriages are complicated. Mom wasn't blameless."

"Oh, good, now he has you sipping the Kool-Aid."

Liam shook his head. "Don't you ever . . . ?" he said.

"Don't I ever what?"

"He lost her, too."

"You should go to bed," Fiona said, standing up. "It's been a long day."

"You're really going to kick me out of your room in the middle of this conversation?"

She crossed her arms over her chest. She was acting like a child, and she knew it, but this felt like one issue that could not be touched.

"I really don't see what else there is to say."

Liam left her room, and a few minutes later, while in her own bed, she heard cooing on the opposite side of the wall that she shared with him. Rebecca was repeating something over and over to Liam in the same soothing tone, like an incantation. It was so calming that Fiona herself fell asleep to it.

When she awoke on Thanksgiving morning, Fiona went for a run, as she'd promised herself she would. The morning was cold but not unbearably so, and by the time she warmed up, she was reminded of why she liked running in this weather: the way it opened up her sinuses, made her breathing so clear and easy; the way it made her lungs feel, large and expansive; the way it turned her cheeks and fingertips cold and red, and how satisfying it was, when she was done, to walk inside and warm them again. Back in the house, she took off her sneakers and skipped up the steps to the upstairs shower but found, to her confusion, the door to Helen's bedroom open.

They kept that door closed at all times. Or at least they had, all the times that Fiona had been home. The matter was never discussed, but Fiona assumed there was nothing to be gained by keeping the door open. It was too awful to consider redoing the room, finally getting rid of Helen's stuff, and just as awful to leave it all there on display. So until Amy or one of the kids tackled the issue of the bedroom, it would, decidedly, stay closed.

Perhaps Amy had been going in to check on things, Fiona thought. Perhaps Amy had made a habit of spending time in there by herself. Perhaps, even, Liam was looking for something—a book or an old photo or another item of nostalgia.

Of course, neither of them would be inside. The Larkins stepped around their grief, not through it.

Fiona peeked into the bedroom, still maintained exactly as it had been, and found, instead, Rebecca, holding and staring at a picture of Helen, ten years old. It was one of Fiona's favorite pictures of her sister. It had been taken after a riding competition; Helen had just won some ribbon or other for jumping. (She was always winning ribbons; Fiona had lost track of them.) In the photo, she was still wearing her black velvet helmet, the strap undone, her yellow curls falling down to her shoulders. She was not looking at the camera but kissing the nose of her horse, Josie. Helen had been a gifted rider—much more so than Fiona—and she loved that horse, Josie, probably more than she loved Fiona. After Helen died, they sold Josie to their summer camp, where she now serviced however many hundreds of keen little girls were learning to ride. Josie would spend the rest of her days plodding in circles in a beginner's arena, around and around.

"Hi?" Fiona said.

Rebecca jumped backward, knocking over a row of miniature horse figurines on the bookshelf. She righted them and then put a hand over her heart.

"I'm sorry," she said. "You scared me." Fiona delighted in seeing the seemingly perfect young woman from the night before now caught in an awkward moment.

"Sorry," Fiona said. "I didn't know who was in here."

Rebecca was still quite beautiful, and she recovered instantly from the awkwardness. She was wearing leggings and one of Liam's T-shirts. Even though she had just woken up, her skin was clear and even, her dark hair was loose and wild, and her features could barely have been enhanced by the use of makeup. In fact, Fiona realized, she hadn't been wearing any makeup the night before, either. Her face had looked exactly the same as it did now. Rebecca was just that pretty.

"No, I'm sorry," Rebecca said. "This was very out of bounds."

"It's okay."

"I was on my way to the bathroom and I got nosy. Incredibly so. I'll go."

"It's really okay. I don't mind."

Fiona glanced down the hallway; all the other bedroom doors were closed. It was only the two of them awake. "It's weird, isn't it," she said, looking around this room for the first time in two years: at all the riding ribbons pinned on the walls, and the trophies lining the bookshelf. A few photographs of Helen's friends, from camp and from school, pinned to a corkboard: middle-school-aged girls looking silly, their tongues stuck out, or pouting, lips pursed, in an attempt to look mature. One poster of the cast of *High School Musical*. The room was a reliquary, an untouched exhibit of the life of a thirteen-year-old girl from suburbia in the year 2006. How long before the posters would have changed, the ribbons been taken down, after Helen had outgrown them and they had become vestiges of immature interests? How long before the photographs of old friends would have been replaced with new ones?

"What is?"

"That we keep the door closed."

"Well," Rebecca said. "Maybe. Nothing about this situation is exactly normal. It's not like there's a manual."

"I think there is?" Fiona said. "In a therapist's office, somewhere."

Rebecca let out a sympathetic smile. "I'm an only child," she said, "so when Liam talks to me about her, I think there's a part of me that might never really understand. I thought seeing her room might help. It's stupid, now that I say it out loud."

Fiona swallowed. "Liam talks to you about her?"

Rebecca nodded.

"And did it?"

"Huh?"

"Seeing her room? Did it help?"

Rebecca looked around, and her gaze landed on a framed photo of the five Larkins, from a ski vacation many years ago, all five of them wearing snowsuits in various neon colors, lined up on top of a mountain, goggles resting on their foreheads. The only picture of the five of them left on display in the whole house. Fiona remembered hating that day, because she had been fourteen and Helen eight, and Helen had already proved to be a better skier than she was. Fiona remembered sulking in the lodge after lunch, after the picture had been taken, not wanting to go back to the slopes, and wishing that someone in her family would ask her what was the matter. But when she said she didn't feel like skiing anymore, her father had simply said, "Suit yourself," and the four of them went back out there, an even foursome, energized and pink-cheeked, the picture of a healthy American family.

"I get why you keep the door closed," Rebecca said by way of response. Then they left the room together, shutting it away behind them.

10.

Liv's house was decked out for Thanksgiving, as it was for every holiday. The long dining table was impeccably set, with the fine crystal and a tasteful array of tall, glowing candles, pinecones, fresh clementines, and dried eucalyptus leaves, arranged fastidiously by one of the housekeepers. A fire was going in the parlor, and above the mantel was a giant arrangement of branches with orange flowers blooming from them. These branches were on every surface in the house, in vases so tall they obstructed mirrors and furniture: not only in the parlor, dining room, and kitchen, but also in the library, in the bathrooms, and on the dresser and nightstand in Liv's bedroom, where they had greeted her upon her arrival earlier today.

When she was very young, Liv never noticed how the flower arrangements changed with every holiday. All of the other houses in McLean looked like hers: sprawling colonials of at least three levels with sloping, manicured lawns out front; in-ground pools and spacious yards out back; tasteful hedging surrounding it all for privacy. All of her classmates in school

also had parents who were high-powered lobbyists—or diplo-
mats, or senators, or cabinet members. It was only when she
began to read novels that she fully understood the scope of the
many worlds outside of her own, learned that most people's
parents did not have jobs that determined, more or less, the
trajectory of the free world. She read *Little Women, Anne of
Green Gables, Little House on the Prairie.* She learned about
class from the March family, learned that girls like Meg and Jo
had to have jobs of their own to support their family, and still
they did not have enough money for gowns as nice as the ones
that the other girls at the ball had.

And so, though Liv understood by age ten or so that her life
was privileged—in comparison not only with the lives she read
about but also with the handful of scholarship students from
the city who attended her middle school—she did not become
particularly grateful for what she had. In comparison with almost everyone she knew, it was the status quo. It was the world
she lived in and enjoyed and the world in which she wanted to
stay. The thought of losing it, or of not having it at all, seemed
preposterous. Her parents had also grown up like this—her
father over in Arlington, her mother in Tokyo. Maintaining a
certain quality of life was important to the Langleys, because
adjusting to a, well, *lower*-quality life was really not an option.

Nonetheless, Liv felt a certain amount of nervousness when
bringing people home with her. In middle school and high
school, she went to friends' houses more often than they came
to hers, mostly because she understood that her family was different. The dynamic in her house was not like that of her
friends', the moms there to welcome them home from school
with snacks at 3 P.M.; her mother was certainly a warm presence, but by the time Liv was in middle school, Kimiko had
gone back to work at the embassy full-time. And when Liv's

parents did come home in the evenings, the atmosphere was unhappy, antagonistic. Sometimes it was silent, or downright awkward. Many nights, her father didn't even make it in time for dinner. Liv had often felt, as a child and as a teenager, that her role was that of conversational lubricant, common interest, mediator, glue. The focus was perpetually on her, and she often sensed that if she ever made a misstep, if she ever strayed from the path they'd set out for her, she would single-handedly break her family in half.

This was the first time she was bringing a boyfriend home since high school, and those visits had been perfunctory and short—Cyrus picking Liv up and taking her elsewhere, Liv always certain to be ready to go upon his arrival. Her parents were dying to meet Brandon, Kimiko had said over the phone (the "we," Liv knew, referred to her mother and not to her father, Robert), and Brandon was also coincidentally from the D.C. area; certainly it wouldn't be too much trouble for him to come over for Thanksgiving dinner? They'd be sure to have the meal late enough in the evening so that he could also eat with his family in the afternoon, as was traditional for them.

Liv wasn't even going to tell Brandon that he was invited, but he'd messed up her plan by inviting *her* to eat with *his* family in the afternoon, and there was no way she'd be able to explain that to her parents without reciprocating the invitation. So they did both meals: first eating with Brandon's entire boisterous extended family in Bethesda—thirty-five people, catered, babies and great-grandparents and everyone in between—and then driving back over to McLean for cocktails and dinner, only the four of them; it was bound to be a humorless evening in comparison.

Brandon put on a suit jacket and a tie for dinner with the

Langleys, which Liv knew her father would appreciate. In their short drive over to her house, she was quiet.

"You recovering from all that mayhem?" Brandon asked. "I know they can be a lot."

In truth, she'd loved how loud and chaotic it was; it was so different from what she was used to, being the center of attention, the one point of accord between her two discordant parents.

"I liked it," she said. "The silence at my house is going to be deafening in comparison."

"Well, good," he said, squeezing her leg as he kept one hand on the steering wheel. "Quiet sounds good."

When they pulled into the driveway, she could tell that Brandon, whose family was upper-middle-class and entirely comfortable, was still impressed by the Langleys' house, which embarrassed her.

Kimiko greeted Brandon with a hug, and Robert with a handshake. Robert held a crystal glass of scotch in his other hand. It was five P.M., a reasonable time to start drinking. Liv hoped this wasn't one of those days he'd started early.

The first thing Robert asked Brandon was if he would like a drink. They walked over to the bar cart, Robert's crystal decanters filled with brown liquids of various shades. He described what was in each one to Brandon, and Brandon listened attentively. Brandon said he would have whatever Robert was having, and Robert poured him a generous helping into a crystal glass that matched his own. He refilled his glass, too, while he was at it, even though it didn't look like he needed a refill.

"Dad, can I have a little?" Liv asked.

Robert looked dubious. "Since when do you like scotch?"

She shrugged.

He poured her one finger's worth. "Try a small amount first."

The glass felt heavy in her hands, substantial. The four of them sat in the parlor now, Liv and Brandon on the couch, and Kimiko and Robert in chairs on the opposite side of the mahogany coffee table. Kimiko was attentive to Brandon, and asked him about his family, his fraternity, and how the law school applications were going.

"Pretty well." He put his glass down on a coaster. "I'm trying to get the applications in a few weeks before the deadline so I won't have to worry about them over winter break. A lot of the decisions are rolling, so the earlier you get the applications in, the better."

Robert nodded in what seemed to be approval.

"And what schools will you apply to?"

He listed them off: all of the Ivies, plus NYU, Duke, Georgetown.

"Georgetown." Kimiko smiled at the proximity to their own house, already assuming that Liv would follow Brandon wherever he ended up.

"That's his safety," Liv said.

"Georgetown's your safety?" Robert said.

"Well, with the way the market is now, I don't see the point in applying to schools that aren't in the top tier."

"What if you don't get in to any?" Robert said.

"Dad. He'll get in."

"It's a fair question." Brandon patted Liv a few times on her leg. It felt like he was trying to mollify her with that pat, unlike the affectionate squeeze in the car. "I feel confident in my LSAT scores and my GPA, but it's true, you never do know. I suppose I would apply for jobs then. And maybe try again the following year."

"It won't come to that," Kimiko assured him.

"There's a lot to be said for security," Robert said. He stood to refill his glass, not offering the option to anyone else. Liv was beginning to feel the first blushes of shame; she worried. She should have known he was going to feel more wound up around her first serious adult boyfriend. She should have prepared more adequately for this.

"Well, what would be your first choice?" Kimiko asked sunnily, trying to gently move the focus away from Robert's naysaying.

Brandon seemed nervous to answer, though. Liv knew the feeling well: too afraid to express what you actually wanted, because it often got shot down by Robert.

"It would be hard to say no to Harvard, Mrs. Langley," Brandon finally said.

Robert hiccupped.

"What if Liv is in New York?" Kimiko said.

That was where Liv was always planning to go after college. It annoyed her, this assumption that they would stay in the same city no matter what.

"There are some small presses in Boston," Brandon said, a point he'd made to Liv more than once.

"That's true," Kimiko said, seeming pleased.

Liv didn't want to go to Boston, and Brandon knew that, but she didn't say so now; she knew that if she expressed her wishes in front of her father, she'd be shut down. *You're an English major, for Christ's sake,* he would say. It wasn't the Victorian age—she was, of course, going to work, but she was never going to make the kind of money that Brandon eventually would. She would simply get a job in whatever city Brandon's top-ten law school was in.

This was how it went: Langley women had jobs—important

jobs, at that—but they were secondary to their husbands' more lucrative careers. Liv's parents had met at the American embassy in Osaka, where her mother was serving as a translator and her father as a Foreign Service officer; they moved back to the States when they learned they were pregnant, because Robert, ever the patriot, wanted their child to be born in America. Her mother worked at the Japanese embassy now; her father was in the private sector, working for a powerful Japanese business lobby, making far more money than he ever could have in the Foreign Service. Kimiko didn't start work in the U.S. until Liv was three, and only returned to working full-time when Liv entered middle school. When Liv was little, Kimiko was always around to take her to playdates, soccer practice, and Girl Scouts. But when Liv was in school, her mother was working. Kimiko was a model of the kind of woman who could do both.

The catch there, Liv realized as she got older, was that her father didn't have to do both. He was never asked to make a choice between his daughter and his job, and then judged for whatever he decided. Meanwhile, Kimiko was forever struggling to balance the scales, trying her best to be equally a professional woman and a nurturing caretaker.

Liv wanted to work: she knew this. And she didn't mind the idea of whomever she ended up with making more money than she did, so that she would be free to pursue a career in publishing, which didn't pay quite enough for the quality of life she wanted.

Ostensibly, the idea of marriage was nice, but it seemed so far in the future. She had only been dating Brandon for six months, and the thought of living with him—let alone marrying him—could not have been further from her mind. It wasn't until Brandon started including her in his discussions about law school locations that she'd considered that trajectory in any immediate way. She liked the idea of having Brandon's support and comfort as a constant in her life, and she liked that she never had to experience loneliness as long as he was around. But the realities of marriage were far from ideal. Thinking about sleeping with the same person for the rest of her life, being held accountable by him, and having to deal with all of his humanness—his insecurities, his snoring, his smells—made her mourn her singleness before she'd even truly lost it.

For dinner, they were each on their own side of the table: Robert and Kimiko at the head and the foot, Liv and Brandon across from each other. Brandon was cutting and eating the turkey the European way, fork in his left hand the entire time, turned with a delicate flick of the wrist when he took a bite, which was a performance for her mother.

"This is delicious, Rosa," Brandon said to their housekeeper when she came out to refill their champagne glasses, and Liv swore she saw Rosa blush. Kimiko made approving eye contact with Liv, a nod to his politeness.

Robert was at that point in the night when he had stopped talking altogether. Instead, he alternated between champagne and scotch, and chewed his turkey loudly.

Liv was not hungry. She pushed the turkey around on her plate. She took a generous swallow of champagne, the bubbles sharp going down her throat. Robert, after draining his most recent glass of champagne, let out a belch.

Liv looked up at her mother, who was looking daggers at her father.

"It's my fucking house," Liv heard him say, in response to Kimiko's warning glances. He had not spoken for maybe an hour, Liv realized, and now he was slurring his words. If Brandon heard the comment, or the quality of Robert's speech, he pretended not to. Kimiko asked Liv some questions about her roommates, her classes, and both women did their best to maintain the bright and breezy level of conversation, diverting attention from the storm cloud that they knew was building at the head of the table.

When they were done eating, and Rosa came out to collect the plates, Liv could see that she was afraid as she rounded the table toward Robert. She gathered his plate and his silverware, as well as the empty champagne flute, knowing quite well to leave the crystal rocks glass with a few sips of scotch left.

"Don't take that," he said, grabbing the empty flute from her.

"Mr. Langley, there's no—"

As he stood and snatched the glass from her with great force, it flew from his hand and against the wall behind him. Rosa let out a shriek, startled, and dropped the silverware and the china plate, which smashed onto the floor into dozens of porcelain-white pieces.

"Goddammit, Rosa," he boomed, grabbing her by the wrist. She shrieked again. There were tears in her eyes; she cowered toward the floor in a position of defense, her free hand covering the top of her head.

"Robert!" Kimiko yelled from across the table. "Let go."

He looked down at the hand holding Rosa's wrist, as if it had been acting independently. He loosed his grip; Rosa, now breathing with great effort, rubbed her wrist with her free hand. Liv could see that it was red, the white imprints from her father's fingers slowly fading.

"Clean this up." He waved toward the dining room, to no

one in particular, and swayed out of the swinging door into the parlor, still carrying his crystal glass with the remnants of scotch in it.

Kimiko went over to shush Rosa and calm her down.

"I'm so sorry, Mrs. Langley."

"It's okay, Rosa."

"It's the good china."

"It's okay." She rubbed Rosa's back. "Go sit down. I'll get the dustpan."

They disappeared through the opposite swinging door to the kitchen, leaving Liv alone with Brandon at the table, in the room fixed between her parents. It felt awfully symbolic, remaining paralyzed in the middle. It had never been easy, that choice: siding with her mother after an incident was always a gamble, because her father's moods were so unpredictable, his propensities toward violence so inconsistent. She had never quite learned when to stand up to him and when to let his storm pass over them and subside, because it was impossible to know in advance when he would let an issue go and when he would retaliate. His behaviors were not constant or methodical, much as Liv had tried, her entire life, to chart them, to unearth their causes and to modify her own actions as a way to thwart his. She remembered, in middle school, when she first recognized that his abuses weren't normal, keeping a journal in which she recorded variables such as type and units of alcohol consumed, time of day, and the inciting incident, hoping to find a pattern in order to be able to change it herself.

She found no pattern. His outbursts did not often correlate in scope with the thing that set them off: a sentence Kimiko said out of turn, a rare B-plus that Liv received on a test. Alcohol was often involved, but how much and what kind didn't seem to matter. Sometimes, in fact, the drunker the better, because his violence would be lazy and inexact, and he would forget the incident the next day.

She'd learned that the best thing to do was behave. Be as good as she could. Only, she'd never had a Brandon in the room with her. Robert tended to reserve these moments for only the nuclear family, and for the people who worked for their family. She had never learned how to account for an outsider.

She could not look at him. She still held her fork, and stared at her plate, all the turkey and mashed potatoes and stuffing that she had pushed around it now inedible. She wanted desperately to be able to say to him, *This has never happened before*. She almost did, almost told the lie, in order to be done with it.

"Hey," he said.

She had been so foolish to think that maybe, with a new boyfriend present, he might have behaved. She had thought there was a chance. At least for a little while longer. Of course, the presence of a new boyfriend only stirred him up more, made him more upset. Changes, as her mother had once told her, were hard for Robert. Changes were to be avoided at all costs.

"Hey."

She heard his chair scrape against the floor, and his footsteps as he walked around the table. She felt his arms on her shoulders, and then she felt him kneeling to her level. Without a word, he took her into his arms, and without moving any limbs, she sank into him, feeling, for the first time, her body relax into his.

II.

UPON HER RETURN from Thanksgiving break, Fiona bought Oliver Ash's second book at the college bookstore: *Dispatches from a Half-Breed*. Though she was meant to be finishing her Lewinsky and modern lit papers, along with studying for her French final and polishing her poetry portfolio, the fact that he had not responded to her email had only fueled her obsession. She checked the bookstore to make sure she didn't recognize anyone before she purchased the book (though, she imagined, she couldn't have been the first young woman for whom the cashier had rung up this paperback). She secreted the book inside the paper bag as if it were a handgun or several ounces of cocaine.

She had come to the point where she assumed Oliver wasn't going to respond to her email, but she had not stopped thinking about him. Her brain seemed entirely too unoccupied without a fantasy of a man to busy it. And how rich her fantasies were about Oliver! Without seeing him in person again, Fiona had begun to construct a great imaginary life around him. The fantasy life began at the dive bar where they'd met, but then stemmed off in a different direction: a night on which Fiona had not drunk too much but had, instead, kept her cool, inching her knees slowly toward Oliver's throughout the course of the night. When he put his hand on the bar and overlaid his pinky finger on hers, she had not flinched.

He would close their tab—paying for her drinks, too—and lead her, with his large hand on the small of her back, to his car. She would ask if he was okay to drive and he would say yes and she would believe him; he would be, in fact, quite capable of driving, and it would make her think of the boys whom she did not trust to drive after a few, and how much Oliver's adultness and competency contrasted with their lack thereof. The air in the car would be laden with the sort of sexual tension that makes one feel jumpy and alive. They wouldn't speak, except for him to offer her a cigarette, which she would decline, preferring instead to look out the window at this city she'd spent nearly four years in and think about how different it looked from this vantage point—from the passenger seat of the car of a married professor, in all of its secretive glory. And what would happen if she caught the eye of someone she knew? She imagined she'd attempt to hide, feigning shame or embarrassment, but in truth, she would have felt proud. She would wonder how many other people they were passing, on the sidewalk or in their cars, who were doing private, illicit things. It would make her feel as if she were entering an aspect of adult life which she'd previously not been privy to.

They would go to his house—she imagined he lived in one of those Victorians on the other side of campus—and from here the fantasies diverged in detail, though they always followed the same rough blueprint: more drinks, kissing, falling on a bed. The greatest thrill came when they saw each other for the first time; for her, it would be almost too much to bear, to square this image of the man she'd built up in her head for months with the flesh version now in front of her. And so, too, would be the tactility of it all—how would she know how to touch him? This was where things got blurry, when Fiona—in her bedroom, often before falling asleep—became not in control of her own thoughts and, afterward, felt somewhat embarrassed by the images she'd conjured seconds earlier.

When the desire was satisfied, the fantasies turned to post-coital bliss, to the things they might talk about: his favorite novelists (she pegged him as a fan of the Russians) and composers (he only listened to classical music, surely). Her own tastes would feel lowbrow in comparison. Maybe, at some point, she would ask about his family, his son. She was not so naïve as to think that he might develop feelings for her or she him, but she imagined, with Oliver, that things would be different than they had been with college boys. More substantial. That he would satisfy her and talk to her afterward, instead of leaving right away. This, she imagined, was what real men did.

Now, Fiona walked down the steps of the bookstore. It was the Monday everyone returned from Thanksgiving weekend, and campus buzzed with the anxiety of exams. It was dark already, even though it was only five o'clock, and students were getting out of their last classes of the day and headed en masse to the library. Every year, Fiona seemed to have temporary forgetfulness when it came to daylight savings, and she felt a pang of sadness when she thought of the sun being out at this time mere weeks earlier. The trees lining the pathways, bare now, were circled with bright lights, which made the campus glow with forced holiday cheer.

She moved against the stream of library-bound students, making her way out of campus and toward her home. The house was dark and silent; they were all at the library, studying for exams and writing final papers. She turned the lights on as she climbed upstairs to her room. She could have sat and read on the couch downstairs or in the kitchen, but she didn't want anyone to suddenly come home and walk in on her. This book, and the fact that she was reading it, felt private. She opened to the first page, and began reading.

> She was standing in her underwear at the foot of my bed, all sinew and limbs, like the baby fat had just been shed. A black thong and a black lacy bra. She wore them like a costume, like a girl playing dress-up, the way she stood there, asking to be appraised by me. What was I to say? That the underwear looked brand-new, purchased for this occasion?
>
> My father had hanged himself that morning. She told me she was eighteen. I had chosen to believe her.

This was supposed to be a novel, but it was impossible not to equate the man with the narrator. It was based on a true story, after all.

She fished her laptop from her bag and opened it. The first hit was his Wikipedia page.

> **Oliver Ash** (born **Levi Abraham Asch**, May 7, 1967) is an American novelist. He is best known for his novels _Adolf_ (1993) and _Dispatches of a Half-Breed_ (2000). _Adolf_ was adapted into a <u>film</u> by <u>Gus Van Sant</u> in 1996.

The page was fairly sparse, with only basic information about his education and the books he had published. The most information came under the subheading "Controversy," which she now studied with greater interest than the last time she'd looked at this page.

In 1998, Ash was accused of sexual misconduct by a former student at <u>Columbia University</u>, Maggie McIntyre. In a civil lawsuit against Ash, McIntyre alleged that Ash had abused his position as her professor to coerce her into a nonconsensual sexual relationship. Ash denied this allegation and mantained that, while there was a sexual relationship, it was consensual. The court found insufficient evidence of coercion, and the case was dismissed.

Ash was fired from Columbia shortly following the controversy.

She envied his transparency, his fearlessness in telling this story. He seemed unconcerned with being found out—or, perhaps because he'd already gotten off scot-free legally, he felt he had the liberty to write about the events. And at the same time, she wondered: Where was this girl now? Where was her critically lauded novel?

She knew how much cognitive dissonance was at play here: despite understanding the unfairness and inequality and sexism involved in this scenario, thinking of him with this seventeen-year-old only made her desire him more. She was learning that attraction didn't discriminate—that often, in fact, it bloomed in the most perverse of circumstances. Was it possible to be both a feminist and to want a man who was bad for women?

She went back to the main search results for Oliver Ash and clicked through his Google images. There was the headshot of him standing in front of a dark backdrop, all sexual intensity, one too many shirt buttons undone, a swath of chest hair peeking out from the open collar. Then there was the "mid-convo" shot, him on a panel somewhere, dressed in jeans and a button-down and in the middle of pontificating, hands in the air as he made a particularly compelling point. And then, one of him smiling, rare among these pictures. He was caught in a conversation at some literary party, wearing a black blazer and a tie and holding a plastic cup filled with red wine, and his interlocutors—two twentysomething women—were facing him, rapt, undoubtedly charmed.

Maybe he hadn't gotten the last email? It dawned on her that she had sent it shortly before the Thanksgiving break, and that he may have been busy with travel. Was it possible he had read it and then forgotten about it, meaning to respond later?

If he was interested enough in her, wouldn't he have remembered?

Where would he have even gone for Thanksgiving, with his family so far away?

She resisted the temptation to write again. Perhaps he would never respond to her email. Perhaps there was freedom in this. After all, she had a class with him in the spring. Perhaps it would be best to keep things professional between them from now on, pretend she had never sent it, start things fresh.

She ought to put the book down, she knew. She ought to finish her papers and study for French. As if the novel were a magnet pulling her into its force field, she reopened it despite her best interests, and kept reading:

She asked me to turn off the lamp. In the darkness of the bedroom of my rented apartment in Morningside Heights, she approached and took her seat next to me on the bed. She reached out, not unceremoniously, into my lap, resting her hand on the top of my boxers. Reason had told me, all my life, that this wouldn't fix things. Today was not really any different. When I entered her she inhaled sharply, like a man gasping for his last breath.

12.

DECEMBER IN BERLIN: a cold, oppressive chill over every-thing. The kind of cold that permeated the layers you wore in a failed attempt to preserve your own heat. It wove itself beneath down feathers and knit cashmere and rested on bare skin, chilling you from the inside out. And the sun? It had been out for eight hours at the beginning of the month, seven now. By the time Simone picked Henri up from school, it was already descending for another long and dark slumber. In Paris, at least there was a liveliness to the cold: the sun stayed out a bit longer, and there was a moisture in the air and a wind over the Seine that made you feel things were still moving, still alive. The winter of Berlin was ceaseless, unwavering. So dead it might as well have not been a season at all.

On Friday morning, Simone called Henri's school and lied, saying he was sick. Then they got on a bus headed to Tegel airport.

On the bus, they talked about what they would do the first weekend Papa was back: go ice-skating at the Sportpark, walk through the holiday markets at Alexanderplatz, go out to nice restaurants and let Henri stay awake past his bedtime. They would spend a week in Paris over Hanukkah to see Danièle and Alex and Simone's mother, and they would celebrate Dani's pregnancy together. Simone felt foolishly hopeful: she knew that things with Oliver had soured recently, but figured their relationship would fall into place when she saw him in person again. He would be with them for four whole weeks. And she felt the break from work might be good for her mental space, might allow her to return to it with new vigor. Oliver was always useful to discuss work with; maybe he would offer some elucidation on her project, which had more or less come to a standstill. She imagined long nights talking at their kitchen table over wine, like the old days.

Inside the small airport, they waited at the arrivals gate.

"What time is Papa getting in?" Henri asked. His big eyes were brimming with expectation. She checked her watch.

"Any minute now," she told him.

Travelers began to stream through the arrivals gate from the flight from Munich, where Oliver had had a connection: an old German couple in khakis, a pair of American college students in oversized backpacks. A whole slew of languages as they waited: Spanish, Italian, Dutch, so many of the speakers under the age of thirty. Berlin had become such a destination, she was realizing during her time here. It was a strike against the city for her: she wanted a place to feel like the place it was, not an amalgamation of the people who had come from wherever else to try to make the place their own. This was what was so unique about Paris: although it was a metropolitan capital, it retained its Frenchness, stubbornly so. No matter how many

Americans moved there, Paris would always be itself. She didn't feel that Berlin could claim the same.

"Where is he?" Henri asked, looking up at his mother. It had been several minutes and several dozens of passengers now; the crowd was beginning to thin.

"I'm sure he's coming," Simone said, though her son's worries began to permeate her. Was there a chance he wouldn't come? The last she'd heard was a text from him in Philadelphia, telling her that he was boarding the Amtrak train that would take him to the airport in New York, for the first leg of his flight.

She felt Henri's hand unclasp from hers then, and she watched him run, her eyes following until they found Oliver, whom Henri had spotted several seconds before she had. Henri was running full speed ahead, past the gates that said "Zutritt Verboten," though there was no security guard there to stop him. In a seamless motion, as if they had choreographed it beforehand, Oliver knelt down and opened his arms to his son, who bounded into them.

She waited, and with Henri still in his arms, Oliver looked up at Simone. He stood and carried his son as he walked toward her with intention. As if he'd choreographed this, too, he moved Henri over to one hip and used his free hand to cup Simone's face and kiss her, the three of them finally all in one place.

That night was one of the wilder ones they'd had in a long time. During some interlude between sleep and sex, Simone asked Oliver to describe to her someone he was attracted to in Pennsylvania. He knew that this turned her on, but it often

made him uncomfortable, especially now, when he was surrounded by students in America. He was, she knew, trying to
be careful.

Only, she liked to feel jealous, a kink that he'd never fully
understood; she liked feeling the sting of envy that preluded
even greater desire. When he was all hers, and she knew he was
all hers, that need to have him faded, however slightly. This
was part of what she had found tedious about her relationship
with Ariel, and what Ariel was never able to understand: he
saw his endless loyalty and stability as virtues, while she saw
them as turnoffs. She could not imagine a life with someone
that was so predictable, so lacking in variability.

In fact, Simone had initially been attracted to Oliver's sharp
edges, his less-than-perfect past, his potential to be unpredictable. As she first read *Dispatches from a Half-Breed*, the scenarios of him with that girl excited her. She always knew there
was a chance that something like that could happen again—
despite his protestations to the contrary, his attempts to be a
reformed man—and the danger inherent in that hooked her. To
her chagrin, he was often self-conscious about the past, and
didn't want to talk about it, partially because it had done so
much to stall his career.

"I can't," he said now.

"Come on," Simone said.

"I'm trying not to think that way."

"No other professors, even?"

He shook his head. "Slim pickings."

This disappointed her.

"Describe a girl to me," she pleaded. "Any girl."

Finally, he assented.

Simone was still on her stomach, and Oliver kissed the back

of her neck, and began to describe a girl: Asian, thin, with dark hair, big breasts, long legs. He kissed the small of Simone's back.

"Tell me what you want to do to her, and then do it to me," Simone said, and he did.

———— // ————

In Paris they cooed over Danièle's growing bump and lit Hanukkah candles and drank champagne and ate pasta with shaved truffles that Alex had procured. The men smoked cigars on the balcony in Danièle and Alex's home, an absurd four-bedroom in the Marais, even though it was freezing out. Her mother had a new boyfriend—she always had a new boyfriend—whom she'd met at mah-jongg. She was sixty-six and he was seventy-nine.

"Think he can still keep it up?" Simone whispered into Danièle's ear at dinner. Danièle swatted her sister on the arm, laughing.

They told Henri he was going to have a baby cousin, and Henri asked, "Can babies play?" and when Oliver responded, "Not in the way you like to play," Henri became immediately uninterested. Danièle worried that the age difference, six years by the time the baby was born, would be too wide for them to ever have a relationship.

"We'll be back by then," Simone said, letting them both indulge in the excitement of her return. They'd signed a one-year lease on the place in Berlin, and would return to Paris in June, just in time for her niece or nephew to be born. Oliver would have little time to spend in Berlin by the time he got back from Buchanan in the spring, and she suspected he might feel sour about this, with that vague idea for a novel that took place in the city, which he'd told her so little about. For Simone, moving back to France was nonnegotiable. He'd gotten to run away to America for a year; now it was her turn to choose.

After Joséphine and her new boyfriend went home for the night, Simone and Oliver put Henri to bed (the apartment was big enough that Henri got his own room) and settled into their own master guest room at Danièle's, since their Paris apartment was being rented out. They got undressed and under the covers and read novels. Simone put one hand on Oliver's chest, mindlessly playing with the tuft of hair as she read. She was deeply content. She had been expecting that the transition might be bumpy, but he'd been back for two weeks now, and they'd yet to have a fight. So far, the time together had been peaceful and romantic, and she was both relieved and suspicious about that.

"This is nice," he said, as if reading her mind.

"I know," she said. "I sometimes forget how easy it is for us when we're together."

He didn't say anything. His jaw was clenched.

"What?"

"Please don't make me feel guilty."

"What do you mean?"

"Sorry," he said. "Maybe I'm already feeling guilty and projecting that onto you."

"I don't mean to make you feel guilty. You're here now, and it's nice, is all I meant."

"Sorry," he said again.

"Why do you keep saying sorry?"

"Huh?"

"Do you have something to be sorry for that I don't know about?"

"No." He seemed offended that she asked. "Nothing, other than the fact that I've been away from my family for four months and that I'm going to be away from them for another four."

"You're here now," she said again, though she suddenly felt annoyed that she had to be the one comforting him about the distance.

"It's just lonely," he said.

"It's lonely here, too." She thought about losing three babies, and wanted to scream at him: *You don't know anything about loneliness!*

"At least you're with our son."

She sat up in bed fully now, head on the pillow propped against the headboard.

"And whose choice was that?"

"No, not this again." He crossed his arms over his chest. "You are not going to spin this into it being all my idea, like you weren't the one who encouraged me to go."

He was speaking entirely in English now, and she in French, which always felt like an obvious metaphor for their discord.

"Because you have no agency, right? You can't make a choice and take responsibility for it. God forbid."

"What do you want me to do? You want me to not go back in the spring?"

"Don't put words in my mouth."

"You sure would miss the money I plunk into our joint bank account every two weeks."

"I don't need that money. Save it for your bar tabs in America. My fellowship pays fine on its own."

He didn't say anything in response to that. He opened his book again and pretended to read.

Had he always been so inattentive to her feelings? She could have sworn that he hadn't. She could have sworn that in the beginning, he listened. Maybe the thrill of a new person after four years of Ariel, plus the pregnancy and all the excitement wrapped up in new parenthood, had distracted her from actually paying close attention to who Oliver was.

She knew how it looked that she was with him. She knew it made her seem naïve, even to her own sister, to be with someone who had a less-than-perfect track record when it came to women. Because on paper there was so much about him that she might have hated, had he not been Oliver. The issue was that there was a disconnect between Oliver-on-paper and Oliver-to-Simone. His Oliverness—at least at the beginning— could not be distilled into a reputation or a news item, or really any words at all. Some might have suspected it was sexual chemistry that kept a smart, accomplished woman like Simone with him, but that wasn't the thing, not entirely. It was more like this: the person you wanted, the person you needed, wasn't necessarily the same as the person who was correct. Ariel had been correct. But she didn't *need* Ariel.

Oliver was the father of her child. She could not intellectualize her way out of that, as much as she tried to. It was innate or primal, which sounded like bullshit, but it didn't feel like bullshit. Single motherhood, she was understanding this semester, was nearly impossible. And when she saw the way that Henri looked at Oliver as he got off the plane at Tegel, it made her feel that pull toward her husband all the more powerfully, as if her son were still inside her, his needs still determining hers.

Perhaps, she was beginning to realize as she lay on her side of this gigantic bed, her husband was not hearing her when she said that she was lonely, too. Henri's needs alone could not sustain a marriage. Not if *her* needs stopped being met altogether.

"Good night," she said, and turned her back to him. The bed was so big that when he tossed and turned tonight, as he was wont to do, she wouldn't feel him move, wouldn't wake, not once.

In the morning, she found herself alone. She walked into the kitchen to find Danièle arranging breakfast for Henri, croissants and baguette and butter and jam. He was sitting patiently, expectantly, at the table.

Simone wrapped her arms around her son and kissed him, and then did the same to her sister.

"Where's Oliver?" Simone asked.

"He left for a walk about thirty minutes ago."

"A walk? It's freezing outside."

Simone made herself a coffee and walked over to a window in the living room. She sat sideways on the arm of a reading chair and peered down at the street below. The sun cut over the tops of the old buildings of the Marais, the muted limestone of the Beaux-Arts homes and the burnt red brick of a sixteenth-century mansion across the way, now serving as a museum or a government building. The freshly washed streets gleamed.

This was her home, this neighborhood; it was where she had grown up, back when it was not so heavily gentrified, still only the Jewish quarter of the city, where Ashkenazim from the pogroms had come for refuge, as Simone's paternal ancestors from Austria had in the late 1800s. In the case of Danièle and Alex, though, and even Oliver, whose apartment had also eventually become her own, living here as Jews had become incidental, not intentional. Danièle and Alex blended in among the rest of the bourgeois of the Marais now, indistinguishable from the other bankers and the independently wealthy gallerists and artists and expats who had settled in the area. Oliver had moved here because of its Jewish history, but also because he had money: by the time he arrived, in the late nineties, prices were already on the rise.

Now the neighborhood was filled to the brim with expensive galleries and boutiques, so sanitized and commercial; it was a far cry from the Marais she had known in the seventies, an insular community where they knew everyone, where Simone went to school with the children of her family's butcher and doctor and pharmacist, and went to synagogue with all of them, too. Her home was becoming a sanctuary for the rich, and she worried that she and her sister and their husbands were part of the problem.

Still, as she looked out onto her city, the neighborhood retained its beauty and its charm—at least now, at nine A.M. on a Sunday in winter, when everything was closed. The storefronts were grated and the balconies across the way were closed, the curtains drawn. Her mother was one of the last vestiges of the old Marais, still living in the place off Rue des Rosiers where Danièle and Simone had shared a bedroom until Simone went away to university. It had mattered to her father to live near the Pletzl, though now her mother stayed in the apartment only because it was rent controlled. Simone's father had been the last of their family to follow religious or ancestral traditions in a serious way; now they were about as secular as could be, celebrating Hanukkah mostly because it was an excuse to give Henri presents. Should Simone be trying harder, for Henri? Should she be fasting on Yom Kippur? Should they be lighting candles every Friday night? What kind of Jewish identity would he end up having if he never experienced any kind of ritual?

She also hadn't been doing these things because Oliver didn't believe in God. He was Jewish by identity, he always said, but not by religion. She wasn't sure if she understood how you could extricate the two. Oliver didn't want to indoctrinate his child with ritual, largely because his father had drilled the rules of Judaism into him out of a sense of duty and anxiety. Out of an intense fear of their people not surviving. It was painful for Oliver to go to services now, or to observe ritual; it made him think of his father, a German refugee who forever treated his Judaism like a scourge.

And Simone had assented. She had not wanted to cause her husband undue pain.

Maybe what Oliver wanted shouldn't play such a giant role in the raising of their child. After all, he didn't seem concerned about her pain. And he was not here this year. He was not even here this morning.

Not a person was out on the narrow gray streets below, except for Oliver, somewhere down there, winding his way through the city alone.

"This is delicious, Aunt Dani," Simone heard Henri say. She turned to see him sipping from a giant bowl of cocoa. He sounded so adult, her boy. When did that happen? How much longer until he wasn't a boy at all?

Danièle, on the other side of the table, beamed at him, and Simone got up from the reading chair and joined them.

PART TWO

13.

THEY CAME BACK for the poorly named spring semester: the trees on campus bare, the frozen dew on the quad crunchy underfoot. Real spring would not arrive until the last weeks of April, when finals loomed and papers were due and sitting on the quad for hours smoking hookahs and drinking clandestine beers was tempting but misguided.

For Liv and Lula and Marley, it was their last semester; their grades and class rankings were more or less set. Marley's grades didn't matter at all; her med school applications were already in, and soon the acceptances would come rolling in, too. Lula and Liv were already networking, figuring out their postgrad jobs.

Fiona, of course, would be back in the fall. She had taken her first semester of sophomore year off.

That semester, she'd stayed in the house in Larchmont for what felt like decades. Neighbors and friends routinely delivered food. Liam kept busy around the house. He was always vacuuming, always mopping, even though there was hardly any foot traffic to clean up after, as Fiona and her mother rarely left their respective bedrooms. All her friends had gone back to school, so no one visited her. She kept her door ajar for Suzy, their yellow Lab.

Suzy was maybe the saddest part of it all. The door to Helen's bedroom remained closed—because keeping it open was a constant reminder she wasn't there, and if it was closed one could make the mistake, for an instant, of believing that she might be doing homework or was on the phone with a friend. For the first several weeks, Suzy slept in front of the closed door. She never pawed at it or cried, just lay there with her head resting forlornly atop her paws. When Liam came up the stairs to take her for a walk, she lifted her head in anticipation—but not of going outside. The brief expectation, before recognizing that the footfalls belonged to Liam, that Helen might be the one coming up the steps. To not be able to explain it to Suzy, that Helen wasn't going to come up the steps again, made Fiona's heart break more than anything else had.

And what was Fiona doing all this time, in her bedroom? Not much. She talked on the phone a lot, to Liv, and to Rachel, the friend who had known Helen best, though she never talked about Helen in these phone calls. She asked the girls questions about their semesters back at school, and the girls reluctantly answered after Fiona insisted that she wanted the distraction. She watched episodes of *The Office* and felt guilty every time she laughed. She heard muffled arguments between her parents at night. Often, she entertained the thought that she should be back at school—she could handle it. But she was struck by inertia. She could barely get up to pee. She ate only after everyone was asleep, walking down the dark, carpeted steps and poking into a casserole dish, lit only by the refrigerator, not bothering to put the food on a plate or heat it up or sit down.

Sometimes she polished off entire Pyrex dishes of cold maca-
roni and cheese, the orange top layer hardened and plastic-
flavored. Nothing tasted good, but that wasn't the point. After
those binges she wouldn't eat for several days, as atonement.
She liked the feeling of hunger as it grew: the gnawing empti-
ness of her insides made her feel clean, new.

She would go days without seeing anyone. Would hear the
door open only when her father left for work in the morning,
close when he came in at night. Some nights he didn't come
back at all. She would hear Liam take the dog out, or hear Liam's car going out of the driveway, then hear him coming
through the front door an hour later carrying plastic bags of
groceries they didn't need.

Her mother did not want to be bothered. Fiona often
knocked on the door, and was told, every time, "Not right
now." Every time, she hoped the response would be different.
She longed, just once, for a "Come in." She longed, just once,
to climb into bed with her mom, the way she had when she was
a kid, only this time she would try to be the person who did the
comforting. She wanted to tell her mother that part of the reason she'd stayed was not because she was unable to concentrate on work—true though that may have been—but because
she wanted to be home in case her mother needed her. Her
mother did not allow herself to need anyone, though. Not even
her only daughter who remained.

Now she wondered what it had even been for, that semester
off. Liam had been ahead on credits at Yale—it was his senior
year; he took one extra class in the spring, and graduated on
time. Fiona was not as smart or efficient as Liam. Everyone
had always known this. So the fact that she had to stay at Buchanan an extra semester, after all of her friends had graduated, was a harsh reminder of that doleful autumn. She had

been left behind then; she'd be left behind again. While her roommates were doing independent studies and taking 100-level classes in art or sociology, because their majors were mostly fulfilled already, Fiona again had a full courseload of English and French classes. They already had one foot out the door. Fiona had no direction but to keep studying. She had no idea, not a single inkling, of what she wanted to do when she was finished.

She had done better last semester than in the previous year. Professor Roiphe loved the Lewinsky paper, deeming it a "fascinating discussion of the sentimental narrative surrounding the Lewinsky scandal, drawing a clear connection to the seminar texts" and giving her an A in the class. She got Bs in everything else, a B-minus in French. The closer her leaving this place loomed, the more she hoped she might find answers in her books, as if expanding her French vocabulary or researching in depth the plight of Monica Lewinsky would bring her some vocational clarity.

"Well, what do you like to do?" Liv asked her.

They were doing work together in Liv's room in February, sitting cross-legged on her bed.

"Watch reruns of *Felicity*," Fiona replied. "Eat breakfast sandwiches."

"Seems professionally viable," Liv said.

"What do *you* like to do?" Fiona asked. "Do people actually get jobs doing what they like doing anymore?"

Liv looked up at her friend. "I mean, yeah."

"In the recession?"

"I'm not worried." The truth was, Liv was such a good student, and so hardworking and well connected and attractive, that she had no reason to be worried. Publishing was dying out, but she'd find a job; they'd make room for her, somewhere. This was how Liv's whole life went—people bending to accommodate her—and why should she expect anything different now?

"My dad didn't become a lawyer because he's passionate about law," Fiona said. "He did it to make a living."

"I think it's different for men," Liv said. "My mom loves her job."

"My mom never had a job."

"She's not working now?"

"I think she's volunteering at the library. I don't know. She has another man taking care of her."

Liv was quiet a minute. "Do you think it's wrong to have men take care of us?"

"No. Did it sound like I did?"

"No. I do wonder about it sometimes for myself."

"Yeah."

"In theory, I want to be my own breadwinner and all that. But when I think about a future, and a family . . ."

"You want to be taken care of."

"Is that terrible?"

"I don't think so," Fiona said. "I think it's feminist to be able to make that decision, right? As long as it's *your* decision."

"Yeah, I guess."

"My issue is I don't ever think I'll like anyone enough to spend my whole life with them. Or they won't like me enough to be willing to take care of me."

"That's not true! You'll find someone."

"That's not what I mean," Fiona said. "I mean I genuinely don't even know if settling down with someone, with the same person always, is what I want. Sometimes it feels like searching is safer. I kind of want to be searching forever."

"That's so lonely," Liv said.

Fiona looked back at the pages in her lap. They were reading a short story by someone else in their workshop, a girl named Sophie whom they'd both shared some classes with. It was about an American girl studying abroad in Paris, like Sophie and Liv both had. Nothing really happened in the story, just trite observations of the city, some French phrases thrown in to show off Sophie's limited knowledge of the language.

On their first day of the workshop with Oliver Ash, he had treated both girls as if he'd never known them at all. Liv's crush on him had seemed to dissipate, but Fiona's wasn't entirely gone. He never responded to Fiona's last email, in which she had asked to meet with him, and this had devastated and embarrassed her. She'd been worried about seeing him on the first day of class and how he might treat her. There was a kindness in his acting like the email had never been sent in the first place.

"Professor Ash is going to tear this to shreds," Fiona said. "'The lights of the Eiffel Tower glittered in the distance.' Yikes."

"I'm trying to be kind in my feedback," Liv said. "I don't want to be ripped apart when it's my turn."

"Yeah, but you can actually write," Fiona said.

Liv shrugged. "Are you done with yours yet?"

Fiona shook her head.

Liv lifted her eyebrows as if to say, *You know it's due tomorrow, right?* Mercifully, she didn't actually say that, because of course Fiona knew it was due tomorrow. What she didn't tell Liv was that she hadn't even started it; the longer she waited, the harder it was to sit down and begin. Oliver would be reading this. And Dave, too, who was also unfortunately in the workshop.

There was so much going on in her head and not enough

ways to get it all out of her. What she didn't like was having to organize those thoughts into stories, narratives that other people would read and form their own opinions of. She knew this was the point: writing was meant to be read. But she wished that it wasn't. She wished she could get an A from the originality of the garbled thoughts in her notebook, an A from the exquisite expression of the private feelings she shared only with the pages of the journal she kept beside her nightstand. She kept a scrim over the work she handed in in the writing classes she took at Buchanan, withheld what she really felt and wanted and believed, got Bs. Wrote fiction that took place in the past or in a vague, dystopian future. Because what could she write about truthfully? She did not want to be known for just one thing; she would rather be disliked or slut-shamed than pitied. And yet, she knew that, at some point, she was going to have to write about Helen. Everything else felt untrue in comparison.

"I want to go to Paris," Fiona then said, to change the subject. "Sophie's observations notwithstanding."

"We should go," Liv said, as casual as if suggesting they go pick up sandwiches from the deli. "Maybe this summer."

"I feel like traveling with friends can be tricky."

"What do you mean?" Liv seemed offended. "We live together fine."

"What about Brandon and New York?" Fiona asked. Brandon had recently learned that he'd been rejected by the law schools at Harvard and Yale, but accepted into Columbia, his third choice.

"I can't go to Paris with my best friend for a week because Brandon will be in New York without me?"

It had been a while since Fiona had heard Liv refer to her as her "best friend." It felt nice.

"You know my aunt Lacy has an apartment in the fourth, right? She's basically never there."

Fiona did remember hearing about this aunt once, a favorite of Liv's: one of her dad's sisters who'd married older and rich, had no kids, and now was widowed and split her time between Paris and London.

"Don't you think it would be a sweet graduation gift to each other?" Liv said. "We could buy each other's plane tickets."

"Yeah. That would be cute."

"You can finally use your French," Liv said, getting excited. "I know the city. I know where to go and where to eat. We'll smoke cigarettes and drink rosé outside at cafés and wear black and read Flaubert and pretend we're Parisian. We'll be walking clichés. It's perfect."

"What about Marley and Lula?"

"Lula's been a thousand times. Marley is all about speaking Spanish. The two of them would have no interest whatsoever." Liv paused for a moment. "You only went the one time, right?" she said. "When you were fourteen?"

Fiona knew what she was going to say, and she didn't want to hear it—the promise her mother had made to Helen. Each girl got a trip to Paris with Mom when she was fourteen.

"Don't bring her into this," Fiona said.

Liv seemed eager and excited enough about the idea of Paris together to be in the mood to challenge this. Back when Helen had just died, Liv was a comfort; she would talk about whatever Fiona wanted to talk about, do whatever Fiona wanted to do. She wanted to push now. More and more she wanted to push Fiona into things she was not ready for, under the pretense that these things were for Fiona's own good.

"Don't you think—"

"What? That Helen would want me to go?"

"Maybe?"

"Helen can't want anything."

Liv looked hurt. But this wasn't Liv's right. It wasn't Liv's family.

"Well," Liv said then, "what do *you* want?"

Fiona snickered. "Isn't that where this conversation started?"

Liv smiled. "Exactly." Then she went back to reading Sophie's bad short story.

Paris with Liv was, in fact, plausible. Fiona had all that money from her dad sitting in her bank account. So far, her only other option for this summer seemed to be sitting around and feeling sorry for herself.

Later, when Liv said she was going to bed, Fiona grabbed herself a leftover can of PBR from when they'd had a few people over the previous weekend. This was what writers did, right? Drink while they worked into the wee hours of the morning? It wasn't fine whiskey, but it would do.

Sitting down at her desk, cracking the beer and opening her laptop, she thought about her options. She looked at the dreadfully blank Word document. She never wrote about herself. In poetry, the previous semester, she had written broadly about love she'd never experienced, about observing others from afar, once recording a conversation she overheard in the coffee shop on campus and transcribing it into a poem.

On the first day of their class, Professor Ash had shared a quote from Ernest Hemingway: "All you have to do is write one true sentence. Write the truest sentence that you know."

"Not literally, of course," he explained. "This is a fiction course. But all of your characters, their sentiments, their feelings, their dialogue—these things should feel plucked from life.

Strive, always, for verisimilitude." Then he wrote this on the whiteboard behind him.

STRIVE FOR VERISIMILITUDE.

She could not give him the dystopian story she had half-baked in her head, or the prototypical teenage heartbreak scenario that she'd been kicking around. Those weren't real, human stories. They weren't memorable.

She thought of her unanswered email to him, dangling there like an unfinished sentence. If she wanted to impress him, she knew, she would have to write about the truest thing she'd experienced. It wasn't her first choice, but she couldn't stand the idea of him thinking any less of her than he did now.

She began to write.

Fiona Larkin
Senior Fiction Workshop/Professor Ash
2/26/09

THE ORDINARY INSTANT

It was eighty-two degrees and sunny on the day that Lucy died.

It is human nature to do this: look back on the day a tragedy occurs and focus on the minute details of it, as if it were impossible that something so massive could happen under circumstances so average. "The ordinary instant," Joan Didion calls it. "Confronted with sudden disaster," she writes in *The Year of Magical Thinking,* "we all focus on how unremarkable the circumstances were in which the unthinkable occurred."

Only, in the case of Lucy, the circumstances were quite remarkable, because the sudden change in weather had everything to do with her unthinkable death. It is remarkable that we all swam at the lake that day. It is remarkable that Lucy's age group—the thirteen-year-old girls—happened to have their swim period last in the day, and that they submerged themselves into the water at the very moment the first cloud made its way across the sky. And it is most remarkable that Lucy's rebellious streak drove her to stay in the lake a whole thirty seconds after the rest of the girls, after the lifeguard's warning whistle at the first sound of thunder—for the lightning, when it struck, could only be attracted to her, where she was gleefully wading toward the aluminum dock while the first raindrops fell on her already wet hair, and her alone.

Her family was told that she died immediately, which was likely untrue, but was a way to put them at ease. "She felt no pain," the doctor at Litchfield General Hospital said in the fluorescent-lit lobby, which was a small consolation for the sudden death of a thirteen-year-old, but a consolation nonetheless.

For her mother, who had spent her whole life praising Lucy, treating her as the favorite of the family, life as she knew it had suddenly, irrevocably ended—not only Lucy's life, but her own. Her entire sense of self-worth was wrapped around being a mother—Lucy's mother, at that. She spent months trying to understand it—reading about lightning striking and the odds of it happening. The chance of being struck in one's lifetime was one in thirteen thousand. And only 10 percent of *those* people actually died. But of course, well, the chances were 100 percent for Lucy.

I still remember the memorial service like it was yesterday: my brother, Sean, going up there to say something in his stoic way, never crying, and never looking up from his paper, either. My aunt who didn't even know Lucy all that well talking about what an angelic girl she was, like she'd never done a bad thing in her entire short life.

And me? What did I have to say for myself? No matter what, it felt like my words were not enough. It made me think about the beginning of *Love Story,* that novel I loved so much when I was sixteen, I read it four times over the course of one year: "What can you say about a twenty-five-year-old girl who died? That she was beautiful. And brilliant. That she loved Mozart and Bach. And the Beatles. And me." Only, Lucy was so much younger than that. Who even knew if what she loved would stick? She loved horses and *High School Musical* when she was thirteen, when she died. She loved summer camp and her friends. She didn't even like boys yet. I'm not sure if she loved me.

But, I went up there too, and talked about Lucy as if she was my best friend, as if we were thick as thieves. I still feel like it was the greatest betrayal of my lif

14.

"Fiona!"

The sound of her own name punched her into wake-fulness. Her neck was sore.

"Huh?" she said, looking around the room and rubbing the back of her neck. She was in her desk chair. Her head had fallen on her folded arms.

"We have to leave for class in five minutes." Liv was dressed, made-up, even her boots were already on. "Did you make copies?"

"What?" Fiona looked at her laptop, the screen now black, and clicked the trackpad. The Word document appeared. The sentence she'd been writing was unfinished. She'd labored over those first two pages, fell asleep likely sometime between two and three in the morning as she thought about what actually needed to happen in this story. "Shit."

Fiona jumped into action, changing from her pajama bottoms to jeans, not bothering to change out of her sweatshirt, no bra underneath. She pulled Ugg boots onto her feet, which she normally did only for Sundays at the library, and threw her hair into a sloppy bun. She printed out one copy of the story and grabbed her tote bag from the back of her chair and her puffy coat from the hook on the door.

"I'll meet you there!" she called to Liv, running down the stairs and out of the house, toward the Writing Cottage.

It had snowed a bit the night before, she was dismayed to learn, and her traction-less boots slipped and slid as she ran down North Abbott Street. She turned right at Phillips Avenue, where more students appeared, and she missed seeing a patch of black ice on the sidewalk, tripping and falling over herself, her arms going first, the rest of her body following. Her puffy jacket cushioned the fall, but her hands, not in gloves, were scraped and dirty and cold.

"Shit!" she heard a guy say from behind her. Across Phillips Avenue, a trio of underclass girls laughed. "You okay?" the man's voice asked, at which point she knew immediately who had witnessed her fall. He reached his hand out to her, and she took it.

"Thanks," she said, and she felt his forearm tighten as she held onto it tightly to pull herself up.

"What's the hurry?" Professor Ash asked. "I never start class on time."

"I have to make copies."

Professor Ash shrugged. "Do it at the break." He frowned at her. "Are you sure you're all right?"

"I'm fine," she said, dusting herself off. "Lucky I'm dressed like the abominable snowman."

"You do look warm," he said, appraising her outfit. They walked the remaining block together making small talk that she tried desperately hard to concentrate on, for fear that she might burst into tears at any moment.

. . . .

The Writing Cottage was a new building on campus that some wealthy parent of an aspiring writing undergrad had funded. It was a two-story house on Phillips Avenue, with a kitchen, a dining room, offices upstairs and, downstairs, a cozy living room with a fireplace—never lit—where writing workshops took place. Students sat on couches and in plush lounge chairs while Professor Ash sat in an armchair at the front of the room, his papers and books awkwardly resting on his lap. The room was surrounded by floor-to-ceiling windows, and during their class period, from ten until one on Thursdays, light streamed in, casting the room in a wintry, white-yellow glow.

They started the class by discussing the short story "Popular Mechanics" by Raymond Carver, which Professor Ash had assigned for homework. Fiona had read it, but, naturally, had forgotten her copy of *What We Talk About When We Talk About Love* in her tizzy that morning. The story was a single scene, a domestic scuffle between a couple. It began with the couple arguing, the man packing his things in his suitcase: he's leaving the woman, or at least threatening to. Then Carver reveals that there's also a baby in the house, and the man and the woman start to fight over who gets to keep it, which turns into a literal tug-of-war over the child. It ends with these three ominous sentences: "But he would not let go. He felt the baby slipping out of his hands and he pulled back very hard. In this manner, the issue was decided."

Professor Ash began. "Does anyone want to start with their initial impressions of the story?"

Liv's hand shot up. She was always the first to volunteer an opinion. Professor Ash seemed to wait a few more moments to see if anyone else would raise a hand. No one did.

"Liv," he said, his voice even.

"Well, I couldn't help but notice that Carver clearly wanted us to come to our own conclusions on that last line. 'The issue was decided'—the use of passive voice is intentional there. It allows us to feel that the fate of the baby is no longer in the hands of this couple; it's now something that's happening to them, beyond their control, whereas the rest of the story is very much character-driven actions. 'He fastened the suitcase,' 'They knocked down a flowerpot,' 'She caught the baby around the wrist,' and so on."

"Yes. Good," Professor Ash said. "The passive voice at the end is not accidental. Though the story isn't entirely in active voice until then. Where else do we see passive voice?" Fiona loved watching him teach: the seriousness in his affect, the furrow to his brow. She held on to their night at the bar, seeing him tipsy, unhinged. She had seen a side of him none of her classmates had.

"The first paragraph," one of the boys offered. The boys never raised their hands. "'Cars slushed by on the street outside, where it was *getting dark*. But *it was getting dark* on the inside too.' Instead of, just 'it got dark' or 'it was dark.' The 'getting' implies something happening in real time *to* the house." Fiona didn't think this was quite right—that wasn't technically passive voice, she thought, but she didn't want to take the chance of being wrong. She didn't have her book with her to confirm it, and Liv was poring too intently over the two pages, underlining and notating, for Fiona to look on with her.

"Also," another one of the girls chimed in. This was Naomi, blond, whippet thin, who only wore expensive black clothes. "The man actually is always active. For him it's 'He gripped,' 'He worked.' While things happen *to* the woman: 'She *felt* her fingers being forced open. She *felt* the baby going from her.' Which actually makes me believe that the man wins the argument and gets the baby. He's certainly winning throughout."

"Yeah, but," Dave said, "why the passivity of the last sentence, then? I don't think either of them gets the baby. If so, it would have ended on 'He felt the baby slipping out of his hands and he pulled back very hard.' That last sentence is used to create more ambiguity, to pull back in scope and even the playing field and to leave us wondering."

"You're all missing the point," said Julia, who Fiona thought was the best writer in the class, flipping her braids over one shoulder. "The point is they both become so focused on winning this particular argument that they use their child as a totem and in the end they both lose. Nothing was going to stop the fight unless something happened to the baby outside of their control. You have two stubborn people who are not going to give up on the matter. Something major had to happen to the kid or else the story would never end. It's not about winning—it's about the inciting incident in and of itself."

Everyone was quiet there for a few seconds, realizing Julia was right. She got to the quick of it under two minutes.

"Let's return to that first paragraph," Professor Ash said, and he read two lines aloud: "'Cars slushed by on the street outside, where it was getting dark. But it was getting dark on the inside too.'" Fiona hated that sort of sparse writing that everyone else seemed to revere. She assumed that Carver thought "it was getting dark on the inside too" was supposed to sound profound, but if she'd read that in a workshop submission, she'd have written next to it, *Cliché*.

After the break—and after Fiona had made copies, flushing with shame as the copier spat out the unfinished story—Professor Ash opened up the workshop on Sophie's Paris story.

"What's working here?" he asked the class, starting, as he always did, with the positives.

"I like the narrative frame of the piece," Liv offered. "The way that Sophie begins in the present, then loops back to the past, then ends back in that present moment."

"Okay. And what did that do for your reading experience?"

"It piqued my curiosity. It made me want to understand why the present moment was so significant."

"But it wasn't, actually, was it?" Fiona asked. "I mean. We have this moment with Natasha waiting for Michel to come over, but then the flashback actually tells us incredibly little about their relationship."

"Isn't there mystery inherent in that, though?" Liv said.

"Not necessarily," Fiona said. "The loop is just about Natasha moving to Paris and meeting Michel once, and we get so little emotional development and understanding of why they care about each other. Nothing about their connection feels authentic or interesting."

"Let's spend a little more time talking about what else is working first," Professor Ash said, clearly attempting to redirect. Fiona shrank back; had she been too cruel? She looked at Sophie, in her boot-cut jeans and sorority sweatshirt. Her face was contorted into ugliness, her brow furrowed in anguish. Fiona supposed she'd been trying to impress Oliver Ash. Again.

At the end of class, she handed out her copies, then grabbed Liv by the arm and led her out of the building before Fiona could register any of their faces skimming over the first page.

——#——

"What's working here?" Professor Ash asked about Fiona's piece the following week. Nearly every hand in the room shot up.

"I think the emotional honesty of it is so raw," said Sophie, whom Fiona had practically eviscerated the week before. "I really felt so sad about Lucy dying. I felt like I knew her."

"Yeah," said Dave. "I agree. It was incredibly sad."

The entire class nodded in assent.

"I also really liked the use of the camp setting," said Julia. "It's this place that clearly holds so much significance and innocence for both the narrator and Lucy, and the fact that the ultimate innocence is lost there adds much more of a sense of tragedy to the piece."

Had these people read the right story?

"Yes, that's true," Professor Ash agreed. "The camp setting resonates. It's clearly important and familiar to the narrator, and through her eyes, we see it clearly. Were there any places that you felt the setting could be utilized more?"

The class deferred this question and instead talked at length about the narrator's relationship to Lucy—how sad it was, how memorable, how *true*. Soon Fiona's classmates were extolling the virtues of the nameless narrator, who we don't know is the sister until the second page—to "allow for more room for personal interpretation at the beginning," Sophie argued— and then, again, back to the emotional honesty of the piece.

"What about the action of the piece?" Professor Ash pushed. "Were there things you would have liked to see happen in the story, other than the backstory of this girl's death?"

It was obvious no one wanted to say that it wasn't good, that it lacked immediacy or urgency. That it was actually unfinished, half-baked crap. For the first time in this class, no one chose to be remotely critical. As Sophie raved on and on about the use of the past tense, Fiona thought about how critical she'd been about *her* story the previous week. Why couldn't Sophie serve the same thing back?

Of course: they were trying to tiptoe around the thing they all knew *actually* happened. Fiona didn't think that even half the people in this workshop knew what had happened to her sister, but Sophie, the gossip-monger, did, and Fiona imagined the truth about Helen spreading among the workshop members like wildfire. And now they were conflating this story with Fiona's life.

Then again, so had Fiona. The way the girl in her story died was not how Helen had died, but every other part of it was true: Her age. The camp setting. The relationship between the sisters. The students seemed to worry that in critiquing the story, they would also be critiquing Fiona's tragedy. While Fiona knew she should have felt gratitude toward them for attempting to spare her feelings, instead she felt anger. She wanted to scream. Why couldn't anyone talk about this like the thing it was: brutal and terrible and *true*? Why did everyone have to tiptoe around Helen like she'd never happened at all? Or like Fiona and Helen's relationship had been perfect and beautiful and that loss was uniformly sad and the response should be uniformly sympathetic, no nuance to it? They only knew that Helen had died; they didn't know that the girls were never friends, constantly bickering, constantly in competition with each other over their mother's love, a competition that Helen was always winning.

After class, Fiona's classmates offered her sad smiles as they returned their copies of the story to her. Fiona approached Professor Ash.

"Can I talk to you for a second?" he asked, waiting for everyone to stream out. Liv stopped at the doorway.

"I'll meet you at home," Fiona said to Liv, who offered a tentative wave on her way out.

"Before I give this to you," he said, "I want to apologize, preemptively, if they're a bit harsh."

"I'm sorry?"

"I, uh." He was rolling the story into a tube. She had never seen him look nervous before. "I had not realized the story was so personal to you. Normally . . . Oh, how do I say this without sounding like a complete prick? You didn't finish the story. You handed in work that was clearly incomplete. And, well, in my experience, the death of a young person, and often of a sibling, is a sort of predictable conceit in my students' fiction. Now I can tell from the way the class reacted to your story . . . Well, it seems that perhaps you have some firsthand experience in this. I don't mean to pry. I just mean to apologize if anything in here is particularly hurtful."

"Bad fiction is bad fiction, right?" she said.

He didn't say anything to this.

"The story was bad. I want objective feedback. I didn't get it from anyone else."

"All right," he said, unrolling her story and then handing it to her. "If you want to talk about it further, I'm here."

"I'm sure that won't be necessary," she said, slipping the copy into her bag. "I'll see you next week."

Outside, once far enough down Phillips Avenue that Professor Ash wouldn't see her, Fiona pulled his copy out and turned quickly through the pages.

"Reductive," he had scribbled next to one sentence. "Why

should we care?" he wrote at the bottom of the piece, a sentiment that was then echoed in more depth in his typed note to
Fiona, stapled to the last page:

Fiona,
I expected more from you. You didn't finish this piece; in
fact, you did not even bother to finish the last sentence.
You didn't meet the page criteria of 6–10 pages. It is clearly
not proofread. It switches from the third-person to the
first-person perspective halfway through. I have to give you
a D simply because you did not meet the basic require-
ments. I will not fail you this time, but you should know
that next time I won't be so generous for such substandard
work.

I'm not going to take the time to critique what is here,
since you didn't put in any time for this piece, either.

—Professor Ash

15.

IT WAS A Friday morning in March, and Liv and Brandon were lying in her bed undressed, their legs tangled around each other's. Liv held one hand on Brandon's chest while his bare foot ran up and down the soft length of her calf. They were sleepy, having just woken up, but their wordless contentment was interrupted by the electronic melody bleating from Liv's cellphone. Her mother was calling.

"It's sort of last-minute," Kimiko said on the other end, "but I thought it might be a nice idea for all of us to go somewhere warm after this long winter. Does Brandon have spring break plans?"

The Bahamas for four nights, she suggested, all four of them. A long weekend to inject some vitamin D into their systems. Liv fast-forwarded to an image of Brandon and herself in bathing suits, coconuts in hand, novels in laps, sunglasses on. They'd never gone to the beach together. But the fantasy was soon marred by scenarios of her dad's potential behavior, looming like a giant question mark. He was so unpredictable, was the thing. He wasn't always as bad as he had been at Thanksgiving; sometimes he was downright pleasant. She imagined the possibility of a universe in which her dad and Brandon went off to play golf together one day, the men returning sunburned and content, full of new in-jokes she would happily never be privy to.

"Let me talk to Brandon about it," Liv said to her mother.

"Will you come, either way?"

Liv said maybe, and hung up the phone.

"Talk to me about what?" Brandon twirled a piece of her hair between his fingers.

"You can say no," she stipulated with the invitation.

"Oh," he said. "Wow."

"It's okay," she said, already defensive, already ready to rescind the offer. "I know it's probably early to go on a trip with my family." Even though she'd wanted him desperately to say yes, to say that nothing in the world would bring him greater pleasure. His acceptance would signal that maybe things hadn't been as bad over Thanksgiving as she'd imagined they were. After all, Brandon had come to their house once more, during Christmas break, without incident. (Granted, her father had stayed in his study the whole time.) And it had been a whole three months since then, and Brandon had never said a word about it. Maybe it wasn't as big a deal as she was making it out to be.

"That's really lovely of them to offer."

"They really like you." Brandon should have understood by now that "they" or "my parents" tended to refer to Kimiko alone, that Robert's nonmonetary contributions were not represented in the rhetoric about the Langley family.

Brandon said, "Can I think about it?"

She felt a constriction in her throat, a choking sensation.

"Of course," she managed, as level-voiced as she could. "I'm going to go either way," she added, as if his decision was completely inconsequential to her.

Later, when he left her house and went to the library to study, she broke down into a gloppy mess of tears and snot and hiccups.

She was going to lose him over this. She just knew it.

——*#*——

On Saturday, they took a day trip to ski in the Poconos. It had been Brandon's idea, a nice way to make use of the unreasonable amount of snow they were getting this late in the season. He was always coming up with sweet ideas like this: picnics when it was warmer, concerts, winter activities earlier in the semester, like ice-skating and tubing. She'd never had a serious boyfriend before, but judging by the college boys she knew—especially the ones in Brandon's fraternity—she couldn't imagine many of them were like this, so romantic and attentive to their girlfriends' needs. On Valentine's Day a few weeks earlier, he'd woken her up with a dozen red roses. The card inside said:

My dear Olivia,
I love waking up with you each morning, and going to
sleep with you each night.
*   You are my everything.*
          I love you,
               Brandon

Only a few months earlier, the nakedness of those sentiments would have made her squirm inside. But her feelings toward him had dramatically shifted after Thanksgiving. She had always expected that if a boyfriend witnessed her home life, he would run in the other direction. Brandon had seen the worst of it, and he hadn't left. Now that he was involved, she could never let him go.

During winter break, she had agreed to the idea of living together, if he ended up getting into law school in a place where she might also find work. Then, a few weeks ago, he'd found out he'd been rejected from Harvard and Yale, but accepted to Columbia. It seemed pretty likely that they were moving to New York.

She'd never skied before, while Brandon was an expert, having spent winters with his cousins in Vermont. But Liv considered herself an athletic person, and thought she would catch on quickly, which Brandon also agreed would likely be the case. On the drive up, they listened to Bruce Springsteen songs that made her feel wistful for things she'd never experienced, and took quiet and winding country highways, the sky blue and bright with white-topped mountains in the distance. Brandon was wearing his Ray-Ban Wayfarers and a beanie. She thought he looked so cute.

"This is a perfect day for a novice," he said, and smiled at her. "I know your feet get cold, but the sun will help."

She couldn't believe there had been a time when she was unsure about him, afraid to settle down with him. She couldn't believe she had flirted with the idea of cheating on him with Oliver Ash. Now it seemed crystal clear that this was the person she wanted to be with. It was so nice, so easy. He was gentle with her, and kind, and giving. If life could be this easy forever, why not let it?

They got to the mountain and picked up her rentals. The ski lift to the bunny slope took no more than two minutes, but she was still excited by it: the swoosh of the lift as it carried them into the air, the way her skis dangled below her, a pleasant heaviness in her legs. It felt like a ride, the way the lift glided through the air, over the tops of snow-dusted evergreens.

Brandon held out his cellphone and snapped a picture of the two of them. The photo was from close up, and silly, the underside of his jacketed arm at the edge of the photo, but they looked happy.

When the chairlift deposited them at the top of the bunny slope, she panicked, bracing her knees, having seemingly forgotten how to turn after Brandon's brief tutorial before they got on. Brandon lifted one of his poles for her and she grabbed it, pulled along by him away from the lift. They were surrounded by children in bright purple and pink snowsuits, padded and gliding awkwardly on the snow, like Technicolor penguins.

They stopped at the top of the hill, which was not steep, Liv knew, but it looked steep from this vantage point, and it scared her nonetheless. "You good?" he asked her, taking his ski pole back, and she nodded. He pulled down his goggles, which cast his whole face in a fluorescent yellow glow. "You go at your own pace. I'll follow behind you."

Liv suddenly felt self-conscious, not wanting to be watched. "Can you go ahead of me?" she asked.

He agreed, even though it didn't make a whole lot of sense, she knew, for the teacher not to watch the student. She didn't like being bad at things—and if she was bad at things, she didn't like anyone to see it. Why had she agreed to this in the first place? Because it had sounded like a nice idea at the time. She couldn't even turn getting off the lift; how was she going to turn going down a mountain?

He went ahead, adept and controlled, and she watched as he

glided across the width of the slope and then back again, sharply rerouting when a stray child crossed his path. His turns were clean, the skis always parallel to each other, slashing through the snow like sharpened blades. Liv found herself squatting but not moving, somewhat afraid to go directly forward, afraid that if she began to go downhill she wouldn't be able to stop.

Brandon stopped about halfway down the hill, a spray of snow from his skis as he stacked them next to each other and looked up at Liv.

"Face the tips of your skis toward each other," he called up the slope. "Like a pizza. Bend your weight forward."

She bent forward slightly, feeling the start of velocity as gravity pushed her forward, and she wedged the skis together, one crossing over the other to lock her in place, letting out a little involuntary shriek in the process. She knew she was going to lose control if she started going downhill.

"You'll go slow," she heard him say. "I promise."

She was paralyzed, stuck at the top of the hill as children whizzed fearlessly around her.

Seeming to realize that Liv was not going to move, Brandon unclipped his boots, gathered his skis over one shoulder, and climbed back up the slope.

"Hey," he said, the cheeks below his goggles flushed.

"Hi," she said, in a wimpy, weak voice.

He laughed. "What's up?"

She shook her head again. "I don't know why I'm so scared."

"It's fun," he assured her. "I promise."

It was not normal, she knew, to be this afraid to go down a bunny slope when you were an adult. It was not normal for even a child to be this scared.

"Do you want to hold onto one of my poles while I go down?"

She shook her head. She would look like a kid holding on to her dad.

"Go," she said. "I'm okay."

"Are you sure?" he asked. His overattentiveness was beginning to irritate her.

"I said I'm fine." She said this more reactively than she'd intended, with a bite to it, her annoyance audible. "Just go."

He flinched, and turned to go down the hill without another word. He didn't stop halfway this time to check on her, and she instantly regretted not accepting his help.

After what felt like several more minutes of standing there paralyzed, once Brandon was a red dot amid the other red and blue and purple dots at the bottom of the snowy hill, Liv pushed herself forward with a little yelp, letting the momentum take over. She kept stopping and starting, the tips of her rented skis clacking as they crossed and uncrossed, and as she awkwardly sidestepped, skis parallel, down the hillier parts. She would have simply taken the boots out of the skis and walked if it hadn't been so conspicuous. Children half her size flew past her, some falling and laughing, brushing themselves off, and getting back up.

"I hate this," she said to Brandon when she got to the bottom of the slope, and made her way toward the ski lodge, forcing him to follow behind.

Liv took off her rented ski boots and warmed her feet by the fire, felt the flames bring blood back into her toes.

"Better?" he asked.

She nodded. They sipped hot coffees in paper cups and didn't speak for a while.

"You should go back out there," she said when her coffee was almost finished.

"You don't want to try again?"

She shook her head. "I have a book in the car."

"I wish you'd told me you were going to be scared. I only suggested it because I thought it would be fun."

"Well, I wouldn't have known that until I got up there. Obviously."

He pulled his head back, like she'd just swiped at him.

"Sorry," she said, a knee-jerk reaction, and then felt mad at herself for saying sorry. Why should she be sorry for not being able to predict the future? For not knowing something about herself because she'd never faced that thing before?

"I don't really want to ski by myself," he said. "Let's go home."

"No, I want to stay," she said. "Maybe I'll go again in the afternoon."

He looked at her, seeming unsure whether she was telling the truth or not. She probably wouldn't try again, but she didn't mind the idea of reading in the lodge. It sounded kind of nice, actually.

"I think we should just go," he said.

"No," she said forcefully. "I said I want to stay."

"I don't—" He sighed deeply, resignedly. "Whatever," he said, and tossed her the car keys. "For your book."

The drive home in the early afternoon was quiet and moody. They'd only stayed until lunch, after which Brandon said he wasn't exactly having fun skiing alone and knowing that she was in the lodge by herself. Liv found this self-serving on his part, even though she knew he thought he was being charitable.

When they were about a half hour from home, Brandon took a deep breath, prepping to say something.

"What?" she asked.

"I was thinking out there. About the Bahamas."

"Don't worry about it. It's not a big deal." She didn't want to hear his reasons for not wanting to go. She wanted to pretend she'd never asked him in the first place.

"I don't think it would be a good idea," he said.

"Because of today?"

"No." He glanced over at her, a look weighted with meaning that she didn't want to unpack.

"I get it. It's early for you to go on a trip with my parents." She thought of how to quickly change the subject, to signal how little she cared about this trip.

"It's not really that," he said, now staring at the highway ahead. "I would happily go to the Bahamas with you and with your mom."

"Oh."

"I know we never talked about it. What happened." It was convenient for him, Liv thought, that he was driving, and didn't have to look Liv in the eye. "I just. I've never experienced anything like that before."

Her heart pounded. No one had ever named this.

"I've been struggling about what to do, or say. I even talked to my parents about it, because I didn't know how much was my place."

"You did *what*?"

He didn't seem to hear her, kept talking. "I couldn't pretend that was normal, Liv. I just couldn't. And I know it's your family, not mine, but I love you. I don't want to see you hurt."

Was she supposed to be grateful to him? She was too shocked to be grateful. It felt like he had taken a hammer and cracked her in half.

"I can't believe you talked to your parents," she said, realizing only as she spoke, as her voice came out broken and wobbly, that she was crying.

"What else was I supposed to do?"

She didn't have a good answer to that. She crossed her arms over her chest. She was shivering.

He reached one hand over to her leg and squeezed her thigh. She pushed the hand away.

"Did he ever . . ." Brandon said, still looking ahead. "Did he ever hurt you?"

She wiped away a tear with the back of her hand. She was so mad at herself that she couldn't stop crying.

"I feel ambushed," she said.

"That isn't my intention."

"No one wants your help," she said, and the strength of that—and the truth of it—steadied her voice. "You don't want to come on vacation with my family, that's fine. But you have some nerve trying to put your nose where it doesn't belong."

He was rendered speechless by this, at least momentarily.

"I thought I did belong," he said.

She could think of nothing to say to that, and they didn't speak for the rest of the drive. When he pulled up in front of her house, she got out and slammed the passenger door firmly shut.

16.

SIMONE HAD STARTED taking Henri to Paris every other weekend. It was mid-March; Danièle was six months along now, and Simone found herself wanting to be there with her more and more often. Alex was traveling so much for work these days, and their mother, loving as she was, doted too much, pitter-pattered around Danièle's apartment asking her what she needed, how much she needed, when she needed it. Was she hungry? Thirsty? Tired? Did she need to throw up? Did she want to go for a walk?

"Please come this weekend," Danièle had first begged Simone over the phone in January, not long after Oliver had left. "She's driving me nuts," she whispered from her bedroom, their mother clearly in the next room.

So, starting then, Simone and Henri went to Paris for long weekends twice a month, flying Ryanair and only bringing carry-on luggage.

Danièle was one of those pregnant women who looked as if she'd swallowed a basketball. While Simone's entire body had swollen when she was pregnant with Henri, and never quite returned to its natural state, Danièle retained her narrow face, her lithe limbs. From the back you couldn't even tell. The only thing that had changed—besides her stomach, of course, which had begun to jut out dramatically, as if independent from the rest of her body—was that her small breasts had gone up to a perfectly respectable C cup, and her long dark hair had grown even more silky and full.

"Where did this all come from?" Danièle asked her sister as they were sitting on the couch, grabbing one of her own breasts with one hand, and a handful of her hair with the other. Simone had arrived that night; they'd just put Henri to bed. "Did this happen to you?"

"My hair changed texture. It used to be sort of wavy."

"And now it's completely flat."

"Yeah, a real joy. And you remember how huge my boobs were."

"They were massive."

"Massive," Simone confirmed. She took a sip of her wine, then handed the glass to Danièle. She was far enough along now, almost in her third trimester, that it was safe to have small amounts here and there. Danièle savored her sip, then passed the glass back to Simone.

"Oliver must have liked that." Danièle said this with a certain challenge in her voice, knowing full well that things were strained between Oliver and Simone right now.

"He did."

For a moment, they were quiet. But Danièle brought out a more talkative side to Simone than she allowed anyone else to see. She had the capacity, with a simple raised eyebrow or pursed lips, to engender in Simone a certain pressure to express herself, to say what she was thinking, when every other person

on earth—except Oliver, sometimes, at least at the beginning—
only made Simone want to retreat further into those thoughts,
and spend time alone in them. Danièle was not an intellectual
in the same way that Simone was, but she wasn't stupid—she
wanted to talk about thoughts and feelings, swim around in
them together.

"We only had sex twice when he was here over the holi-
days," Simone said.

"That's not so crazy. Every couple is different."

"After not having seen each other for three months?"

Danièle considered this.

"You know how we used to be."

"All over each other."

Simone nodded.

"Maybe it's a phase," Danièle said.

"It doesn't feel like a phase."

"Sometimes when couples don't sleep together for a while it
creates this kind of no-sex homeostasis. It's harder to start having sex again after you've lost your momentum. What about
phone sex? Or, there's Skype now."

Simone didn't want to say that she had asked Oliver once or
twice to have phone sex, and that he had turned her down for
some reason or another—the time difference, too tired, there
was always something.

"I guess I'll try it," she said.

Danièle sighed.

"What?"

"He makes me mad. It makes me mad that he's probably not
concerned about any of this, keeping the relationship healthy,
maintaining your sex life."

"That isn't fair." *What about your nonexistent marriage?*
she wanted to ask her sister. Simone wasn't the only one aban-

doned, and *she* wasn't six months pregnant. Yet here they were, married women who only seemed to have each other for company.

Danièle reached out for the wine, took another sip, gave it back.

"I guess I don't understand why you don't ask for more from him."

"Well, what do *you* want from *your* husband?" Simone tried.

Danièle looked uncomfortable. "What do you mean?"

"Doesn't it bother you that he hasn't been around more during the pregnancy? This thing you guys have been wanting for so long?"

Her face flushed. "He's working."

Simone wanted to say, *On the weekends?* Dani wasn't dumb; she knew, of course, that Alex probably wasn't working—not on all of the weekends that he was gone, anyway. But it made her upset that Dani, her kind, caring, beautiful sister, would end up with someone who wasn't caring for *her* constantly—who, in fact, did quite the opposite.

"I chose this, Simone," she said, as if to thwart whatever accusation Simone was about to lob about Alex. "Don't think I don't know what I got myself into."

How did Danièle come to terms with that? How could she choose money and affairs and absence over a real, living and breathing relationship? How could she be this person who seemed so concerned with healthy relationships and communication, and yet who ended up with an entirely absent partner? It was always so much easier for Danièle to talk to other people about their problems than to deal with her own. This had always been their dynamic: Danièle as the teacher, the one who knew best, the sister who had it all together, and Simone as the lost and confused one, the overthinker. In actuality, they both knew that Simone only seemed to have a lot of problems in comparison to her sister because she was the only one facing them.

Simone didn't actually know if Danièle wanted Alex to be around more. She'd never asked.

Danièle lifted up her shirt, showing Simone her stomach. They were having a girl. "Look," she said.

Simone looked at the stretched flesh, the knots and bones of the fetus moving around in there. She put a hand over the round of Danièle's belly. She felt the baby churning violently inside, as if desperate to get out.

17.

Every Thursday night during that spring semester they went for drinks at the bar at the new boutique hotel down the street. Liv had christened it Fancy Lady Night. A farm-to-table movement had sprung up in their college town; downtown, there were at least three restaurants with organic local kale on the menu, and young artists were beginning to move to the small city for the cheap studio space. The hotel, called the Jefferson, was only a ten-minute walk from their house; it had opened right around Christmastime. The converted cork factory was now outfitted with red deco furniture in its lobby, where the original wooden rafters and exposed brick were intact; it cost $195 a night to stay in one of the uniquely designed rooms. The hotel attracted mostly visiting parents of Buchanan students, and businessmen passing through the city. But for Fiona and her roommates, and a select few other seniors and professors, the bar continued to be a well-kept secret.

Lula had discovered it originally, going for a drink by herself after her senior anthropology seminar one Thursday af-

ternoon, as she sometimes did. It made sense that she of all of
them had found it: Lula had a way of seeking out the more
upscale corners of a city, of finding the most creative and in-
novative people in a particular place and being invited into
their ranks. After all, Lula had that air about her: she was
New York rich. She didn't wear her money like a badge; she
was more refined than that. It was as if you could smell it on
her instead, or pick it up little by little: from the way that
clothes accentuated her gamine legs, her delicate features, her
Lula-ness—she wore her clothes so naturally that even the
most expensive items appeared disposable—from the way she
kept up with the cultural events of the city, like the current
opera season at the Met or a Shaw revival at the Public, expecting everyone else to follow her as if they were as much part of
the common conversation as, say, the NBA playoffs or a Bat-
man movie that had been recently released.

The difference between Lula and the other city kids at Buchanan, though, was that, though her peers seemed continually
disappointed by an America that did not live up to their home-
town, Lula knew that New York would always be in a league
of its own, and so she allowed herself to be charmed by small-
town pleasures. And even though the Jefferson was hardly
glamorous by the standards of what Lula had experienced in
her lifetime, she enjoyed that they had beer on tap that was
brewed right here in the county, that she could be surrounded
by other well-dressed people, and that their happy hour menu
allowed her to drink a top-shelf martini for $7.

Fiona always ordered a drink called the Colonial—a rasp-
berry margarita, a specialty of Joseph, the bartender. It was not
on the menu; Joseph had offered it to Fiona one day when she
had trouble picking something on the happy hour list that ap-
pealed to her. Now she relished her Thursday-night cocktails:

flirting with Joseph, who was tall and tattooed up and down his biceps, and spending time with her roommates. The opportunities for such evenings were quickly diminishing.

Now that it was April, and graduation for the rest of them was on the horizon, time seemed to move exponentially faster. She wanted desperately to hold on to it. Senior year of college was meant to be the best, but she felt she could not enjoy it anymore because she was so focused on the inevitability of it ending. Once her friends were gone, she alone would be back at this school. She hoped she could go unnoticed, could walk through campus like a ghost. She would need to take only three classes that semester; she could stay in her room the rest of the time, or go home on the weekends, or go stay with Lula and Liv in the city. As of now, she was trying to take advantage of the time they had left.

Thursday nights were her favorite nights to dress. Tonight she wore a black bodycon dress, high heels, and a faux-leather jacket (which she'd bought at Marshall's after wearing Lula's real one that night at Zeta). This was one of the points of Fancy Lady Night—to look nicer and more refined than you would at, say, Truckstop, and to be *treated* in a nicer and more refined way, too.

Fiona watched Joseph's upper arms flex as he shook her drink. He was in his usual head-to-toe black—well-worn black jeans, leather boots, and a black Hanes T-shirt that ran tight around his biceps. A bit of dark chest hair peeked out from the V-neck. His tattoos, which he had designed himself, seemed random—there was a wolf in a pink tutu; a broken umbrella with cobwebs drawn between the spokes, like a spiderweb; a dead ladybug, oversize, the red on her shell mingled with spatters of her blood, so you couldn't tell which was which. His left hand had BITE spelled out on it, one letter on each knuckle. It must have been really hard to think of a tattoo that felt original. Everything had been done already.

"To us," Lula said, once Joseph had finished making their drinks, and the four of them clinked their glasses. Fiona took a hearty first sip of her Colonial. The first sip was always the best; she missed this drink pretty much every other time she drank something different, and she didn't know if it was because of the taste, or because of the bartender who had made it, or because of the place where she drank it, feeling dressed up and unencumbered.

Fiona asked Liv, "What's Brandon up to tonight?"

Liv took a sip of her own Colonial. "Zeta pledge stuff."

"Elephant walks?" Fiona asked, smirking.

"What's that?" Liv asked.

Marley made a face. "You know, think of elephants—four legs, and their tails . . ."

"Ew," Liv said. "No. Nothing like that."

"Just good old-fashioned toxic masculinity, then," Lula said.

"I don't know," Liv said. "I don't ask, actually. I don't really care."

"Drinks all right, ladies?" Joseph asked, wiping down the space on the bar next to them.

"Great," they all said in unison. Fiona locked eyes with him and smiled.

When she turned back to her friends, Liv was batting her eyelashes at Fiona.

"Stop," Fiona said, quietly.

"What?" Marley asked.

"Nothing," Fiona said, because truthfully only Liv was privy to Fiona's crush. Fiona hadn't even told her; she had picked up on it one Thursday night, and now Fiona felt as if she were under Liv's microscope. What was all the judging for?

It wasn't like Liv hadn't made some misguided romantic decisions herself, hadn't been secretly emailing with Oliver Ash all those months ago, too. Not that Fiona had ever told Liv she knew about that.

At that moment, Liv turned her head to the door, and Fiona followed her gaze: Professor Ash and Professor Roiphe were entering the bar together—Ash in a charcoal blazer, and Roiphe in a satin vest over a button-down shirt, pressed tightly against her breasts as if to flatten them. It never ceased to amuse her that her English professors dressed exactly as if someone in a novel were writing them.

"Look who it is," Marley said quietly to her friends, and brought her beer to her lips as she watched the two of them move toward two open stools. It was a square, open bar, with the bartender station in the middle, and so by the time the professors found seats, they were directly across from the girls, where they were impossible not to notice.

"Hi, ladies," Professor Roiphe called out, lifting a convivial hand. Professor Ash smiled with his mouth closed, seeming entirely displeased by the encounter. Liv said hello back, and Fiona lifted her drink in salute. Then the girls turned away from the professors, and toward one another.

"You better not make a scene, Marley," Liv said.

"Come on. Give me a little credit."

"How's your class with him, anyway?" Lula asked quietly. "Is he any good?"

"Yeah, he is," Fiona said. "He's really smart."

"He's not bad." Liv shrugged. "A little harsh, maybe." Fiona knew that Professor Ash had given Liv less than glowing notes on her most recent short story.

"I think he's fair," Fiona said. She had not told Liv about his comments on *her* story. Though he had apologized to her for being harsh, she had, in fact, treasured the criticism. He was right.

"I don't know how he lives with himself," Marley said.

"Marley," Liv hissed. "He's right there."

"We don't know what really happened," Fiona said. "It could have been consensual, for all we know."

"Consent doesn't really exist when there's that kind of power dynamic," Marley said.

"How old was she again?" asked Lula, who actually couldn't care less about Oliver Ash and was clearly impatient for a subject change.

"Seventeen."

"Not proven," Liv whispered. "She turned eighteen that fall, and it's unclear when exactly he was sleeping with her."

"I mean, he implicated himself in his book," Fiona said. "I'm actually shocked he didn't get into bigger trouble."

"It was technically fiction."

"Seventeen!" Lula said too loudly, and Liv shushed her. Lula lowered her voice. "I was having threesomes by the time I was seventeen. Seventeen-year-old girls are far more mature than any of you are giving them credit for."

"It's wrong," said Marley, definitive in her assessment of the matter.

Fiona looked over at him, sipping a brown liquid from his rocks glass, nodding intently at what Professor Roiphe was saying. It surprised her that the two of them were friendly, Professor Roiphe being such a feminist. She felt this was a boon to Professor Ash's reputation, maybe even proof that he wasn't as bad as Marley thought he was. Fiona lifted her empty glass to Joseph, and he nodded, began making her another.

Marley straightened on her barstool. "So, I actually have news."

"Oh my God," Fiona said. "Schools?"

Marley nodded, beaming. "I got into Duke."

They erupted: they jumped up, drinks still in hand, splashing over the rims and onto their hands and onto one another, hugging her around the neck, the waist, wherever they could get their hands on her.

"I'm soaked!" Marley shrieked.

"Joseph!" Lula reached across the bar. "A bottle of champagne, please!"

He smiled, revealing the tiny gap between his teeth that Fiona was so charmed by. "Any preference?"

"Your finest!" Lula said with aristocratic affectation, which meant that she would be putting it on her father's credit card.

"What are we celebrating?"

Fiona practically had her arms around Marley's neck in a choke hold. "Our girl just got into her first-choice medical school."

"Impressive," Joseph said, raising his eyebrows. "Congratulations."

"Thank you," she said, her cheeks pink.

When he popped the cork they cheered, already tipsy from their first drinks, and he poured it into glasses, the foam rising exactly to the top and no further.

"Joseph, take a glass!" Lula said, and he did, clinking his glass against theirs.

"So, where to, then?" he asked Marley.

"Only one of the best schools in the *country*," said Fiona. "This girl is going to save lives."

Fiona realized that her second Colonial had come, sitting fresh and untouched alongside her glass of champagne, and she pulled it toward herself. She heard Professor Ash's voice carrying from across the bar, and looked up to see that he was speaking to them.

"What?" Fiona called back.

"I said, What are we celebrating?"

"Oh," Fiona called, "Marley got into her first-choice med school."

Professor Ash lifted his glass.

"Congratulations," said Professor Roiphe.

"Join us!" Lula called out.

"No, no, that's all right," said Professor Ash.

"There's tons of champagne," Lula said. "Right, Joseph?"

He lifted the bottle from the ice bucket to reveal that there were still a few glasses' worth left.

"Yeah, come over," Lula said, beckoning to him. Whether she had momentarily forgotten Marley's vendetta against him or was trying to use this moment to bridge some kind of a divide, Fiona was unsure. Or perhaps Lula was just bored, as she was wont to be, and was trying to make the night more interesting.

Professor Roiphe was the one who assented. Well-loved professor to Fiona and Liv—and also to Lula and Marley during their forays into lit classes freshman year—she had nothing to lose from a friendly celebratory drink with her outgoing seniors. Professor Ash stood up and followed.

They were in a row—Lula, Marley, Fiona, then Liv—and the professors took the two seats to Liv's right. Joseph poured two more glasses of champagne. Immediately, it was awkward.

"Again, congratulations, Marley," Professor Roiphe said across the bar, and they all lifted and clinked. "And what will you specialize in?" she asked. "Or is it too soon to know?"

"I'd like to do women's health, I think," she said. "And be an ob-gyn. If I can hack it."

"Really?" Liv said. "You never told me that."

"You never asked."

"I'm so awed by the number of students here who end up in professional schools immediately following graduation," Professor Roiphe said. "I've had several English majors over the years who have gone on to become doctors."

"I'm sorry to break it to you," Fiona said, "that I will not be one of them."

She smiled kindly at Fiona. "And what about the rest of you? Any plans shaping up for next year? Or maybe it's too early."

This was a sore subject. Liv and Lula had interviews scheduled—Lula at the Natural History Museum and at the Smithsonian; Liv at a couple of publishing houses in New York—but Fiona would, of course, be back to school in the fall.

"Oh God," Lula said, graciously sparing Fiona this discussion. "Absolutely not."

She leaned forward and waved across the line of them to Professor Ash, who had largely remained silent. "Hi! I'm Lula!"

"Oliver." He waved back.

"What's your plan, Professor Ash?" Liv asked, turning toward him. "You're only here for the year, right?"

"Yeah," he said. "I'm headed back to Berlin in May."

"Are you writing a book there?" Lula yelled down to him. With six of them in a straight line, and the bar beginning to fill up, it was getting harder and harder to hear.

"Sort of," he called back, and left it at that.

"What's it about?" she called. She pointed to Joseph for a refill on her champagne. He refilled hers and then Marley's, finishing the bottle.

"Another?" Joseph asked her.

Lula nodded.

"You know what, I'm gonna come over there so I can hear," Lula called to Professor Ash.

Marley stayed where she was, and Fiona noticed that while Professor Ash began to give a roundabout description of a family epic, Joseph brought the new bottle of champagne to Marley and filled only her flute. He leaned across the bar then, and they began to chat, just the two of them, their faces closer than Fiona's had ever been to his. Meanwhile, to her right, Lula, Liv, and Professor Roiphe were listening intently to Professor Ash. All three of them had looks on their faces like he was saying the smartest thing they'd ever heard.

"So it sort of probes into this idea of what constitutes a 'survivor.' Did one have to go to a camp, or be in hiding, or do the European Jews who fled count, too? So there's some research there, about the narrative of the Jews who escaped in time, and how they fit into the question of survivorship, tied in with the notion of inherited trauma and framed by a more personal story of the relationship between this narrator and his father."

"Is the father a survivor?" Liv asked. They were discussing this narrator and father like they were fictional, but Fiona, who had read Professor Ash's second novel, knew it had to be inspired by his own life.

He took a sip of the champagne before answering. "That's the question, I guess. Who gets to call themselves that?"

"My grandfather fled Poland when he was a baby," Lula said. "1937, I think."

"Are you Jewish?" he asked. Lula was black, and it'd be hard to guess that she was half-Jewish if you didn't know that her last name was Rosenberg.

"Sure am," she said. "Well, not *technically*. Wrong side and all that."

"Same here," he said, seeming particularly touched by this information.

"I'm also a halfie," Liv chimed in, and Lula turned to her, perplexed. "Half-Japanese," she clarified.

"Oh," Professor Ash said, "I see."

Fiona felt suddenly out of place in this conversation. She had nothing at all to say to him in comparison with these two, who were urbane, sophisticated, worldly. She felt provincial in comparison. She checked on Marley, to find her still talking closely with Joseph, whose forearms were now on the bar, his head close to hers. A customer a few seats down from Marley was trying to get his attention. Neither of them noticed; Marley laughed in response to something he said.

"Joseph!" Fiona called to him, and he turned slowly, both surprised and annoyed to be interrupted. When they locked eyes she pointed at the middle-aged woman lifting her empty glass of wine to be refilled.

"Thanks," he mouthed, though he didn't seem particularly grateful, and she swore she saw him roll his eyes in Marley's direction before removing his forearms from the bar and attending to the woman.

"Well," Professor Roiphe said, replacing her empty champagne flute on the bar and looking at her watch. "I actually should be going."

"Seriously?" Fiona said. "It's only nine! You old lady."

"Guilty," Professor Roiphe said, putting her hands up. "It was so nice running into you all." She looked over at Marley—

Joseph was still chatting with her while he refilled the glass of wine—and saw that this wasn't a moment to interrupt. "Please tell Marley I say congratulations again."

"I'll walk with you, Joan," Professor Ash said, also standing. "Fridays are my writing day, and I'm afraid I would stay out far too late chatting with you lovely people if I didn't leave now."

Lula gave both professors air kisses on the cheek, and Liv, as if taking notes, followed suit. Fiona did the same. She tried to hide her disappointment that Professor Ash wasn't staying and drinking more. He'd held tight to his formal, teacherly persona.

"I'm gonna go, too," Liv said, checking her phone after the professors had left.

"What?" Fiona said. "Already?"

"Yeah, I'm gonna head over to Zeta."

"Is that safe?"

"Totally," Liv said. She took forty dollars from her wallet and put it on the bar.

"That's way too much," Lula said, pushing a twenty back across to Liv. "The champagne was on me."

"No way," Liv said. Liv did this sometimes; even though Lula was impossibly rich, Liv had to assert that she had money, too. Lula shrugged and took the bills.

"Bye, Mar!" Liv called to her friend, then smiled, because Marley didn't hear her.

Lula reached across the bar, took the champagne from its ice bucket, and finished off the bottle, filling her flute and Fiona's to the top. Joseph didn't notice. Lula clinked her glass with Fiona's once more.

"To us," she said.

"To us," Fiona repeated, and took a sip. She didn't need this last drink, but she wanted to keep drinking, for the ritual of it, for spending more time out with her friend.

"It's so rare we do this," Lula said. "Just the two of us."

"It is," Fiona agreed. "I can't believe it's almost over."

"It is not," Lula said.

"You know what I mean."

"Oh, don't be gloomy. Let's enjoy it while we can."

"Okay," Fiona said.

"That Oliver Ash is quite a specimen," Lula said, raising her eyebrows.

"Tell me about it," Fiona said.

"How do you concentrate? Those shoulders."

Fiona sighed. "Don't do this to me. It was hard enough to turn it off in the first place."

"So you did have a thing for him."

"Who wouldn't? I've never even heard you express your attraction for a man before."

"That's . . . yes, that's probably true." Lula laughed.

"I won't tell," Fiona said. "I wouldn't want them to take away your gold star."

"But, Fee," Lula said. "The way he was *looking* at you."

"What do you mean?"

"You don't see it?"

"I don't see it because you just made it up."

Lula shook her head, held her champagne flute aloft.

"He was staring at you. Everything he was saying, he was saying it to you, fishing for your reaction."

"No way."

"Yes way."

"He's married."

"Like that's ever stopped a man from getting what he wanted."

At this, Fiona thought of her father, then felt uncomfortable at the perverted train of thought. She thought back to her conversation with Liam at Thanksgiving, how he'd said the situation between their parents was "complicated." That their mother wasn't totally blameless. It was true that Fiona knew little about Professor Ash's home life, about his marriage. Certainly it couldn't have been rock solid, given that he'd decided to be here all semester. But he was a father, too. In all of this fantasizing, she had not once put herself in the child's position. Moreover, she had not thought about the fact that she *was* the child in this position, that her father had cheated with a perhaps unknowing woman, or several women. She didn't know the specifics. Things were bad between their parents, according to Liam, before Helen had died. And then Helen blew it all open. How possible was it that the woman her father had an affair with knew anything about his home life? Fiona suspected she knew very little, that she was just an outlet for the issues in his real life, a person he could go to who knew nothing about him at all.

Lula's father, too, had been a cheater, though they rarely talked about the similarities in their home lives. Fiona wanted to ask Lula if she was talking to her dad these days, but she thought perhaps it was best to keep the train of thought, from sex to fathers, to herself.

"Did you really think so?" Fiona said, looking over at Marley and Joseph again. Now their hands were intertwined over the bar.

"I think you could fuck him tomorrow if you wanted to," Lula said, draining her champagne. "Come on, let's go." She stood up, and Fiona finished her own drink and followed suit. "Bye, Marley!" Lula singsonged. Marley didn't even look up.

18.

LIV WRAPPED HER arms around herself, underdressed for the chilly April night. She walked down Phillips Avenue, well lit by the street lamps, past the admissions office, the registrar, and other administrative offices—two-story stone and slate houses, matching brass nameplates out front—lined up in an official row between centuries-old elm trees. The light cast eerie shadows of the trees, which still had no leaves on them, and their silhouettes looked like twelve-foot-tall men, the long prickled branches like translucent black arms reaching out to one another. She walked a few blocks down the avenue—past the International House, where she once accepted an award from the French Honor Society; past the Writing Cottage—and turned onto her street. The houses grew smaller, cheaper, and the streetlights were decidedly less bright. The sidewalks were littered with bottle caps and cigarette butts.

When she got to their house she was startled, at first, to see a woman sitting on their stoop. As she got closer, she realized it was June.

"Hi, June," she said to their next-door neighbor. She was sitting on the top step with her tabby cat in her lap.

"Hi, honey," the woman said in her raspy voice.

The two-family house that Liv and her roommates lived in was split down the middle; June, her daughter, and her granddaughter lived on the other side.

"You all right, hon?" June asked. Liv realized that she had stopped in front of the house, not planning to go inside, but was standing on the sidewalk contemplating it.

"I'm fine," she said. "I'm actually going for a little walk."

"Careful," June said, patting the cat.

"I'll be fine," Liv said, and she turned on her heel and kept going.

The Zeta house was still a ten-minute walk from her house; it was far away from the rest of the frat houses, which were closer to campus, though it was the oldest and biggest of them all, and farthest from campus public safety, and therefore— though she was partial—threw the best parties. She turned right when she hit West Pine, passing brick townhouses all in a row, connected to each other, the porch lights yellow and dim.

There was no one out; this was the block where that student had been shot Liv's sophomore year. It was past nine. She knew the pledging event had started at seven, and she figured the boys would be almost done by now. Brandon was supposed to call her when he was done; she hadn't heard from him yet.

Things between them had been tense over the past month. Liv had gone to the Bahamas over spring break, with her parents and without him. As she had hoped, her father was placid and quiet, on good behavior, and it made her angry with Brandon for making such a giant deal over what turned out to be nothing. Nonetheless, she was putting in an effort at making things good again between Brandon and herself: bringing him snacks at the library when he was studying, delivering six-packs of fancy beers to the house when he was spending the night with brothers, or—like now—surprising him. All in an endeavor to forget that day at the ski mountain. He was the one who continued to be distant, who'd barely texted her while she was in the Bahamas and didn't even ask how the trip was when she got back. He didn't seem to want to have sex with her anymore, either, always putting it off or saying he was too tired.

Brandon had officially accepted his place at Columbia Law, while Liv had secured an editorial assistantship at a publishing house in midtown. Even though before spring break they had both been gung ho about the idea of living together, Brandon hadn't brought it up since it became clear they were both going to be in New York. Liv worried, though she wouldn't say so to Brandon or to anyone else, that he was having second thoughts. There were only two months until her move to the city, and time to find an apartment was running out, but she was afraid to bring it up with him, for fear that he'd changed his mind.

West Pine sloped sharply downhill, and she crossed at a traffic light, arriving at the Zeta house on the corner. The houses were bigger over here. The frat house itself was three stories, with an overhang above the front porch connected to the second floor and held up by staid brick columns. The porch lights were off; she opened her cellphone and used the blue light from the screen to guide her up the front steps, concave with decades' worth of foot traffic from frat brothers and partygoers. At the heavy front door, she rapped on the brass knocker three times and waited. She peered in through the slim window beside the door; the main entrance, too, was dark and empty. They must be in the basement.

She called Brandon; his phone went straight to voicemail. Rather than being concerned about standing on an unlit street alone at night or considering that perhaps she should return home and wait for Brandon's call, she found herself indignant. How dare he not be available? What were boyfriends for, if not this?

She knocked again, in vain. Called again and left a voicemail: "Hey, B. I'm standing here outside Zeta, and it's really fucking cold."

After she hung up, it dawned on her to try the door. To her amazement, it opened.

She walked through the dark entryway where she'd attended many a cocktail hour. The main stairs were ahead, a wide staircase with wooden banisters on both sides. She could go up to Brandon's room and wait there. Though she had no right to go down to the basement—pledge rituals were of the *highest* secrecy, Brandon had stressed, many times—she had to admit she was curious. She assumed that whatever they were doing was stupid, and secret for the sake of secrecy but not out of any particular need to obscure the inappropriate or unlawful. They were probably just forcing the poor freshman boys to binge-drink and run around in circles until they puked.

So she tiptoed just to the top of the basement steps, where she began to hear yelling and cheering, and as she got closer it was an immense roar, as if seventy-five college-aged boys were watching a horse race in which they all had money at stake. The door to the basement was closed; she attempted to see if that, too, was unlocked. The knob didn't budge when she tried to turn it.

She went up to Brandon's room, the door to which was also unlocked. The lights were on, and the bed was unmade. There was a recently smoked bowl on the bedside table. She sat on the bed, propped a pillow up behind her head, checked her phone. It probably wouldn't be much longer; he would be happy to see her. She opened the drawer of the nightstand— condoms, a big bottle of Lubriderm lotion, a lighter, and the thing she was hoping to find: a Ziploc bag of weed.

She emptied the burnt remnants in the bowl onto the night-stand and packed a new one. She had never done this herself, wasn't even really much of a smoker, but she'd seen Brandon do it a million times, and what else was she going to do right now?

She pinched a few pieces of the weed between her fingers and pressed them into the round part of the bowl until they were packed tightly. She cocked the lighter back with her thumb, and held the flame to the weed, trying to get it all lit. She burnt her thumb three times before she succeeded, the embers glowing orange. She went to take her first hit, and sucked in far too hard; a giant whiff of smoke entered her airway and filled her lungs so fast that she coughed dramatically, repeat-edly, beating her chest to get it all out. Immediately high, she looked around for water, or a glass to fill; in the mini-fridge by his desk, there was only beer, so she cracked open a can of Budweiser, taking a long sip, and then returned to the bed. Her coughing abated. Normal Budweiser was actually pretty good.

The moment she sat back and brought the beer to her lips to take a second sip, the door creaked open.

Brandon was shirtless, in basketball shorts, and covered from head to toe in a rainbow's array of paint. Liv burst out laughing.

"That's what your secret ritual is?" she said when she caught her breath. "Paintball?"

He looked angry in the open doorway. It was hard to take him seriously when his face was splattered with hot pink and electric green.

"I'm sorry, I'm sorry," she said. "You just look so funny."

"What are you doing here?" He swayed a bit on his feet.

"Aren't you happy to see me?"

"I told you I would call you when I was done." His eyes were bloodshot.

"You're high, aren't you?"

"Why aren't you with the girls?" The paint was starting to mingle with the sweat on his forehead, and it was running down his face, clownlike.

She shrugged, took another sip of the beer. "It got boring."

He looked at the area around her, the beer, the pot.

"Did you go through my stuff?" he asked. "Did you smoke my weed?"

She giggled.

"I can't handle this right now." He ran a hand through his hair, also soaked in paint, and turned his back to her. "I have to shower."

"Brandon!" she called at him as he began to walk away.

He turned around again in the doorway, hands slack at his sides.

"Do you wanna order wings?"

She swore she detected a small smile on his face, which quickly turned into a much more sinister expression.

"No. I do not want to order wings."

"Geez Louise."

"You know what I really want?"

"What?" She thought he might say pizza, or subs from Antonio's.

"I want you to leave."

"What?"

"You can't walk into my house, come into my room, and go through my stuff when I'm not here."

"You *were* here. You were just—"

"I said I would call you. I was going to call you when I was ready. I wasn't ready."

"I thought you would like being surprised," she said quietly.

He let out a groan so loud it made Liv jump.

"You've been making this really hard for me."

Her insides lurched.

"Making *what* hard?"

He gestured between them. "This. Us."

"I don't get what's hard about it."

Now she started crying, and his face softened into empathy, or pity. She couldn't tell if there was a difference.

"Oh," he said, in a sorry voice that matched his expression. "I'm gonna get in the shower, and then we'll talk."

She listened to the water running, still confused. A month ago, he would have liked this. He would have wanted her to surprise him. How had the tables turned so quickly? How had she gone from being the one who held all the power in this relationship to the one who was now at his mercy?

He came out in boxers, rubbing his hair with a towel, and sat down on the edge of the bed, next to her, and took her into a hug. His chest was warm and damp. Then he pulled his face away and looked at her.

"I do like being surprised," he said now, seeming to choose his words carefully. "But you've been doing that a lot recently."

"Doing what?"

"It feels like you are so scared to lose me that you will find me at all hours of the day without thinking about the fact that I might need to actually study, or hang out with my friends, or sleep, when I say I'm going to do those things. I'm really not trying to be harsh. I love you. But I am also worried about you. And about, you know, about the family stuff. I think they might be related."

"Oh, great, here comes the psychobabble."

"Do you really think this is psychobabble?"

"You're not a doctor."

"Do you want to talk about this like adults or not?"

She thought she *was* talking like an adult. She didn't know how to talk about things the way he wanted to talk about them. It felt like he spoke a language she didn't have access to.

"I think there are some things you still need to work out," he said.

"Why is it all on me?"

"It's not," he said. "But it has to be a little on you. There is shit that . . . that you need to take care of. And I can't do it for you."

"Are you breaking up with me?"

"No. No."

"Because it sounds like—"

"I'm not breaking up with you. But I think, I think we need to take it slower. We're still so young, you know? Like, maybe . . . maybe it's too soon to live together. In New York."

She began sobbing now, and couldn't stop. She was a puddle, mouth agape. Why didn't she have any say in this relationship anymore? Who was the child, really? She couldn't talk to him anymore. Everything she said got turned around in his mouth, made wrong. He made her words meaningless, or made them mean something other than she'd intended. How could she live with someone who didn't hear her? Didn't believe her? She'd wanted to surprise him; that was all.

She stood.

"Where are you going?" he said.

She walked out of his bedroom.

"Liv!" she heard him calling from behind her. She didn't turn around, and he didn't come after her. She walked down the wide stairway of the Zeta house sobbing uncontrollably while the brothers, covered in paint and barely fazed by her, were walking up them.

19.

I T WAS A little chilly for May, but at least it wasn't raining. All week it had been drizzling, and the last thing they wanted was for their college graduation to be inside the gymnasium: all that fluorescent lighting, all their parents complaining about how untimely the rain was, as if having spent nearly $40,000 a year on their children's tuition should have bought better weather, too. Liv, Lula, and Marley had gone to pick up their caps and gowns a few days earlier; it was clear they were trying not to talk about graduation inside the house, but after a certain point, it became impossible to avoid the fact that the three of them were leaving. Fiona was staying in the house that fall, with three junior girls—one she knew from French classes, and two of that girl's friends, who were essentially strangers to Fiona. It didn't matter; she only had to live with them for one semester, and then she'd never see them again.

Things started to slowly disappear from the house—a throw pillow here, a cutting board there—and the graduating girls began to deconstruct their bedrooms, wrapping picture frames in newsprint, stacking books in boxes that they'd picked up from the liquor store. Fiona kept offering to help, to no avail.

"I'm totally fine!" Liv would say.

"I'm almost done anyway," said Lula.

"Wanna sit on my bed and keep me company?" asked Marley.

Fiona had wanted to skip graduation, but that felt too cruel. They had all left the house by nine the morning of, so Fiona got ready alone: putting on a pretty floral dress, a cardigan over it, and making loose waves in her hair with a curling iron. She wasn't graduating but she might as well look nice, like she'd made an effort to be there. It would lessen the embarrassment if she was deliberate in her attendance, rather than attempting to hide it.

The white chairs on the quad, in front of the stage, were reserved for the graduates; behind them sat anxious parents, hard-of-hearing grandparents, unenthused siblings. Fiona had not bought a ticket for a seat, so she stood at the back of the crowd, where underclassmen gathered, the ones who had stayed on campus to watch their significant others or teammates walk across the stage, and some of the professors who lived locally. She smiled at a girl she knew from poetry class, who waited for her boyfriend with a digital camera ready in her hands.

When the band started to play, and the graduates began to walk down the stone pathway toward the quad, everyone stood and turned, oohing and aahing, as if they were watching five hundred brides proceed toward the altar. The graduates moved down the middle of the quad, bisecting the standing crowd and the rows of white chairs. Fiona would not walk when she received her diploma that fall. She had the option to do so the following spring, as the ceremony was held only once a year, but she did not imagine she would come back for that. She knew at some point she'd have to tell her mother that she would not be attending her college graduation ceremony, and she wasn't sure if this would break her mother's heart, or if it would bring relief instead. One less thing to watch Fiona do that Helen never would.

Marley grinned and waved at Fiona as she passed, then again at her parents and several siblings closer to the front. They were yelling and screaming her name. Liv and Lula followed, proud and composed and far less excitable, their parents similarly beaming with pride, but not in the showy way Marley's family was. Lula's father wasn't with her mother and sister; Fiona wondered if he was even there.

There were opening notes from the dean, words from the college president. Their keynote speaker, a CNN anchor, was pompous and unfunny, but received many polite laughs. The assistant dean began to read off the names, and each graduate paused for pictures—first shaking hands with the president, then posing at the end of the stage with diploma in hand. Fiona clapped extra loudly when Marley crossed the stage— announced as magna cum laude—and then Liv, cum laude. She wanted to scream out for them, but didn't want to draw attention to herself.

"Why aren't you up there?"

She looked to her right, and then up. Professor Ash was in a tie, crisp white shirt, khakis, no blazer. His grayish hair— grayer than when the year started, Fiona swore—was cleanly pushed behind his ears.

She tried to think of something witty to say, but came up short.

"I . . . uh . . ."

Fiona could see from the sudden change in Professor Ash's

face as she stumbled over words, from joviality to seriousness and empathy, that he thought the reason she wasn't up there was a sad or embarrassing one. Then he shifted again into lightheartedness, kindness.

"Too good for it. I didn't walk at my graduation, either."

"Really?"

"I hated college." He put a finger up to his mouth as if this were a secret, as if all professors had to be self-proclaimed lovers of institutional learning themselves.

"Where did you go?"

"Penn. I swear I was the only nonathlete or non–frat boy there. I called myself a 'GDI,' a—"

"A goddamn individual," Fiona finished. "We still say that."

Lula crossed the stage—gliding, tall, with impeccable posture, somehow managing to make even a cap and gown look glamorous. Fiona clapped.

"How come you stayed for graduation?" Fiona asked Professor Ash. "Shouldn't you be back in Berlin?"

"Good memory." He seemed surprised. "I guess I've grown nostalgic with age. For the past I didn't have. I don't know. Anyway, I fly home tomorrow."

"That's nice," she said. "You must be looking forward to seeing your family." She would have thought he'd fly home to them the minute his classes concluded.

He was quiet for a moment, as if considering this notion. "I am," he eventually said, realizing the comment required a response. "You up to anything fun this summer?"

"Actually, yeah. Liv and I are going to Paris next week. Before our jobs start." Only Liv had a job lined up. Fiona had no idea what she would do during the summer when she returned home.

"You'll have a wonderful time," he said. "Paris in May," he said with a mock wistfulness, and trailed off.

"I'm looking forward to it," she said. In reality, she wasn't all that excited. The significance Liv had placed on Fiona's making a return visit, as a sort of homage to Helen, felt forced and fatuous. And now that Liv and Brandon were broken up, the vacation was turning into a rebound trip for Liv. But it was a trip to Paris, which anyone was supposed to be excited about—and a trip her father's money was paying for, at that—so she feigned enthusiasm, too guilty to present otherwise.

Professor Ash looked ahead to the stage. They were at the very end of the alphabet—the ceremony was almost over, after which Fiona would find her friends, socialize with their families, then go back to her empty house, change, and drive home to Westchester. She would stay there for the next week, packing for Paris and waiting for the trip to begin.

"Will you write while you're there?" Professor Ash asked.

"In Paris?"

"Yeah."

"I don't know. I hadn't really thought about it."

"Your revisions were strong for your final portfolio. I was impressed by that."

She had worked hard on them, trying to make up for the D from earlier in the semester. "Thanks," she said. So she had, in the end, managed to impress him.

No more graduates were left to walk across the stage. The dean announced that they were now, officially, graduates of Buchanan College, and the caps went up in unison, came back down in a frenzy, none seeming to return to their original owners.

Professor Ash turned to face Fiona, and put a hand on her

shoulder. "Enjoy Paris," he said. "If you end up making it to Berlin, give me a ring." She could feel his hand warm and heavy as he held it there, and he maintained his eye contact with her. She felt both excited and uncomfortable. He rubbed the area between her shoulder and neck with his fingertips for a few moments, as if trying to work out a knot in the muscle. Then he removed his hand, said goodbye, and turned. Fiona watched him as he walked across the grass, past the empty Adirondack chairs, down the stone pathway that traversed the campus, and turned a corner behind a brick building.

—— // ——

All of Fiona's belongings surrounded her in suitcases and duffel bags. For the week she had at home in Larchmont before her trip, she emerged for jogs around the high school track and for dinners with Ed and her mom; otherwise, she stayed in her childhood bedroom, among the packed bags, clicking away at Facebook, texting with Marley and Lula about how much they missed each other already, talking to Liv on the phone about their trip. The house felt far too big, too empty, for Fiona to spend any time in its unoccupied rooms. Thanksgiving and Christmas had been okay, with Liam and Rebecca around. Now it was only her and her mom and Ed, who spent almost every night there.

Amy had not been thrilled to learn about Fiona's trip to Paris. They'd had an argument about it over the phone a month earlier, after Fiona told her she had booked the flights.

"And what money will you be using?" Amy had asked, her voice fraught with what sounded like jealousy. Fiona knew she would have to tell Amy now about the money that her father was depositing into Fiona's bank account each month.

"A *thousand* dollars?" Amy shrieked. "Who the fuck does

he think he is?" Fiona rarely heard her mother swear. "That is so typical. Flexing his muscles the only way he knows how."

"Well, what else was I supposed to use it on?" Fiona said.

"You shouldn't have *taken* it in the first place," Amy said. "He pays your tuition and your rent. You have a part-time job at school. What more could you possibly need? You're a college student, for Christ's sake."

"Don't be mad at me for what *he* did," Fiona said.

Amy came around and apologized for overreacting, and was now doing her best to act excited for Fiona, though Fiona knew it was insincere. And there was of course the other, unspoken thing: this was supposed to have been Helen's trip. Wouldn't it have been nice if Fiona went back with Amy, instead of with Liv, the snooty girl from Buchanan whom Amy had never really liked?

Fiona humored Ed at dinner, though he had so many questions. How were her classes this past semester? What kind of writing did she like to do the most? Would she like him to set up an informational interview with his brother, who was an editor at the *New York Post*?

"Oh, Fiona, that would be an incredible connection," Amy said.

"I'm not really interested in journalism," Fiona said. "You know that."

"Still. You have to start somewhere, right?" Ed said.

What Fiona wanted to say was that the *Post* was a gossip rag at its best, but she didn't want to insult him. She still did like Ed, after all, and she liked how he made her mother happy, but she wasn't used to a father figure lavishing so much attention on her. It made her uncomfortable.

"That's true," Fiona said, and assented to the idea of the interview, to end this particular branch of the conversation.

"I have something to tell you," Amy announced on the last night before Fiona left for Paris. "Well, *we* have something to tell you, actually."

Fiona stuffed a forkful of salad into her mouth.

"What's that?" she said, mouth full.

Amy took Ed's hand.

"We're moving in together."

Fiona swallowed her food.

"Oh," she said. "That's exciting."

Both Amy and Ed were looking at Fiona with big, glassy eyes. She took a swig of her white wine.

"Don't you think the house is kind of big for the two of you?" she asked.

"I'm selling the house, honey," Amy said, still clutching Ed's hand. "I'm moving into Ed's condo."

Fiona put her wineglass down.

"There's a spare bedroom," Amy spoke fast, "so you can stay as much as you want. I promise there will always be somewhere for you to come home to."

"I thought Ed stayed here all the time."

"Actually," Ed said, "your mom and I usually stay at my place, because it's a closer commute for me to get into the city. But when you and Liam are around, of course we stay here."

"Well." Fiona lifted her glass of wine for a cheers. "Congrats, then."

Amy's mouth was pursed. Perhaps she'd been expecting Fiona to make a scene. What could Fiona say? The house was of no use anymore. She wasn't so sentimental as to not understand that.

Amy and Ed looked at each other, and then raised their glasses as well.

"Thank you, sweetheart." Amy smiled.

The three of them clinked their glasses.

"To new beginnings," Ed said.

Fiona drained the last of her wine, and then cleared her plate.

"I gotta pack," she said, even though she knew Amy had seen the suitcases, and was fully aware that she'd never unpacked them in the first place.

Upstairs, Fiona plopped onto her bed, took out her laptop, and logged on to Facebook. She had a friend request from Sophie from her workshop this past semester, the one who had written the bad short story about Paris.

She accepted the request, and then a list of People You May Know popped up. The first name, she was surprised to see, was Oliver Ash.

"You have two mutual friends," said the smaller print beneath his name.

She clicked on his profile. It was sparse, at least if you weren't Facebook friends with him. The profile picture was of him with a toddler in his lap. Oliver Ash was looking at the camera, not quite smiling, but contented. The boy was looking up at him in wonder.

She clicked on the list of his Facebook friends, and saw that their two mutual friends were Professor Roiphe, and now Sophie. If he'd accepted Sophie's friend request once the class had ended, surely he would accept Fiona's. And after all, she was friends with Roiphe, too. She clicked the Request Friend button and watched it change instantly to Friend Request Pending.

PART THREE

20.

Fiona was reading *A Moveable Feast* on the plane; it was the quintessential Paris book, so everyone said. She was mostly unimpressed so far by the way Hemingway wrote, sparse and without sentimentality. What was so wrong with verbosity, with lyricism and description? With talking about your feelings? Hemingway seemed to be allergic to it. Occasionally, beautiful sentences sprang out—like, "When spring came, even the false spring, there were no problems except where to be happiest"—and she kept reading to find more of those. Liv, on the other hand, was reading Duras, *The Ravishing of Lol Stein,* in the original French. She hadn't turned the page in at least five minutes.

They were supposed to sleep soon; they were flying into morning. Fiona still felt like a kid when she flew, amazed that she was sitting in a long skinny tube cutting through the stratosphere, crossing over the Atlantic, thirty thousand feet above it. She watched two rom-coms in a row, and drank the free wine, and didn't even bother closing her eyes.

....

In the Paris morning, Fiona was bleary-eyed and slightly nauseated when the cab took them to Liv's aunt's apartment in the Marais. For a long while it was gray highway billboards, no different from any other city besides the billboards being in French. Every airport she'd been to felt more or less the same, an underwhelming entrance to your destination. It was usually outside of the city, and it took a long while for the place to take on its own identity.

In the outskirts of the city, there were whitewashed apartment buildings with graffiti on their sides and men in green boilersuits picking up trash from the sidewalks with long poles, depositing it into matching green bags. It was a Monday morning: young people walking toward the Métro, Arab men stacking fruit in crates outside produce shops, old ladies leaving boulangeries with baguettes in their arms.

"Look." Liv pointed, and out the opposite window, Fiona could see Sacré-Coeur on a hill, the white basilica with its trio of spires.

"This is the eighteenth," Liv announced, though Fiona didn't know the significance of the arrondissement numbers.

Soon the road turned narrower and the buildings prettier—older limestone houses with large wooden double doors, the tops to the entrances rounded and ornamented with sculpted faces that looked like cherubs or Greek goddesses. Flowers in window boxes decorated the balconies protected by wrought-iron railings. This was the Paris she vaguely remembered and had been hoping to return to: roads so narrow that a taxicab could barely pass through; cafés on the corners, with red awnings covering glossy wicker seats that faced out toward the sidewalks; dark-haired women in big scarves and with cleanly scrubbed faces, walking with purpose, not seeming to notice anyone around them, the women like themselves who they passed, unimpressed by the centuries-old streets where they lived. Were they going to work, all these beautiful women? What did it feel like to be one of them, surrounded by other women like you, so content and confident with your beauty that it was almost boring?

They passed the Pompidou, the monstrous modern art museum with bright blue and green and red tubes on the outside.

"We're almost there," Liv said.

She told the taxi driver where to pull over, and he deposited their suitcases on the narrow sidewalk outside of an ornate red door with a brass knob in the center. The air was dry and warm and smelled like dish soap. After paying the driver, Liv typed a code into a modern touchpad; the door clicked open, slamming loudly behind them as they made their way through a courtyard and into another building, where Liv typed in another code. They ascended marble steps, their heavy suitcases banging behind them on the stairs as they climbed, and finally landed at the third floor, where Liv stopped, retrieved an antique-looking key from under the mat, and turned the lock.

Insane, the kind of money Liv's people had. A foyer with a brass coat hanger and a velvet fainting couch, a huge abstract painting on the wall behind it. Then the living room—an expensive-looking midcentury couch, facing velvet upholstered chairs that matched the chaise in the foyer; a white marble coffee table and side tables, crown moldings on the pristine white ceiling, a chandelier hanging from the center of it. French windows that opened directly onto Rue Vieille du Temple. A kitchen with sleek appliances, black granite countertops. All of the rooms decorated with art, the cost of which Fiona could only hazard a guess: gigantic Cubist nudes, lit-up neon shapes that were plugged into the walls. There were two bedrooms: the master and the guest room.

"You can sleep with me in the king if you want," Liv said, dropping her own suitcase on the tufted bench at the foot of the four-poster bed. "Or in the guest room, if you want your own space. Up to you."

Fiona wandered into the extra bedroom and found a queen-sized bed covered with a thick comforter, fluffy and white. A huge modernist painting, reminiscent of Rothko, hung on the wall opposite the bed. A dark chestnut midcentury dresser in the corner. Minimalist heaven.

She flopped onto the bed, exhaled.

"I'll stay here," she called out to Liv, and rested her head on a down pillow, just for a minute.

She awoke to the sound of the heavy front door closing.

"Fiona?" Liv called from the foyer. "Are you up?"

Fiona lay on the bed for a moment, feeling the mattress, warm beneath her, her head swimming in that mélange of heaviness and guilt that can only come from sleeping for a long time in the middle of the day. She strained to open her eyes, looked at the clock on the nightstand. Three P.M. They had arrived at the apartment at 9:30 in the morning.

Fiona groaned. Liv appeared in the room, made up, hair down and shiny. She had changed into a simple A-line dress and was carrying a matte shopping bag with the word "Chanel" embossed on it.

Liv reached her hand toward Fiona, and brushed the matted hair away from her forehead.

"Why did you let me sleep?" Fiona asked.

"I tried to wake you up. You practically clocked me in the face."

"I don't remember that."

Liv shrugged. "You know how you are when you need your sleep."

"Now my internal clock is going to be all fucked-up."

"I don't know what to tell you. You should have slept on the plane."

"I couldn't," Fiona said, sitting up in the bed. "What did you do? What did you buy?"

Liv reached down into the Chanel bag. "My mom gave me a shopping budget. I'm trying not to blow it on the first day, but I couldn't resist these." She opened a shoe box and showed Fiona a pair of quilted black flats with interlocking gold Cs on the toe. They were nice, nothing special. Liv had clearly bought them so she could say that she'd bought a pair of Chanel shoes in Paris.

"Cute," said Fiona, yawning.

"And then I went to the Pompidou, because it's like five minutes away. I hope you don't mind that I went without you? I figured I would stay local, in case you woke up. There's an amazing Kandinsky exhibit. I'll go back with you."

"Okay," Fiona said.

Liv grabbed Fiona's hands. "Time to get up! We're in Paris!"

They sat at a table in a square somewhere, smoking the Camel Blues Liv had bought. They ordered their kir royales in French, but of course they were tourists—only tourists drank kir royales, especially at four P.M. on a Monday. If they had been Parisians they would have ordered beers and rolled their own cigarettes. If they had been Parisians they would have been at work.

This did not deter them from pretending, imagining even, with great detail and clarity, that this was what life would be like if they lived here.

"This is the dream," Liv said, leaning back after the first exhale of a freshly lit cigarette. Fiona nodded in assent. It was seventy-five degrees outside, mostly sunny, and they had nowhere else to be. A moped sped along the narrow street beside them. At the next table, an older British couple were consulting a map.

"I wish I could get paid for it," Fiona said.

The waiter brought their drinks. Liv clinked her glass against Fiona's.

"*Santé,*" she said, and they sipped. It tasted like vacation.

Liv took a cleansing breath through her nose. "Helen would have liked this, huh?" she said, a wistfulness to her voice.

"I guess," Fiona said.

"I wonder what she would have been like," Liv said. Liv had never even met Helen. She only knew about her from what Fiona had told her. What did it matter to her what Helen would or would not have become? The whole notion of coming here because Helen would have liked it, because Helen deserved it, felt so forced, yet Fiona had gone along with it. Sometimes it just felt easier to give in to the platitudes than to fight them.

For dinner that night, they ate foie gras and chèvre toasts and côte de boeuf so tender it dissolved in their mouths. They split a bottle of Côtes du Rhône and reached across the table to each other's plates, stealing bites, groaning with pleasure at the buttery flakiness of a thinly sliced fried potato, the torched top layer of a crème brûlée. They flirted with their waiter in French.

In the morning, Fiona suggested they walk across the Seine to Shakespeare and Company.

"Why?" Liv asked. "It's not like we can't get English books at home."

"We haven't been to the Left Bank yet. We could walk."

"The Rive Gauche is for tourists and old people," Liv said. "All the young people live on the Rive Droite."

"Who cares?" Fiona said.

"You can go if you want," Liv said. "I'm going to check out some of the galleries around here. Apparently there's an amazing one with some up-and-coming French artists in the Place des Vosges."

So they did split up, and Fiona got lost among the labyrinthine side streets in the Marais as she wound her way toward the Seine. She didn't mind not knowing exactly where she was; this was an attribute she had inherited from her mother, who liked getting lost. It drove her father crazy that Amy enjoyed these more ad hoc moments of family road trips, as she tried to dissuade him from asking for directions ("We'll figure it out eventually," was her stance, whether outside of Acadia National Park in Maine or in a small town in Virginia on their way to the Outer Banks). Getting lost was the best way to get to know a place, Amy reasoned, but they never stayed lost for long; Fiona's father always wanted to know exactly where he was, and he would pull over onto the side of the road and get out one of the many maps stashed in the glove box and study it with complete concentration until he had his bearings again. It took Fiona until her teenage years to realize how little sway Amy held in their family.

She turned from street to charming street, looking up at the balconies too narrow for any person to stand on, only an inch or two of concrete in front of the French doors, some with vines tangled around the wrought iron. Nineteenth-century streetlights jutted from the old apartment buildings, and the sidewalks were so narrow, too, that Fiona had to turn her body sideways or walk into the street whenever a person passed. Eventually she found her way to the Rue des Rosiers, a wider, two-way expanse, busier, with Parisians waiting at bus stops, and *tabacs* and stylish boutiques lining the streets. Tall, spindly trees shadowed her as she walked, their yellow-green leaves dotting the horizon. She wished she was the kind of person who knew how to identify trees.

And then, to her right, was the Seine. It was more majestic than she'd remembered it from when she was fourteen; in fact, she hardly remembered it. She'd been so focused on the antiquity and foreignness of it all then that she hadn't had the capacity to register the city's beauty. She crossed a bridge with all the other tourists, stopping, like them, to take pictures of Notre Dame, on its own little island, to her right.

On the other side of the river, she found the narrow street with the bookstore. The green chalkboard set up outside of Shakespeare and Company read:

PARIS BOOKSELLER LOOKING FOR OUTDOOR GIRL TO
BUILD CABIN IN NORTH WOODS. IF SHE WILL COOK
HIM TROUT FOR BREAKFAST EVERY MORNING HE
WILL TELL HER DOG STORIES EVERY NIGHT.

Upon entry, she found a whole section on a shelf with above it the sign "Lost Generation Writers." Several different editions of *A Moveable Feast*. Novels by Fitzgerald, Stein, Pound. It was by far the busiest section in the store, with what appeared to be mostly Americans swarming around it.

"You know, I read that Gertrude was actually really shitty

to Alice," one girl with a pixie cut, around Fiona's age, said to her friend as she paged through a copy of *The Autobiography of Alice B. Toklas.*

Fiona walked past them, past the hardcovers laid out on a table in the new fiction section, and up the creaking wooden stairs, where she encountered, painted on one of the rafters: "Be not inhospitable to strangers lest they be angels in disguise." She browsed the spines in the poetry section. She wasn't well versed in poetry. She pulled out a collection of Sylvia Plath, another writer she'd always meant to read but never had, opened to a poem called "The Babysitters," read the first stanza, and paused at these lines:

That summer we wore black glasses to hide our eyes.
We were always crying, in our spare rooms, little put-upon
    sisters

She found a little desk, in the borrowed-books room, and sat behind it, hidden away from shoppers. There was a typewriter in there, and little notes people had typed out and posted on the corkboard above her head.

Fiona descended the winding staircase and picked out four postcards toward the front of the store: for her mother, Liam, Marley, and Lula. At the register, two employees—an American guy and a British girl—were chatting about the girl's love life.

Fiona handed the guy the Plath poems.

"Would you like a stamp?" he asked.

She did, in fact, need stamps, to send the postcards.

"Actually, yes. How much are they?"

He lifted the rubber stamper in his hand. "Stamp. For the book."

"Oh," she said, embarrassed. "Sure."

He dipped it into the ink, stamped the inside cover of the Plath, then took her credit card.

"Do you want to pay in dollars or euros?"

"Um. Dollars, I guess."

While they waited for her debit card to process, she asked, to make polite conversation, "Where in the States are you from?"

"California," he said, not reciprocating the question. He gave back her card. "You're all set."

With her book, she sat outside at a café on the Boulevard Saint-Germain. The waiter came by. She ordered a croque monsieur, in French.

"Okay, sure," he responded, in English.

She opened the Plath. The stamp inside was a bust of Shakespeare's face, and the words "Shakespeare and Co., Paris, Kilometer Zero" in a circle around it. Liv was right; why, indeed, buy an English book in Paris? Wasn't that really the most American thing to do—flock to the one place in a foreign city where you could find people like yourself, and books you could buy at home?

She turned to the first page of the poems. Her croque monsieur came. All around her she heard American English, a group of four girls her age a couple of tables away.

"I'm so thirsty. I'm so tired of having to *buy* bottled water everywhere."

"What you pay for in water you make up for in the wine. Wine is cheaper than water here."

"My friend who studied here was telling me that if you spend more than, like, four euros on a bottle then that's a splurge."

"Can you imagine?"

She bit down on her croque monsieur. It was salty and hot, and her stomach groaned in approval. She washed down bites with her wine and got greasy fingers on her new book as she turned through the poems. So many were depressing and dark, hard to follow. Full of morbid images, because this, she recalled now, was what Plath was known for.

Flies filing in through a dead skate's eyehole.

Daddy, I have had to kill you.

Who buys Sylvia Plath poems on vacation?

She found "The Babysitters" again and read it in full. It was the one poem in the book she liked, about sisters who had once been close but grew apart.

O what has come over us, my sister!
On that day-off the two of us cried so hard to get
We lifted a sugared ham and a pineapple from the
     grownups' icebox
And rented an old green boat. I rowed. You read
Aloud, crosslegged on the stern seat, from the Generation
     of Vipers.
So we bobbed out to the island. It was deserted—
A gallery of creaking porches and still interiors,
Stopped and awful as a photograph of somebody laughing,
But ten years dead.

The bold gulls dove as if they owned it all.
We picked up sticks of driftwood and beat them off,
Then stepped down the steep beach shelf and into the water.
We kicked and talked. The thick salt kept us up.

I see us floating there yet, inseparable—two cork dolls.
What keyhole have we slipped through, what door has shut?
The shadows of the grasses inched round like hands of a clock,
And from our opposite continents we wave and call.
Everything has happened.

Growing up, Fiona observed the ways other sisters interacted
with each other and wondered what she had missed. She had
cousins, Beatrice and Zelda, the big-eyed, dark-haired daugh-
ters of Amy's artist brother, who flanked Fiona in age. They
were quiet, witchy girls, forever whispering to each other,
speaking in what sounded like tongues, a language the sisters
had invented for themselves. When Fiona was a child, with
Liam ringleader of the boy cousins and Helen not yet born, she
found herself the third wheel to Beatrice and Zelda at family
parties, following behind her cousins as they ran through the
woods behind their grandmother's large property in Connecti-
cut, traversing the trails hand in hand while Fiona pretended
not to feel left out. Once, playing a game of hide-and-seek,
five-year-old Fiona crouched behind a pine tree for half an
hour before she came to the realization that Beatrice and Zelda
were never planning to look for her. She peed herself in fright,
pants soaked and face tear-streaked by the time she was re-
united with her very pregnant mother.

When Helen was born, Fiona was optimistic at first: they
could become like Beatrice and Zelda one day, with a secret
language of their own. But, as a baby, Helen wanted nothing
to do with Fiona; Fiona's holding her or patting her head only
made Helen cry harder. Once Helen began to walk and talk,
she became unnerved by Fiona's presence, often toddling away
in the opposite direction whenever Fiona approached her; she

knew how a mother and father and big brother could serve her needs, but Fiona, too old to be a playmate and too young to be a caregiver, was of no use whatsoever. Fiona was awkward with Helen and sensitive to her indifference, which Helen seemed to be able to smell on her; the harder Fiona tried to impress her little sister, the silly faces and the overly affection-ate squeezes ("Too tight!" Amy would warn, loosening Fiona's well-intentioned grip around Helen's neck), the less Helen wanted to do with her.

No one seemed to feel bad for Fiona for being in this pre-dicament; Helen's every action was, to her parents and to Liam, precious and warranted. Fiona had no choice but to begin hating her.

As Helen got older, Fiona had little flashes of hope for their relationship: *Once she starts going to school,* Fiona would think, *we'll become friends.* Helen made friends at school in-stantly, though; she didn't need an extra one. By middle school, Fiona gave up trying, and the chasm between them cemented over. By that last summer at camp, they barely spoke except in situations of absolute necessity. They were all but strangers to each other when Helen died.

Fiona actually had no idea if Helen had even cared about taking a trip to Paris. She'd never asked.

Over the next three days, Fiona tried everything to get Liv to spend time with her exploring the city. She suggested the Louvre and the Orangerie and the gardens. She suggested a day trip to Giverny.

"Giverny in May?" Liv responded. "It'll be crawling with tourists."

Liv was only interested in the things that she thought real

Parisians did, which was to say: Not see any of the city, really. Sit outside cafés and smoke a million cigarettes and speak French, even to each other—which was absurd, frankly. Begin a three-course meal at nine-thirty at night. Go to niche galleries; shop at boutiques and spend hundreds of euros; meet other French people at bars, at concerts, and find a way to get invited back to their house parties.

Fiona wanted to go back to the Louvre. She wanted to stroll past the booksellers along the Seine, maybe walk down to the river with a picnic. She wanted to lie down in the Tuileries Garden with no plans. She wanted to stand in front of the *Water Lilies* in the Orangerie and cry. So what if these were things that Americans did? They were American girls.

And she wanted to do these things with her friend, not by herself. Because that outing to Shakespeare and Company had been too sad alone. So Fiona tagged along with Liv, because she preferred to be with someone, anyone, even if it meant doing things she didn't want to do.

Fiona also felt like she owed Liv time together in light of the breakup with Brandon. Even though Liv had not mentioned him once, Fiona got the sense that Liv's real feelings were percolating somewhere underneath her shiny, happy veneer. It couldn't have been easy, considering how serious they had been and their plan to move to New York together. Fiona and her roommates had been shocked by the news back in April, a couple of weeks before graduation, but Liv had refused to talk about it. They didn't know why it had happened, or even who broke up with whom.

Liv didn't like talking about her problems. She only liked talking about other people's problems.

On day four, sitting outside a café with Liv, who was smoking something like her tenth cigarette that day, Fiona read in *A*

Moveable Feast: "Never . . . go on trips with anyone you do not love."

After another overpriced dinner, the two girls went to a bar in the Latin Quarter. (Liv had consented to go to the Left Bank for this particular bar, which she'd read about in some list online.) It was packed with French college students.

Liv ordered them both glasses of champagne. She handed her card to the bartender.

"Cash only," he said to her.

"Shit," she said. "Fiona? Do you have euros? I'm out."

Fiona reached into her purse, put a twenty on the bar. "That's all I have left," she said to Liv.

"That's okay," Liv said. "We'll find some gentlemen to buy us the next round."

Fiona saw then, across the crowded bar, a face that looked familiar to her. At first she could not place it—it was easily transferrable, handsome but Waspy, plain, almost suspiciously blank. The man was tall and tanned and speaking to a captive audience of two young men his age. She figured she could not know him, because who did she know who was Parisian?

"Oh my God," Liv said then, her mouth next to Fiona's ear.

So she did know him. Maybe he was famous.

"He's someone, right?"

"That's . . ." She looked at Fiona, waiting for her friend to fill in the name. "You don't know?"

"I can't place him."

"It's Gabriel Benoit." She said his name in a hushed tone.

Suddenly the memories rearranged themselves around her, and she was taken back to that drunken night in the fall, nearly a year earlier. Waking up parched in the middle of the night, desperately groping for water. Him waking up, too, holding her captive when all she wanted was a drink of water. The next day she'd felt prideful, but something had been off. Liv had warned her about him, and Fiona hadn't wanted to admit that Liv was right, so she had secreted the memories away. The pain of his fingers inside her. His limp dick, no condom on it. Rasping, "Stop," the scratch of the word against her dry throat. His hand gripped tightly around hers, forced tightly around him, while she stared at the ceiling. She looked at him now, at his smarmy grin. It made her queasy.

"He's French?" Fiona managed to say.

"One of his parents is," Liv said. "I forget which one," she added, as if that mattered. "We should talk to him, right?"

"I'm not sure he'll remember me."

"Really? How did you guys leave things?"

Here's how he had left Fiona, anyway: feeling dirty and base. For drinking too much; for sleeping over; for not quite being able to tell him what she wanted, or didn't want; for being cripplingly hungover the next day; for hoping, even after all of that, that he'd text or call. Because if he called, it would prove her wrong, and the night, in retrospect, wouldn't be as bad as she'd thought it was. She had not told Liv this at the time, and she certainly couldn't tell her now, here in this bar, on their Parisian vacation.

So she said, instead, "I don't really remember," and shrugged. "Nothing really came of it."

"No harm in saying hi then, right?" Liv asked.

"Don't you hate him, though? What happened to him being bad news?"

"I don't know. You slept with him and said he was fine, right? Besides, maybe his friends are cool."

There it was: the way that Liv's priorities bent to her own

needs. Then, she could play at being responsible, like she was looking out for Fiona; Fiona realized now, in this Parisian bar, that it had only been an act back in the fall, only a way for Liv to assert her power over Fiona: maybe a way to get her kicks, or maybe an expression of her own jealousy of Fiona being single, of Fiona having the choice to sleep with whomever she wanted. But had it been a choice, even? Wasn't it the illusion of choice? Hadn't Fiona gone home with Gabriel *precisely* because Liv had told her not to?

Before Fiona could respond, Liv was walking across the room and approaching the men. Fiona could see from the way Liv's mouth moved that she was speaking to them in French, and then, by their mouths, that they responded to her in English.

She turned and beckoned Fiona over to her. Slowly, Fiona made her way through the crowded bar.

"Hi," she said to all of them, and the three men looked at her, appraising. She was wearing tight jeans and a tank top with no bra, and she regretted it; she could feel the men's eyes on her nipples. Each of them gave her *bises* and said his name as he did so. When she got to Gabriel, he kissed her on the cheeks and introduced himself no differently than the other men had.

"Fiona," she said back, a bit stunned. The moment passed in which she might have asserted herself, said something to the effect of "You don't remember me?" But she had not acted fast enough, and now she had to pretend that she was meeting Gabriel for the first time.

"You go to Buchanan, too?" he said to her.

"Yeah," she said. Liv looked at Fiona, confused, her mouth parted as if she were about to interject and clear things up herself, but Fiona shook her head once, and Liv closed her mouth.

"What are you girls doing in Paris?" one of the Frenchmen asked. He was smirking, with a dark five o'clock shadow. He said "girls" like "gahhuls," the back of his throat sticking on the nonexistent "h." And he also said "gahhuls" with disdain, as if by virtue of being young women they were miniature, insignificant, and squashable beneath his large French feet.

"Vacationing," Liv said, as if vacationing was a thing she did all the time, like studying or going to work.

"See anything good so far?" the other Frenchman asked. He was more handsome, with freckles and full lips.

"Well, we've both been here before," Liv was quick to say. "It's mostly been a lot of shopping and relaxing."

"She saw the Kandinsky retrospective at the Pompidou," Fiona said.

"I saw that, too," the handsome Frenchman said. "I didn't love it."

"Yeah, it was okay," Liv said, even though she'd told Fiona that she'd adored it. "A little bit, I don't know, reductive. Not as all-encompassing of his career as I would have liked."

"Those were my thoughts exactly," he said.

Now Fiona could tell Gabriel was looking at her as if he was trying to place her.

"We've met at Buchanan, right? Did we have a class together?"

Now was her chance. Now she could say to him: *Yeah, you stuck your limp, unprotected dick inside of me. Don't you remember me telling you to stop? Or is that so commonplace for you that I wouldn't stand out from the others? If I called you an assaulter, or even a rapist, would you be genuinely confused?*

Instead, Fiona said, "No, I don't think we did." Because, what if he denied it? What if she seemed crazy? She was just tired. Of this trip. Of this city. She didn't feel like expending her remaining energy on him. It seemed too hard.

"How do you guys know each other?" Fiona asked Gabriel and the smirking one, to change the subject.

"Boarding school," the smirking one said. "In Switzerland."

Of course Gabriel had gone to boarding school in Switzerland. Why come to Buchanan, then? Why not Harvard or Yale or the like? He was a bad student, probably. Fiona could imagine him getting caught snorting coke off the desk in his dorm room.

For several more minutes, Fiona engaged in painful conversation with Gabriel and the smirking friend, in which they discussed their boarding school exploits ad nauseam—the girls they fucked, the drugs they did, the crazy places on and off campus in which they partook in both sets of activities. She noticed Liv and the cute guy walking away and then returning with fresh drinks, just for the two of them.

At a natural pause in the conversation, Fiona excused herself, and walked over to Liv. She tapped her friend, who was speaking very closely to the cute Frenchman, on the shoulder.

Liv turned her head.

"Oh, hey," she said, surprised, as if she didn't know anyone else in the bar who might talk to her.

"I think I'm gonna head home," Fiona said.

"Really?" She turned. "You're not having a good time?"

Fiona looked at the French guy, then blocked her body away from him.

"I just don't really love these guys."

"What are you talking about? They're fun!"

"Gabriel doesn't even remember me," Fiona whispered.

"To be fair, you hardly remembered him."

"I'm gonna go," Fiona said. "You stay."

"Come on," Liv whined. "We're in Paris." Fiona was so fucking tired of being reminded by Liv that they were in Paris.

"You don't need me to be your wingman. You know how to get home."

"I don't *need* you," Liv said, looking a little stung. "But I *want* you to stay. Because you're my friend."

"Well, you're not talking to me, so I don't see what the difference is."

Liv took a step backward. "Just go, then. I'll see you tomorrow."

Fiona walked home in the dark night, back over the Seine and now through the Île Saint-Louis, the quaint little island between the Left and Right Banks. All the store windows were shuttered; a few diners sat lingering over their late meals at outdoor cafés, but it was nearly midnight, and most of the restaurants had stopped serving food by now. She passed a brown, shuttered storefront that read "Berthillon" in gold medieval-looking lettering, and remembered, with a start, lining up around the block with her mother for an ice cream cone on the first day of their trip. "This is the best ice cream in Paris," her mother had assured her, and when their turn came, her mother ordered a pistachio cone for herself, and Fiona, stracciatella. Fiona didn't remember what the ice cream tasted like, but she did remember her awe as her mother ordered the ice cream in French. Amy's French came out garbled and slow, like she had stones in her mouth—she hadn't spoken it since her semester abroad in Paris, a decade and a half earlier—but hearing her mother speak in another language was the first time Fiona had considered Amy's life before Fiona's own existence. It was the first time she saw Amy as a person with a past without children, as a college girl exploring her first foreign city, flirting with Frenchmen, untethered to any kind of family or responsibilities. She was amazed that the ice cream vendor understood Amy's French and handed over the counter the exact two cones she had ordered: one white and speckled with brown, one a pale green.

The next morning, a Friday, Fiona awoke to the heavy door closing. It was going to be a hot day; she had broken into a sweat in her sleep. Not wanting to talk to Liv, she feigned sleep as she heard Liv walk past her own bedroom, slow her footsteps then knock on Fiona's door.

Fiona didn't say anything, and Liv opened the door anyway.

"Hey," Liv said, and Fiona pretended to wake up, though it was obvious, she knew, that she was faking it. Liv was in her outfit from last night: a satin sheath and the new Chanel flats.

"Hey," Liv said again.

"How was last night?"

"It was fun," Liv said.

"Did you spend the night at what's-his-face's?"

Liv made a face—pursed lips, rolled eyes. "If you're going to judge me then we don't need to have this conversation."

"I just asked an innocent question."

"It wasn't that innocent."

"What?" Fiona said. "Jesus. You are impossible."

"*I'm* impossible?"

"Yeah, you are," Fiona said. "Why did you even want me to come on this trip with you?"

Liv stepped farther into the bedroom. "Are you serious?"

"We've only been doing things you want to do, and nothing I want to do," Fiona said, sitting up straighter in the bed.

"That's not true," Liv said. "We're sharing this experience together. And I thought it meant something to you."

"You *forced* it to mean something to me. I am not just your friend with the dead sister. I am trying to move *past* that, not toward it."

"Well, you certainly don't seem to be doing a lot in that regard."

"Fuck you."

"Excuse me?"

"I said—"

"No, fuck *you,* Fiona. You've been miserable this entire trip. You do nothing but complain. You only want to do touristy shit. I didn't force you to come, and I certainly did not use your sister as a ploy to get you here. What kind of fucked-up person do you think I am? You chose to come here, too."

"Can I tell you something about Gabriel Benoit?"

"Here we go."

"I'm being serious."

Liv took a deep, labored breath. "What."

"I was drunk. But I remember I didn't want it. I know that."

Liv looked as if Fiona had just struck her across the face.

"I hadn't thought about it all year," Fiona continued. "But seeing him last night, it came back."

"Okay," Liv said slowly. "Once you say this, you can't take it back."

"What do you mean?"

"I mean . . ." She was clearly trying to figure out how to say this delicately. "Are you sure? Don't you think, the last few years, you and guys and alcohol, they haven't been the best combination? Sometimes when you're drunk, you come up with alternative histories. You fill in the blanks."

"You were the one who told me he was bad news."

"He definitely has a past, but . . ." She trailed off. "You didn't remember him, Fiona."

"So I'm different than the girl he *actually* raped, huh? The one he got suspended over?"

"I didn't say that."

"You don't believe me because you think I'm just as much bad news as he is. You think I wanted it. Or was too drunk to know any better."

"I never said that. It seems like there's a lot of gray area."

"Gray area," Fiona said. "That's rich." She got up from the bed and started emptying the drawers. "Listen. I'm gonna go."

"Where?"

"I have another place I can stay."

"Hold on. We're just talking."

"I guess I don't really feel like talking, then."

"Where are you going?"

"I'd rather not say." She didn't know, actually, but she wasn't going to let Liv in on that.

"Please don't do this." Liv's eyes were beginning to fill with tears.

How had Fiona not seen it until now, how much she fulfilled for Liv, and how little she got in return? Liv needed to be better than everyone she came into contact with; she loved having a mess of a friend like Fiona because she could be constantly reminded of how intact her life was in comparison. She never had to take into account her own shortcomings if she was too busy counting Fiona's. It didn't fit into this narrative, then, that Fiona might have been a victim of someone *else*'s wrongdoing. Everything had to be Fiona's fault, or else Liv's worldview would crumble.

"I guess you only have yourself to worry about now," Fiona said to her friend, not without pity, and zipped up her suitcase.

21.

SIMONE GOT THE call from Alex on Friday morning: Danièle's water had broken, five weeks early.

Henri and Oliver were on the floor in the living room, playing with the truck that Oliver had brought back for Henri from America—one of the many toys he'd brought back. Simone had been halfheartedly reading a novel on the couch, but she wasn't paying much attention to it—she kept getting distracted by Oliver and Henri, how obviously delighted Henri was to have his father back, how utterly attentive Oliver was to his son.

Simone and Oliver, though, had been fighting. They were moving back to Paris in a little over a week: their lease in Berlin was up on June 1, and their subletters in Paris would be leaving then, their apartment free again. Oliver was less than excited about the move. He wanted to stay another year in Berlin: his new book took place there, and he needed time to do research. The city was cheaper than Paris, he reasoned. No one was moving into the Berlin apartment after them, and they could easily re-sign the lease for another year.

For Simone, Paris was nonnegotiable. Her research project had been a complete bust, and she had to return home. She'd ended up mining one Polish woman's letters for interesting if not very elucidating correspondence between her, at Ravensbrück, and her sister, who was forced into sexual slavery at one of the *Sonderbauten*. Neither woman had survived.

Simone had spent months trying to find more on the woman at the *Sonderbau* but came up short; there was barely enough for an article, let alone a book-length project. She'd yet to tell Oliver or the museum any of this; she was so ashamed that she had convinced them of the import and viability of this project when there was nothing there.

So she would return to her regular teaching job in the fall. She might have to give back the fellowship money; she didn't know how they would handle her total failure. There was no way she was going to ask for an extension, and spend another year in that lonely office behind the stacks. There was no way she was going to put Henri through another year in that hellish school. They would return to France, where her family was.

"I just got here," he'd said in their kitchen in Berlin during his first week back. He was drying a serving bowl with a dish towel; they had just put Henri to bed. "I want a little more time in this city. I need to write, and I know I'll get the work done here."

"What do you want me to do about it? Our lease is up. Our Paris apartment is ready. Danièle is due in a month. This isn't the time."

"It wouldn't be so crazy to stay for the summer. What if we tried to extend the lease for two more months, until August? We'd still be back in time for school."

"And what about the baby?"

"What about me?"

"What about you?"

"I'm your husband."

"She's my sister."

"She has a husband. And your mother."

"I'm not having this conversation," Simone said. Just be-cause he didn't have siblings or living parents didn't mean that hers meant nothing. "This is my family we're talking about."

Oliver hung a dried saucepan on a hook above the sink.

"I thought we were your family," he said, appearing hurt.

"You are," she said. She wrapped her arms around his waist from behind him. "I had this vision of us all being together in Paris. Why can't that happen?"

He'd assented, but she knew he wasn't happy about it, knew that there were still some wheels turning, that he was still trying to come up with ways to stay in Berlin. Since that conversation, he'd grown sour—withdrawn, moody, quiet. More than once in the week since, Simone had asked him what was the matter, but he only said that he was tired. He still wasn't interested in sex, even though they hadn't seen each other since the winter.

She wasn't without guilt; she could understand that Oliver was still jet-lagged, and had just gotten back after a year away, and probably wanted to stay in one place for a bit. But she couldn't help the current circumstances, even though he was treating her like she could.

Alex was flying back from London in an hour, Simone man-aged to piece together on the phone now, and their mother had already taken Danièle to the hospital, but Joséphine wouldn't be the best caretaker alone, in her late sixties and with a bad case of sciatica in both legs.

"Should I come?" Simone said.

"It's up to you," Alex said, his voice shaky.

"I'm getting on the next flight," Simone said. "She's going to be okay."

She hung up the phone, Oliver looking up in alarm. "What is it?"

"We have to go to Paris." Simone frantically opened her laptop to pull up the Ryanair website. "Her water broke."

He was doing calculations in his head. "How many weeks early?"

"Five."

He nodded. "She's going to be okay."

"You don't know that." Did he not remember how painful the loss of each baby was? She couldn't imagine how afraid Dani was right now, having grown that child for so much longer than Simone had during her unviable pregnancies. Danièle had felt the baby moving and kicking and eating. She was going to give birth; she was going through labor no matter what. Could Oliver not comprehend how gigantic this was? That there was nothing truer than this, someone at the precipice of living or dying, someone whom you'd grown inside of yourself, who belonged only to you?

"Five weeks is, I think, within the realm of mostly healthy deliveries."

She ignored him, clicked through the flights.

"There's one at noon." She checked her watch: ten A.M. They could make that easily. "Can you be ready in forty-five minutes?" she asked Oliver. "Henri, sweetie, can you go get your little suitcase from your closet?"

"Wait a minute," Oliver said.

She looked up from the computer. "What?"

"Do you think it's a good idea for him to go?" Oliver asked, his voice lowered.

"Who would he stay with?"

"Well maybe . . . maybe I would stay with him here."

"What?" The possibility seemed so remote that she had trouble comprehending it.

"What's the matter with Aunt Dani?" Henri asked, in a voice more curious than concerned.

"Henri, go get your suitcase," Simone told him.

The boy looked to his father for confirmation.

"Henri," she said again. Oliver nodded, and Henri went into his bedroom.

"I'm not sorry that my family is important to me," Simone said in a hiss, angry but not wanting Henri to hear her. "And it should be important to you, too. And to him. I want him to grow up in a family whose members care about one another."

"You know I'm concerned about your sister. But he's too young for all that. It could be traumatizing."

"We don't have time to fight. We have to go to Paris right now." She went into their bedroom to get her own suitcase out, and he followed.

"It's not a fight. I'm trying to reason with you."

"You can come or not come, but Henri and I are going."

He took a deep breath, like he needed all the strength he had left to endure her. She was so tired of feeling like she was difficult and needy. He treated her like everything she wanted was beyond what was appropriate. Too much. She wanted too much.

"Maybe it's best you go without me," he finally said.

She looked up at him, the duffel bag open and empty in her hands. "What?"

"You gave me a choice," he said, steeling himself. "And I'm choosing to stay here."

She suddenly felt a deep and unwavering hatred for the man standing in front of her. She did not understand how this could be what had become of the person she'd decided to be with, raise a child with, spend a life with. How did the man she'd once loved—or thought she had loved—turn into this? Or had he always been like this, and she had just never noticed?

"When did you become so cruel?" she asked him, her voice cracking a bit from the pain, the disbelief.

"I have to get out of this apartment," he said, and did.

—#—

The hospital room, with its shining linoleum floors and bad overhead lighting, was buzzing with nurses adjusting sonogram equipment, IVs, heart monitors. Danièle was lying in the hospital bed, head propped up on a pillow, sipping water through a straw. Alex was sitting at the edge of the bed, rubbing her feet, and Joséphine was arranging a bouquet of flowers in a vase on the windowsill.

"Sister," Danièle said, her smile calm and beatific. "Nephew."

Henri was scared, clutching Simone's leg.

"It's okay, sweetie," Dani said to him. "I'm okay."

Simone's eyes filled with tears as she pushed Dani's hair back from her sweaty forehead. She'd never seen her little sister in a hospital bed.

"I'm fine," Dani said, still smiling.

"She's on lorazepam," Alex told her.

"Is that allowed? For the baby? Is the baby okay?"

"She had to calm down. She wouldn't stop screaming."

"Henri, why don't you go with Bubbe," Simone suggested after kissing her mother and handing her a bag of toys. "Go play in the waiting room." After they had left the room, she turned to Alex, confused. "Is she having contractions? Is the baby okay?"

"Everyone's fine," Alex said, still rubbing his wife's feet.

Danièle didn't seem to hear them. She was looking out into the middle distance, her eyes fluttering. "Their heart rates are normal. She's not in labor. She wasn't dilated."

"Why would her water break if she's not in labor?" Simone asked.

"It's a premature rupture of the amniotic sac," Alex said. "Apparently it happens especially in high-risk mothers, because of the fertility treatments and her age."

"She's only thirty-five," Simone said.

Alex shrugged. "I guess that's considered old with babies." Simone felt slightly offended by this comment, even though she knew it was simply fact.

"So what now?"

"They want to keep her overnight and make sure she doesn't lose any more fluid and also monitor her for any signs of infection. She's on antibiotics and steroids."

"What are the steroids for?"

"They make the baby's lungs stronger. If she doesn't go into labor on her own in the next twenty-four hours, then they'll have to induce her. Most likely, they won't need to do that."

"She still has five weeks before her due date."

He shrugged. "The baby has other plans. Where's Oliver?"

"He couldn't make it."

Simone wondered, during this past year, if Oliver was worse than Alex for leaving for an entire year. Surely Oliver wouldn't have left if *Simone* were pregnant. Or would he have?

"That's too bad," Alex said, not seeming particularly bothered by the fact that Oliver wasn't there. He kept rubbing Danièle's feet, even though she had now dozed off and was breathing softly, asleep.

22.

Fiona checked into a boutique hotel in Saint-Germain-des-Prés that she'd found, in a hurry, on Yelp. She was determined to stay on the Left Bank in order to not run into Liv before she left. There was only one room left, and it cost over three hundred euros a night to book it so last-minute. She had two nights to go before her flight home. She paid for one night for now, figuring she'd decide in the morning what to do for the following night, and felt more than a twinge of guilt about spending more of her absent father's money as she signed the receipt.

She carried her heavy bag up the spiral marble staircase and turned the antique-looking key in the door. The room was tiny, but charming. The bed was covered in an embroidered white quilt, and above the headboard was an oval painting of some woman from centuries earlier, her skin fair and her cheeks blushed pink, the portrait framed in tarnished gold. There was a mirror in a similar gold frame on the opposite wall, and Fiona looked at herself in it. Her face was flushed from the heat, and her hair was matted against her forehead. She was wearing a blue-and-white-striped dress, no makeup. She was still buzzing with adrenaline and fury from walking out on Liv. She was surprised to see that she looked pretty.

The room was stifling, and she opened the doors to the balcony, which looked out onto a narrow side street. There was a boulangerie across the way, and an art gallery next to that, though they were both closed now. There were all sorts of things she could do by herself this weekend. The Musée d'Orsay was only a few blocks away, and she remembered loving that when she was fourteen. The Luxembourg Gardens were also close.

How, she wondered, would she deal with sitting next to Liv on the plane?

She opened her laptop and got onto the hotel's Wi-Fi network. She sorted through her junk emails and saw, after deleting them, a single email from her mom. She had replied to Fiona's last email, a short message checking in and saying she was having a great time. "Sounds wonderful," Amy had written back. "Be sure to get Berthillon for me. Call whenever you have a chance—I want to hear your voice." She thought about emailing Marley, telling her what had happened with Liv, but decided to save that until later, until she could write about it with a clearer head. And then there were two messages from Facebook. She was about to delete them when she noticed the name "Oliver Ash" in the message preview.

"Oliver Ash has accepted your friend request," read the first email.

She opened the second: "Oliver Ash has sent you a message." She hurriedly logged on to Facebook.

"How's Paris?" was all his message said.

It had been sent only an hour earlier, at 4:30 P.M.

She stared, bug-eyed, at the screen, squatting on the bed like a praying mantis. She felt that this could not be happening. Was this actually happening? This thing she had been fantasizing about all year? Her heart raced, and she felt sheer glee. She typed back right away, her fingers jumpy hitting the keys.

"Paris has its challenges," she wrote back. "And Berlin?"

She stood from the bed, paced around the small room. She took a pillow to her face and shrieked into it. She watched for a change on the screen; no change came. Although she was not much of a smoker, she wanted a cigarette. She left her laptop open and took her key and ten euros and walked to the *tabac* on the corner. There was a line of several Parisians, in their thirties, in expensive suits and dresses, buying their cigarettes before the *tabac* closed in ten minutes. When it was her turn, she ordered a pack of Camel Blues and the woman handed it to her without flinching. It never ceased to excite her that she could make herself understood in another language, even for a thing as minor as buying cigarettes. *"Et un briquet, s'il vous plaît,"* she added, pleased with herself for remembering the French word for "lighter."

She smoked outside the hotel, leaned up against the painted blue exterior. Smoking was supposed to calm one's nerves, though she supposed that only applied to people who were addicted. It made her more jittery. She couldn't finish the cigarette, so halfway through she stubbed it out and ran back upstairs to check her computer.

And, *voilà!* A new message had appeared below hers. She stood squinting at the bright screen, reading the message as fast as possible, then reading it again, and again.

Berlin also has its challenges. The transition at home hasn't been quite as smooth as I'd hoped.

"I'm sorry to hear that," she wrote back immediately, not bothering now to wait. He was at his computer, and so was she, and they were having a live conversation. "Transitions are hard."

OLIVER: Indeed, they are.
FIONA: how long have you been back now?
OLIVER: Two weeks or so. At least I'm not jet-lagged anymore.
FIONA: haha, yeah are you traveling or anything this summer?
OLIVER: Maybe to Paris. Don't think I'll overlap with you,
   though. Do you leave soon?

She was foggy headed from disbelief but struck with a sense of purpose so clear it felt compulsive. He was baiting her. Wasn't he? Was this allowed? Was this simply the kind of person he was, pouncing on his students the minute they left his class? Or had he been having issues in his marriage since he'd gotten back, and she was the first, easiest girl to flirt with? Was he fishing for some sort of temporary hit during some temporary marital problems?

Or was it her, and only her, that he wanted?

It suddenly all seemed so easy, so obvious, what she needed to do next. She had money left. She had time, no job, no responsibilities back home. Flights were easily changeable. And besides, if she came home from Berlin rather than Paris she wouldn't have to see Liv again. Maybe ever.

What was stopping her was some small voice in the back of her head that said: *This is dumb. Don't do this.* She had only two days left, after which she could go home and try to forget about this awful trip. She could tell her mother everything— and Marley, and Lula, they were still her friends—and get a summer job. Maybe it wasn't too late to get work at the *Post* through Ed's brother, but she could go back for her final semester and move forward with her life, leaving Liv and the promise of Oliver Ash in the past, where they were meant to stay.

And then there was a second, louder voice that said: *You could stay here another two days, exploring the city you felt alone in all week, or you can do what you've been wanting to do for a very long time.* And this voice was so loud, so insistent, that she felt she had no choice but to listen to it right away. She was losing time by the second and she had only now to seize on it. She pulled out her cellphone.

"Lula!" she texted. "More catching up later, but you have friends in Berlin, right?"

She watched the computer screen, desperate to respond to Oliver, worrying that he was sitting on the other side of the screen waiting for her answer, near to giving up. Maybe he'd already signed off and she'd lost her only chance. Her phone dinged, and she jumped at the sound. It was Lula texting her back.

Lula: miss you too, asshole ;) yeah, i do. why? you going?
Fiona: do you think you could put me in touch with them? do
    you think they'd let me stay with them for a few nights?
Lula: course.

Then Lula forwarded the number of Avi, one of her best friends from New York, who had graduated a year above her at their prep school.

Fiona went back to her Facebook messages. Oliver's question to her was still hanging there.

"I'm actually coming to Berlin this weekend!" she typed. "Visiting friends. Sort of last-minute." She went back, deleted the exclamation point, turned it into a period. Read it over

once more. Hit Enter. Waited. Thought of texting Avi, to introduce herself and check if it was okay to stay with him for a
night or two. Thought of looking at flights. Then decided it
was best to see what Oliver said first. He probably had weekend plans with his family. It was already Friday, after all.
Maybe he was going to say he was busy, and she would say,
"No big deal," and then she could go home and put this whole
Oliver Ash thing to rest, telling herself that at least she'd tried.
She was starting to get used to this idea, patting herself on the
back for asking, and already preparing for—and beginning to
welcome—his rejection, when his message appeared below
hers.

Wow, that's wild. Well, you'll have to let me buy you lunch.

Lunch?
Just lunch?
Was "lunch" lunch? Or was "lunch" a euphemism?
She supposed he couldn't exactly say over the Internet if he
wanted anything more than lunch. Berlin seemed worth visiting anyway. Didn't it?
In fact, she knew little about it. She knew of its reputation
as a young city, famous for its clubs and its artists and its grit.
She knew it was cheap. She knew you didn't really need to
know German to get by.
And she knew, looking at flights on Ryanair right now, that
it would cost only 76 euros to fly one-way from Paris to Berlin
at six the following morning.

23.

SIMONE STAYED AT the hospital for a few more hours. Alex didn't leave Danièle's side. In the waiting room, Henri complained that he was hungry. Simone realized she hadn't fed him since breakfast, and it was now early evening. She was, she decided swiftly, a terrible mother.

She said good night to Danièle, who was still fast asleep, got a key to the apartment from Alex, and took a cab back with Joséphine and Henri, Joséphine insisting she stay at Danièle's apartment with Simone and Henri.

"I won't be able to sleep anyway," she said.

At home, Simone fixed them all pasta with olive oil and dried herbs from Danièle and Alex's limited pantry—it was too late to go shopping, and she was too tired to make anything else. Henri fell asleep mid–pasta bowl, facedown on the dining room table.

She tucked him into his bed and watched him sleep, his chest rising and falling, his little lungs doing their work. Her one and only baby. If he came from a broken home, would he survive it?

She shut the door quietly; her mother was doing the dishes, the television tuned to Canal+ in the background, on mute. She thought about calling Oliver, but what was there to say?

Joséphine saw Simone coming into the kitchen. She dried her hands on a dish towel and took her daughter into a long hug. Simone began to cry. At first she was able to hide her sobs but soon they came out in violent, gasping jags.

"Oh, my love," Joséphine said. "I'm scared, too."

She pulled her head away from her mother's neck and wiped her eyes. "Are you okay here with Henri for a little while?"

Joséphine nodded.

24.

THE APARTMENT FELT so big, and Liv so small. Fiona had been gone for several hours now; it was becoming clearer with each passing minute that she wasn't coming back.

Liv thought about calling Paul, the guy from last night, then decided against it. The first person she'd slept with since Brandon, and though it was supposed to be fun and carefree—a rebound!—it had just felt sad. Paul's roommates had still been awake when they arrived at his apartment around one in the morning. The roommates were playing a video game, and rather than take Liv directly to his bedroom, Paul sat down with them. His roommates only briefly looked up and said hello to her, intent as they were on the screen in front of them. Paul offered Liv a beer, which she took to have something to hold while she sat on the stained corduroy couch and watched them play in silence, some shoot-'em-up game in a series of gray brick rooms where enemies hid in dark corners. Paul yelled advice at his roommates, called out in anguish when one of their characters got shot. One of them rolled and lit a spliff;

Paul partook, then remembered to pass it to Liv only as an af-
terthought. She knew, more or less, where she was—far, far
north of Aunt Lacy's apartment—but wasn't sure she could
find a cab at this time of night. They'd taken the Métro there,
Paul complaining the whole time about how Gabriel had made
them travel halfway across the city to see him. She didn't know
when the trains stopped running.

She had sensed that she was about to make a bad decision
by sleeping with Paul, that he had not earned it, had not done
anything to deserve sex with her. She supposed, as she tuned
out the hyper-fast, slang-ridden French the boys spoke to one
another, that she could be wrong. Sometimes bad decisions
turned out to surprise you, turned out to be rewarding, fun,
memorable. No matter how it went, this was a story she'd always be able to tell. Sleeping with a gorgeous Frenchman who
picked her up at a Parisian bar a month after her breakup with
Brandon, proof of the fact that she was over him, that she was
resilient, that she'd bounced back like a rubber ball.

In a few long gulps, she drained the beer she'd been holding,
then grabbed Paul's hand and told him to lead her to his bedroom. At least she would always have the power to be more
alluring than video games. She saw the hint of jealousy in his
less attractive roommates' eyes as they briefly glanced up at her
when she said good night.

It was, unsurprisingly, not good. He finished too fast, then
made a half-assed manual attempt on her that exhibited a
shocking lack of skill. Or perhaps it was fitting: the really
good-looking ones had to try even less than the average man
did. She told him it was fine, and he seemed relieved to be off
the hook, kissing her once and falling asleep on his back. She
laid her head on his chest, and he made a sort of satisfied stir-
ring noise. He wasn't anything, but she could, for the time that

she was awake and he was asleep, pretend that he was. It was
a warm body. It was something.

Now, in the windowsill of her aunt's empty apartment, she
drank a glass of Sancerre by herself, watching people move
along Rue Vieille du Temple—mostly tourists, mostly Asian,
eating falafel and snapping pictures of themselves. It made her
think of Paris syndrome, a phenomenon Kimiko swore that her
sister, Liv's aunt Ayumi, who fetishized Paris, had experienced
in full when she first traveled to the city back in the nineties:
she'd reportedly become paranoid that French policemen were
following her, and so physically ill—vomiting, becoming dehy-
drated, hallucinating—that she'd had to be hospitalized. The
physical manifestations seemed like bullshit to Liv, and she
doubted that Ayumi, who was prone to hyperbole, had actually suffered from the syndrome, considering how rare it was.
Still, she understood the psychology behind it: severe culture
shock at the discovery that the city was not as glamorous as it
was supposed to be. There were tourists, just as there were in
every city, and trash on the sidewalks, and neighborhoods that
got worse the farther you moved from the Seine, and plenty of
French people who did not look like they'd just stepped out of
an editorial spread.

Paris was not, she knew, what Fiona had hoped it would be,
either. Liv had only wanted them to have a good time, to forget
about their problems and the fact that their lives were about to
go in separate directions. Fiona didn't want that, it seemed. Liv
couldn't fix Fiona's problems by wishing them away, much as
she wanted to.

So let Fiona think that Liv was a grief vampire. Liv knew it
had never been about that. It was about the externalization of
pain, which she herself never learned how to do. Liv both ad-
mired and feared Fiona's ability to put all of her hurt on the

table. It fascinated her. Liv had always curbed her own pain: through hard work, through forgetting, through telling herself that everything was all right. Everything could be all right if you made it so. She really believed this.

The thing about Gabriel—Liv didn't know what to believe. She had warned Fiona about him back in the fall, but Fiona hadn't wanted to listen. So Liv had been right. But why wait a whole year to tell her what had happened? Because Fiona hadn't wanted to *admit* that Liv was right? That felt unnecessarily spiteful. Then again, who knew what she even remembered? She had been so drunk that night, which made the whole thing more complicated. Liv didn't know the line, that murky gray area, where consent started and ended. She found the talks the administration had given them during freshman orientation laughable. "No means no." But what about when no meant yes? What about when refusal could be sexy, when the fun lay in the gray area itself? Or, the reverse: what about when you allowed sex to happen, and it was terrible, and regrettable, as last night had been?

It was nine P.M. and the sun was still setting, the Paris sky a dusky gray-blue, the street lamps just turned on. Liv hadn't eaten dinner yet. She was craving a juicy, rare steak.

She drained her Sancerre, leaving the glass on the windowsill, and made her way down the stairs and toward the main drag of Rue Vieille du Temple. She walked down the street for a few blocks, looking for somewhere to eat. These nights, the weather had been perfect, with the slightest chill in the air. Soon she found a busy bistro on a corner, people drinking and smoking at outside tables, a tea-light candle on each one, and a chalkboard listing the evening's specials: *magret de canard, moules-frites, entrecôte bordelaise.*

She took a seat at an empty table outside, next to a woman who was also by herself, and ordered a martini from the server. She lit a cigarette while she waited for her drink. Smoking, these past few weeks, was the only thing that allowed her a deep and unwavering sense of calm. It was meditative, how she was able to focus on only the cigarette, its glowing orange tip when she sucked in, the ash that cumulated before she gracefully tapped it away. She exhaled, contented. She worried she was getting addicted.

The server brought her a rocks glass filled with ice, a rosy red drink inside and an orange rind floating on top. It wasn't what she had been expecting. She took a sip; it was overly sweet, and musty, what she imagined mothballs tasted like.

"*Excusez-moi,*" she said to the server, as politely as she could. "I asked for a martini."

"*Oui,*" he said. "This is a martini."

"Like with gin?" she tried. "And vermouth?" She did not know the French word for vermouth, so she said that in English, and he didn't understand it.

"You asked for a martini. This is a martini."

"Excuse me?" she heard the woman next to her say in English. Liv turned: she was one of those French women who looked glamorous without a hint of makeup. She had a long, elegantly defined nose, and she wore head-to-toe black linen, her dark curly hair cut into a blunt bob. The tables were only a whisper away from each other. "Are you American?"

"Yeah," Liv said.

"When you order a martini here, they bring you sweet vermouth. You have to order a *martini sec* for what you want."

"Oh." Liv looked into her glass, not wanting to drink what was in front of her and not wanting to send it back with the snooty server either. She was annoyed that she'd outed herself, that she hadn't thought about this before. Of course the French didn't drink the same martinis that Americans did.

"I'll take it if you want," the woman said, gesturing to her own empty wineglass. "I quite like it."

"Oh," Liv said. "Really?"

"Sure." The woman ordered a gin martini from the server.

"With a twist?" Liv said.

"*Avec un zeste de citron,*" the woman added.

"That's very kind," Liv said. "On me."

The woman shrugged. "Whatever you say."

When it came, they swapped their drinks, and clinked the glasses.

Liv went back to her cigarette, and the woman to her sweet vermouth. Liv took the first sip of her martini. It was not quite as good as in the States—too heavy on the vermouth—but it still had that hard bite she loved, almost industrial in its flavor. It reminded her, fondly, of her father. She used to ask him for sips of his martinis and he would oblige her. She was regularly disgusted by them, but she loved the burn in her chest, the sensation of heaviness lifting from the top of her head. Her father was impressed that she liked them, so he started making them for her when she was in high school, during the cocktail hour that preceded dinner. She pretended to enjoy the taste until, eventually, she did. Learning to drink martinis was, like life, hard work that paid off.

When she thought of her father now, she thought of what Brandon had asked her, on their ride home from the ski lodge. Whether her father had ever hurt her. The memory would always leave her as quickly as it arrived, intruding for a simple, gut-stabbing second, and then going back where it came from, into the ether where it best remained unperturbed.

She would savor the martini first, and then order the *entrecôte,* paired with a glass of Bordeaux.

A couple of men sat down at the table on the other side of her. The one closer to her turned and began to appraise her.

"Hello," he said. He was young and unattractive, with greasy black hair, wearing a faux-leather jacket. She could smell his cigarette breath, and began to feel self-conscious that her breath smelled the same. "What is that you're drinking?"

"A martini," she said.

"That's not a martini."

"It's an American martini."

He smiled, apparently charmed.

"An American girl."

She nodded.

"What are you doing in Paris, American girl?"

"Just visiting," she said.

"Just visiting," he mimicked, attempting the American accent of French. "So cute."

The server brought them beers, and the second friend, pint in hand, now also turned his attention to Liv.

"Hello," he said, smiling. He was equally unattractive, with a wiry goatee that resembled pubic hair.

"Hi," she said, and looked into her glass.

"You don't want to talk to us?" the first guy said.

"I'm trying to enjoy my drink," she said.

"Why are you by yourself?" the second guy said.

"She doesn't want to talk to you." Liv heard the same woman's voice, calling over to the young men.

Both guys smirked.

"Mind your own business," the first one said, eyes still on Liv.

The woman then let out a stream of expletives, only some of which Liv recognized. They guys looked at the woman agog.

"Such a filthy mouth for a lady," one of them said, which had them both in hysterics. But it worked; they decidedly turned away.

"Bitches," the other one murmured, laughing, and they left Liv alone.

Liv looked to the woman with gratitude. She actually, Liv realized now, appeared to be a bit drunk, her eyelids sluggish, though she was still put together, sitting tall with that sort of effortless poise that Liv wished she had herself. She always felt like she had to put in so much effort, in everything she did.

"You like that stuff, huh," Liv said in French, pointing to the sweet vermouth. She felt like she ought to make conversation with her now.

"My mother adores it," the woman responded in English. "She drank it as an aperitif. It was the first alcoholic drink I enjoyed. It reminds me of my early teenage years." Her English was only slightly accented, mostly British with a hint of a French lilt.

"How do you speak English so well?" Liv asked.

"My ex-husband is American," the woman said. "Are you visiting the city for a while?"

"Only until Sunday."

"By yourself?"

Liv nodded.

"Traveling by yourself is really lovely," the woman said. "You end up meeting lots of interesting people that way. More so than if you're with a companion." Liv didn't feel so lucky to be alone; in fact, she felt quite the opposite. "I admire that at your age. I'm not sure I would have had the confidence."

"I find it lonely," Liv allowed, the martini half-finished now and making her talkative.

"Loneliness is a hazard of living," the woman said. "You get used to it."

Maybe with age Liv would become more comfortable with loneliness, like this woman, who wore her solitude like a favorite dress.

"What's your name?" Liv asked the woman.

"Simone. Yours?"

Liv told her. "Are you Parisian by birth?" she asked.

"I grew up here," Simone said with some pride. "What about you?"

"I'm from Washington, D.C."

"I have never been. Only to New York."

"I'm moving to New York soon."

"To do what?"

"To be an editorial assistant at a publishing house. I start in one week."

"How exciting," Simone said, with a tinge of jealousy in her voice. Liv wasn't so sure how excited about it she was, now that living with Brandon was no longer part of the plan. She was going to sleep in the guest room in Lula's mother's apartment on the Upper East Side while she looked for her own place. It wasn't ideal. And she wondered how long it would take for Fiona to regale Lula and Marley with the story of what had happened between them earlier today, if she would pit them against Liv, and if Lula would still want Liv to stay in her home afterward.

"Maybe you can spend some more time in New York one day," Liv suggested.

Simone made a face.

"I don't think so," she said. "Paris is home."

When the woman's bill came, Liv insisted on paying it. Simone thanked her and said good night. Liv watched her walk up the Rue Vieille du Temple, lit by the ancient streetlights, her arms free and swinging.

She was alone again. What if she didn't want to wear her solitude like a favorite dress? She did not want to get used to it. Another pang, sharp and achy in her chest: she wished she and Fiona were still together, cigarettes dangling between their lazy fingers, matching American martinis side by side. Liv imagined an atmosphere of honesty in which she might tell Fiona everything, about her dad, about how things had ended with Brandon. Liv would say about Gabriel: "I believe you," would not rub it in Fiona's face that she had, last fall, been right. She would listen to her friend in turn. She would say she was sorry.

It was a fantasy, those things being easy, tumbling from her mouth. It would never happen. But she could entertain it for now. For tonight, it would keep her company.

25.

FIONA GOT OFF the plane at Tegel Airport, eyes buggy with exhaustion. It was not yet nine in the morning. Out of excitement, she had not been able to sleep at all the night before, nor had she slept on the plane, what with the fluorescent overhead lights on the whole time and the vinyl seats that reclined an entire inch.

Her flight had been filled with mostly people her age, and she waited now with similar travelers at the baggage claim. Three twentysomething French guys stood next to her, bearded and unshowered, talking about their plans for that night, pulling out packets of tobacco and rolling their cigarettes, to be smoked the minute they got outside.

Once she got her suitcase, she exited the airport and found a cab. All the taxis were identical black Mercedes. She showed the driver, who didn't speak any English, the address of Avi's apartment, and he nodded, repeating it in German. How she'd thought the street name was pronounced and how he'd said it sounded like two entirely different words.

They took the highway. Everything was industrial and gray, the buildings low and unremarkable. But soon they were inside the city, with its wide streets, its stylish blond women on bicycles, its green trees filtering the sun, the sidewalk dotted with morning light. Between German DJs speaking impossibly fast and the driver occasionally laughing at something they said, the radio played American songs. When Lou Reed came on, Fiona found the song to be a strangely apt pairing with the scene out her window. And when the girls went *Doo doo-doo doo-doo doo-doo doo-doo,* the bass line picking up, Fiona felt like she was in her own movie, the heroine following a dangerous man to a foreign place, watching the new city through the window of her taxicab. They passed a giant park—more like a forest, really, it looked so dense and endless. And then they crossed the canal, passing cyclists on their way to work, and there was endless grass on the other side, and more rows of trees, and the sun kissed the water like a promise.

Then, quite suddenly—or it seemed sudden—the driver pulled onto a quiet street, the road paved with glossy cobblestones. Tall apartment buildings, painted the palest pink, lined the block, their high windows ornamented with ornate lintels, balconies with herbs and houseplants jutting from each unit. It looked like a block where people enjoyed living.

The driver repeated the address and pointed to the door next to the car's passenger side: oxblood red, with a giant gold knob in the middle that appeared more ornamental than practical. She handed him thirty euros and he helped her take her suitcase out of the trunk. She thanked him in German, one of three words she knew.

Avi had said that he and his roommate would both be home, and Fiona looked down the list of last names next to the buzzers, all of them printed in a uniform font, and rang the buzzer labeled "Green/Koehl," as she had been instructed to do.

She heard the door click and let herself in and went up the wide stairs, carpeted in the same oxblood red as the door.

"Fiona?" she heard an American voice call, and then she saw a man, shirtless, appear at the top of the stairs. He was stunningly beautiful, which Lula had not mentioned, Adonis-like in his height, his wide shoulders and V-shaped torso highlighted rather well by the blue jeans that cinched right atop his hips. He had a large, wide nose, and chin-length brown hair.

"Stop there," Avi ordered, and hopped down a level to the landing where Fiona waited. He was barefoot. "First, hi," he said, kissing Fiona once on each cheek and then taking her into a tight, heartfelt embrace. She had had no idea how much she needed that, and she resisted the urge to let out a deep sigh. He moved his face back to take a look at her. "It is so good to meet you. Lula adores you and I adore Lula." He lifted her bag, which she had felt was heavy, with one arm.

"Welcome," he said, pushing wide the cracked-open door to his apartment and ushering Fiona in first. There was a short hallway—a skinny Persian rug lining the way—which opened into a gigantic living room: potted palms and meandering vines everywhere, vintage-looking mahogany furniture, and mismatched, framed drawings over a giant, well-worn sectional couch. The French doors to the balcony were wide open, allowing in the morning sun and a slight and temperate breeze.

"You are lucky you came this weekend and not a minute sooner. Berlin is winter nine months of the year and it *just* turned. Do you smoke? Let's smoke."

She said it was too early for a cigarette but she would love a coffee, and he delighted in the task, insisting she settle on the balcony while he made it. She sat in one of the wrought-iron patio chairs, looking out onto the street. It was ten on a Saturday morning and the street was nearly empty, aside from a few old women walking their dogs. One bike passed, a girl around Fiona's age transporting two sizable sacks of groceries, one in the front basket and the other strapped to a rack over the back wheel, but the girl was wearing a sundress and pedaling the bike as if it weighed nothing at all.

Avi came out carrying two matching white mugs. "Do you take anything?" he asked. "Milk? Sugar?"

"Black is fine," Fiona said.

"Good, 'cause we don't have either." Avi plopped down in the chair across from Fiona's, placing a pack of Gauloises on the table. He lit a cigarette and inhaled deeply, turning his head toward the street as he let out a puff of smoke. He made smoking look admirable.

He leaned back in the chair, crossing his legs.

She took the first sip of her coffee. It was strong and hot and delicious. "Wow, that's good."

He nodded knowingly. "So how was gay Par-ee?"

"Oh. Sort of a mess."

He lifted one eyebrow.

"I went with my other friend from college? Liv?" She hesitated to share too much, but he was listening, and she was desperate to talk. "It's a long story, but I told her something sort of personal and she didn't handle it well and it got messy."

"That happens." Avi ashed his cigarette over the balcony. "So now, Berlin."

She nodded. She had only told him over text messages that she was "passing through on her way home"—though of course Berlin was not at all on the way home.

"It's certainly a good place to get away from things, if that's the kind of weekend you're looking for."

"I really wanted to experience it," Fiona said. "And, you know, I had to get out of Paris."

Avi nodded his head emphatically. "I hate Paris."

"What do you do here?"

"I'm a photographer," Avi said. "I freelance. And I'm in art school, part-time. School is so cheap in Europe."

"So work brought you here?"

"Honestly, no," he said. "A guy brought me here."

"Your . . . Stu?" Avi had mentioned the name in his texts to her.

Avi laughed. "God, no. He's not *my* Stu. He's just my roommate."

"Oh, sorry," Fiona said. "Maybe I was confused from the texts."

"Please don't apologize. He *was* my Stu, for a time, but not anymore. He's my best friend."

"Where is he?"

"Asleep," Avi said. "He's a server at this restaurant in Mitte, right on the canal. We have to go there, maybe tonight. He's off, I think. Anyway. It was an older guy I followed here. So clichéd to say it now. I met him in the city while I was still at NYU. I really believed we were in love." Avi rolled his eyes. "It all worked out in the end. I came for the guy, but I stayed for me. This place is like Neverland. You'll see."

"Dinner sounds fun," Fiona said. She felt honored that Avi wanted to spend time with her; she'd assumed that he and Stu had their own things going on, that they were going to provide a couch and nothing else. "I actually have lunch plans," Fiona said, looking at her watch. "At one. But I'm free tonight."

Avi raised one eyebrow again. She allowed a sly smile as she brought the coffee cup to her lips.

———#———

Oliver chose an Italian restaurant that was also in Mitte, in the former East. As she got off the U-Bahn, the first thing she saw was a row of clothing stores she might have found in America. Tourists carrying shopping bags spoke loudly in their own languages while they moved from store to store. She left the main drag and found rows of short white and brick buildings butted up against one another, some restaurants with patio tables out front, and cyclists moving confidently down the cobbled bike lane. There was a park on the corner; it seemed there was a park on every corner, even in the busiest parts of this city. She spotted a giant green-domed building over on the canal, shining bronzelike in the afternoon sun. She made a note to herself to find out later what it was.

She was the first to arrive, and told the maître d', who spoke impeccable English, that there would be two of them. The restaurant was designed with white walls and angular lines, a gleaming white barista station in the corner, and a wood-topped bar along the front window. The maître d' seated her toward the back, beneath a wall of Italian wines. He asked her if she would like anything to drink while she was waiting.

"I'll take a look at the wine list," she said.

She looked around the restaurant, at the young family sitting next to her, at the twentysomething freelancers working on a pair of silver MacBooks. Everyone wore dark, muted colors, and long pants, like it wasn't seventy-five degrees outside. None of the women seemed to wear dresses, as she did, and even though hers was simple, a dark cotton shift, she felt overly formal. She had wanted to look put together but also like she wasn't trying too hard—even though she was, of course, trying too hard. How much time had she spent throughout her life, she wondered, trying to look like she wasn't trying too hard?

She ordered a glass of white wine—the third from the top on the list, a tactic she often used so as to seem like she knew more about wine than she did—and the waiter told her it was an excellent choice. She thanked him and watched the door. Several middle-aged men came in, some in pairs, all handsome, and each time she stopped breathing, as if any of them might be Oliver, as if his face might have changed completely.

The wine arrived before he did, but not by much. As soon as she brought the first sip to her lips, she spotted him. He was searching the room, his face pinched with worry. When he found her, his expression turned from worry to certainty, and as he looked into her eyes a beat too long for it to be comfortable, she knew, instantly, that he understood why she had come here, and that they wanted the same thing, that they were at lunch for the very same reason.

"Fiona," he said, and she stood to greet him. He kissed her once on each cheek. "Welcome to Berlin."

Her heart was beating fast and she did her best to disguise her nervousness by smiling too widely. "I hope you don't mind I started without you."

"No, no," he said as they sat. "I'm glad you did. How is it?"

"Delicious," she said. "Would you like to try?"

She handed the glass to him, and he swirled the wine, stuck his nose deep inside the mouth of the glass, and sniffed the wine before drinking it.

"Yes," he finally decided.

He picked up the wine list sitting on the table. "Should we get a bottle? You're on vacation, right?"

"Sure," she said. He wasn't on vacation, though, she thought. He beckoned the waiter and ordered in German.

Over the bottle of pinot grigio, they went through pleasantries about her time in Paris, and she left out most of the details. She said she was visiting friends for the weekend in Berlin. She wondered if he knew yet that that wasn't true. He seemed so interested in her, so ready with every follow-up question, that she never had the chance to reciprocate by asking him anything about himself. Maybe this was intentional, a tactic. As they started on their second glasses, picking at an antipasto, they began to gossip about people they both knew: professors, students. The people in their class together, the ones who could write and the ones who couldn't.

"I felt bad sometimes," he said. "There were a lot of people at that school who desperately wanted to be writers. A lot of people who, throughout their whole lives, were always told yes."

She did not ask him if she was one of these people.

"Will you ever come back?" she asked instead.

"Probably not," he said. "I need to be here."

She felt tipsy and daring enough that she simply blurted out her next questions.

"Your family?"

He nodded. "And also the book I'm working on now. It takes place in Berlin."

"What about your wife?"

He looked into his wine, swirling it aimlessly. They were nearing the bottom of the bottle.

"I never knew this before I had a kid," he started. "Being a parent does a number on you. Before this year, I seemed to think I would be okay with being away. I was certainly okay with being away from her. I had done it before. But with him. You don't understand. It supersedes all else."

He had not answered her question. She wondered if she should ask it again, or let the issue of the wife drop. They both knew she existed, and that they were here, at this lunch, in spite of her existence. Where was she right now? Was it of any consequence to Fiona to know? The woman wasn't her responsibility, but in front of this man, in the city where he lived with his family, she began to feel guilty about his wife for the first time. What about female loyalty, the sisterhood? Did those things apply to complete strangers? This woman might be a good person who loved Oliver very much, with zero suspicions about where he was right now. Then again—being married to someone like Oliver, who was gone for the whole year, how could you not have suspicions?

She decided to ask again.

"What about your wife?"

He looked at her searchingly, trying to gauge her: her curiosity, where it came from, why it existed. Finally, he sighed, as if acknowledging that the question was an annoyance, a burden on him.

"They're away for the weekend. At her sister's. It's been complicated."

"Complicated": an adult code word for *I don't want to talk about it*. Was this what adulthood was—knowing someone was in the wrong, but never saying so? Ignoring the issue of morality to get what you wanted? Or did that only apply to Oliver?

"I see," she said. She supposed the question of morality was only relevant to him. Where was her mistake? She was not the married one. She was the single one, the childless one. She would not be the one in the wrong.

The issue was that this was Oliver Ash, the man she had wanted for so long, who now, she finally understood, wanted her back. It was easy to sweep wrongdoings and misgivings under the rug when they were yours, when the moment to be seized was dangling in front of you, asking to be plucked. He had just given her permission to do what she wanted without feeling bad about it.

The wine was doing its work, and she found herself uninterested in food when their pastas came. He watched her take a bite, shook his head in disbelief.

"Fiona Larkin," he said.

"What?"

"I just . . ." He was looking at her with a real sexual charge in his eyes now, fully appraising her. It made her feel both turned on and deeply unnerved. "Nothing. Aren't you hungry?"

"Not really," she said, knowing that now they could go, now they could get the check, dash out of there, find a hotel or a dark alleyway or a park, for that matter—this was Berlin, after all. But she could not bring herself to suggest movement. She was paralyzed by him. She could only follow his lead.

"Me neither," he said, and called for the waiter. He paid the bill himself, sliding his credit card into the assigned slot quickly and discreetly, which made her feel like a concubine, a kept woman. A coquette.

They walked down a busy street, a tram line running through it, and toward the canal. The sidewalks were so crowded that she and Oliver had to walk single file, him in front of her, leading the way. She felt like people were looking at her, though they probably weren't. It was both magical and disquieting to be wine drunk in the daylight, in a city she didn't know, at the mercy of Oliver Ash.

They came to a park just before the canal. A man with dreadlocks and a Jamaican-flag beanie approached them: "Hashish? Want hashish?" Oliver shook his head. She could see a skinny tower above the tree line, like a disco ball with a stake poking from the top. Soviet-feeling in its cold silver gleam, its spire shooting toward space.

Oliver led them to a bench in the shade. He took out a pack of cigarettes, offered her one. She took it. He lit hers first, his hands cupping the flame, their faces close. They didn't say much as they smoked. There were a few more dreadlocked men, standing together and chatting, then dispersing to approach potential clients who were traversing the park. There was an old man a few benches down, wearing a flat wool cap and holding a newspaper open, though his chin was against his chest as if he was asleep. There were young people on blankets on the grass, lying on their stomachs, feet kicking the air aimlessly, puffs of smoke rising above their heads and into that bright Berlin sky.

"This city really comes alive in the summer," Oliver remarked.

When they finished their cigarettes, he said her name again, and looked at her with intention.

"Yeah?" she said.

He had nothing to say in response, and he leaned in to kiss her, placing one hand on her thigh. His lips were rough but the kiss was softer than she'd expected, romantic-aspiring but almost lifeless in actuality. He whispered her first name again, and nuzzled his nose against hers, an action of forced intimacy which made her recoil.

"I can't believe I'm kissing you," he said, the emphasis on *you*, as if he'd wanted her the whole time.

It was a line, but she wanted to believe him enough that she did. It felt too good to buy into this fantasy springing to life, the notion that he had wanted her, and only her, all along—that during all those nights when she was fantasizing about him, he was fantasizing about her, too. During the school year, she hadn't believed she stood a chance with him. She hadn't planned this far. So it seemed inconsequential, now, that she felt tentative, that she hadn't already melted to the ground. It seemed wise to ignore that his breath was not great, that as they kissed more it felt like he could be kissing anyone, that this was just the way he kissed his students: softly at first, as if to show them he was sensitive, and safe; hands on their faces; careful to whisper their names over and over as if reminding himself of them.

It was easiest and most desirable and most life-affirming to believe that he wanted Fiona and only Fiona, that she was not just one of his students but the only one of her kind. That she was different. That she, Fiona Larkin, had made an impression.

She kissed him back, imagining that he was the man from her fantasy, and filling herself up with pride. *She* had gotten him. Not Liv. That, she assured herself, was worth feeling good about.

He took her in a cab to a trendy hotel, and bought a bottle of wine at the lobby bar to be brought upstairs. The hallways were black and the only light came from the strange experimental videos playing on screens mounted on the corridor walls. The room was white and bright and very small, with only a full-sized bed pushed up against a corner, and a toilet, and a shower with no door. The windows looked out onto the center courtyard of the hotel, which was busy with guests who were uniformly good-looking and wearing spotless white Vans, playing Ping-Pong and lying in hammocks reading novels, while servers delivered cocktails and espressos and miniature sandwiches to them: it was a youth hostel for the late-twenties set.

Oliver took glasses from the bathroom, then opened the bottle of wine and poured. She didn't need to drink any more, but didn't say so. They clinked, and she took the smallest sip. He closed the window curtains, though it was still bright in the room, and still loud outside. Techno music was playing full blast, which they could hear perfectly despite the windows being shut.

They fell onto the bed and fumbled over each other's clothes. His large hands were moving frantically over her body, as if he were searching for something. She tried to shut off her mind, and the suspicion that he'd known to come to this hotel too quickly, that she was not the only woman he had brought here in the middle of the afternoon.

As Fiona went to unbuckle his belt, she felt that one of the belt loops in his jeans was ripped. She unbuttoned him and found that his smell was unpleasant, and that he was not groomed. Sometimes men's smells could be appealing to her, and sometimes even when they were unshowered they smelled desirable to her: pheromones doing their biological work. Oliver's didn't. He only smelled unclean.

He flipped her over, pulled her underwear down, and kneeled between her legs. He made an excited sound as he pressed his tongue into her. Immediately, she hated it. He was doing this clinically, like she could have been exactly anyone. His tongue was cold and slobbery and reminded her of the cold wet muscle of an oyster. She hated oysters.

"Wait," she heard herself saying. He didn't seem to hear her.

"Wait," she said louder.

He looked up. "Huh?" His face was flushed, and he seemed annoyed with her for interrupting. She saw now, as he looked at her with impatience and indifference, that he was not the Oliver Ash of her imagination. He was not interested in pleasing *her*. She was not special. Maybe she could have ignored that if she felt turned on by him, if she was enjoying this. The thing was: she wasn't. She didn't want him, either.

"I don't want to do this," she said, pulling up the sheet and covering herself.

"What?" he said. "What are you talking about?" He came up on the bed to sit closer to her, trying for tenderness, and smoothed a piece of her hair behind her ear. She pushed his hand away.

"I don't want this," she said. She heard her voice shaking. "I don't want you."

"I don't understand," he said, annoyance creeping back into his voice. "You were all systems go a minute ago."

"Well," she said, "I changed my mind."

She gathered up her clothes, which were strewn around the bed, still trying, in vain, to keep herself covered with the bedspread. She turned her back to him to fasten her bra.

"Where is my other shoe?" she said, and turned to see that he was holding it out to her. She took it.

He laid his head back against the white pillow of the hotel bed and put one arm up over his head.

"I don't understand why you're doing this," he said again.

Dressed, she looked at him, shirtless and defeated in the bed. She asked herself if she would regret this.

He squeezed his eyes shut and rubbed his temples, as if willing away a migraine. He did this for several moments, and Fiona thought about leaving while his eyes were still closed.

Then he opened them, and looked around the room, and at her again. It was like he was seeing all of it for the first time, disbelieving its existence. He shook his head.

"I just saw myself," he said.

She didn't respond. She didn't want to stay suffocated in this shoe box of a room a minute longer than she needed to.

"I saw what this looks like. What a fucking creep I am," he said. "You must think I do this all the time."

She might have shrugged, or nodded.

"I was good all year. I wanted you, you know. But I was good."

"Congratulations," she said.

"Poor me, right?" He looked like he was going to cry. "It's falling apart," he said. "My life has completely fallen apart."

She almost felt sorry for him. She assumed his marriage was failing, that he felt like a mostly forgotten writer, that he was just trying to hold on to the last scrap of his youth. Just trying to feel desired again, through her. And she was depriving him of that. It almost made her feel bad enough to change her mind.

"I thought I could hack it."

"Hack what?" She couldn't help but ask out of curiosity, even as she felt herself being pulled toward the door.

He threw a hand up, as if to imply *all of it*. "Nuclear family life. Teaching again. Et cetera."

"You're not cut out for it," she confirmed. He nodded. She understood the feeling: that you didn't fit into any of the paths set before you, that your own life was uncharted, that no one like you had ever lived before. The world could feel so imposing, so square.

"Why are you telling me this?"

He shrugged. "I figured you would get it."

She did get it, and felt momentarily flattered, and yet: did he really mean her? Or would he have talked to any young woman who would listen? There was, perhaps, no way to know the answer, to know if she, Fiona, was special to him, or simply another girl.

She could give in to her ego, believe that she was, in fact, special to him. But what did that actually matter? All year, she'd been thinking about what men thought of her, but she had never stopped to ask herself what she thought of them.

She patted him on the leg, more maternal than romantic, and then walked toward the door. She took one last look at Oliver Ash, lying supine on the hotel bed he had paid for.

"Good luck, Professor," she said to him, meaning it, and she left him there and struck out on her own into the foreign city.

26.

OUTSIDE, FIONA REALIZED she had no idea where she was. She checked her cellphone: it was five P.M. It felt like it should be so much later; she'd hardly slept in the last twenty-four hours. She wondered if she was still invited to dinner with Avi and Stu. But it was early, and she had no idea, anyway, where dinner was. She hadn't bought a German SIM card, and she didn't want to turn on her international roaming and have to explain to her mother why she took a last-minute trip to Berlin. She should have asked for the restaurant's name and location before, but she'd only thought as far as Oliver.

She had a spare key to the apartment, though, and she knew the address by heart now. She crossed the busy road to the nearest U-Bahn station. The U7 ran here; she had taken the U7 to meet Oliver for lunch. On the outdoor platform, she looked at a map and guessed which direction to go. She couldn't remember the name of Avi's U-Bahn stop.

She studied the map for several minutes, allowing a train to go by before she worked up the courage to ask someone for directions. A girl her age had been eyeing her, and Fiona could not tell if she had been checking her out or was pitying her, the poor lost American. The girl was wearing Doc Martens, baggy jeans that stopped right above the boots, and a tight, cropped T-shirt. Her hair was cut close to her scalp, and platinum white. Fiona would have looked absurd in this outfit, but this girl, with her defined cheekbones and bright eyes, appeared effortlessly cool.

She waved at the girl to get her attention, smiling, because she didn't know how to say "Excuse me." She asked, *"Sprich du English?"*—sure she was butchering it.

"Yes?" the girl said.

"Can you help me? I'm trying to get to Kreuzberg."

"Yes, where in Kreuzberg?" She pronounced the name of the neighborhood differently than Fiona had, like "Croytsberg."

"Um. The stop starts with 'G-n'?"

"Gneisenaustrasse?"

"Yes!"

"You can't take this train there."

"Really? I thought I was supposed to take the U7."

"You are. This is the S7." Her English was perfect, with the slightest and most charming German lilt to it.

"What's the difference?"

"They're very different. What is the street in Kreuzberg?"

Fiona butchered the pronunciation of that, too, but eventually the girl figured out where Fiona was going, and told her she would need to take the U1 to the U6, and that *that* platform was a few blocks away. (She pointed vaguely behind them.) She showed Fiona on the map the name of the station where she would change—Hallesches Tor—and Fiona thanked her profusely, aware that people were looking at her. (She was probably talking too loudly, didn't all Americans talk too loudly?) She walked up the steps and over toward the underground platform, boarded the train when it came, and sat in a carpeted seat facing a pair of canoodling teenagers. She heard the automated lady's voice say the name of the stop over the train's speakers—it sounded completely different than it was written, like "Halaishes Towar"—and soon she saw the words in German as the train pulled up to a busy station. Fiona got off there, victorious, to change to the U6, which she would now take to Platz der Luft-something. Aboveground, she guessed a direction, and was soon proven right, coming upon Avi's street.

"Hello?" she said tentatively as she walked into the apartment. She was elated that she had found her way here, and wanted to share her excitement with someone. The lights were on, and she heard Whitney Houston playing from Stu's bedroom. She knew that he could not hear her, because she could hear him singing along, uninterrupted by her entrance. They used to play this song all the time at frat parties—eighties songs were popular; frat boys loved the nostalgia of the eighties. They loved the bright colors and the cheesy synth lines and the cocaine.

"Hello?" she called, louder.

Stu appeared at the end of the hallway then—or slid, rather, out of his bedroom—in his socks and boxer briefs and a white Hanes T-shirt.

They moved toward each other down the hallway. He wore tortoiseshell glasses and had curly brown hair and full lips. He was thin and freshly shaven, and when he took her in for a long hug she could feel how smooth his cheek was against hers. His cologne smelled like the woods, like a freshly extinguished campfire.

"Did you just smell me?" He pulled away, looking at her outfit. "What are you wearing tonight?"

"Not this," she said defensively. "I need to shower."

"Do you have leather pants?"

"No?"

"I'm on the list, so you'll get into the place we're going after dinner. But you'll still want to look the part. Go shower and then we'll talk." He checked his watch. "We're meeting Avi at the restaurant at seven."

After her shower, she dressed carefully, in a different, simple black dress—thin satin, almost like a slip, and short black motorcycle boots. She appeared in front of him and he pursed his lips to the side, thinking.

"Take the bra off."

She did as she was told; then he appraised her again.

"It's still a little feminine. You don't have black jeans?"

She shook her head.

"The boots are good," he said. "Wait." He took his T-shirt off, threw it to her. "Wear that under the dress."

"Under it?"

"Yeah. And no makeup."

"None?"

"Maybe black eyeliner. That's it. Your whole pigmentless white-girl vibe is good, but we need you to look less American."

The restaurant was fancier than she had been expecting, and she felt underdressed.

"It's a casual city," he assured her.

They arrived before Avi did and sat, sharing a cigarette, on the ledge outside the restaurant, which overlooked the canal. Stu was from Frankfurt, she learned, and had lived in Berlin since he was eighteen (he was "in his thirties" now). He had started as a server and worked his way up, and now he was managing one of the nicest restaurants in the city. Often during the course of their conversation, he paused midsentence to hop up and greet someone middle aged and expensive-looking, moving seamlessly between English and German, always sure to introduce Fiona to them. He greeted one couple in English, and they responded to Stu in American accents.

"Hi, darling!" said the woman. She was gray haired and wearing an elegant silk shawl. She kissed him on both cheeks. "We have to get a cocktail soon, okay? Just the two of us." She winked at him.

"Of course, darling," Stu said back to her. "Your table is ready."

The man opened the door for the woman.

"That's the U.S. ambassador to Germany and his wife," he whispered to Fiona.

"Are you serious?"

"I had to go to their place for Thanksgiving last year and wear a tuxedo. It was so boring." He raised his hands and waved at Avi, who came skipping down the steps.

Avi kissed Stu on the lips, then Fiona on both cheeks. He put his palm out to Stu. Stu made a *tsk* and pulled a cigarette from his back pocket.

"I'm not buying them anymore," Avi explained to Fiona. "I'm trying to quit."

Stu rolled his eyes. "He's been trying to quit since the day I met him."

They went inside and had cocktails at the bar before sitting for dinner. Avi asked Stu how work was (a headache); Stu asked Ari how his photography class was (long but useful). Then Avi turned to Fiona.

"How was lunch?" he asked pointedly.

Stu looked at her. "What was lunch?"

Ari looked to Fiona, not wanting to explain for her.

"My professor," she said. "Former professor."

"I'm listening," Stu said.

It was strange: Fiona had the impulse to share every detail of her day with these strangers, even though she knew it might be uncouth.

"Well," she said. She wasn't sure how to begin. She had told Avi the basics earlier—that he had been her professor in college and that he lived here now. When he'd asked if she wanted to sleep with him, she'd obliquely replied that she wasn't sure what would happen.

"Did you?" Avi asked.

She shook her head. "I couldn't."

"How come?"

"It just . . . it didn't feel right," she said.

They both nodded, letting her continue.

"I guess I felt like I was doing it for the story."

"That makes sense," Avi said.

"You never slept with him in college?" Stu asked. "Wait, did you come here for him?"

"No," she said, leaving it unclear which question she was answering, and they didn't pry. Of course, they understood that she had come here for him. What other reason was there to book a spontaneous trip to a foreign city and ask strangers to let her stay with them on a moment's notice? But she understood implicitly that they would not judge her for it even if she were to admit it out loud. It wouldn't make her appear weak to them. Just human.

"I'm sorry I don't have a more interesting story for you," she said.

Stu waved a hand.

"It sounds like you did what was right for you," said Avi, putting his hand on top of hers. The conversation topic was thus changed. She could have cried at their kindness.

The plates at dinner didn't seem to stop coming—buttery artichokes and garlicky mussels and a giant chateaubriand with a side of béarnaise sauce. The wine was a cold, full-bodied white.

"What is this wine *called*?" she asked, declaring it her new favorite.

Avi reached across the table to fork another piece of steak. "I'm so full, and yet."

"Slow down," Stu said. "That won't feel great in an hour."

"Oh God," Avi said. "Remember Tim?"

"We have a lady in our presence," Stu said.

"It's fine, she's American," Avi said, proceeding to regale Fiona with a story about a friend of a friend who had eaten a large dinner followed by one too many lines of coke at the club.

"He . . . on the dance floor?"

Avi and Stu broke into hysterics.

"He disappeared to the bathroom for like half an hour to clean himself up," Avi was saying as he tried to catch his breath. "We thought he was getting head."

Fiona felt her chest fill, and she let out a giant laugh, joining them. They all sighed at the bottom of their laughter in unison, which sent them into another fit.

Stu paid for their cab to the club, which was not what she had been expecting. She had thought it would be a giant, bright discotheque in the middle of a city street; this was very much the opposite. The taxi had to let them off in what looked to Fiona like an abandoned parking lot, and as soon as they got out of the car, Avi and Stu removed their dress shirts and revealed matching black muscle Ts, transforming themselves instantly from buttoned-up dinner dates to Berlin clubbers. Avi collected both shirts and stuffed them into his backpack.

There was a wide dirt path in front of them, and people were waiting in a long line, silently smoking cigarettes and passing green bottles of beer back and forth. Ahead was a giant bunkerlike structure. It looked abandoned, with graffiti all over the exterior and barbed wire on the high fences around its sides. There were several giant German men manning the door and as they got closer, Fiona could hear pounding bass from inside. The people waiting on line were dressed in a hodge-podge of outfits, all of them representing a sort of minimalist, goth aesthetic: a woman in a black leotard with no pants and four-inch platform boots; a man with green hair and a black mesh top, the rings on his pierced nipples gleaming; an androgynous trio in nondescript black T-shirts and black jeans and black sneakers. As they approached the entrance, Fiona watched a straight couple—tattooed, clad in leather—being appraised by the doormen. Two of the men murmured to each other, then looked back at the couple and shook their heads, the bouncer closest to the door gesturing a hand away from the entrance to send them on their way. Fiona was confused—they looked the part to her. Maybe this was the club where Liv had waited in the cold for two hours and then didn't get in.

They stood off to the side, until one of the bouncers—the one with the tattoos on his face—noticed Stu and greeted him amiably. They had a quick conversation in German; then the man checked a list on his clipboard.

He looked up at Fiona and asked her something. She looked to Stu for translation.

"He wants to know how old you are."

"I'm twenty-one," she said.

The bouncer exhaled in disappointment, waving them in anyway, patting Stu on the back as they walked through the door.

"What?" she said quietly to Avi.

"It's young," he said. "This is more of a late-twenties-and-up crowd."

Inside, a strong-nosed woman patted her down, barking orders at her in German.

"What?" Fiona said, wishing desperately that she could understand the language. She hated being marked as an American everywhere she went.

The woman told her again, impatient, in German.

"Turn around," Avi said to her, being patted down himself by a male bouncer.

Fiona did so, and the woman patted her bottom perfunctorily, though what she was checking for Fiona wasn't sure. She imagined that a place like this looked the other way when it came to drugs.

"*Telefon?*" the woman said. Fiona took her phone out—was the woman going to confiscate it? Instead she put a hot pink sticker over the lens on the flip phone's camera. "*Keine Fotos,*" she said, shaking her head and making a "No" signal with her hands, like "Do not cross." Fiona nodded in assent. She would do whatever this woman told her to.

They paid for their tickets and went inside. Fiona felt the bass reverberating throughout the dark ground floor, though the music was coming from the upper levels of the giant building. Avi went to drop the backpack off at the coat check, and when he came back he took both Fiona's and Stu's hands and said, "Shall we?"

They walked through the bottom floor toward the steps, passing silhouettes of pairs in dark corners, behind columns or on benches along the walls. Fiona saw the shadow of one man standing against a column, holding the head of another who kneeled below him. Avi and Stu seemed not to notice the outlines of the people they passed.

They climbed a wide staircase to the second floor, and the music grew louder with every step. She knew nothing about techno music, or about clubbing, and she could not have characterized what she was hearing if she'd tried. It sounded like darkness and glee and sex and intensity rolled into an overwhelmingly deep and bodily bass line, and layers that kept piling on top of that: drums and cymbals and synthetic, man-made loops that weren't quite melodies, really. It sounded as if computers had found God. At the top of the steps there was a mass of people moving in time to the music, steady as a heartbeat. The strobe lights pulsed and lit the smoke rising above their heads and into the rafters. It was so loud that no one was talking; there was no point in trying to be heard.

Avi grabbed her hand and brought her to the bar, where they could hear each other better, and where he bought them sodas called Club-Mate and shots of vodka.

"It's German Red Bull," he said, drinking a bit of the maté-flavored soda to make room for the vodka. She followed suit, sipping hers and then pouring the shot in. It tasted like cream soda.

"Let's look around," he said into her ear. "Do you want to take anything?"

"Like drugs?" she said.

"Yes, like drugs." He laughed. "Like a pill?"

"Ecstasy?" she mouthed. She had only ever done psychedelics; she was scared for her heart. As if it were only a matter of time until she, too, would succumb to the same disease that killed Helen.

He nodded. "Have you ever?"

She shook her head.

"Well, if there's a place for it, this is it. It's sort of a perfect pairing with the music. We could split a pill to start, if you're nervous."

"Is it bad for your heart?" she asked.

He said he didn't know, and then made a face that denoted sudden realization. Lula had told him about Helen; of course she had.

"Let's not do anything you're not comfortable with," Avi said.

"No," she said, because she didn't want, yet again, to be marked for this tragedy. "Let's do it."

"Are you sure?"

"Yes," she said, even though she wasn't.

"Actually, I know that guy has it," Avi said, gesturing toward a dark-haired man wandering the bar area. He was wearing black eyeliner and a lacy vintage wedding dress. "Want me to get us some?"

Fiona nodded, and she waited alone at the bar while Avi conversed with the dealer, then walked out of the bar area with him. Someone next to her was smoking and she asked to bum a cigarette. Wordlessly, he handed her one, and then lit hers with the butt of his. "*Danke,*" she said, and he nodded and turned toward the crowd to watch them dance.

. . . .

When they took the pills Avi said, "I won't leave your side," and she believed him. When they got on the dance floor the music felt like lights inside her body. It was hard to know where the music ended and the drugs began. She saw her arms moving up into the air like she'd always seen ravers do in nineties movies, holding those silly glow lights, which no longer seemed so silly. Avi's eyes were closed and he was moving his hips like a salsa dancer. They looked like they were drawing figure-eights; she could see the psychic marks his hips left in the empty space all around him. They'd lost Stu a long time ago. Fiona wanted to reach out and touch Avi's hip bones, so she did. They felt hard and human under her fingers, the bones rotating under flesh. Bodies were amazing, the way they knew exactly what to do. Why couldn't she always feel this sense of wonder? He had taken his shirt off and his skin was warm and slick and taut and she moved her palms in experimental circles around his abdomen. He leaned into her touch. They kissed, their tongues playing off each other like instruments. Why couldn't she always do things for the sake of doing them, for the sake of the way they felt, and nothing else? Why did everything always have to be attached to so much meaning? And then they were done kissing, and were smiling at each other, dancing like they were exactly as young and high and beautiful as they felt. Soon Avi was kissing a boy in the mass of the dance floor, and she watched them, curious and removed, and it reminded her of being six, in the playground with her mother, seeing a couple making out on a park bench and feeling a spark of excitement that she immediately understood she wasn't supposed to feel. When else, until now, had she ever been given permission to watch someone? She had always implicitly understood that she, a young woman, was meant to be the appraised, and never the other way around. In here, femininity was neither a virtue nor a burden. In here she was anonymous and free. She knew she could leave Avi, could wander the upper floors of this place or be with someone in the dark rooms downstairs. They would find her eventually. But all she wanted, really, was to stay in this giant mass: one in a thousand, an easily replaceable blood vessel in the heart muscle of the dance floor, no one and everyone.

— // —

They got home around eight in the morning on Sunday, and Fiona awoke on her last day in Berlin at two in the afternoon.

"I feel like shit," she said, walking into Stu's room, where he and Avi were lying in bed, watching a show on Stu's laptop. Avi moved into the middle of the bed and patted the space next to him.

The three of them lay in Stu's bed for hours, eating stale gummy candies and watching reruns of *Friends*. Stu and Avi laughed at nearly every joke. Fiona knew when the jokes were coming, she had seen the episodes so many times, but sometimes she laughed as well, because of the delivery or a bit of physical comedy or simply out of a sense of comfort and a desire to laugh for the sake of laughing. She knew she should go outside, go see the city, go to the Pergamon or Checkpoint Charlie or see parts of the Wall along the canal. It was another beautiful day outside.

"Should we order food?" Stu asked them.

"I'm not actually hungry," Fiona said.

"Me neither," said Avi.

Fiona checked the time; it was five in the evening. Her flight home to New York was at seven the next morning.

"I should probably pack soon," Fiona said.

"Don't leave," Avi said to Fiona, snuggling into her.

"I don't want to," she said.

"Stay forever," said Stu. But she had her mother to see, a house to help pack up. It was Amy's birthday next week. She wanted to talk to Marley, and to Lula. Tell them everything that happened. Maybe she would reckon with Liv. Maybe not. She had a semester to finish. She wanted to stop spending her father's money, or else tell him that she was spending it. She felt guilt now—about her dad, Helen, all of it. She had taken his penance and run away, even spending his money on drugs to make her forget.

But she had felt so good last night. The source of the feelings was synthetic, but didn't it mean that those feelings were inside her, somewhere? Even without drugs, or anything else? They hadn't come from nowhere. The experience almost made her believe she could learn how to do the healing herself. She suddenly felt anxious to see her mother, to tell her about this trip. Maybe she could even share the Oliver parts, obscure some of the details. She wanted to figure out a way to show Amy: Look at the adult decisions I'm making. Look at this good person I'm becoming.

"How's your heart?" Avi asked her.

"It's okay," she said. "It's good."

He put his hand on her chest, and held it there.

27.

THEY DIDN'T NEED to induce Danièle after all; her contractions began naturally at one o'clock on Sunday afternoon. While Joséphine and Alex were in the delivery room with Danièle, Simone had to stay in the waiting room with Henri. It took all of Simone's might to focus on the boy in front of her as he zoomed his toy trucks around the room with intense concentration. She thought she could hear Danièle's screams, even though the delivery room was past a set of swinging doors and all the way at the other end of the hall. She could practically conjure the pain of her own delivery almost six years earlier, pain unlike anything she'd previously thought possible: the internal twisting, as if her organs were being ripped apart from one another; the searing sensation in her lower back, like someone was stabbing it over and over. She'd been determined to deliver without an epidural, which she came to regret as she endured thirty sleepless hours of labor, a constant stream of contractions with no end in sight. But she was too stubborn, and as much as she'd been tempted, she didn't give in to the drugs.

Not for a second was Simone worried about the health of her baby when he did come. He was on time, at exactly forty weeks, and the sonograms had shown nothing but a perfectly healthy little boy. The risks were so much higher for Danièle: the baby might not be strong enough, might not have lungs that worked properly. This little girl, five weeks early, would be more prone to infections or any other combination of terrifying possibilities than Henri had been. What did it feel like for Danièle, the fear for the baby's health and well-being on top of all of that excruciating pain?

Surely, Simone reasoned with her anxious self, the baby wouldn't come if it wasn't ready to?

It didn't always work like that. *We are at the mercy of these tiny creatures*, she thought, *who themselves are at the mercy of chance*. Who decided who survived? Her father would have said that God decided, that we are all at his mercy. Oliver, if he had ever met Hugo, would have responded that there was no God, that life was only a string of random events that we attempted to ascribe meaning to.

Simone had once believed in God because her father believed in God, and she had thought that if a man who lost his parents in the Holocaust still believed in a god, then he must know something she didn't. But it was hard for Simone to believe in a god after her father died of cancer, too young, before getting to meet his grandson. It was harder to believe in a god after losing three babies. It would be nearly impossible to believe in a god if something terrible happened to Danièle's baby now or to Dani herself. Simone certainly did not believe that God had brought her Oliver, this man who had caused her so much pain over the past year. Everything reasonable in her said that God did not exist.

It also felt callous, in a way, to be so defiant about God's nonexistence. How could a person obstinately rule out that which we might never have an answer to? Maybe God was randomness itself, the moments of despair and joy, the things we would never understand, in coexistence with one another. Maybe God was Henri playing on the floor with his trucks, single-mindedly focused on the task in front of him. Maybe God was the voice that had referred to Oliver as her ex-husband last night, to that American girl at the bistro, words that had come out of Simone before she even had a chance to consider them. Or maybe God was none of these things. Did it matter, having an answer?

If she believed that God was a man in the sky who listened to prayers, then she would certainly be praying to him now, for the health of her sister and the baby. This, she was almost sure, wasn't what God was. And so instead she sat down on the floor, took a toy truck, and chased her son's truck with her own until he began to giggle. If she could not be in there holding Danièle's hand, wiping sweat from her forehead, and if she could not have the chance to endure that pain all over again herself, then at least she could be here, playing with the boy who was already hers.

One hour later, Alex came out, tears in his eyes, to announce the birth of their little girl.

They named her Maya, for the month she'd been born—not the month she'd been expected. The "M" was also after Joséphine's mother, Madeleine. She was ushered almost immediately to the NICU to be put on a feeding tube and respiratory support, and to protect her from infection. No one except Danièle had been able to hold her yet. Simone and Henri went in to see Danièle before visiting the NICU, and they found her in the hospital bed where she'd delivered Maya, sobbing.

"They *took* her from me," Dani was crying. "She was so hungry, and I tried to feed her, but it wouldn't take, and then they *took* her."

"They're simply making sure she's up to her regular weight," Alex said, dipping a washcloth into a cup of cold water and placing it on Dani's forehead. "She's going to be okay. They've already said so."

"I don't trust them!" Dani screamed out, her face red and full of fury. Henri grabbed Simone's leg and hid behind it. Simone remembered this, too, all of the hormones coursing, how obsessed with and attached to and fearful for Henri she'd felt in the minutes following his birth, and yet how no one seemed to understand her, how unreasonable everyone else was. She patted the top of Henri's head, told him everything was okay.

"Should I take him out?" Joséphine asked, which caused Henri to grasp Simone's leg more tightly.

As much as she wanted to stay with Dani, tell her everything was going to be okay, tell her she understood exactly what she was afraid of, Simone knew she had to choose her son now. "No, we'll go," she said.

"It sure would be easier if Oliver was here," Joséphine said under her breath, just loud enough for Simone to hear it.

Right before he fell asleep, Henri asked, "When are we going home to Papa?"

Simone hadn't booked a return flight. She had been too

overwhelmed by fear for her sister's health to think that far into the future. Too angry with Oliver to think about returning to him, ever. It was already the twenty-fourth of May; they would be returning to Paris in a week. They only had to go back to Berlin to pack up the apartment, ship some boxes. All of their important furniture had remained in Paris. The thrift-store or Ikea items they'd bought for the Neukölln flat were already posted for sale on Craigslist. What they didn't sell Simone planned to put on the curb; she was too tired to bar-gain.

Most surprisingly—or maybe not surprisingly at all—she hadn't heard from Oliver. He hadn't checked in about the baby, and she hadn't kept him updated. It felt as if they were making a simultaneous decision to give up on each other, which felt anticlimactic despite the massive repercussions. Perhaps the magnitude of this would hit her later. Perhaps there was a blowout waiting for them in Berlin, or perhaps Oliver would already have his bags packed, waiting for them to return. Perhaps—quite the opposite—his things were still in their drawers, having been unpacked mere weeks earlier; perhaps he'd decided to stay in Berlin indefinitely. This seemed the more likely option. What it came down to was how much he wanted to be near his son. Simone was sure that only Oliver knew the answer to that.

"When are we going home to Papa?" Henri asked again, thinking she hadn't heard him.

"In a few days," she said, and gave his hand a tight squeeze.

"That's so long," said her sad, sleepy boy.

"They'll go fast. I promise."

He nodded, swallowing back his tears. He got that from Oliver—the ability to secrete away the things that really hurt him, and save them for a rainy day.

....

As she waited for Joséphine to return to the apartment, she opened up her laptop, which she hadn't done all weekend, to answer some overdue emails. Logging into her account, she had the false hope that, perhaps, there would be a message from Oliver. A long email apologizing, or even simply explaining himself. He was a writer, after all; he was always better at expressing himself on paper than in person. He had written so many letters to her at the beginning of their relationship—love letters, erotic letters, admiration letters. She'd saved them all, pushed them to the back of her underwear drawer.

But there was nothing in her inbox except a couple of emails from her university in Paris, about her fall schedule, and one from her fellowship advisor, whose notes she'd been ignoring for nearly a month now, asking about progress. Could they take their money back? She didn't know. She'd unequivocally failed at her Berlin year; she wasn't sure she'd ever failed so spectacularly. Soon, she would be able to erase it, pretend that it had never happened at all.

Her phone buzzed, and she jumped, half hoping; it was only her mother, saying that she'd be home for the night around ten, if Simone wanted to go back to the hospital when she returned.

So was this it, then? Was this how their relationship ended—not with a bang but with a whimper? She wondered how he was busying himself in Berlin that weekend instead of coming with her. Packing up all his stuff? Going out to a club, finding someone in a dark corner, staying anonymous? How little she knew about this man she'd spent the last six years of her life with. She was starting to feel like they'd been a dream—a hazy, sometimes sexy, sometimes traumatic dream—that she was only now waking up from. A dream that had left her a son, one who was very real.

Joséphine came home to relieve Simone, and when Simone got to the hospital and walked toward her sister's room, she cracked open the door to find Danièle fast asleep. She wouldn't wake her; Dani needed rest.

She made her way toward the NICU nursery instead; she'd yet to see Maya, for fear of scaring Henri with all those infants hooked up to life support. The hallway was badly lit, fluorescent lighting that reflected off the cheap linoleum flooring, and there was only one person standing there looking at the babies. It was Alex.

He was looking down at the sea of minuscule humans plugged into their various contraptions: oxygen tanks and feeding tubes and heart monitors. Some of the babies were no longer than Simone's forearm. She followed his gaze to one of the bigger babies, relatively speaking, in the third row. She was pink-skinned and wrinkled, with what looked like a gas mask covering her face. She had a feeding tube coming from her belly button, and she was fast asleep.

"Is that her?" Simone whispered, and Alex jumped, putting a hand over his heart.

"You scared me."

"Sorry."

He placed a finger on the glass, pointing her out. "Fourth from the left."

"She's beautiful," Simone said, though truthfully she looked terrifying, hooked up to all of those machines that had the capacity to give her life as easily as they could take it away.

"She's going to be okay," he said, with a certain amount of overconfidence to his voice, as if convincing himself of it.

"She will be," Simone said.

"Thanks for being here," he said.

"I wouldn't miss it."

He turned to look at Simone.

"Does Oliver hate Danièle that much?"

"No," Simone said. "I don't know. I think I'm the problem."

"Why?"

"I ask too much."

"You're his wife."

She shrugged.

"I know I'm not perfect," he said. "But it's changing now. I've decided."

"You say that."

"I don't understand how . . . with a baby, how can you leave your baby?"

"Some people can."

She knew that Oliver was going to break Henri's heart, the way Oliver's parents had broken his. She mostly expected, when they returned to Berlin, that Oliver wouldn't be there. That kind of trauma—they say it's inherited. She had borne a boy with trauma in his blood.

But maybe there was a chance that she alone could save Henri. Maybe he would always be a little bit broken, and maybe she had capacity enough, as his mother, to mend the broken pieces.

If not her, who?

28.

FIONA HAD SLEPT the entire flight from Berlin to New York. Although they took off at seven in the morning from Germany, it was only nine A.M. when she got home, having flown backward in time. She hadn't told her mom that she was flying in from Berlin, not Paris, and that she had changed the flight for a whopping fee two days earlier; the Berlin flight had landed in New York at nearly the same time as the one from Paris.

Fiona made her way through customs to find Amy waiting for her. She looked nervous, as if waiting to meet a blind date. Fiona greeted her mom with a long hug, and she thought she heard Amy sniffle.

"Mom, are you crying?"

She appeared to wipe away an errant tear. "No," she said. "I'm just happy you're home."

"I was only gone for a week," Fiona said, throwing an arm around her mom while she pulled the suitcase with the other.

On the drive back to Larchmont, Fiona resisted the heavy

pull of her eyelids, determined to stay up in order to beat jet lag. She felt a sort of culture shock despite having been away for such a short period of time: she was struck by how wide the highways were, how big the cars, how ugly the drive, the gray and smoggy industrial turnpikes through Queens and the Bronx.

The house was filled with boxes, some packed up already, labeled KITCHEN and DINING ROOM and OFFICE. The bookcases in the living room were empty, the open boxes filled with novels. Fiona left her suitcase in the living room, afraid that if she brought it up to her bedroom she'd immediately collapse on the bed.

Fiona sat down at the kitchen table; Amy made scrambled eggs and a pot of strong coffee, and turned on the little TV on the kitchen counter for background noise.

On a morning news show, there was brief footage of Secretary of State Hillary Clinton in El Salvador, attending the inauguration of the country's new president. She was dressed head to toe in a royal-blue pantsuit, shaking hands with Salvadorean men in identical black suits and bending to accept presents from local girls in school uniforms. The red carpet she walked down was lined with soldiers in red uniforms, standing to attention. Hillary's blue pantsuit stood out against the red and black that surrounded her; she was, Fiona thought, brave to dress like that, setting herself apart from the crowd. After all, she was already a woman in power, already set apart enough.

Fiona took the first sip of her coffee, watching Secretary Clinton and thinking about her Monica Lewinsky project. Her mother placed a plate of eggs and toast in front of her and sat across the table with her own mug of coffee. It felt like a lifetime ago, that project, and a lifetime ago for Hillary, too. The humiliated wife who'd gone on not only to survive but to thrive. That project was, ultimately, the only work Fiona had truly cared about last year. Oliver's notes on her final portfolio now seemed false and insignificant. In the end, she'd only wanted to do well in the class because of him. But she would have spent another semester, another school year, an entire graduate degree studying Monica and women like her—women who were betrayed by other women, ruined by the patriarchy, and forced to go into hiding because they decided to have sex with a powerful man.

Did it make Fiona a better person that she hadn't chosen to sleep with Oliver? What might have happened to her if she had? Maybe, if she'd kept it a secret, nothing would have happened. This sort of thing occurred all the time. The only thing that varied was which women chose to speak out about the things they came to regret. Imagine all the women who didn't, who went on with their lives carrying around a secret. Was it possible that any of Oliver's previous conquests recalled their trysts with nostalgia or erotic longing rather than shame? In a way, she hoped so. She hoped that some of them had gotten what they wanted. She hadn't slept with him because, ultimately, she didn't want to, not because it was the "wrong" thing to do. That in itself, she believed, was a victory.

"I wonder what Monica Lewinsky thinks about all this," Fiona said to her mother.

Amy looked confused. "About what?"

"About Hillary. It can't be easy, watching her thrive."

"It wasn't easy for Hillary, either," Amy said. She gestured to the TV. "This shows resilience."

Fiona wondered if Amy saw herself in the secretary, finding fulfillment again after hardship. Only, Amy had not just been cheated on but had lost a child, too. She seemed to be doing so well these days that sometimes Fiona could forget that they had endured the same loss. Why was Amy so good at moving on, and Fiona so bad at it?

Maybe it wasn't a competition, how one grieved. Fiona could never know what the depths of Amy's despair looked like, because she'd never shown them to her. And maybe that was okay. The point was, Amy had gotten herself out of the bedroom she'd hidden in for months. She was here for Fiona now, and she was moving forward.

Maybe they needed to pretend to be doing better than they were. If only for each other.

"Are you going to tell me about Paris?" Amy asked.

She could leave out the fight with Liv. She could speculate on the things that Helen might have loved: the flower boxes over the balconies, the sumptuous queen bed, the crème brûlée and the satisfying crack of the spoon as it broke the burnt surface. They could talk about what Helen could have been, the impossible possibilities of her.

Fiona and Helen might not have grown to love each other. But they might have loved each other. There was no way to know.

"I went to Berlin, too," Fiona said, after a pause.

Amy didn't look mad; on the contrary, a small smile crept in, conspiratorial. She leaned forward in her chair and put her hands around her coffee mug.

"You did?"

Acknowledgments

I AM GRATEFUL TO many people for their support in the writing of this book, and this is by no means an exhaustive list.

Thank you to my visionary agent, Meredith Kaffel Simonoff, and to my brilliant editor, Andrea Walker. I'm grateful to Emma Caruso, Allyson Lord, Melissa Sanford, Andrea DeWerd, Katie Tull, Janet Wygal, and the rest of the lovely people at Random House for their hard work at all stages of publishing this book. Thank you to everyone at DeFiore and Company, especially Reiko Davis and Jacey Mitziga.

I am grateful to the following works and institutions: *The Coquette* by Hannah Webster Foster, with commentary by Cathy Davidson; *The Culture of Sentiment* by Shirley Samuels; *The Last Jews in Berlin* by Leonard Gross; *Amelia, or The Influence of Virtue* by Sally Wood; the Jewish Women's Archive; the Jewish Museum, Berlin; Yad Vashem; and *The Washington Post* and *The New York Times,* for the Monica Lewinsky transcripts.

Thank you to my former professor Dr. Robert Battisini, who generously allowed me to pluck readings and themes from his Love, Lust, and Loss syllabus for the purposes of this novel.

Thank you to my Berlin people. All of you live in this novel in ways obvious and not. I'm especially grateful to Jacob Schickler and Moritz Estermann, for their hospitality and wisdom; David Levitz, for the apartment in Neukölln; and Greg Bryda and Bora Sirin, for the fun.

Thank you to Ben and Nicole Daniel, for the trip to Paris and the apartment in the Marais, without which I could not have written the neighborhood so clearly; and to Ellie Hunzinger, for Montmartre after: My love for you and my love for France will always be intertwined.

Thank you to Katie Abbondanza, an all-time great reader, editor, accountability partner, and friend. Thank you, Julia Bosson, for conversations about Berlin in New York, for help on the Simone chapters, and for telling me to cut Oliver's POV. Thank you to Kea Krause and Lauren Pagano for reading early drafts of this novel and being nonetheless kind about them. And thanks to the loved ones who helped me to understand subjects about which I was clueless: my dad, Tony Berman, for teaching me about life in finance in 2008; my dear friend Dr. Lauren Covington, for explaining the medical complexities of premature births; and Lauren Pagano and my brother, Sam Berman, for legal nuances and terminology.

For the space and time to write, I'm grateful to the Brooklyn Writers Space, the Virginia Center for the Creative Arts, The Wing, and the Wellspring House.

Thank you to Fiona Apple and Monica Lewinksy, patron saints of this novel.

Forever, for all things, thank you to Mom, Dad (again), Sam (again), Mimi, Kelsey, Laura, and Lauren (again).

I happen to live with an unofficial Holocaust scholar, a sharp critical reader, and the kindest person I know. Zachary Solomon: Thank you, thank you, thank you. I love you and I like you.

ABOUT THE AUTHOR

MANDY BERMAN is the author of *Perennials* and *The Learning Curve*. Her writing has been published in *The New York Times*, *Time*, and *Poets & Writers*. She teaches creative writing at Montclair State University and Manhattanville College, and lives in Brooklyn.

mandyberman.com
Twitter: @mandyberman
Instagram: @mandykate

ABOUT THE TYPE

This book was set in Sabon, a typeface designed by the well-known German typographer Jan Tschichold (1902–74). Sabon's design is based upon the original letter forms of sixteenth-century French type designer Claude Garamond and was created specifically to be used for three sources: foundry type for hand composition, Linotype, and Monotype. Tschichold named his typeface for the famous Frankfurt typefounder Jacques Sabon (c. 1520–80).

5-21-19
10-31-19 -12-23-21
12 23 (CLND)